Praise for the C

"*Rosemary and Rue* will surely appeal to readers who enjoy my books, or those of Patricia Briggs."

—Charlaine Harris,
#1 *New York Times* bestselling author

"McGuire has never lacked for courage in her writing, and this eighth entry in the phenomenally inventive October Daye series showcases her narrative daring and ingenuity beautifully. By forcing Toby to question her own identity and loyalties, McGuire highlights what a truly strong character Toby has always been, and what a remarkable heroine she has become." —*RT Book Reviews*

"The plot is strong, the characterization is terrific, the tragedies hurt . . . and McGuire's usual beautiful writing and dark humor are present and accounted for. This has become one of my favorite urban fantasy series, and I can't wait to find out what happens next." —FantasyLiterature.com

"An urban fantasy detective series featuring a resourceful female detective . . . [October Daye] should appeal to fans of Jim Butcher's *Dresden Files* as well as the novels of Charlaine Harris, Patricia Briggs, and similar authors."—*Library Journal*

"It's fun watching [Toby] stick doggedly to the case as the killer picks off more victims and the tension mounts."

—*LOCUS*

"With *Ashes of Honor*, McGuire has crafted a deeply personal and intense story that will keep you on the edge, hoping to be pushed over. In my opinion, it is, hands down, the best Toby to date." —The Ranting Dragon

"These books are like watching half a season of your favorite television series all at once. . . . More than anything else, it's the fun of it all that's kept me returning to McGuire's books, and to this series, long after I've stopped reading other mainstream titles." —SF Signal

"I love that Toby is a strong, independent—yet still vulnerable—heroine. I love that this is a world where people die, where consequences matter. I love the complex world-building and mythology. I love the almost film noir tone of the series. I love that each book leaves me wanting more. If you dig urban fantasy, this is one of the best out there." —CC2K

DAW Books presents the finest in urban fantasy from Seanan McGuire:

***InCryptid Novels*:**

DISCOUNT ARMAGEDDON

MIDNIGHT BLUE-LIGHT SPECIAL

HALF-OFF RAGNAROK

POCKET APOCALYPSE

CHAOS CHOREOGRAPHY*

SPARROW HILL ROAD

***October Daye Novels*:**

ROSEMARY AND RUE

A LOCAL HABITATION

AN ARTIFICIAL NIGHT

LATE ECLIPSES

ONE SALT SEA

ASHES OF HONOR

CHIMES AT MIDNIGHT

THE WINTER LONG

A RED-ROSE CHAIN

*Coming soon from DAW Books.

AN OCTOBER DAYE NOVEL

DAW BOOKS, INC.
DONALD A. WOLLHEIM, FOUNDER
375 Hudson Street, New York, NY 10014

ELIZABETH R. WOLLHEIM
SHEILA E. GILBERT
PUBLISHERS

www.dawbooks.com

Cover art by Chris McGrath.

Cover design by G-Force Design.

Interior dingbat created by Tara O'Shea.

DAW Book Collectors No. 1706.

Published by DAW Books, Inc.
375 Hudson Street, New York, NY 10014

First Printing, September 2015
1 2 3 4 5 6 7 8 9

DAW TRADEMARK REGISTERED
U.S. PAT. AND TM. OFF. AND FOREIGN COUNTRIES
—MARCA REGISTRADA
HECHO EN U.S.A.

PRINTED IN THE U.S.A.

For Brooke.

I am so lucky to have you in my life.

ACKNOWLEDGMENTS:

Every new Toby book is an adventure for me as a writer just as much as it (hopefully) is for you as a reader. *A Red-Rose Chain* was a surprise from start to finish, and that's the best kind of book for me, as a writer. I learned things that excited me, and I'm so glad that you're still here.

As always, there are people who need to be thanked. Thanks to the Machete Squad, for tireless support and editorial assistance, and to the entire team at DAW, without whose faith in me this book would not exist. Thanks to Talis, Teddy, and Amal, for hosting me at various spots around the United Kingdom while I finished this book, and to my entire Parisian crew, for not drowning me in the hot tub located in the basement of our Murder Palace.

Thank you Vixy, for continuing to put up with me; Amy, for continuing to love me; and Shawn, for clicking on all those axolotl pictures I send you. Thanks to Patty, for understanding that sometimes I am just going to become God's problem, and to Robert and Rachel for emergency staffing duties.

Sheila Gilbert remains the best of all possible editors, Diana Fox remains the best of all possible agents, and Chris McGrath remains the best of all possible cover artists. While we're on this track, my cats are the best of all possible cats. So are yours, if you have them. All hail the pit crew: Christopher Mangum, Tara O'Shea, and Kate Secor.

My soundtrack while writing *A Red-Rose Chain* consisted mostly of *Songs About Teeth*, by Cake Bake Betty, *Caffeine & Big Dreams*, by Kira Isabella, the soundtrack of *Ghost Brothers of Darkland County*, endless live concert recordings of the Counting Crows, and a really awesome playlist made for me by Amal. Any errors in this book are entirely my own. The errors that aren't here are the ones that all these people helped me fix.

Welcome back.

OCTOBER DAYE PRONUNCIATION GUIDE
THROUGH A RED-ROSE CHAIN

All pronunciations are given strictly phonetically. This only covers races explicitly named in the first nine books, omitting Undersea races not appearing or mentioned in book nine.

Afanc: *ah-fank*. Plural is “Afanc.”
Annwn: *ah-noon*. No plural exists.
Bannick: *ban-nick*. Plural is “Bannicks.”
Barghest: *bar-guy-st*. Plural is “Barghests.”
Blodynbryd: *blow-din-brid*. Plural is “Blodynbryds.”
Cait Sidhe: *kay-th shee*. Plural is “Cait Sidhe.”
Candela: *can-dee-la*. Plural is “Candela.”
Coblynau: *cob-lee-now*. Plural is “Coblynau.”
Cu Sidhe: *coo shee*. Plural is “Cu Sidhe.”
Daoine Sidhe: *doon-ya shee*. Plural is “Daoine Sidhe,” diminutive is “Daoine.”
Djinn: *jin*. Plural is “Djinn.”
Dóchas Sidhe: *doe-sh-as shee*. Plural is “Dóchas Sidhe.”
Ellyllon: *el-lee-lawn*. Plural is “Ellyllons.”
Gean-Cannah: *gee-ann can-na*. Plural is “Gean-Cannah.”

Glastig: *glass-tig*. Plural is "Glastigs."
Gwragen: *guh-war-a-gen*. Plural is "Gwragen."
Hamadryad: *ha-ma-dry-add*. Plural is "Hamadryads."
Hippocampus: *hip-po-cam-pus*. Plural is "Hippocampi."
Kelpie: *kel-pee*. Plural is "Kelpies."
Kitsune: *kit-soo-nay*. Plural is "Kitsune."
Lamia: *lay-me-a*. Plural is "Lamia."
The Luidaeg: *the lou-sha-k*. No plural exists.
Manticore: *man-tee-core*. Plural is "Manticores."
Mauthe Doog: *mwa-th doo-g*. Plural is "Mauthe Doog."
Naiad: *nigh-add*. Plural is "Naiads."
Nixie: *nix-ee*. Plural is "Nixen."
Peri: *pear-ee*. Plural is "Peri."
Piskie: *piss-key*. Plural is "Piskies."
Puca: *puh-ca*. Plural is "Pucas."
Roane: *row-n*. Plural is "Roane."
Satyr: *say-tur*. Plural is "Satyrs."
Selkie: *sell-key*. Plural is "Selkies."
Shyi Shuai: *shh-yee shh-why*. Plural is "Shyi Shuai."
Silene: *sigh-lean*. Plural is "Silene."
Tuatha de Dannan: *tootha day danan.* Plural is "Tuatha de Dannan," diminutive is "Tuatha."
Tylwyth Teg: *till-with teeg*. Plural is "Tylwyth Teg," diminutive is "Tylwyth."
Urisk: *you-risk*. Plural is "Urisk."

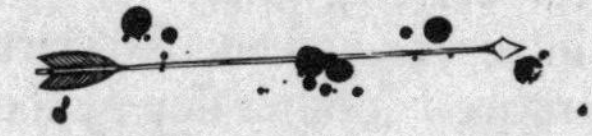

ONE

March 11th, 2013

Thus he that overruled I oversway'd,
Leading him prisoner in a red-rose chain:
Strong-tempered steel his stronger strength obey'd,
Yet was he servile to my coy disdain.
—William Shakespeare, *Venus and Adonis*.

"SO HOW LONG ARE you and the kitty-cat plannin' on doing this whole 'engagement' thing?" Danny punctuated his words with a sweep of one heavy hand. The motion neatly swatted the enormous black dog that had been leaping for my head out of the air, sending it crashing to the ground. It yelped. Danny pointed at it, saying sternly, "Stay down, ya big mutt!"

"Could we focus on the Mauthe Doog for right now, and talk about my engagement later?" I asked, as I swung my sword at another of the shaggy canines. It dodged easily. They all had. I wasn't as good with a blade as Danny was with his hands, and in the end, I was just too *slow*. "I don't want to be torn to shreds because you're planning floral arrangements!"

I would normally have felt bad about attacking dogs

with swords. I like dogs. Most dogs aren't feral teleporters the size of small ponies. Human animal rights groups have very different problems than fae ones. For one thing, most human animal rights groups don't have to worry as much about being eaten.

"I'm just sayin', maybe you need to start talking about dates." Danny grabbed another dog by the tail, scolding, "No. Bad. We don't eat people."

The dog snarled and snapped at him, not quite managing to twist around enough to sink its teeth into his arm. That was a pity. Danny's a Bridge Troll, with the solid, concrete-like skin to prove it. If the dog had tried to take a bite out of him, it would have probably broken several teeth, and made itself a lot less dangerous to *me*.

With most people, it's unfair for me to expect them to play shield. I heal faster than anyone else I've ever met, to the point where if I watch closely I can actually see my skin knitting back together—and trust me, that's even more unnerving than it sounds. Danny is one of the few exceptions to this rule. He's huge, imposing, and virtually indestructible. He heals slower than I do, but that doesn't matter, because there's almost nothing that can actually injure him. All of this makes him uniquely well-suited to being my partner when I have to do something ridiculously dangerous—like, say, clearing out a pack of Mauthe Doog that should never have been roving the salt flats of Marin.

Not that we were out there alone. My squire, Quentin Sollys, and my boyfriend-slash-fiancé, Tybalt, were about fifty yards away, dealing with their own contingent of black dogs. Quentin had his sword, and was handling his share of the problem with a grace and finesse that I will probably never possess, even if I live to be a thousand—although he hadn't managed to land a hit, either. The dogs were just too fast for something as clumsy as a sword. Tybalt was having better luck. He had shifted far enough into his feline mien that his hands had become heavy with claws and his mouth bristled with teeth, and he was taking out his share of the Mauthe Doog in the classic cat-meets-dog fashion. I could hear his feral snarls, and the dogs' pained yelps, all the way down the beach.

Mauthe Doog are native to a few small islands in Avalon, one of the deeper realms of Faerie. All the deeper realms were sealed by Oberon centuries ago, as part of the process of locking up the house and hiding the valuables before he went on an extended vacation, leaving his descendants to fend for ourselves. Most of the really dangerous monsters fell under the "valuables" category, and were shut off from the rest of us, leaving our asses unchewed and our pets uneaten. Unfortunately, there'd been an incident about nine months ago involving an uncontrolled, overpowered teleporter named Chelsea Ames. Chelsea was strong enough to rip holes in those closed walls between the realms, leading to leakage from all the deep, dark places into the Summerlands, the last accessible Faerie country. Which also happened to be the one closest to the mortal world. Which meant that once something was *there*, it could easily wind up *here*.

We'd managed to stop Chelsea before she could completely destabilize Faerie, leading to the loss of the Summerlands, or worse. That didn't do anything to stuff whatever had already managed to come through back into the places where it belonged. Sylvester, my currently semi-estranged liege lord, wound up adopting an Afanc, a docile lake creature big enough to squash cars. The local pixie tribes swelled by a factor of five, and promptly began battling each other for territory, shrieking in hypersonic voices and stabbing each other with tiny poisoned spears. And those of us unlucky enough to be on-call as knights errant or heroes of the realm got to spend a lot of time playing mediator between the warring swarms.

Guess what I do for a living. Lucky me.

"Toby, watch your back!"

Danny's shout caused me to whip around, sword raised defensively. The leaping Mauthe Doog rebounded off the blade with a yelp, leaving a smear of red-black blood behind. The fae dog retreated a few steps, alternately whining and growling. I stared in surprise at the blood on the blade. It smelled like hot copper and distant fens, a rich, boggy smell that was as familiar as it was foreign.

They had been moving too fast before for me to draw blood. Danny had been doing a lot of damage, but it had all been blunt force trauma. Not much blood in that sort of fight.

"Danny, cover me," I said, and brought the sword to my mouth.

"You're not gonna—aw, shit, you are. That's gross," grumbled the Bridge Troll, and moved to shield me from the remaining dogs as I licked the blood from the side of my sword.

Faerie is a funny place. There are hundreds of different types of fae, all descended from the First Three: Oberon, Maeve, and Titania. We can look different enough from one another that it's impossible to believe we could be related, much less share the same origin, but it's true. And all of us have our own special talents to help us survive. Some are shapeshifters, like Tybalt. Others are built to last, like Danny. The rest of us have to depend on subtler magic. Like blood.

My kind of fae, the Dóchas Sidhe, are the best bloodworkers of all. The fact that I'm a changeling—part human, part fae, although the fae part of me is getting stronger all the time, at the inevitable expense of my humanity—has never been enough to keep me from accessing the magic my lineage is heir to, even when I would have been better off leaving that magic alone. The fact that I hate the sight of blood is neither here nor there. If anything, it's proof that the universe has a sense of humor.

The Mauthe Doog's blood was tart and faintly bitter, like it had been tainted by some unknown substance. I closed my eyes as I swallowed, trying to find something—anything—that would tell me what the dogs wanted, or how to make them stop attacking joggers and eating people's housecats. Instead, I found my own face, distorted by the Mauthe Doog's fear until it became the visage of a monster. Danny loomed behind me in the red blood haze of memory, a walking mountain that dealt out death with every blow.

"They're terrified," I said distantly, only barely aware that my lips were moving. I swallowed hard, trying to chase away the shreds of blood memory. A faint headache was growing in my temples, warning me that I was pushing the limits of my powers again. Blood magic is hard on a body—harder, it seems, than regenerating most of my skin, or repeatedly healing broken bones. Louder, I repeated, "They're terrified!"

"What?" The low rumble of Danny's voice pulled me all the way back into the present. I opened my eyes and dropped my sword in the same motion.

The sound of the blade hitting the ground seemed louder than it was. Even Tybalt stopped his snarling, head whipping around as he stared in my direction. His ears were better than mine under the best of circumstances, and in his partially-transformed state, his hearing would be especially sharp. That was a good thing. I didn't want to yell.

"They're scared," I said, lowering myself to a crouch. The three Mauthe Doog who were in any shape to fight watched me warily, but didn't attack. I think they were just relieved that I wasn't holding a sword anymore. "We've been acting like they were animals because they're not shapeshifters, and that was sort of right: they *are* animals. They're monsters. The Law doesn't protect them, because they can't claim its protection. But they're not *dumb* animals, and they're not attacking people out of malice. They're doing it because they're scared out of their minds."

"What do you mean?" rumbled Danny.

"Imagine going from one of the deep realms—a place where there's never been an Industrial Revolution, no people, no pollution, no cars—to modern-day Marin in the blink of an eye, just because you were standing in the wrong place at the wrong time." I extended my hand toward the nearest Mauthe Doog, fighting not to let my nervousness show. I could probably grow back any fingers the big dog decided to bite off. Probably. I'd never actually experimented with regenerating limbs before, and this would be a lousy way to find out where the limits of my healing powers were.

"So you're sayin' that these are somebody's pets?" Danny actually sounded halfway excited now. He had a big heart to go with his big body—and given that he was almost eight feet tall, that meant he had a *lot* of heart. He also ran the only Barghest Rescue Society in existence. He was supposedly trying to find homes for all his semi-canine, scorpion-tailed monstrosities, but since most Bridge Trolls didn't live in houses with backyards and everyone who isn't a Bridge Troll has issues with venomous pets, he hadn't managed to adopt one out in the whole time that he'd been keeping them. I wasn't sure he really wanted to anymore.

"I'm saying they used to be, a long time ago, before we went away and left them all alone." Sometimes I questioned Oberon's wisdom in sealing the deeper realms. Yeah, he kept the kids away from the guns and liquor, proverbially speaking, but he'd also kept them away from their quiet spaces and favorite toys. More, he'd locked them out while locking their companion animals in. Even fae creatures can live forever, under the right circumstances. How long could an abandoned fae dog wait for its master before it decided to turn loneliness into rage?

I turned my attention to the injured Mauthe Doog. "Hi," I said, as gently as I could. "I'm sorry we hurt you. You scared us."

Danny snorted. "They did more'n scare us."

"Danny, hush," I hissed—but he was right. Queen Arden Windermere in the Mists had asked me to gather my friends and take care of the Mauthe Doog problem in Marin after the third mortal jogger had come staggering back to his car raving about disappearing dogs with teeth like daggers. The fact that he'd been lucky to encounter the Mauthe Doog instead of something nastier—they're not the only breed of fae dog, and some of their cousins are venomous—probably didn't occur to him. He'd been so focused on convincing people that he wasn't crazy that he'd actually managed to stammer his story to a local newscaster before he was whisked off to a hospital. Arden had called me immediately. I was a hero of the realm, after all, which made this my problem, whether I wanted it to be or not.

I had turned around and called for backup. Which is maybe not a very heroic thing to do, but is definitely the sensible thing to do, and if there's one thing my friends and allies have been pounding into my head for the last four years, it's the need for support when I'm going into a dangerous situation. Some people call it personal growth. I call it the slowly dawning understanding that I enjoy being alive, and that it's easier to stay that way when I have people to help me.

The Mauthe Doog was still watching me warily, its ears pressed down flat against its head. All of them were about the size of healthy Rottweilers, but with thick, shaggy black coats that would have looked more at home on a Muppet. The other two had fallen back farther, whining in confusion. At least they weren't attacking us anymore.

"Tybalt, I know you can hear me, since you're all kitty-kitty right now," I said, raising my voice only slightly. I didn't want to scare the Mauthe Doog again if I could help it. "I want you to start falling back toward me. Bring Quentin along. Defend yourselves if you have to, but stop attacking. Don't make any aggressive moves." I paused before adding, "Trust me."

It was probably a good thing I couldn't hear whatever Tybalt said in response to my instructions, since it was almost certainly profane and laced with comments about my intelligence, or lack thereof. Tybalt's been just about everything I could ask for in a lover, which is why I agreed to marry him when he asked, but he doesn't like my habit of charging headlong into danger when there are people he likes less who could be doing it in my place. It's hard to argue with that sort of logic.

The Mauthe Doog slunk closer to my outstretched hand, its head hanging low and its ears slanted forward. I didn't know enough about dogs to know whether that was a good sign.

Dogs. That was it. Tybalt was a King of Cats, which was all well and good, but wasn't going to help calm a bunch of fae dogs. Luckily, Tybalt wasn't our only option. "Do you remember the Cu Sidhe?" I asked the Mauthe Doog. Its ears seemed to prick up a bit. I decided to take that as a good sign, and kept talking. "They're here, with us. You're on Earth now, on the other side of the Summerlands. That's why things are so strange here. But we can help you get back to the Summerlands, to the Cu Sidhe. You don't have to be alone anymore."

What we couldn't do was help them get back to Avalon. Those doors were sealed, and had been since we stopped Chelsea from her panicked flight through Faerie. She couldn't teleport at all right now, thanks to an alchemical potion that had blocked her powers, and was going to keep blocking them until a year had passed. When it wore off—and it would wear off soon; she only had about three months to go—she would have a normal Tuatha de Dannan's limitations. No more shredding the fabric of Faerie for Chelsea, and no way home for the Mauthe Doog.

The Mauthe Doog closest to me whined. I heard footsteps approaching from behind me. Experience told me that they belonged to Quentin, not Tybalt—my squire might have the grace and elegance of a pureblooded Daoine Sidhe, but Cait Sidhe are in a league of their own when it comes to sneaking up on people. The day Tybalt did something as common as stomp would be the day he turned in his proverbial whiskers.

"These are my friends," I said, gesturing toward the sound of footsteps and hoping that the gesture would encompass all three of the guys. "We're all sorry we fought with you. We didn't know."

"I'm not sorry," said Quentin. "One of them tried to take my throat away from me. With its teeth. I'm not you. I *need* my throat."

"Whine about missing body parts later, talk nicely to the poor confused doggies now," I said, keeping my eyes on the Mauthe Doog. "This is one of those moments when I could really use Etienne's powers back in working order. Danny, call Muir Woods. Tell Arden we need a door from here to there, and tell her that Madden needs to be waiting on the other side."

"I think attacking the Queen with a bunch of monster dogs is treason, Toby," said Quentin, starting to sound concerned.

"Good for me, I haven't committed treason against this monarch yet. I'm trying to complete the set. Danny?"

"On it," rumbled the Bridge Troll, and moved away, his steps thudding against the ground like tiny boulders falling.

I stayed where I was, keeping my hand stretched out toward the dogs and making quiet, soothing noises. More Mauthe Doog slunk around us to join the three I'd started with, forming a pack of wary canines. There were seven of them, all told; I didn't know how many we'd killed, or how many of them had teleported away and were now making their way back to check on their pack mates. I've never really been much of a dog person.

The smell of blackberry flowers and redwood bark drifted over me, out of place this close to the water. I twisted to look over my shoulder. Arden was standing behind me and not behind me at the same time, since there was no rational way of folding geography that put Muir Woods "behind" the Marin salt flats. A glimmering circle in the air marked the division between her location and ours.

"What in the world—" she began.

I cut her off. "Is Madden there?" It's good to be on speaking terms with the Queen: it makes rudeness a little easier to forgive. But only a little. I had to be careful not to push it.

Arden frowned, apparently not used to people interrupting her anymore. I was definitely pushing it. All she said was, "Yes, he's here. Madden?"

"Coming!" The voice was followed by a large, shaggy man in jeans and a black T-shirt with the Borderlands Café logo on the front appearing in the frame of Arden's portal. He would have looked completely out of place next to Arden, with her perfectly groomed hair and the dress that could have been lifted straight from the Italian Renaissance, if not for the red streaks in his otherwise snow-white hair and the wolfish gold of his eyes. Madden looked mostly human, but the parts of him that weren't human were pure canine. "Hi, Toby! Hi, Toby's friends!"

"Hi, Madden," I said. "Can you step through for a second? I have some folks here who really want to meet you."

"All right," said Madden amiably, and bounced through the portal. Then he stopped, staring at the Mauthe Doog with open-faced delight. "Hey! Cousins!"

The Mauthe Doog perked up instantly, their ears going straight and their shaggy black tails beginning to wag. I straightened up and stepped back as Madden stepped forward. That seemed to be their cue: the Mauthe Doog who weren't too injured to jump began jumping all over him, dancing up onto their hind legs to make it easier. Those who were too injured pressed themselves against his calves and ankles, sighing heavily, the tension going out of their bodies.

I turned to the portal. "They're not monsters, Your Highness; they were attacking people because they were scared and confused. But they come from the same realm as the Cu Sidhe, so once I realized they weren't actually hostile, I figured Madden was the answer."

"You didn't tell me they were Mauthe Doog, Arden," said Madden, sounding hurt. I glanced back to find him standing behind me, one of the injured canines cradled in his arms. It had its neck bent at an improbable angle, and was calmly licking the underside of his chin. "I would've said they were good dogs, if you'd told me."

"I didn't know," said Arden. "All the reports we had said 'shaggy black canines,' but they weren't specific enough to let us figure out what *kind* of fae dog we were dealing with."

"They're good dogs," said Madden. He turned to me. "They'll come with me now. If that's okay with you. I can call my brothers and sisters, and they'll come to Muir Woods to get the Mauthe Doog that were here and take them back to the house before we come back and start looking for the rest. Any that are missing, we'll find, once the pack trusts us."

Cu Sidhe like to live in large family groups, almost like packs, but without the social posturing and structure that humans have tried to assign to the word. They just want to be with other dogs. I could understand that. It's nice to be around people who understand you. "Sure, Madden," I said. "Do you need us to help you carry them?"

"There's only two who don't feel like they can walk so

good, and I can get them," he said. "Arden, can you hold the door?"

"For you, the world," she said, with a faint smile. Arden and Madden had been friends since long before she had come back to Faerie and allowed herself to become a Queen. Their relationship wasn't romantic, and that was probably a good thing; she needed a friend more than she needed a lover. I knew what that was like. "Sir Daye, I'm going to need you and your people to come by the knowe to give me a full report. Shall I see you tonight?"

"As soon as we finish cleaning up here," I said. None of us had physical magic, but we could kick away the footprints in the sand and bury the blood, making it look like the salt flats had been invaded by a bunch of kids playing soccer or something, not a group of heavily armed fae having a pitched battle with supernatural dogs. That, too, was part of my job. The human world and Faerie were separate for a reason, and I had to help hold that line.

"Can I come visit the doggies?" asked Danny, looking at Madden.

Madden smiled. "We will welcome you," he said. He stooped to lift the second badly injured Mauthe Doog onto his shoulder, and then he stepped through the portal. The rest of the black dogs flowed through at his feet, vanishing from the salt flats and reappearing in the shadows of Muir Woods. Arden looked briefly nonplussed. Then the last dog was through, and she lowered her hand, closing the portal.

Danny, Quentin, Tybalt, and I stood alone on the sand in silence for a few moments. Two dead Mauthe Doog lay further down the beach, their necks broken, the blood running from their open mouths tinting the ground where they had fallen. The night-haunts would come for their bodies soon enough; we just needed to take care of the tracks.

Quentin spoke first. "So this was fun."

"Yeah," I said.

"We should do this every week," he said.

"I will drown you in the ocean and send your parents a very nice card to tell them how sorry I am," I said.

"Be sure you include a gift card for Tim Hortons," he said. "That's how we say 'sorry for killing your firstborn son' in Canada."

I laughed. So did Quentin. Tybalt just snorted, while Danny looked confused. All in all, it was a pretty normal night for us, and the fact that we had to clean up our own mess just continued the theme.

"All right, boys, let's kick some sand around before we go to visit the Queen," I said, and sheathed my sword. A hero's work was never done.

TWO

FAE TEND TO BE nocturnal by nature. That's probably the only thing that's really protecting us from being discovered—or rather, rediscovered—by humanity. We used to show ourselves a lot more, which explains all those fairy tales and folk stories and popular ballads about the merry, merry greenwood ho. We also used to steal livestock and "borrow" human women to raise our children. And we used to find ourselves burnt and stabbed and killed with iron on a regular basis, because while our worlds may have been meant to coexist, they were never intended to do it peacefully.

So yes, not being chased by angry mobs is a benefit of the nocturnal lifestyle. The other nice thing about it is the people, or rather, the lack thereof. We didn't bother spinning human disguises for ourselves before we got in the car: there was no one around to see us. The normally ninety-minute drive from Marin to Muir Woods only took about an hour. Quentin spent the whole time complaining about the fact that I wouldn't let him change the radio, while Tybalt spent it staring through the windshield, fingers clenched white-knuckled against the dash. It should probably have been reassuring that there was *something* that scared him, apart from my tendency to rush headlong into certain doom. Instead, Tybalt's reaction to cars just reminded me of how much older he was than me, and left me feeling uneasy and off-balance.

Danny had left us in the parking lot in Marin where I'd stowed my car and he'd stowed his cab. "It's not that I don't like the new Queen an' all, but every time I go with you to visit royalty, somebody winds up dead or exiled or whatever," he'd said, with disturbingly accurate logic. "I figure if I just go on home, you won't have to worry about it."

"I'll call you later," I'd promised, and endured his clumsily patting me on the shoulder before he turned and lumbered back to his cab. Bridge Trolls can't be physically demonstrative with most denizens of Faerie. There's too much of a chance that they'll accidentally break us.

There were no cars visible in the parking lot at Muir Woods when we arrived. There could have been anything from junkers to horse-drawn carriages hidden under illusions and complicated don't-look-here spells, but since most of those also come with mild aversions and "please don't park on top of me" suggestions, I didn't worry overly much as I steered my car into a parking space and killed the engine.

"All right, everybody out," I said.

Tybalt didn't have to be told twice. He practically kicked his door open, retreating to the edge of the parking lot while he waited for me and Quentin to follow him. Quentin snickered, but there was no malice in the sound. He was just amused, and he knew he was safe enough that he could get away with expressing it. It felt good to know he was that relaxed. Not many Crown Princes get to grow up feeling like they're allowed to be happy. Not in Faerie, anyway.

The thought reminded me of something. I glanced at Quentin as we got out of the car and walked toward

Tybalt. "Hey," I said. "Don't you have a birthday coming up?"

"I'll be eighteen on Lughnasa," he said.

"Is there anything you wanted to do for your birthday this year? Eighteen's a pretty big deal. We could have a party. May loves parties."

"Eighteen's a big deal for humans, maybe," said Quentin. He grinned, the light from the lamps around the parking lot throwing gold highlights off his dark bronze hair. He'd looked like a dandelion when we first met, all pale yellow fluff with no real substance. Now he was taller than I was, and finally starting to fill out. It was unnerving. My squire wasn't supposed to grow up. "Ask me again when I come of age."

"So we hold off on the grand bacchanal until you turn thirty. Got it." I looked back to Tybalt, allowing my face to relax into a wide, only slightly mocking smile. "You know, you're going to have to get used to riding in cars eventually. I'm never going to learn how to teleport, and that means I'm going to keep driving everywhere."

"Must you taunt me so cruelly?" Tybalt asked.

"Yes, I must," I said, and offered him my hand. He took it, tucking it gently into the crook of his arm. It was an old-fashioned way to walk, but it made him happy, and I was all in favor of things that made Tybalt happy. He shook his head, still feigning offense at my comments about the car, and started walking toward the woods. Quentin followed close behind us, for once not ranging wildly ahead. Fighting a bunch of disoriented fae dogs and cleaning up the signs of the struggle had tired him out, at least for the moment. Knowing Quentin, he would bounce back soon. In the meantime, I got to keep everyone where I could see them.

The trees loomed around us like sentinels, filled with dancing lights as pixies soared from tree to tree and Will o' Wisps danced above the water. I wondered idly what the human rangers who ostensibly controlled the park thought of the changes that had occurred over the course of the past seven months. Knowes—better known as "hollow hills" in the human world, which has had a long time to forget the proper names for fae things—have a tendency to weaken the walls between the Summerlands and the mortal worlds when they stand open. Not to the point where monsters can slip easily through, but in more of a "pixies in the backyard, strange whispers in the water, Dryads in the trees" sort of way. Fae communities grow up around them, because we know we're safe there. We can always run for the Summerlands if things turn sour.

Up until seven months ago, no one knew that there was still a knowe in Muir Woods. I'd known that there had *been* a knowe there, once upon a time, but I had assumed it was one of the lost ones, so old and so weakened that it had become nothing more than a shallow scrape in the space between worlds. It turned out the knowe was perfectly healthy and structurally sound. It was just waiting for its actual owner to come back and give it permission to open. Enter Arden Windermere, daughter of Gilad Windermere, rightful Queen in the Mists. She had been in hiding since before I was born, choosing safety and obscurity over the dangers inherent in taking the throne.

We would never have found her if the woman who'd been holding the throne of the Mists hadn't been a psycho bitch who decided to banish me from the Kingdom for the crime of asking her to stop selling drugs that killed changelings. That didn't sit well with me, or with my allies, and we'd ended up asking some pointed questions about how a woman with no Tuatha blood could be the rightful heir of a Tuatha de Dannan king. One thing led to another, and we'd managed to find Arden, talked her into retaking her Kingdom, and brought her back to the knowe that had been patiently waiting for more than a century for her to come home.

We walked down the carefully-maintained paths through the flat part of the park, across streams and over tiny ponds that still made my skin crawl if I looked at them too closely—I don't like water much, and I don't like pools of standing water at all—and began to climb the hiking trail that wound its slow way up the side of the hill. Tybalt let go of my arm as the path narrowed, taking up a position directly behind me. He'd learned the hard way that if he let me out of his sight when we were checking in with the nobility, I'd probably find a way to dump myself in a mud puddle, cover myself in blood, or otherwise render myself completely unpresentable. To be fair, I never did it on purpose. It was just a talent of mine.

The path leveled off, and we stepped into the small clearing that preceded the entry to Arden's knowe. The doors in the big redwood that served as the knowe's tie to the mortal world stood open, like they were welcoming us home. Many knowes require complicated rituals or motions to get in. Not this one. This was the royal seat of the Mists, and its doors were never closed to the people of the Kingdom. The pixies clustered in the trees here so thickly that they illuminated the area like so many pastel Christmas lights. Guards in Arden's livery stood to either side of the doors. I waved. One of them—a diminutive Glastig with hair the color of walnut shells—waved back.

"Evening, October. Quentin. Your Highness." She bobbed her head to Tybalt, which was as close as any member of the Divided Courts would come to bowing to a Cait Sidhe. The fact that she called him by his title at all said a great deal about relations between Arden's Court and the Court of Cats. "The Queen's expecting you, and said that we were to send you right on in when you arrived."

"Evening, Lowri," I said, with a quick smile. It was safe for Arden's guards to stand outside like this: given the strength of the illusions hiding the knowe, they were probably rendered invisible to searching eyes just through proximity. "Where did Madden go with the Mauthe Doog?"

"You mean the big black dogs that pop in and out of view like bad special effects?" asked Lowri, her faint Welsh accent making the question sound even more surreal than it probably should have. The other guard—a Coblynau I didn't know by name—put a hand over his mouth, concealing a smile.

"Those are the ones," I confirmed.

"He took them home to meet his siblings," said Lowri. "Said some of them need proper medical care that's based on dogs, not on people. He looked awfully sad about it, too, and said that if you asked, we were to tell you he didn't blame you, since you didn't know any better."

I winced. There was something especially unsettling about being chastised, even secondhand, by someone who was essentially a dog. The Cu Sidhe liked to cultivate a simpler way of life, eschewing the complexities of fae politics and human manners. That doesn't mean they're rude or stupid: Madden couldn't have been Arden's seneschal if he wasn't a smart guy. It just means they don't hold grudges or go on vendettas, or host dinner parties that require knowing when to use multiple forks.

"We shall make it up to him later," said Tybalt.

"Yes, we will," I said. "Is Arden inside?"

Lowri wrinkled her nose at the informality, which was funny, considering that when we'd met, Lowri had been working in the private guard of the false Queen, who had called Arden things that were far worse than her actual name. "As she said to send you in, I believe that is a fair guess, yes."

"Cool. See you in a bit." I waved to the other guard and walked inside, with Quentin and Tybalt following.

Arden's knowe was a redwood wonderland, perfectly suited to the woods outside. The floor and walls in the entry hall were all paneled in the stuff, and the smell of it suffused the air. Elaborate carved panels on the walls sketched out the history of the Kingdom of the Mists all the way up to the present day, and while new panels seemed to have been added every time we came to visit, none of the old panels seemed to have disappeared. I made a mental note to ask Arden whether the hall was getting longer, or whether it just somehow knew which panels it was safe to hide when I was looking. Either option seemed reasonable. The knowes are alive, and while they may not think like people do, they have opinions about things, and will generally do what they feel best.

The hallway let out on the throne room, where Arden was sitting on her throne, wearing the same purple-and-silver velvet gown that I'd seen through her teleport window, playing with her mobile phone. She looked up at the sound of our footsteps. Then she smiled and unfolded herself from her seat, standing. "Hey. Did you have any trouble getting here?"

"None," I reported.

"Cool," she said, and tossed her phone onto the cushion on her throne.

Arden Windermere might not sound much like a queen, but she certainly looked the part, especially these days, now that she had a proper staff of handmaids and clothiers to help her present the appropriate image to her people. She was tall, slim, and elegant in her carriage, standing a few inches taller than Tybalt, who was in turn a few inches taller than me. Her purple-black hair was pulled into a high chignon, secured with loops of amethyst, and her jewelry was all silver, accenting the vibrant colors of her mismatched eyes: one vivid blue, the other liquid mercury. She could easily have walked among the kings and queens of our past, as long as she kept her mouth closed. Not that I'm one to criticize the speech of others, but when Arden talked, it was more Haight Street than High Court.

Maybe that was a good thing. A lot of the problems faced by the fae nobility come from the collisions between our world and the human world. Arden had spent most of her life in the human world. While she wasn't going to broker a lasting peace or anything, she at least understood what I and her other changeling vassals were talking about when we brought human problems to her attention.

Now that she was standing, it was time to observe the niceties. I curtsied, dipping as low as practice and training allowed. Quentin bowed with equal depth and solemnity. Tybalt inclined his head, but otherwise stayed upright. That wasn't as disrespectful as it looked. As a King of Cats, he was technically Arden's equal, and it would have been inappropriate for him to bow to her. He was already showing her a great honor by following the rules of her knowe, and not insisting that she treat him as visiting royalty.

Quentin was also visiting royalty, being the Crown Prince of the Westlands and all, but that wasn't something we talked about much. Arden knew—High King Aethlin and High Queen Maida had been the ones who came and validated her claim to the throne of the Mists—but as Quentin was technically untitled while he was in fosterage, she didn't let it affect her reactions to him. Quentin's rank was secret from most of Faerie, and it needed to stay that way if he was going to stay safe.

"You may rise," said Arden, sounding faintly bemused, like she still didn't understand the point of all this bowing. At least she wasn't trying to make us stop anymore. Centuries of training don't die out that quickly.

"Lowri told us Madden took the Mauthe Doog home," I said, as I straightened. "Will he be back tonight? I'd like to apologize for not realizing what was going on quicker."

"He should be," said Arden. "You did well tonight. The Mists appreciate your service."

There are some pretty strong taboos in Faerie against saying the words "thank you," which has made us all incredibly good at talking our way around our gratitude. "It was sort of fun, in a 'big angry black dogs trying to kill us' kind of way. I'm just sorry we didn't figure out that they weren't hostile sooner. We could have saved the rest of them. As it stands, I don't know whether any managed to teleport away."

"Madden will look for them," said Arden. "How many died?"

"Two," said Quentin. "It might be a good idea to tell Madden to go back over there before tomorrow night, to make sure none of them were wounded and went to ground. But I don't think any of them were. They were all pretty dedicated to attacking us."

"I listened for the sound of pups hidden in the high grass," added Tybalt. "No such sounds came to me. I believe we found them all."

"That's good," said Arden. "They were becoming a nuisance."

"They just needed someone to tell them they weren't alone," I said. That wasn't an uncommon situation, in Faerie. For every Court like Arden's, which welcomed changelings and shapeshifters as well as the more "courtly" members of the fae, there were three Courts like the former Queen's. She had run a very formal house. No changelings unless they were servants; no shapeshifters, because she didn't allow animals around her nice things. The Mists had been losing good people since that woman took the throne, driven away by her insistence on a form of courtliness that had no bearing on the modern world. Arden was starting to get some of those people back, but it was going to take a long time before the Kingdom had fully recovered.

"They're not alone now," Arden said. "Madden and

his family will take good care of them until we can figure out a permanent place—and Mauthe Doog used to be popular companions among the Tuatha de Dannan. I may be able to settle them here at my Court, depending on how well they remember their time with my people."

"That would be excellent," I said. Tybalt made a face. I laughed and elbowed him lightly in the side. "Don't worry, I'm not going to get a puppy."

"I should certainly hope not," he said stiffly.

"Actually, while you're both here, there was something I was hoping to talk to you about."

Arden's words were casual, but if there was one thing I'd learned in my years of dealing with the nobility, it was that nothing that included the phrase "I was hoping to talk to you" was ever as casual as it seemed. Tybalt and I exchanged a look. Quentin winced, looking wary.

She was my Queen. Tybalt belonged to a different political structure and Quentin was going to outrank her someday. Swallowing my sigh, I turned to face her, and said, "Yes, Your Highness?"

To my surprise, Arden groaned. "You know, sometimes being the Queen isn't all it's cracked up to be. I don't want to give you an order or send you on a quest or make your lives harder, I swear. I just want to ask you a favor, and have you really think about it before you answer either way. I don't want you to say 'yes' and hate me, and I don't want you to say 'no' before you've heard me out. All right?"

"All right," I said, more slowly. "What's up?"

"I would like you to consider choosing Muir Woods as the site of your wedding," said Arden.

I stared at her. Tybalt stared at her. Arden reddened.

"I know, I know, we need a better name for this place, but I feel silly saying 'the Court of Windermere,' which is what my father called it, and I can't go the easy route and call it 'Mists,' because this whole Kingdom is the Mists and right, sorry. Babbling. I don't do it often, but when I do, I can win valuable prizes." Arden shook her head. "Look. October, you're a hero of the realm. You mean something to people around here."

"Yeah, I mean they're about to get in trouble," I said.

Arden ignored me. That was probably a good choice on her part. "And Tybalt, you're a King of Cats. Do you know how long it's been since a titled member of the Divided Courts has married into the Court of Cats? It's incredibly unifying, and that makes it incredibly important. I know you were probably considering Shadowed Hills for the ceremony, but I'd like you to please give some serious thought to doing it here."

Apparently taking our stunned silence for criticism, she put her hands up in what was probably meant to be a reassuring stance. "I promise you, we have the space—you haven't seen the entire knowe. *I* haven't seen the entire knowe. The more we clean it out, the more rooms we find. The staff here is superb, and they're itching for more opportunities to prove themselves. The Yule Ball went off without a hitch, in part because my staff was so eager to show off how amazing they can be."

"Yes, but that was a ball," I said, choosing my words carefully. "We sort of have road maps for those things. Like, we know where to put the refreshment table, what kind of band to hire, and how many guests we're expected to invite. Our wedding is a whole different can of worms." And complicated as hell, for many of the reasons Arden had already mentioned. Tybalt being royalty meant we were at risk of having it turn into a state wedding, which could result in six hundred guests, a cake the size of a small car, and me spending what should have been the happiest day of my life hyperventilating in a closet. I don't *like* big parties. The idea of being the center of one . . . thanks, but no thanks.

"I know," said Arden. "I just want you to think about it, all right? Like I said, I know Shadowed Hills is your first choice, but I think you could be really happy here."

“We will consider your most generous offer,” said Tybalt, before I could say anything I was going to regret. I shot him a grateful look. He inclined his chin, very slightly, and said nothing.

Shadowed Hills is the Duchy I’m sworn to serve, and my oaths are held by Duke Sylvester Torquill, who has been a part of my life for as long as I can remember. He was the one who gave me the Changeling’s Choice, back when I was seven years old and still standing balanced on the knife’s edge between the fae and mortal worlds. He was the first pureblood to take a chance on me, allowing me into his court and even making sure I got knighted when I earned it. For years, he was the closest thing I had to a father. I still loved him like one. I couldn’t stop.

Not even when it turned out he’d been lying to me the whole time, and that he’d been taking care of me in part because his brother had been married to my mother since before I was born, which technically made Simon my stepfather. Simon Torquill was also the man who’d kidnapped Sylvester’s wife and daughter, and turned me into a fish for fourteen years, effectively destroying my relationship with my own daughter. Why hadn’t Sylvester told me any of this?

Because he had promised my mother that he wouldn’t. He had put his promise to a woman who had all but abandoned me ahead of his relationship with me, and he wouldn’t—or couldn’t—give me a good reason why. I hadn’t spoken to Sylvester in three months. As far as I was aware, he still didn’t know Tybalt and I were engaged, and I was happy to keep it that way.

I don’t trust easily. Abuse that trust, and I don’t see why I should keep giving it to you. Sylvester had more credit with me than most people—he’d been building it for decades—and I loved him very much. Probably always would. I just needed some time before I’d be able to deal with him again.

Arden smiled, looking relieved that she hadn't just been shot down cold. "Excellent. Is there anything else I can do for you tonight? The kitchen's still open, if you're hungry after all your hard work."

"I could eat," said Quentin.

"October would greatly appreciate a sandwich," said Tybalt. "Or perhaps a banquet that you happen to have lying around going uneaten."

I shot him a mock-glare. "Stop trying to feed me."

"Stop trying to starve yourself to death for no apparent reason, and I will consider it," he replied.

Arden laughed. "Well, since you put it that way—" she began.

A commotion from the entryway cut her off. Arden turned, amusement giving way to confusion and then alarm. The rest of us turned to follow the direction of her gaze. Lowri and the other guard from the entryway staggered into view, bent under the weight of the big red-and-white–haired figure they held between them. Madden was limp, his feet dragging behind him like a dead man's.

"Madden!" cried Arden, shoving me out of the way as she flung herself across the throne room to reach her seneschal. She grabbed his head, lifting it so that she could stare into his face. His eyes were closed, and if he felt her hands against his skin, he didn't react to them. He didn't react at all. "Madden? Wake up!"

"He was dropped through a portal into the clearing, Highness," said Lowri. Her voice shook as she spoke, her accent growing stronger in her dismay. "Whoever left him for us, their magic came and went too quickly. We didn't have time to recognize it."

"Why won't he wake up?" moaned Arden. She didn't look like a Queen in that moment: she looked like an ordinary woman, on the verge of a breakdown over the thought that her best and oldest friend had been hurt. "Madden, please. Please wake up, Madden, please."

"He won't," said Tybalt. He strode over to Arden, pushing her aside as he bent to pull Madden's jacket open. Quentin and I followed him, although we didn't touch Arden. He could get away with a certain amount of manhandling the Queen, since she had no authority over him. Quentin and I weren't so lucky. Arden was our friend and all, but that wouldn't stop her from getting pissed if we touched her while she was already distraught.

Tybalt felt around inside Madden's jacket, Arden looking on in wide-eyed dismay, until he hissed with displeasure and pulled out a short, almost stubby-looking arrow. The tip was damp with blood, but only the tip; the arrow had done little more than scratch Madden's skin, based on how much blood was there. The smell of it hit me as I was walking toward him. I gasped, clapping a hand over my mouth.

Blood knows everything. Blood is where memory is stored, and where magic lives . . . and when someone is poisoned or enchanted, the blood knows that, too.

"As I suspected," said Tybalt sadly. He turned the arrow in his hand, careful to avoid the point. The shaft was fletched in deep pine green and silver—the same shade of silver that appeared on the arms of the Kingdom of the Mists, in fact. That was odd. There are only so many colors in the world. Some duplication is unavoidable, but people mostly try to avoid using the colors that have been claimed by neighboring Kingdoms when they can possibly help it. There's just too much chance of winding up with an angry monarch on your tail, questioning your fashion choices.

"Elf-shot," I said, voice muffled by my fingers.

Arden's face, which had been teetering on the edge of despair, crumbled. It was like watching a bottomless pit open in what had been a perfectly happy woman. "What?" she asked, eyes flicking to me. "No. It can't be elf-shot. No. I'm . . . I am the *queen*. I became queen so that my people would be safe. Madden is my people. He's my best people. I mean, he's my best friend. He can't be elf-shot. I won't allow it." Her voice broke on the last word, and my heart felt like it broke a little too, in sympathy.

Elf-shot is either one of Faerie's crueler weapons or one of Faerie's kinder weapons, depending on how you look at it, and how you feel about hundred-year naps. It allows the purebloods to wage war without killing each other, since killing a pureblood is a violation of Oberon's Law. Killing changelings *doesn't* violate the Law, naturally, and just as naturally, elf-shot is fatal to us, because who cares if some mongrel foot soldier dies on the battlefield?

I care. And everyone I know who's effectively lost a friend or loved one to elf-shot cares. A century is a long time, even for a pureblood.

Maybe my reasons for hating the stuff are more personal than I like to admit. Elf-shot killed Connor, who was my lover and my friend and an important part of my life. Elf-shot forced my mother to shift my blood away from human and toward fae, disrupting the fragile balance I had managed to build for myself and sending me into what has sometimes seemed like an inevitable spiral toward the pureblood side of my heritage. And it was elf-shot that forced me to turn my little girl human, taking her away from me forever. So yeah, I hate it. I figure I'm allowed.

Arden was shaking her head, eyes still fixed on my face. "You're wrong," she said. "Why would someone use elf-shot on Madden? He's . . . he's the best. He's the sweetest person in the world. No one wants to hurt him."

"Unless, through hurting him, they might hurt you," said Tybalt gently. Arden whipped around to stare at him. "You know as well as I do that the throne carries a heavier cost than we would choose, if it were up to us. So often, that cost is borne by the ones we care for."

"Green and silver are the colors of the Kingdom of Silences," said Quentin.

We all turned to stare at him—even Arden, who had started to cry. Quentin was undaunted.

"Silences is the Kingdom to the north of us, right? Their colors used to be green and red, to symbolize the evergreen forests and the roses they grow there, but when they lost the War of Silences, the Queen of the Mists—I mean the one who wasn't really Queen, Your Highness, it's just that we never got a real name for her, so I don't have anything else to call her—took the red away from them. She said they no longer had the right to claim the blood of those who had died in the name of their false cause, and that they should always know who the superior Kingdom was. That's why she made them match the silver in the arms of the Mists." Quentin bit his lip before continuing, "I mean, I'm just saying. Those are their colors."

"Oh, oak and ash," I breathed. Silences wasn't just the Kingdom to the north. It was the only Kingdom whose monarch had been chosen by the Mists, after the War of Silences had left their ruling family broken and their surviving heirs, if any, scattered. It had been a Tylwyth Teg demesne before that. But the man who had been given the throne had been a Baron in the Mists before he became a King.

And he was Tuatha de Dannan.

"If Silences was behind this attack . . ." I began.

"No," interrupted Arden, shaking her head. She was still crying, and her face was pale. "No, no, no. I remember that war. Nolan and I were still just kids when it happened. We were in hiding, but we still knew about the war. People died. Not just on the battlefield. Poisonings and assassinations and all the things I walked away from the throne to escape. I promised my brother that we would never, ever get involved with anything like that."

I looked at her, seeing not a Queen, but a frightened

bookstore clerk who had managed to wind up way over her head. I even felt a little guilty about that. If Arden was in over her head, I was one of the people who had put her there. "We don't know for sure that it was Silences."

"Yes, we do," said a weary voice from the entryway. I turned. An unfamiliar Cu Sidhe woman was standing there, her red-and-white hair pulled into low pigtails on either side of her face. She was wearing a green linen peasant blouse over jeans—all she needed was a flower crown and some wire-framed glasses and she would have looked like she had just stepped out of the Summer of Love. She held up a parchment scroll. "They left this so they could be sure we'd understand their message. I don't blame the guard for missing it. I had to sniff my way around the whole clearing before I located the admission of their crime."

"Um, hi," I said. "You are . . . ?"

"My name is Faoiltiarna. You may call me 'Tia,' as that will probably be easier on you." The woman looked at me solemnly, her eyes large and liquid and filled with the sorrow that only dogs seem to have access to. "Madden is my brother. He was snatched from the yard of our home. We knew it must be an act of violence brought against him for his association with Queen Windermere. Cowards have always struck at brave rulers through their canines."

Arden put her hand over her mouth again, and didn't say anything. She seemed to have frozen under the pressure, which wasn't the most useful reaction out of a monarch. I tried to swallow my anger. Inexperienced Queens can't be expected to get everything perfect right out the gate. Her reign had consisted of one rebellion where she didn't have to do much, a lot of cleaning, and a couple of parties. It wasn't surprising that she was overwhelmed now.

"Can I see that?" I asked, taking a step toward Tia and holding out my hand.

"Certainly," she said. She dropped the scroll into my palm, her sorrowful gaze flicking to Madden, who still hung motionless between the guards who had carried him inside. "My poor brother. He'll have a good long sleep, and when he wakes up, we'll be waiting to tell him about everything that's changed in the world. May he slumber here?" She looked back to Arden. "Our mother told us when we followed her to the Mists that King Gilad had a chamber for sleepers such as this. It would be best if Madden could sleep in safety, with no need to fear the march of progress."

"We haven't finished opening the knowe, but if that room is here, we'll find it," said Lowri. Her voice was calm and even; of everyone in this room, she had the most experience serving in a royal court. "If Queen Windermere consents, we can place him in his own room while we search. He'll be comfortable there."

Queen Windermere wasn't consenting. Queen Windermere wasn't saying anything at all. She was still just standing there, frozen and silent.

I swallowed a sigh and unrolled the parchment, careful to avoid paper cuts. There was no guarantee that whoever had left us the message would be enough of a dick to poison it, but there was also no guarantee that they *wouldn't*. Better safe than joining Madden in a century of sleep.

I skimmed the parchment, reading it twice over before I said, "The Kingdom of Silences is declaring war on the Kingdom of the Mists, in answer to our most treacherous and unkind act of treason. They want to depose Arden and return the 'rightful Queen' to the throne—their words, not mine. As per tradition, we have three days to give our final answer, or they attack."

"What rightful Queen?" asked Quentin.

"Who do you think?" I held the parchment out toward him. They didn't name their chosen monarch—of course they didn't, no one ever had; no one had ever known her name—but they called her "our fair lady of the Mists" and "the Siren of the West." It was pretty clear they intended to put the former Queen back in the position she'd held for more than a century, just like it was clear that we needed to stop them.

"But High King Sollys confirmed Queen Windermere's claim to the throne," said Quentin, sounding confused. "That means she's legitimate."

"He also confirmed the nameless usurper's claim," I said. "That means she can try to take it back. Your Highness, we're not going to—" I turned toward the spot where Arden had been standing, and stopped. The smell of blackberry flowers and redwood bark was hanging in the air and the guards were staring, open-mouthed, at nothing.

The Queen was gone.

THREE

"WHERE DID SHE GO?" demanded Tia. The rising note of rage in her tone was completely at odds with her flower child exterior. "My brother has been elf-shot because he was in service to his Queen! Loyalty cuts in both directions. Where did she *go?*"

"Away," I said. I had some ideas about where "away" might be, but I wasn't going to discuss them with an angry Cu Sidhe. Not before I'd had a chance to find and talk to Arden myself. I turned to Lowri. "You've been with royal courts for years, right?"

"Most of my life," she said, sounding uncertain. She looked worried, but not angry. That was a good sign. Her loyalty was to the Queen who held her oaths, not to the people who got hurt because they were in that Queen's orbit. That might seem cold, but in the moment, I was grateful for her relative objectivity. "Why?"

"Because the Queen just went for a walk and the seneschal is down for the count. Sorry to do this to you, Lowri, but this is where you step up and show what you've learned from all those years of service."

Lowri's eyes widened. She took a half step backward, her hooves making a staccato tapping noise against the floor as the implications of my words sank in and anchored themselves to her bones. She was the only person in the room with the experience and the training necessary to do what needed to be done, especially if we were facing a declaration of war: after all, she had served in Silences both before and during the war. She knew it, and I knew it, and the only way for her to avoid it would be to break her oaths to the throne—something I didn't think she was capable of deciding to do.

Normally, I would have felt bad about essentially strong-arming someone into taking a position in someone else's court, however temporarily. This wasn't a normal situation. Arden had turned tail and run. Madden was asleep, and he was going to stay that way for the next hundred years. The Mists might be an old kingdom, but Arden's court was very young, and it didn't have that many trained options.

Lowri swallowed. "All right, but I'm only doing it until the Queen finds someone more suited to the role," she said.

I wasn't sure whether she was trying to convince me, or convince herself. "Of course," I said. "Now, what are your orders?"

As seneschal—even acting seneschal—Lowri was the voice of the Queen. That was why attacking Madden was such an effective declaration of war. Take out a random member of a royal court, and there's a measure of "that was offensive, let's talk it over." Take out the seneschal, or worse, the heir, and it's on.

Lowri took a deep breath. Then she turned to Tia, and asked, "Will you help get Madden settled until we can locate the room you spoke of? The knowe is still being reopened, but I promise you, his quarters are more than suitable, at least for the time being. The Queen's brother sleeps in a room very much like his."

"Yes, of course," said Tia, not looking particularly mollified. She glared at the space where Arden had been, nose wrinkled in canine disgust, before walking over to slide her shoulders under Madden's arm, supporting his weight. Lowri stepped clear. Tia turned her glare on the diminutive Glastig. "We are not happy. We understood the risks of Madden's involvement with this court, and were glad of them. It's rare that the Cu Sidhe are recognized as helpmeets and pack mates by Kings and Queens. But I speak for our entire family when I say that we assumed loyalty would be met with loyalty, not with running away."

"I understand," said Lowri. "We're going to fix this." She glanced pleadingly at me.

Much as I might want to put up my hands and say, "Hell, no, I didn't sign on to get involved with any wars," I knew better. Part of being who and what I am means that things like this are never somebody else's problem. In the end, they always wind up being mine.

"I'm going to find the Queen and bring her back," I said. "You have my word, as a hero."

"Good," said Tia. Her gaze flicked to Tybalt. "You consort with cats, but Madden spoke well of you despite that."

Tybalt raised an eyebrow. "How flattering of him," he said, voice flat.

"And on that note, we're out of here," I said, taking Tybalt's arm. "Quentin, you're with me. Lowri, you have my number. Call if anything changes."

"I will," she said.

"Good." I started for the door, pulling Tybalt along with me. He came without resistance, and Quentin followed close on our heels. That wasn't what I'd been expecting to spend my night doing—I'd sort of been planning to go home and watch some television after we dealt with the Mauthe Doog—but that just goes to show that I shouldn't allow myself to expect things. I'll always wind up disappointed.

I paused in the clearing outside the knowe, sniffing

the air to see whether I could pick up any traces of the person who had shoved Madden though the portal. There weren't any. How long magic lingers depends on a lot of factors, including how powerful the spell was and how much time the person using the magic spent in the area. Whoever opened the portal for Madden had done it from a distance, and might never have set foot in this clearing in their life. They'd left me nothing to work with, and that just aggravated me further. I stormed onward, down the hill and into the park.

We were almost to the exit when Tybalt asked, "Did you intend to take the arrow and its associated message with you? I assumed you had, but as you now seem too angry to be rational, I thought it bore asking before we had gotten much further."

I looked down at the parchment scroll and unbroken arrow still clutched in my left hand, and shook my head. "No, but now that I have them, I'm going to put them to good use," I said. "Walther's an alchemist, and if we're on the verge of war, I'm not going to feel bad about drafting him. He may be able to extract something from these that will tell me more about who left them here, and since we have next to no information on Silences right now, that's data we very much need." Walther Davies was Tylwyth Teg, an alchemist, and a chemistry teacher. He'd been a big help to me more than once. He wasn't as fond of charging headlong into danger as I was, but if I needed lab work done, he was more than happy to act as my private forensics department. In many ways, he was more useful than an actual forensics team could possibly have been. Human police don't know how to look for magic.

Yes. A stop at Walther's, or at least a phone call, was definitely in the cards, after we had managed to locate Arden and get her back to her own court. If we were going to war, we were going to have our Queen front and center.

"Silences plans to march upon us," said Tybalt. "They used to be a Kingdom in the holding of the Tylwyth Teg. It's entirely possible Walther has ties to the area, and has simply chosen never to discuss them."

"I don't know that I would have discussed them, given the way their current government came to power," I said. The War of Silences was something I had only ever heard mentioned by the older fae, usually in hushed, haunted tones. "I've never been there. Given the reasons for the last war, it didn't seem like a good place for someone like me to go for a vacation."

"I know that Silences invaded the Mists, and I know that the current King was chosen by the false Queen after their old monarch was overthrown, but I thought it was just a territory dispute," said Quentin, stepping around a large fern that had decided to overgrow the path. He frowned at me, looking honestly puzzled. "Why would that be a bad place for you to go?"

Much as I love Quentin, sometimes it was easy to forget that he was, and had always been, a pureblood. He didn't understand what it had been like to be a changeling under the old Queen of the Mists, or what it was still like to be a changeling in most of the world. I took a breath and paused, trying to figure out how to explain things to him.

Tybalt saved me from needing to. "King Gilad was a good man, and one who understood that the changeling children of the Courts are still precisely that: our children. They belong to us, because we create them. While he lived, the Mists were a healthy place for changelings to live—unequal, because equality has never been a priority among the Divided Courts, but still, a place where those of mortal blood could thrive. When he died, his successor began to change that. Rapidly. She reversed all the gains that he had put in place, and quickly created the unhealthiest kingdom in North America for those among us with human blood in their veins."

"So?" asked Quentin blankly.

"So it was the abuses of the rights of changelings that caused the old King of Silences to get pissed off and invade," I said. "The dude who currently holds the throne was put there by the old Queen because he agreed with her, and since all their sitting nobility was taken out at the same time, you didn't get any Duchies like Shadowed Hills, where the people in power said 'it's nice that you're a bigot and all, but we're going to keep doing what we're doing, and we don't care what you say.' Silences is not a safe place for a changeling to be."

"Oh," said Quentin. He hesitated before saying, "That wasn't part of the history lesson I got."

"Changelings rarely are, even though we've been part of Faerie practically since the beginning," I said. "Funny thing, that." We had reached the edge of the woods while we reviewed the history of Silences. It was late enough that there was little to no chance of finding humans there, but I still paused when I saw a figure sitting on the hood of my car. For one giddy second I thought it might be Arden. Maybe she hadn't run as far as I had feared; maybe she was going to give us our orders and then head back to her knowe to oversee whatever came next.

Then I took another step and realized that the figure, while female, had hair that was too pale and clothes that were far too informal. Tuatha de Dannan can teleport, but they can't change their clothes magically, as a general rule. If Arden had cast an illusion to make her court clothes look less formal, the smell of her magic would have been filling the parking lot. All I could smell were redwoods, and the sea.

Tia slid off the hood as we drew closer. "I want to come with you," she announced, without preamble.

"No," I said.

"How did you get down here ahead of us?" asked Quentin.

"I didn't have any bipeds to slow me down. A dog

moves faster in dense wood than a man. Your cat could have done the same, if he'd been willing to leave you behind." Tia's attention swung back to me. "What do you mean, 'no'? My brother will be asleep for a hundred years. I have the right to know what the woman who claims his fealty is going to do about it."

"Yeah, you do, but you can wait until she's back at home before you ask her," I said. "Arden will be here. I don't care if I have to carry her myself, she'll be here." Tuatha de Dannan are good at running away—something about them being capable of bending space—but slap a blindfold over their eyes and they're as stuck as anyone else.

Tia frowned at me. "That isn't good enough."

"It's going to have to be," I said. "I *just* met you, and you carried in a declaration of war. I pretty much believe that you're Madden's sister, but since he can't vouch for you right now, you'll forgive me if I don't hurry to put you in my car."

Tybalt, bless him, didn't say anything. I knew how hard that had to be: he was normally one of the most sarcastic people I knew, especially when it came to things like riding in cars with dogs. He just stood there, silently lending support to my position.

The side of Tia's mouth curled up, exposing her teeth. It was less a sneer than it was a silent snarl, and it had no place on a human-seeming face. "This is unfair," she said. "My brother isn't a bad dog, and neither am I."

"No, and I understand that you're upset, but right now the best thing you can do for Madden is stay here, in the court that he loves, and make sure everything keeps working the way it's supposed to," I said. "Let us take care of finding Queen Windermere and bringing her home. We'll figure out what's going on, and we'll handle it. It's my job, remember? I'm a hero of the realm. Let me do my job."

Tia continued to eye me mistrustfully for a few seconds more before her face relaxed, turning into a neutrally mournful expression. "I will sit by my brother's bedside until you return," she said. "I will not eat, or sleep, or stray."

"Um, okay," I said. "You do that. Just try not to starve yourself or anything, all right? Lowri doesn't need another crisis on her hands." I walked past her to unlock the car doors. She didn't stop me, which was a relief: I had been half convinced that she was going to grab my wrist and resume demanding to come with us as soon as she had the chance.

Quentin and Tybalt got into the car without incident. The last we saw of Tia was her reflection in the rearview mirror as we drove away from Muir Woods, turning ourselves toward San Francisco.

"Where are we going?" asked Quentin.

"Borderlands," I said. "I can't think of any better place to start the search."

"It's two in the morning," said Quentin. "They're not going to be open."

"I can pick locks, and Tybalt can carry us through the shadows," I said. "I think we'll be fine."

When we'd first gone looking for our missing Crown Princess, the trail—augmented by some magical homing fireflies provided by the sea witch—had led straight to an independent bookstore on Valencia, less than a mile from my house. Borderlands Books sold science fiction, fantasy, and horror, which I guess made it a uniquely well-suited place for a fairy princess to go into hiding. Arden had been living in the store's basement, in a cunningly well-concealed makeshift apartment. Her brother, Nolan, had been there too, sleeping off the slow decades of his own elf-shot poisoning.

The old Queen had been the one to have Nolan elf-shot, in an effort to keep Arden from seeking the throne that was hers by right. It sent a message: "I can hurt you." Elf-shooting Madden sent the same message. It was difficult not to think that the messages had been penned by the same evil hand.

There was no traffic on the roads, and Valencia Street was pretty well deserted. I pulled up right in front of Borderlands, stopping the engine. "All right, here's how we're going to play this," I said. "I will scout the front of the store for an alarm system. If they don't have one, I pick the lock and we go in the front door. If they do have one, Tybalt opens a passage through the Shadow Roads, and he and I go straight through to the basement. Either way, Quentin, you're going to stay with the car."

My squire gave me a wounded look. "Why?"

"Because I seriously doubt Arden is going to agree to go back to Muir Woods the slow way, and Tybalt doesn't know how to drive." I pulled the key out of the engine and passed my keychain over the back of the seat to Quentin. "I'll call you if I need you to move the car."

"I think I liked it better before I had my license," Quentin grumbled. "You didn't make me play valet nearly as much."

"Before you had your license, we needed to get May involved if we wanted to have a backup driver," I reminded him. "Do you really want to go back to that world?"

Quentin blanched. "I'll drive."

"Good squire." I grabbed a handful of shadows from the roof of the car, weaving them into a makeshift human disguise. The smell of cut grass and copper rose to fill the cab, only to be beaten back by the smell of musk and pennyroyal as Tybalt did the same. His disguise was much better than mine: he looked like an actual human, while I just looked blurry and somewhat less pointy than I usually did. I didn't want to spend the magic or time to spin something more believable, not when we were going to be spending at most five minutes on the street.

"If you see anything unusual, or if the police come by and seem too interested in why you're sitting here, drive away," I said, before opening my door. "I don't want you casting a don't-look-here on the car. You may need that magic later."

Quentin nodded. He didn't argue. That was good. I wasn't sure I could handle arguing with him right now.

The last thing I wanted was another war—and when I said "another," I really meant "my first." The only other time in my lifetime that the Mists had almost gone to war, I had managed to avert it by finding the missing sons of the local Undersea Duchess. This time, I didn't think there was going to be an answer that easy.

Tybalt met me on the sidewalk. We moved toward the bookstore together, only to find a small, carefully displayed sign in the front window cautioning us that the property was protected by a local alarm company. "Oberon's ass," I muttered. "So much for picking the lock. I'd been hoping to avoid this, but—Tybalt? Could you?"

"It will be difficult, as my pride has been wounded by your hopes to avoid my contribution, but I think I can manage," he said, with a hint of amusement. "Take a deep breath."

I did. He took my hands and pulled me with him as he fell gently backward, into the shadows that pooled around the bookstore door. We toppled into absolute blackness, second only to the absolute cold that suddenly surrounded us. The Shadow Roads were lightless, airless, and most of all, freezing. They're among the most accessible of the secret paths that run through Faerie, and strange as it might seem, they're also among the gentlest: the Rose Roads are almost impossible to access, and roses have their thorns; the Blood Roads will drain you dry and leave your body as a warning to others. Nothing comes without a price. Not even passage.

We fell through another wall and back into the world of warmth and air, although not much more light: we had emerged in the Borderlands basement, where there were no windows to cut the darkness. I was just glad we weren't standing on the stairs.

I put out my hand, finding Tybalt's chest, and pressed my palm flat against his shirt. He froze, understanding my intent without a single word needing to be spoken. I smiled despite the situation. How I loved that man. Not bothering to close my eyes, since I couldn't see anything anyway, I sniffed the air.

Blackberry flowers and redwood bark. Arden was here.

"Arden, it's October and Tybalt," I said, letting my hand fall away from Tybalt's chest. There was no point in trying to sneak up on her. If she didn't know it was us, we might spook her, and I had no idea where she'd go from here. If she did know it was us, well . . . we still might spook her. It was hard to say. "We need to talk to you. Can you please come out?"

There was a long pause—long enough that I began to worry that I'd misinterpreted the scent of her magic. Maybe she had been here for so many years, casting illusions in an enclosed space, that the smell had worked its way into the walls. Then the air on the other side of the room seemed to crack open, revealing a thin band of extremely low light, like the glow from a nightlight. It was still enough to make me squint and turn partially away after the darkness of the past few minutes.

"Why did you follow me?" Arden's voice was tense and tight. I didn't need to see her face to know that she was a flight risk. Maybe she always would be. "Get out of here."

"We came to bring you back to your court, *Your Highness*," I said, stressing her title so hard that it became a weapon. "I understand that this is all sort of overwhelming for you, but it's overwhelming for everybody. Lowri is trying to hold things down—she's doing the 'temporary seneschal' thing, in the absence of better options—but we need you there. We need you deciding how the Mists will respond."

"No, you don't," she said, an edge of hysterical laughter in her words that set my teeth on edge. If she panicked, if she ran . . . "I don't know what I'm doing. I can't do this."

"Begging your pardon, Queen Windermere, but none of us know what we are doing when we begin," said Tybalt. "It is the role of each monarch to find their way, and the way of their people, even when the world seems set against them. We have no choice."

"But see, I do have a choice," said Arden. "I could abdicate. I could step down. This could all be someone else's problem, and the people I care about would stop being hurt."

"Once." The word was cold, heavy with fury, and it took me a moment to realize that I was the one who had spoken it.

"What?" Arden sounded confused. "What do you mean?"

"I said, once." I took a step toward the narrow sliver of light that hung in the basement air. I could see Arden's face when I moved. She was framed by darkness, by the two pieces of the illusion that protected her little bolt-hole here in the bookstore basement. It was just magic painted on canvas, but it had kept her hidden for years, before I came and dragged her out of her chosen obscurity.

I had wanted to feel guilty about it when it happened, but I had had no real choice: the Kingdom had needed her. And she had accepted it. She had taken her oaths before the High King of the Westlands, and she had addressed her people. She had promised to do better. She'd *promised*. Faerie isn't fair, but we take our promises very seriously.

"You get to make that threat once," I said, taking another step forward. "You get to play that card once. You get to imply that your throne, your people, your *Kingdom* are somehow less important than your personal comfort *once*, and you just got your shot. Boo-hoo, Madden is asleep. That sucks. I'm going to miss him until he wakes up. But he *will* wake up, because the people that attacked him used elf-shot. They did that for a reason. They did it because they wanted to scare you. You're really going to let them win?"

"You have no idea what you're talking about," Arden spat. The smell of blackberry flowers and redwood bark began to gather in the basement air.

I lunged forward, wrenching the two sides of the illusion apart and revealing the small, shabby apartment where our Queen had spent so many years. Arden, still in her fancy royal gown, gaped at me. I grabbed her hands before she had a chance to move, pinning her in place. She couldn't open a portal without moving them. She was trapped.

"You're not going anywhere without me, *Your Highness*," I snapped. "If you open a portal, you're taking me through, or you're not going. This isn't a conversation that you get to run away from."

"Unhand me," she said, and her voice was frozen anger and Arctic command. It was the voice of a Queen.

"If you're running away, you're not the Queen in the Mists anymore," I said. "I don't have to listen to some random bookstore clerk who doesn't want to do her thrice-damned job because it turns out that being in charge is sometimes difficult. If you're not running away, then yeah, I'm probably going to get punished for touching you without permission. I'm cool with that. Do whatever. But don't run, Arden. Don't do this to your people, and don't do it to yourself. We deserve better. You deserve better. The Mists deserve better."

Arden stared at me for a moment, eyes wide and shocked. Then, weakly, she tugged against my hands, and said, "You can let go now." The commanding tone was gone, replaced by resignation and shame.

"You won't run?" I asked.

"I won't run."

I let go.

Arden took a step back, wrapping her arms around herself so that her hands were pinned against her body, where I couldn't grab them again. That was all right. I had never seen her open a teleport gate without using her hands. I knew she was capable of it—I had borrowed her magic once, to save both of our lives—but most people fall into patterns with their spells and find it difficult to deviate. By hiding her hands, Arden was promising she wasn't going to run.

"I can't do this, Toby," she said, looking down at the floor. Her shoulders slumped, making her the perfect picture of defeat. "When you told me I had to . . . that I had to come and be Queen, I thought you were kidding at first, and then I thought maybe I could do it. Maybe I could finally live up to my father. I know he has to be disappointed in me. So I tried. Isn't that enough?"

"Maybe in the mortal world," I said. "That isn't how things work for us, and you know it. You're Queen in the Mists. The High King accepted you. The knowe of your father opened for you. You're stuck with the job, Arden. It's yours until you die, or you have kids to pass it off to. That's how this *works*."

"What's more, you knew that when you accepted the crown," said Tybalt, voice pitched low. "None of us who are raised in the halls of power can come to adulthood ignorant of what we will one day be expected to become. You were not an innocent. You were not tricked. You were a princess born, and have aged into what you were always meant to be."

I noticed that he didn't use the word "grown." Arden still hadn't grown fully into her position—if she had, we wouldn't have been standing in the basement of a human business, trying to convince her to come home. She was still growing. I just hoped we'd all survive long enough for her to finish the process. "We don't have anyone else," I said. "The false Queen was a vindictive bitch *before* we knocked her off your father's throne and put you in her place. If she gets this Kingdom back, everyone who moved against her is going to be in a lot of trouble. And the changelings . . . oak and ash, the changelings. She never defended us. She never raised a hand to welcome us into Faerie. But at least for most of us, she never stood against us the way she did right after she took the throne. Power mellowed her. We were allowed to exist. You really think she's going to stay that understanding after the way I helped you take your throne?"

"She will also be set against the Court of Cats, of that I am sure," said Tybalt. "She cannot raise a hand to me directly, but there are things she could do, if she came back to power. Purebloods have always been fond of controlling mortal legislation. There could be culls of the feral cat colonies, restrictions placed upon the humans who claim to own us, even closures of local shelters and rescue organizations. She could easily destroy my Court, all without crossing the lines that Oberon once drew."

I glanced at him, startled. What he was saying made sense—so much sense that I had no doubt it was true—but I had never considered it before. Sometimes I can get so wrapped up in Faerie that I forget how dependent we still are on the mortal world, and how many purebloods know how to work it to their advantage. It's odd how good they are at pulling those strings. These are people who don't understand telephones or cars or cable television, but if you show them something and say "this makes you powerful," they'll figure it out. My liege, Sylvester Torquill, owns enough real estate in the Bay Area to make him a millionaire a dozen times over; his court employs a small army of accountants and investors to keep that money moving and prevent attracting attention. And he's by no means unique among the truly long-lived.

It's weirdly easy to underestimate the purebloods, to

think that their power ends at the boundaries of their courts. That's a good way to get into a whole lot of trouble.

"What do you want me to do?" demanded Arden. "I'm painting targets on everyone I care about!"

"Be better," I said. "That's what we want from you. We don't want you to be perfect, and we don't want you to be above reproach, but we want you to make an effort. We want you to be our Queen."

Arden looked at us both for a long moment. Then she turned to look at the little living space behind her. Everything was still there, except for the carved redwood wardrobe that had once dominated an entire side of the room. She must have moved that to Muir Woods as soon as she got settled there. The wardrobe had belonged to her mother. It made sense that she would want it with her. But the rest—the television, the small rack of videos, the ancient, roughly-constructed bunk bed—were all still in their places.

"It was simpler when I lived here," she said. "I kept Nolan from getting covered in cobwebs. I made coffee when I worked at the café, and sold books when I worked at the bookstore. Jude and Alan were always nice to me. I miss them. I miss knowing that as long as I did my job and kept my head down, they would have my back. I miss Ripley. I miss my *life*. You know that's what you took away from me, right? You took away my *life*."

"We gave you back the life that was supposed to be yours all along." I shook my head. "Change sucks. No one's going to argue about that. Change is hard and painful and sometimes we wind up losing things we wanted to keep forever. You can't go back to the life you had when you lived here. You made promises. It's time to keep them."

Arden looked at me for a moment before looking down at the floor. "Everything got so hard when you showed up."

"I have a talent for complicating situations," I said. "Your Highness, will you please return to Muir Woods before poor Lowri has to organize a response to a declaration of war with no one to support her?"

"Yes," said Arden. "You're coming with me."

I had been expecting that. I still raised an eyebrow and asked, "Why?"

"Because you put your hands on me without permission, and that means you have to be punished," said Arden. There was a smile in her voice that unnerved me as she continued, "Don't worry. I know exactly what I'm going to do to you."

She lowered her arms before raising one hand and tracing a circle in the air. The smell of blackberry flowers and redwood bark rose as the portal opened, showing the entry hall at her knowe in Muir Woods. "If you would come with me?" she said.

When a Queen tells you to come with her, there isn't much room for argument. I pulled my phone out of my pocket and pushed the button for Quentin's number. When he answered, I didn't wait for him to say anything: I just said, "Bring the car to Muir Woods," and hung up, putting the phone away again. Taking a deep breath, and with Tybalt beside me, I walked through the portal, and toward whatever punishment my loyalty had earned me.

FOUR

I WAS SITTING ON THE trunk of a fallen redwood only feet away from the open doors of the Queen's knowe, wondering whether I could find myself a new career, when Quentin came racing up the side of the hill. He stopped when he saw me, his eyes going wide as he took in my slumped, despondent posture. Tybalt was standing a short distance away, giving me my space. That, more than anything, explained Quentin's cautious approach. If Tybalt, who was rarely afraid of anything, was standing out of hitting range, I was a clear and present danger to everyone around me.

I held my silence until Quentin was closer. Then I lifted my head off my hands, leaving my elbows resting on my knees, and said, "I need to ask you a question, and I need you to give me an honest answer. Not the answer you think I want to hear, and not the answer you want to be true, but the actual answer. All right?"

"All right," said Quentin uncertainly.

"I'm not kidding, Quentin. If you lie to me, I will kick your ass all the way back to Toronto."

"All right," said Quentin again. He sounded more

confident this time. If he was getting ready to lie to me, at least he was planning to do it with conviction.

"Would your father approve of you accompanying me to Silences right now? Because guess who's just been appointed the ambassador in the Mists." I jerked a thumb toward my chest. "Arden seems to think the best way to negotiate peace with a Kingdom that hates changelings is to send in your most irritating changeling knight."

"And her Cait Sidhe fiancé, pray do not forget that," said Tybalt. There was an edge to his words. "If you attempt to creep out while you think I am not looking, you will come to direly regret your actions."

I leaned back until I caught his eye. "We've gone over this. I'm expected to bring a retinue. Since you're a monarch in the Mists, you can either come as a King of Cats and thus officially throw your Court of Cats in with the Divided Courts, or you can stay here and not commit your people to a war they don't want any part of."

"I threw my lot in with the Divided Courts when I threw my lot in with you, and I will not take it back," said Tybalt tersely. "I mean to accompany you, whether you will it or no."

"He's getting all Shakespearean," I said, leaning forward and looking back to Quentin. "That means he's coming with me. The question is, are you?"

"I . . . I don't know," said Quentin slowly. "I think this may actually be one of those situations where I need to call home and ask my dad. I can see where me being involved with negotiating a cease-fire could be really useful later on, you know? But I think my parents will be pissed off if I wind up sleeping for a hundred years."

"Most people's parents would be," I agreed, and stood. "Come on. We need to get back to the house and tell May what's going on. You need to call your folks, and I need to call the Luidaeg. She should know that I'm about to leave the Kingdom."

Quentin blinked. "If we're just going to turn around and go home, why did you have me drive all the way out here? I could've met you at the house."

"Because I will not be accompanying you upon this leg of your journey," said Tybalt. "Even as you must inform your companions of your intent to travel—"

"Is it really my intent if I'm doing it against my will?" I asked.

Tybalt rolled his eyes and continued without missing a beat: "—I must inform my Court that I will be away for a short time, pursuing a guarantee of their safety. I can convince them to be patient. Kings are not so vital in the day-to-day operation of a healthy Court that they will not let me go. Some may even be relieved by my absence, however brief. It can be difficult to feel as if you are truly wild when there is a keeper forever watching over you."

I blinked. In all my dealings with the Court of Cats, I had never stopped to think about it that way. The Cait Sidhe made up part of their Court, but the rest consisted of runaway house pets, feral cats, and the changeling children of the Cait Sidhe themselves. Anyone who's ever known a cat knows how much they prize their independence. As King, Tybalt was essentially cast in the role of caretaker. He set rules, provided food for the weak and defenseless, settled disputes, and generally did all the things for the Cait Sidhe that they didn't want to do for themselves.

In an entire Court of the free, the King was the only one who was captive.

"Are you going to leave Raj in charge?" I asked.

Tybalt snorted. "No, for a great many reasons. He is not ready. He will be ready soon. Until that day arrives, I will not leave him on my throne. There is too much chance that his returning it to me would be seen as weakness, and prevent him from later claiming it as his own. I will leave Gabriel and Opal as my representatives.

Gabriel has been of my guard for long enough that his presence will be accepted, and Opal is more adept at using the telephone than most of my people. Alazne is old enough now that she can be coaxed into one form over another if her mother puts in sufficient effort."

Alazne was the only survivor of Gabriel and Opal's first litter. Her three siblings had been killed when Oleander de Merelands poisoned the meat supply of Tybalt's Court. It had been touch and go for Alazne for a long time, but she was finally growing out of her early medical issues, and into the rest of her long, long life as a pureblood Cait Sidhe. She was a good kid.

"Sounds good," I said. "Meet us back at the house?"

"As soon as I may," he said. "Should you need to relocate in the interim, please leave a note of some sort. I would hate to have to go looking for you."

I smiled. "Will do." I stood, leaning over to kiss him quickly before I started walking toward Quentin, and away from the knowe. "Come on, kiddo. Let's go home." A faint waft of musk and pennyroyal from behind me told me that Tybalt was gone. It was time for us to be gone as well—time, and past time.

Quentin was quiet as we navigated the hill back down to the park, and walked through the park to the lot where my car was waiting. He stayed quiet—uncharacteristically so—as we got into the car. I cast a quick don't-look-here and started the engine, pulling out onto the main road. I glanced at him a few times, but decided to wait until we were on the freeway. If he hadn't at least turned on the radio by then, I would ask him what was wrong.

We reached the freeway with the silence still hanging between us like a knife on a string. I cleared my throat. "Okay, what's wrong?"

"I don't want to let you go without me." His voice was very small. "I hate that you have to treat me like . . . I never wanted you to know. Not until I was ready to leave my fosterage and take my family name again. I didn't want you to treat me differently."

"Oh," I said.

Quentin was the Crown Prince of North America. One day, he would control the continent. And I hadn't known that when he became my squire. He'd been sent to Shadowed Hills on a blind fosterage, which meant that no one other than Sylvester had known who his parents were, and that none of the rest of us were allowed to try to find out. For a long time, I'd assumed he was minor nobility at best, since his parents seemed perfectly cool with letting him become a changeling's squire and run around the Mists getting shot at and hanging out with the sea witch. It had been . . . well, a shock to discover that actually, his parents thought spending time with me would make him a better King one day.

"I've tried really hard *not* to treat you any differently," I said carefully. "It's been difficult sometimes. But you still have to do the dishes when it's your turn, and I took you to fight the big black dogs without going 'oh no, I could hurt the Crown Prince.' Honestly, I would have wanted you to stay behind even before I knew—I would probably have insisted. It's only the fact that you're going to be High King someday that makes me think this is something you should see."

"It still feels like I'm being punished for being a prince," he said.

"Let me ask you something. If this had come up while you were still concealing your identity from me, and if I had been temporarily out of my senses enough to ask you to come along, would you have been willing to just grab your things and follow me to Silences? Or would you have called home and asked your parents if they'd mind?"

His silence was answer enough. He would have checked in. That was reassuring—it meant I hadn't completely converted him to my particular school of "go ahead, rush straight into danger, it's fun." It also put a lot of past events into a new perspective. If he'd been checking in all along, the High King and Queen must have really believed in the idea of preparing their heir for anything.

"So see? The only thing that's changed is that now I ask you to call them, rather than you having to sneak around and do it behind my back. I've never been happy about hauling you into danger, and I've never pretended to be." I flashed him a quick smile. "I think this is a good thing. I like it when we're not keeping as many secrets."

Quentin smiled hesitantly back. "I guess so." He paused before asking, "So why is Arden making *you* go to Silences? I mean, it's not like you have any ambassadorial experience."

"Funny thing: I don't think anyone in the current nobility *does*," I said grimly. "Sylvester is busy in Shadowed Hills, and he's our most experienced hero. If we actually go to war, Arden is going to need him here to organize the troops. Li Qin is a scholar. April is . . . April is April. Even if she could travel that far, she's more likely to accidentally start a war than intentionally prevent one. We could ask Saltmist to loan us someone, but they don't really do diplomacy, unless you count Dianda going 'stop hitting yourself' over and over again. There may be some diplomats in Wild Strawberries or Deep Mists or someplace, but none of them will have seen any action since the War of Silences, when they were working for the woman who's now trying to declare war on the rest of us." Simon Torquill had been a diplomat, once upon a time: that was part of why he had a title but no lands. As the less martial of the brothers Torquill, it was his job to solve problems before they got out of hand and required Sylvester to come along with an army. Unfortunately, Simon was asleep, and was going to stay that way for a century. He wasn't going to help us with this war.

Sometimes I think Faerie goes to war as much because we can't find anyone who'd rather talk things out as for any other reason. Diplomacy is not a valued skill among the Courts. Most of our nobles would prefer to do the dance of manners and then slide a knife between someone's ribs. It's more fun than actually discussing trade sanctions and why it's rude to kill your neighbors.

"Okay, I guess, but why you?" asked Quentin. "You're . . . not really that diplomatic."

"You mean I'm a blunt instrument being sent to do a scalpel's job," I said. Quentin nodded. I shrugged. "When I found Arden, she and I had an argument about how to handle things. I sort of grabbed her without her permission. So she's punishing me."

Quentin looked suitably horrified at the idea that I had grabbed the Queen in the Mists without her consent. He shook it off and pushed on, saying, "Maybe, but she's not stupid. If she thought that punishing you like this would result in a war, she wouldn't do it. So she must think you can argue your way out of a war."

"I did it once, I guess," I said dryly, before leaning forward and turning on the radio. "I want to think. Feel free to critique my taste in music."

"I always feel free to do that," said Quentin, and promptly changed the station.

He was right about one thing: if Arden wanted me to be the ambassador in the Mists, she had to think it would somehow benefit the Kingdom. It was too specific to be a punishment she'd come up with on the spot. Fine, then. How could I benefit the Kingdom? Well, I could yell at the King of Silences until he agreed not to go to war. Awkward, but potentially effective. I could try to talk some sense into the former Queen of the Mists. I could—

Wait. "Quentin, do ambassadors get diplomatic immunity?"

"Yes," he said. "It's the only way to prevent assassinations at major court functions. Not that it actually *prevents* them, but it makes them less common than they would be otherwise. No one wants to deal with a dead body on the dessert cart."

"And people say I'm desensitizing you to violence," I said. "So here's a theory for you: Arden is sending me because this way I'll have diplomatic immunity, which means the King of Silences can't arrest me on the spot. That gives everyone back here time to come up with a better plan for getting through this alive. In the meanwhile, we're in Silences with the former Queen, who *hates* me. That means she's a lot more likely to lose her temper and do something that violates hospitality." Which I would probably survive, given my own nigh-indestructability.

It was only nigh, not complete, which meant I wasn't entirely comfortable with this plan, but I could see the logic. If my presence could provoke the former Queen into doing something inappropriate, we might be able to call this whole thing off—High King Sollys couldn't prevent his subordinate kingdoms from going to war, but he could step in if one of them broke the rules of engagement. Of course, I could get stabbed a few dozen times in the process. Sadly, as I had come to learn, sometimes being a pincushion is my purpose in life.

The kitchen light was on when I pulled into the covered parking space next to our house. We lived in a beautiful old Victorian that had been purchased by Sylvester Torquill shortly after it was constructed, and used as a rental property until the day I agreed to let him move me into something safer than my apartment. Most of the neighbors hated us in an offhand sort of manner, since we had twice the space they did, plus a parking area and a small yard—all things virtually unheard of in modern-day San Francisco. I was sure they'd change their minds if they knew how much I'd bled to earn that house.

Or maybe not. Reserved parking is hard to come by in this city.

Quentin, as always, walked ahead while I locked up

the car. Arden's promised snack hadn't materialized, due to Madden having been elf-shot, and Quentin was probably starving. Keeping a teenage boy away from food for the better part of a night isn't *actually* torture, but it can definitely seem like it to them. I followed at a more decorous pace, tucking my keys into the pocket of my leather jacket. If there was one thing living with Quentin had taught me, it was not to get between him and the refrigerator at moments like this.

May and Jazz sat at the table in the breakfast nook, polishing off the remains of what looked like an ice cream sundae the size of my head. It's good to have goals. They were looking up when I arrived, courtesy of Quentin, who was already digging through the fridge with the manic intensity of a man who had just been informed that there was never going to be food ever again.

"Long night?" asked May sympathetically. As my former death omen, she was unique in all of Faerie: a Fetch whose existence was no longer directly tied to any one person's survival. Amandine had somehow severed the bond between us when she shifted the balance of my blood away from human to save my life. This had left May with a copy of my original face, all soft changeling edges and bluntly-pointed ears, and a level of indestructability that even I couldn't match. She seemed pretty happy about the situation.

We'd been living together since she first appeared. People used to mistake us for each other, but that hadn't happened in a while. It helped that May's style was best described as "*Jem and the Holograms* meets Rainbow Brite." Her spiky brown hair had been bleached to within an inch of its life and dyed in a variety of pinks and purples, and she was wearing a tie-dyed cotton sundress. Between that and the increasing sharpness of my features, anyone who could mistake us for each other was either legally blind or had recently been hit in the head.

"Long, and getting longer," I said. "Nights like this, I wish I still drank coffee. Quentin, can you make me a sandwich, too, while you're rooting through the fridge like—Oberon's ass, I don't know, something that roots. I'm too tired to insult you."

"Wow, you *are* tired," said Jazz, May's live-in girlfriend. She was a Raven-maid, with long black hair, warm brown skin, and eyes rimmed in avian gold. The band of black feathers tied in her ponytail held her fae nature; without it, she would have been as human as any of our neighbors. Skinshifters are somewhat odd, even by fae standards. Raven-maids and Raven-men are even odder, since they're diurnal when most of the rest of Faerie is nocturnal. May and Jazz's relationship was a love story about missed sleep, compromises, and working around differences. In that regard, it wasn't that different from my relationship with Tybalt.

At least we all got along, for the most part. Not bad for a changeling, a cat, a death omen, a bird, and a prince in hiding.

"Yeah, well." I leaned up against the counter, half watching Quentin as he emptied the fridge onto the table. We were apparently having leftover pot roast sandwiches, with mashed potatoes and cranberry jam. I'd eaten stranger. "I don't really know how to give the short version of this, so here's the badly edited one: the Kingdom of Silences has declared war on the Mists for the crime of unrightfully deposing our former Queen. One of their people elf-shot Madden—I have the arrow that came with the message, I'll be taking it to Walther this afternoon. Arden tried to run. We tracked her down, things got a little heated, I grabbed her without permission, and as my punishment, she's making me go to Silences as the ambassador in the Mists. Hopefully, we can get this all sorted out before I convince them that they should slaughter us all in our beds."

May blinked. Jazz blinked. Both of them stared at me

like this was the most ridiculous thing they had ever heard.

Finally, Jazz spoke. "They're sending *you* as a *diplomat?*" she asked, with exquisite care. Right then, she proved that she was more of a diplomat than I would ever be. "Did you explain to Queen Windermere why that might not be the . . . smartest choice?"

"I tried," I said. "She's pretty set on the idea. I think she's trying less for 'Toby goes to Silences, smooths everything out, hooray,' and more for 'Toby infuriates them so badly that they can't remember which end of the sword to use.' It's a terrible plan."

"I don't know," said May. "I was a diplomat once—well, a couple of times, but only once that I really remember. Super-annoying ambassadors have their place, too. Sending someone you know the other side will hate keeps them from being too comfortable during the negotiations, while also letting them know that they can't just dismiss your emissary. If they do, you can claim that they never really wanted to work in good faith, and that justifies burning a lot more stuff down."

"And in the meantime, Arden and Lowri can get together with the local nobles and come up with a plan for getting through the war alive, if it actually happens," I said. Before she became a Fetch, May was a night-haunt, one of the dark secrets of Faerie. They eat the dead, and because memory is hidden in the blood, they take on the faces of their meals. The night-haunts remember things that happened to people who they never really were. "If you were a diplomat, you died. How did you die?"

"Um. Poison once, and I sort of got stabbed the other time." May's cheeks reddened. "Maybe that wasn't as encouraging as I wanted it to be."

"No, it was totally encouraging, if you're encouraging me to get stabbed." I sighed, running a hand through my hair. "I need to call the Luidaeg. She's going to be pissed at me for finding a new way to try to get myself killed, but maybe she can give me some advice."

"Pretty sure her advice will be 'don't go,' " said Jazz.

I chuckled bitterly. "Pretty sure you're right."

May pushed her chair back from the table, standing. "I'll go pack."

"Uh, what?" I stared at her. "No, you will not. Sit your butt back down. You're staying here."

May raised one eyebrow, an expression so familiar that I didn't need to wonder what it meant. "I'm sorry, but it sounds like you just told me to stay here in the Mists while you run off to Silences to get yourself killed. Is there a planet where that would work? I'd love to visit there sometime, just to see what it's like."

"We're *on* that planet," I said firmly. "Sit back down. I need you to stay here."

"Because . . . ? Seriously, Toby, I want to know why you think leaving your indestructible, incredibly useful sister behind is a good idea. I won't lie, I'm not feeling it." May crossed her arms and glowered at me. "I should be with you on this one. I have actual experience."

"You have someone else's experience," I said. "You've told me yourself that most of your memories come from either me or Dare, since we were the last two people you shared blood with as a night-haunt. We color everything you remember. Neither one of us was ever what you'd call a diplomat." I'd improved since the cutoff point between May's memories and my real life—I hadn't been given much of a choice—but the woman I'd been when May tasted my blood and took my face had never been forced to learn how to rein herself in. That woman was long dead, thankfully, buried under the weight of the experiences I'd had since then, but part of her lived on, in May.

"And? You have to take backup with you, or we're getting you back in a box."

"I'm going to call home and see whether my parents

want me to go with Toby," said Quentin, walking over and handing me the plate with my sandwich. "I'm going to do that now." He waved to May and Jazz as he walked out of the kitchen, presumably to make his phone call someplace that was more private, and maybe quieter. The fact that he'd be out of the blast radius was nothing but a bonus.

May didn't say a word. She just pointed after Quentin, her arm stiff and trembling slightly with anger.

"Quentin is my squire," I said. "It looks stranger if he *doesn't* come with me than if he does. No one knows about where he comes from but us, Tybalt, and Arden. Nobody in Silences is going to stand up and say, 'Hey, that kid looks the way the Crown Prince was rumored to look back before his parents hid him. Let's take him hostage.' "

"They *might*," snapped May. "You're being stupid. You need to take me with you."

"I'm already taking Quentin—maybe—and Tybalt," I said. "Since there's a good chance Arden will want to send someone with me to keep an eye on things, I'd say the party is about full. Bringing you and Jazz along starts to look like an entourage."

"Hang on there," said Jazz, looking suddenly alarmed. "Who said anything about me coming with you? I'm not going with you. I'm staying right here to feed the cats and Spike and *not* get used as target practice by some Silences archer who thinks ravens make good stew."

I blinked. "I'm sorry, Jazz. I just assumed . . ."

"You can stop assuming, honest. I love May. She's a big girl. A big, indestructible girl. I am *not* an indestructible girl. When there's a war, I stay away from the battlefield until the killing is over and the scavenging begins." May and I gave her matching appalled looks. Jazz shrugged. "When I'm a woman, I eat Pop-Tarts and vindaloo. When I'm a big black bird, I eat eyeballs and spleens. It's all part of the glorious contradiction that is me."

"Ew," I said.

"She brushes her teeth before I let her kiss me. She brushes her teeth a *lot*," said May. She turned back to me, sighed, and said, "I didn't want to play this card, but here it is. You're either taking me or you're taking Stacy. Who would you rather have with you in a dangerous Court? Your roommate who can't be killed, or your thin-blooded best friend with five kids who depend on her?"

I frowned. "Why would I take either one of you?"

"Because you don't know how to style your own hair," said May, with a shrug. "You're bad at doing makeup, your idea of 'court formal' is actually offensive, and you usually look like you forgot how to operate a hairbrush. We're used to you around here—you're even sort of endearing, since you're all 'local girl made good' and 'Duke Torquill's pet project'—but in Silences? Where they already think of changelings as being inferior to purebloods? You have to be better than you have ever been. Better groomed, better prepared, and better braced for what's going to hit you. You need a lady's maid, October. Given your friends, it's either me or Stacy. Now pick one."

I stared at her for a moment, open-mouthed and stunned into silence. I had never even considered how I was going to dress for the Court of Silences, or how they were going to judge me on things like how I wore my hair. It was stupid, and shouldn't have mattered when there was a war on the horizon . . . and May was right. It *did* matter.

"Go pack your things," I said finally. "We're going to get some sleep, and we'll head for Muir Woods as soon as we wake up. Arden will open a portal to Portland for us. After that, we're on our own." I pushed away from the counter, taking my untouched sandwich with me.

"Where are you going?" asked May.

"To call the Luidaeg," I said. "I figure I may as well let everyone yell at me at once." I didn't look back as I walked out of the kitchen, leaving the two of them behind.

FIVE

"*WHAT?*" THE LUIDAEG'S VOICE was essentially a snarl, filled with the kind of irritation that should have earned her an apology and a quick disconnection.

It was too bad for her that I had learned to see through some of her disguises. She was never as angry as she sounded on the phone; her tone of voice was one of the few deceptions she had left, thanks to her big sister geasing her to always tell the truth, and so she always answered like she was going to kill whoever had called. Everybody needs a hobby. "Luidaeg, it's me," I said, sitting down on the edge of my bed. The bedroom door was closed, buying me at least the illusion of privacy.

"Toby?" The anger faded immediately, replaced by pleased surprise. "I thought you weren't coming over until later this week."

"I'm not, or at least I'm not planning to. I have a problem."

She chuckled, low and dark, like bones rolling on the bottom of the sea. "Don't you always have a problem? The day you don't have a problem, you'll probably decide that *that's* a problem, and go looking for one."

"I can't say you're wrong, but this is a real problem."

I described what had happened at Arden's as quickly and concisely as I could without leaving anything out. It was easier than I had expected it to be. I've had a lot of practice at describing bad situations over the past few years.

When I finished, there was silence from the other end of the phone for several seconds before the Luidaeg sighed. "I should have seen this coming," she said. "Silences has been a danger ever since your last Queen decided to put her patsy on the throne. Don't underestimate him just because he's a fool, October. Rhys always knew how to play the political game. He was going to be King one way or another. Silences just gave him a throne that didn't require a wedding ring to go with it."

The thought of the false Queen marrying *anyone* was startling enough to throw me off for a moment before I said, "I have to go. I don't have a choice."

"No, you really don't. Once you put your hands on Arden, your fate was sealed." The Luidaeg chuckled humorlessly. "Really, you just lie awake all day coming up with new ways to screw yourself over, don't you?"

"Sometimes even I'm not sure."

"Regardless, I'm assuming you called because you want my help."

"The thought had crossed my mind. I also thought you might want to know that I was leaving the Kingdom. The deadline you gave the Selkies—"

"Is mine to worry about. I'll tell you when you're needed." Her tone left no room for argument, and honestly, I didn't mind.

The Luidaeg was the Firstborn daughter of Maeve and Oberon, and like every Firstborn I had ever met, she had been the mother of her own race: the Roane, shapeshifters and fortunetellers who manipulated storms and lived happily in the waves. They were almost extinct in the modern day, thanks to a betrayal by her elder sister, Eira Rosynhwyr, better known as "Evening Winterrose."

She had given knives and instructions to a group of people with more greed than sense, and they had skinned the Roane alive. Those same people's children had returned the pelts to the Luidaeg after killing their own parents. They had begged her for mercy, and she had shown it, in her way. She had transformed them into Selkies, entrusting them with the burden of keeping her children's magic alive.

According to her, the Selkies' bargain was almost up, and their time in the sea was almost done. I was going to play a part in ending them. I didn't know what that part was; I was honestly afraid to ask. But as long as she wanted to keep putting it off, I was happy to delay.

"Okay," I said. "Got any advice for me?"

"Don't drink the water; don't trust the locals." She paused. "Actually, amend that: you *need* a local, one you can trust. That alchemist of yours, Walther? Take him with you. He'll help you make it back alive."

I blinked. "Walther? He's not from Silences."

"Yeah, he is. He just doesn't talk about it much."

"And you know this because . . . ?"

"Because I pay attention. Because I remember the War of Silences. And because Silences trained the best alchemists in the Westlands. He's Tylwyth Teg, just like the old ruling family of that Kingdom. He's an alchemist skilled enough to keep a changeling alive through a goblin fruit addiction. He's from Silences, sure as fish have bones. It's going to be hard enough without going in blind. Take him."

"People aren't like loaves of bread at the store. I can't just go 'oh, I'll take this one.'"

"Can't you?" Now she sounded almost amused. "Figure it out. Stay alive." The line went dead in my hand.

I lowered my phone, glowering at it. I couldn't call her back. For one thing, if she'd had anything else to say, she would have said it. For another, poking the Firstborn when they don't want to be poked is a good way to pull back minus a hand, and I liked both of mine. Sighing, I pulled up my address book, and dialed again.

Sunrise was at least twenty minutes away, and the campus wouldn't be open for hours. The phone was still answered on the second ring. "Professor Davies' office, Professor Davies speaking. I'd ask why you were calling at this ungodly hour of the morning, but maybe you've met me." Walther sounded almost offensively cheerful for a man who had doubtless been locked in his lab, inhaling chemical fumes all night.

"Academic standards for how you answer the phone get lower after midnight, don't they?" I asked.

"All human standards get lower after midnight," said Walther. "Hey, Toby. Long time no hear. What's up? Do you need another alchemical miracle? Because I'm warning you, I may start charging you by the ounce soon."

"I don't need a miracle right now, but I'll keep that in mind," I said. "I *do* have an arrow and scroll that I'm going to need analyzed. I hope your schedule's free." Walther was the best alchemist I knew. He'd kept me from eating myself alive when I was addicted to goblin fruit, and he'd created the power-dampening potion that had allowed us to save Chelsea when she was teleporting uncontrollably through the various realms of Faerie. He wasn't my most frequently used Hail Mary pass, but he'd done the job often enough to be a very valued ally. "Why are you at work this late? I was sort of expecting to get your voicemail at this hour."

"I'm working on a few private projects. Even the most dedicated grad students give up by midnight, or sometime shortly after; that leaves me the hours between two and six for getting things the way I want them. A lot of alchemical tinctures need to be hit by the first rays of the rising sun to really crystallize their effects, so I like to have them finished right before dawn. That way I can pack them in before the human students show up and why are you calling if it's just a standard analysis? You'd normally bring that by the lab. Are you actually being social for a change?"

He sounded so delighted by the idea that I felt a pang of guilt when I had to say, "No, not really. I do need that analysis, but there's . . . there's a problem, and I think I also need *you*. Not your work, not your potions, *you*. Is there any way you can get out of your classes for a while? A week or so?" It wouldn't be more. After a week, we'd either be at war, or everything would be back to normal.

Walther hesitated before saying, warily, "There's a flu that's been going around campus. I have grad students who can take my classes and sick time saved up for the actual time off. But you're going to have to give me a damn good reason that I'd want to do that."

"Silences has just declared war on the Mists."

Walther didn't say anything.

"Queen Windermere, in her brilliance, has decided that I would be the ideal diplomatic ambassador from the Mists. I leave tomorrow to try and make this war not happen. The Luidaeg says I need to take someone who actually knows Silences with me. She suggested you."

Walther didn't say anything.

"Please."

"Do you understand what you're asking me to do?" His voice was lower now, almost pained. "If the Luidaeg told you I was from Silences, she must have told you that I never wanted to go back there again. I can't do this."

"Why not?"

"Why not?" He laughed unsteadily. "Because they came for my family, Toby. They killed or arrested everyone I had ever given a damn about, and they did it because they didn't like the way we thought. I barely got away. I haven't spoken to my sister or to any of my cousins in years. I don't even know if they made it out, and I can't go looking. It's not safe for me to talk to people from Silences, not with that murderous bastard on the throne. You're asking me to walk right back onto the killing fields."

"I'm asking you to help me keep the killing fields from coming here. Please, Walther. The old Queen—the one whose rulings about changelings started the first war, the war you're talking about now—she's there, with their current King, and she's the one who wants us to start killing each other again. She wants her throne back. I don't think that would be good for *anybody*, but I get the feeling it would be especially bad for people who have known connections to me."

There was a long pause before Walther said, in a soft voice, "That's low. You know that, don't you?"

"I do." Sometimes the high ground is reserved for the people who think honor is more important than living. "I'm sorry, if that helps at all."

"It doesn't."

"I didn't think it would." I stopped talking, waiting for him to break the silence between us.

It stretched out for long enough that I began to think he wasn't going to. Finally, he said, "Pick me up from my office before you go. I need time to get my kit together."

"Okay," I said. I felt bad about pushing him this way, but it was going to have to wait. He was going to come. My diplomatic team, such as it was, was nearly complete. "We'll see you then. Open roads, Walther."

"We're going to need a lot more than open roads," he said, and hung up.

"That could have gone better," I said, lowering my phone and looking at it like it should have somehow warned me. Then I sighed and tucked it back into my pocket as I stood. Walther was coming with us. Ruthless as it might seem, I was willing to upset him if it meant he was going to play native guide to the ins and outs of the Court of Silences. Everyone's lives might depend on his temporary unhappiness . . . and as I had come to learn over the past few years, sometimes ripping away the bandages was what allowed the soul to finally heal. He might come out of this stronger than he had ever imagined.

Assuming he—and we—came out of it at all.

Quentin was in the kitchen making more sandwiches when I came back downstairs. I paused in the doorway, arching an eyebrow upward. "Well?" I asked.

"My father says I should go with you, because this is important stuff for me to know and understand," he said dutifully, looking over his shoulder at me. I kept my eyebrow raised until he sighed and added, "He also says I should be prepared to run if it's necessary to save my own life, because he needs an heir more than I need an education."

"Great," I said. "I'll ask Arden for some blood before we leave."

Quentin paled. If there was one area in which I had not been good for my squire's education, it was his understanding and use of blood magic. I hadn't quite managed to pass along my revulsion at the sight of the stuff, but he'd been fostered with Sylvester, who never did very much blood magic, and then squired to me, who had a tendency to either wind up covered in the stuff or try to ignore it completely. I'd made a few efforts to get him accustomed to what would be his greatest strength when he was a King, but it was hard to keep my own prejudices from shining through.

I was going to have to try harder. I owed it to him, and to the Kingdom that would one day be his to hold. "Walther is coming with us," I explained. "He can make blood charms. Blood from Arden will hold her magic, and by having Walther preserve it, we can keep an escape route open the whole time." Blood from her sleeping brother, Nolan, would have been even better. Their power was roughly equal, but he had less opportunity to use his, and it built up in his veins like wine. I just didn't think she was going to let me bleed him for the sake of our escape.

Then again, she *was* shipping me off to stop a war. I made a note to ask her about it.

"Make sure he makes enough for everyone," said May. She was still sitting at the table.

I turned to look at her. "Didn't I tell you to go pack?"

"Yes, and I stayed right here to make sure you weren't going to try to sneak out of the house while I was distracted," she said amiably. "I figured it would be harder for you to ditch me once you'd said that I was allowed to come along in front of Quentin. Besides, I'm a great alternative escape plan. Let them fill me with arrows while you run. I'll catch up later."

"What if they're using elf-shot?" asked Quentin.

"Now that is an interesting question that I would almost like to know the answer to," said May. An edge came into her voice, accompanied by the strange, nameless accent that she sometimes had, usually when she was talking about—or to—the night-haunts. "A few centuries ago, this woman decided she wasn't going to let us have her husband. I'm not sure why. Someone had told her we were evil, or that we perverted the bodies of the dead or something."

"Maybe someone told her that you ate them, sweetie," said Jazz.

"Maybe," agreed May. "Anyway, this lady met us standing over her husband's body with a crossbow and a whole quiver of elf-shot arrows. She started firing at random into the flock, trying to scare us off, or take hostages if she couldn't manage it. She was a pretty good shot, too. She hit half a dozen of us before she ran out of arrows. And not a single night-haunt fell."

"So night-haunts are immune to elf-shot?" I asked.

May nodded. "Yeah. I just don't know if Fetches are. Could be interesting to find out."

Jazz punched her in the arm. "Don't do it on purpose. I have no interest in sitting and weeping by your bier for a hundred years or more."

"Yes, dear," said May.

Quentin, meanwhile, had a more important question. He frowned and asked, "What happened to the woman?"

"Oh, her? She had raised a hand against us, and willingly entered our circle. We ate her." May stood, leaning over to kiss Jazz's cheek before she added, "I'm going to go get my things ready. Don't leave without me!"

"We wouldn't dream of it," I said, staring after her as she sashayed out of the kitchen. May and I were close. Sometimes I even thought of her as my actual sister, not the result of a complicated series of choices and magical bindings. I definitely loved her. But there were still times, like this one, when I was reminded that she was unique in all of Faerie, and that there were legitimate reasons for her to scare the crap out of me.

"That's my girl," said Jazz. She sounded faintly amused. She pushed her own chair back, stretching, and said, "I'm going to go help May pack. I'll probably be asleep when you leave."

"Okay," I said. "There's cat food in the hall closet, and mulch on the porch."

"I know where everything is," said Jazz. Her amusement faded. "Bring her back safe, Toby. And bring *you* back safe, too. I'm not sure she could live with herself if she let you get hurt."

"I'll do my best," I said.

"That's all I ever ask," she said, and left the kitchen, leaving me alone with Quentin.

He looked at me. I looked at him. He shrugged. I sighed, and said, "I bet this isn't what you were expecting when you asked to be my squire, huh?"

"It's better," he said, with a brief grin. "By the time I'm King, there won't be anything left that can surprise me."

"I guess that's a good trait, in a King." I pushed away from the counter. "I should pack, and you should, too. Leave behind *anything* that might let them figure out who you are."

He blinked at me. "You never figured it out."

"I wasn't looking, and I'm not a hostile monarch getting ready to go to war against the Court you represent," I said. "For all I know, you carry a handkerchief with the logo of the Westlands on it, and seeing it would let any servant in Silences know that you're the missing prince."

"I think that's the plot of a Disney movie," said Quentin slowly. "But okay. I'll make sure I don't pack anything that could give me away."

"Good," I said. I retrieved my neglected sandwich from the counter. "Let's go get ready to do something incredibly stupid."

"Business as usual, then," he said, and fled the kitchen, laughing, before I could swat him. I followed, a smile on my face. That was the nice thing about sharing my home with people that I loved: even when things were bad, I could generally find something to smile about.

Quentin beat me to the top of the stairs and was already in his room by the time I reached the hall. I paused for a moment, listening to the sound of him opening drawers. He would be done packing well before I was. Unlike the stereotype of the teenage boy living in mess and chaos, Quentin kept the tidiest room in our house. May's bedroom was always an explosion of fabric and makeup and bright colors. And my room was, well . . .

I turned and opened the door, revealing the battered outline of my secondhand bed, rescued from being a spine-breaker only by the addition of a memory foam mattress topper, and the heaps of unfolded laundry that always seemed to sprout up around my dresser and nightstand, like strange mushrooms. Spike, my resident rose goblin, was asleep in one of those piles of laundry, curled into a tight ball with its nose resting on its spiny tail. The cats were equally asleep, on the bed.

Spike had tried to sleep in the bed with me, Cagney, and Lacey when I first brought it home. Unfortunately, being a rose goblin meant that it was completely covered in thorns. I'd only needed to roll over on top of it once to know that it needed to sleep elsewhere.

"Hey, guys," I said quietly, and walked across the room to the closet. "Jazz is going to be taking care of you for a while, all right? Try to be nice to her. She's probably going to be pretty stressed out." Cagney and Lacey, as expected, ignored me.

Spike was another story. The rose goblin clambered to its feet, stretching in a languid, catlike manner before rattling its thorns at me and making an inquisitive keening noise in the back of its throat.

"What?" I asked, opening the closet and beginning to paw through my growing collection of ball gowns. I was going to need to bring them *all*. The irony of wearing dresses created by the false Queen's magic to a Court where she was currently in residence did not escape me. After a pause, I also dug out the black spider-silk formal I'd worn when I went to prevent our war with the Undersea, and the silver spider-silk gown I'd worn to Arden's Yule Ball.

"I know there's some sort of a rule against wearing the same dress to two court functions, but it's a stupid rule, and I'm pretty sure it doesn't extend across Kingdoms," I said, dumping my armload of formalwear on the bed. Spike, still watching me intently, rattled its thorns again and chirped. "Okay, seriously, *what?*"

"It wants to come with you," said Tybalt, from the bedroom door.

I turned to look at him, raising an eyebrow. "Please don't tell me you speak rose goblin now. That would be one weird thing too far for my delicate nerves to handle."

"I do not," said Tybalt calmly. He folded his arms, causing the red flannel shirt he was wearing to wrinkle interestingly across his chest. "I do, however, speak fluent housecat, which is a frequently nonverbal language. Your resident felines are hoping you will acquiesce to its request and allow it to accompany you on whatever journey you are undertaking, as otherwise it will pace and rattle and disrupt their sleep."

"Right. Because my cats speak rose goblin."

Now Tybalt allowed himself a very faint smile, the corners of his mouth tilting almost imperceptibly upward. "They have had occasion to learn, given the close quarters they once inhabited."

"It's not my fault I kept them in an apartment for so long! I couldn't afford the rent on anything larger." My objections sounded weak even to my own ears, and when Tybalt's smile grew, so did mine. I shrugged. "Okay. So I liked my apartment. It was the home I made for myself after I came back from the pond. You know? I liked having a place that was *mine*, that didn't have to be anyone else's."

"But it didn't remain yours alone for terribly long." Tybalt lowered his arms and prowled into my room, moving close enough that I could smell the lingering traces of pennyroyal and musk on his skin. It was a heady perfume, and one I had become very accustomed to over the past few years. "It began with the cats—almost immediately—and then came the rose goblin, and then May . . . however did it take you so long to realize that you were not made for solitude?"

"What can I say? I'm a slow learner." I leaned up and forward, pressing my lips to his. Tybalt's arms slunk around my waist and pulled me close, until my heels left the floor and I was balanced on my toes. His hands found a home at the small of my back, fingers clenched tight against the ridges of my spine. I closed my eyes, sinking into the moment. We wouldn't have it for very long. I knew that; I always knew that. Kisses like this were meant to be stolen, captured around the edges of the things we couldn't run from.

There had been a time when I hadn't even been willing to admit that I loved him, or more terrifyingly, that he loved me. And now he was going to marry me, assuming we both lived long enough to let that happen.

Spike's low keening caught my ear and caused me to finally pull away, looking down at the thorny little thing. The rose goblin narrowed its bright yellow eyes and rattled its thorns at me, clearly impatient.

"Yes, you can come along," I said, removing my hands from Tybalt's shoulders, where they had somehow come to rest. "Just try not to get me into any trouble I wasn't going to find on my own, okay?"

Spike rattled its thorns and made a warbling noise before trotting out of the room, presumably to do whatever sort of preparation an animate rose bush needed to do before going on an adventure.

"You're right about one thing: I'm not good at being alone," I said, raking my hair out of my eyes as I turned back to Tybalt. "Even when I'm trying to go on a dangerous diplomatic mission, I wind up bringing half the Kingdom of the Mists with me. Walther's coming, too. He knows Silences, and the Luidaeg thought it would be a good idea."

"We worry about you," said Tybalt. He reached out and brushed back a lock of hair that I had managed to miss. "Your predilection for racing headlong into danger has left us reluctant to allow you to wander unobserved."

"A girl's got to have a few talents," I said, with a smile, and took a step backward before turning and opening my dresser. "I'm bringing a couple of ball gowns, but I figure I can probably get away with a few pairs of jeans, too. I look silly in tights, and I can't fight in a dress."

"Fashion is ever your nemesis, isn't it?" asked Tybalt, sounding amused. I glanced over my shoulder to find him studying my open closet. "It's a miracle we can make you presentable as often as we do."

I paused, looking at him carefully. He was still considering the bed, but there was a tension in his shoulders that I recognized all too well. "You're really worried, aren't you?"

"I am following my fiancée, an alchemist, a half-trained squire, and a death omen to a hostile Kingdom, currently being influenced by a woman who has every reason to wish the lot of us dead," he said, sounding oddly subdued. "A woman who, I feel I must remind you, once compelled me to tear your throat from your body."

"Tybalt—" I began.

He raised a hand, motioning for me to be quiet. I stopped. For a long moment, silence held sway over the room, so thick with what wasn't being said that I could barely breathe. Finally, he sighed, looking at me gravely. There were shadows in his malachite-banded eyes.

"We have not spoken of this, mostly, I feel, because I did not wish it, and you did not force the matter. You know I was under her control; you know I would die before I would harm you of my own volition. The matter, such as it is, is closed for you. I have known this since the moment you embraced me in Queen Windermere's hall, and please do not doubt that I am grateful. All I have ever wished is your good regard."

"That's not true," I protested. "You were alive for centuries before I was even born." It was a stupid thing to say, but I needed to say *something*, and it was the only thing I could think of.

Tybalt smiled. It didn't chase the shadows from his eyes. "True enough, and I won't pretend the life I lived before you was somehow the lesser for your absence. There was no hole waiting for you to come along and fill it. I loved often, if not always well. I fought, I fled, I ruled my people, and I thought myself content. But since you have returned to us—since the waters of the Tea Gardens gave you up, and gave you back to me—not a day has passed without my considering the fragility of your smile, or the color of your eyes. You insinuated yourself into my heart like a worm into an apple, and I am consumed by you."

I didn't know what to say to that. I just blinked at him, struck silent by his words. Sometimes I could forget that Tybalt was a contemporary of Shakespeare, that his language wasn't archaic because he was putting on airs, but because that was the way he'd learned to speak: all flourish and metaphor, and an anguished search for understanding.

"When the false Queen sang, all I heard was her voice; all I knew were her orders," he said, expression all but begging me to understand. "I could no more have denied her in those moments than I could deny you now. I felt no love for her, thankfully—if I had, I think I might have died on the spot, my heart torn in two by the depth of my betrayal."

"You did what you were compelled to do," I said, finally feeling like I was back on solid ground in this conversation. "She was part Siren. You couldn't help yourself." She had *been* part Siren, then. She wasn't anymore. I had ripped that part of her heritage away from her as cruelly as a battlefield surgeon hacking away a limb. I hadn't felt bad about it then, and I couldn't bring myself to feel bad about it now. She was the one who had chosen to use her fae gifts to turn my allies against me, and to try to hold a throne that she knew damn well wasn't hers to have. She'd deserved what I did to her.

"But I *knew*." The bitterness in his voice stopped me cold. "I *knew* what I was doing, even as I could not help myself. I had been pushed into the wings of my own existence, and my understudy allowed to take the stage. Don't you understand? I wasn't controlled so completely that I didn't see your face as it crumpled, as my claws came away red with your blood. I could have killed you. I *would* have killed you. And I would have lived the rest of my life knowing that I had destroyed the woman I loved. I have lived with that knowledge, October. It was a bitter pill to swallow when Anne died, all independent of my actions. I could not have lived with it a second time. So yes, I'm worried. I'm worried that we're walking into a situation I cannot predict or control, orchestrated by a woman who has used me as a weapon against you once before. I'm worried that when I see *her* face, I won't be able to stop myself from taking my revenge. And I am equally worried that were I to stand aside, were I to let you go without me, you would not come home again."

"Oh, oak and ash, Tybalt." I crossed the distance between us in two long strides, putting my arms around him again. This time, I was the one to pull him tight, and he was the one who folded into me, pressing his face to my shoulder as he cried. I just held him, stroking his back with one hand and staring at the wall while I tried to sort through all the things I wanted to say—the ones I shouldn't say, the ones I couldn't say, and the ones that would have to be said eventually, but would do us no good in the here and now.

Finally, I said, very softly, "I don't blame you. I made the choice then not to blame you, and I stand by it. You would never have hurt me if she hadn't forced it to happen, and I got better. I always get better. That's the thing you have to remember, okay? No matter what happens to me, I will do my best to get better, and I will not leave you. I love you. I love you even when my blood is on your hands. And I'm not going anywhere, you got that? I am not going *anywhere*."

Tybalt didn't say anything. He just stayed where he was, crying into my shoulder. I closed my eyes as I held him close, and hoped more than anything else in the world that I wasn't lying to him.

SIX

I DIDN'T SLEEP LONG, BUT the sleep I got was sweet, tangled as I was in the welcome cage of Tybalt's arms. The light of the afternoon was coming in around the edges of the blackout curtains when I finally opened my eyes and blinked, bewildered, at the dimly lit ceiling above me. "What time is it?"

"Later than it could be, earlier than it should be," said Tybalt. I turned to find him sprawled next to me, his head propped up on one hand. "Did you rest well?"

"As well as can be expected, given what we're about to go and do," I said. His hair was artfully disarrayed, like it had been arranged by some supernatural stylist while he slept. Mine, on the other hand, was a bird's nest of tangles, halfway blocking my eyes. I shoved it out of the way. It flopped right back down again. I sighed and gave up as I asked, "Do you need to go back to the Court of Cats for anything?"

Tybalt shook his head. "No. I made my farewells and my arrangements before I came to you. There was a chance that Arden might have ordered you to leave at sunrise, giving me no time to double back. I'm all yours, both now and until you'll no longer have me."

"Forever. Forever's good." I kissed him quickly before rolling away and out of the bed. There wasn't time to get distracted; Walther needed to be picked up, which meant driving in the exact opposite direction from Muir Woods. We'd already kept Arden waiting. It wasn't a good idea to do that more than we had to.

I stretched, causing my muscles to grumble and groan. I recover fast from injuries, but there are still consequences for my actions. Thank Oberon for that. Without consequences, I'd probably be worse about plunging headlong into danger than I already am. "I would kill a man for another six hours of sleep," I said.

"And here I was assuming that beginning quests while exhausted had become perfectly normal," said Tybalt, sliding into a sitting position. He was naked. I could see the ghosts of his cat-form's stripes on his back, narrow bands of darker skin. They weren't always there. Like all Cait Sidhe, Tybalt had some control over the places where his Sidhe and feline forms met. Unlike most, his control was absolute—he looked as Sidhe as any child of the Daoine when he wanted to, and the face he usually wore only had a few telltale feline elements, which he could have hidden if he'd ever wanted to. The fact that he was comfortable enough with me to let me see his stripes was a great honor, and it just made me more determined to do right by him.

By both of us. "Did you bring a suitcase?" I asked. "Because much as I like this look, I don't think it's suitable for Court, and you can't wear the same flannel shirt for three days."

Tybalt snorted, shooting me an amused look. "I appreciate that you felt the need to inform me of that. I might have been unaware."

I shrugged. "Just making sure."

"Yes, I packed a valise for this trip, and it contains all that I'm likely to need during the time we have available. I am fortunate to have been born a member of the sex whose fashion requires less space; had I the need for ball gowns and elaborate footwear, I am sure I would be traveling with a steamer trunk too heavy to shift on my own. I definitely would not smash them down to make more space in a single container." He turned to smirk at my hard-shelled suitcase. "I have always been more interested in clothing than is perhaps ideal."

"Whereas I'm just happy when my ass isn't cold." I stretched again. "Okay. I'm going to grab a quick shower, and then we can wake up May and Quentin and get on the road."

"I have a better idea," said Tybalt. "While you shower, *I* will wake the others, as they may also wish to cleanse themselves before getting into the car. The more we can accomplish at once, the more quickly we will be able to depart."

"I wasn't aware that you were in such a hurry to go," I said.

He leaned over and caught my hand, giving it a brief squeeze before releasing it. "I assure you that I'm not. I am in a deep hurry to return home, safe and sound and with all of this behind us. If this must be done—and it must—then it is best that it be done quickly."

"I love it when you misquote Shakespeare," I said, earning myself a wry look before he grabbed his trousers off the floor, pulled them on, and prowled, bare-chested, out of the room. May was going to get a surprise.

Ah, well. She could handle a few surprises. I took my bathrobe off the back of the door and made my way to the master bathroom.

Showering only took about ten minutes. It wouldn't have taken even that long if I hadn't needed to wash my hair before going to visit hostile royalty. It seemed polite. Packing my toiletries and cosmetics—such as they were—took me even less time. I stepped out of the master bathroom to find that Tybalt had not yet returned. I dropped my cosmetics case into my backpack and was in the process of zipping it up when my eye caught on the bottom drawer of my dresser and I stopped, just looking at it, feeling my heart beating too hard against my ribs.

There was a time, when I was more human than I am now, when I carried two knives everywhere I went. A silver knife, received from Dare before she died, and an iron knife, received from Acacia, otherwise known as the Mother of the Trees. The iron hadn't burned me then, although I'd needed to handle it with care. Iron kills magic. It's the only thing that can reliably be used to destroy the fae—all save for the Firstborn themselves, who must be killed with iron and silver together. It's not forbidden, exactly, but it's viewed as a cheater's weapon.

And I wanted to take it with me so badly that it hurt. I wanted the safety it would afford, even if I never took it out of its case. I couldn't carry it in my bare hands anymore; it would blister my skin and poison my blood if I tried. The closest comparison in the human world was pure uranium.

In the end, I turned away, and left the dresser drawer closed. There would be a time for iron. This was not that time.

I dressed the way I always did: jeans, a tank top, and my leather jacket, which was the only armor I'd ever worn into battle, and sometimes felt like the only armor I would ever need. Then, with my hair still damp against the back of my neck, I picked up my suitcase and walked out to face my fate.

May, Tybalt, and Quentin were already in the kitchen when I came downstairs. Quentin was at the breakfast table, his face pressed against the mat. May seemed slightly more alert, but only slightly. She was wearing jeans and a brown cable-knit sweater. At least one reason for her exhaustion was immediately evident: the streaks of color were gone from her hair, leaving it the plain, no-color brown that she'd inherited from me when she took my face and form. I blinked at her before raising an eyebrow.

"What did you do to your hair?" I asked.

"I figured anything I could do to not draw attention to my appearance would be a good thing," she said, before smothering a yawn behind her hand. "I'm not going to lie about what I am, and there's a good chance Nameless McBitchypants will tell the King of Silences that I'm a Fetch as soon as she realizes who I am. But if we can pass me off as a changeling member of your retinue for at least a little while, that's what we should do."

I blinked at her again. "That's . . . a really good idea," I said finally. "Good thinking."

"I was up until an hour before he," she jerked a thumb toward Tybalt, "came to pry me out of bed. This is a terrible plan. Why can't we sleep until six? We can prevent the war after six happens."

"Arden wants us there before we're expected," I said brusquely, leaving my suitcase in the doorway as I walked to the fridge. I yanked the freezer door open and rummaged until I found my waffles. "This way we arrive while they're all still getting ready for the day."

"And this won't make them shoot us on the spot?"

"That would be undiplomatic. Look, I figure they're already going to be pissy and hard to deal with. Maybe if they're pissy, hard to deal with, and exhausted, they'll slip up." I dropped my waffles into the toaster. "Or maybe we will. Hell, I don't know. Do whatever you have to do to wake yourselves up. Swallow a bottle of No-Doze. Lick a bee. I have no useful suggestions here."

"Nor do you have any actual nutrition in your planned meal," observed Tybalt.

"Why mess with a good thing?" I threw the empty waffle box at the back of Quentin's head. It hit him squarely. He sat bolt upright, twisting around to give me a betrayed look. "Up. It's time for wakefulness and energy, not drooping like a wilted flower."

"I hate you," he said.

"Weren't you enrolled in human high school at one point? They would have made you get up *much* earlier than this."

"I was going to bed earlier when I did that, and fewer things were trying to kill me on a nightly basis," he said, before yawning enormously. "Can I sleep in the car?"

"Until we get to Muir Woods, yes, you can sleep in the car," I said. My waffles popped up, somehow managing to be soggy and burnt at the same time. I plucked them out of the toaster, juggling them from hand to hand as I waited for the hot parts to cool off and the frozen parts to warm up. "It's not too late to back out, you know. You could stay here with Jazz. No one would blame you."

His sleepy expression hardened into narrow-eyed suspicion. "Are we leaving this early because you don't want me coming with you?"

"No, but it's a good idea," I said. I finally got both waffles settled in one hand, and walked to recover my suitcase. It was heavier than it looked. Spider-silk compacts small. It's still heavy as hell. "My sword is in the car; this is all I need. Do the rest of you have all your things?"

"Yes," said May.

"Yes," said Tybalt.

"I really hate you," said Quentin.

"Good. Get your stuff in the car." I started for the door. Spike—having crept into the kitchen at some point when I wasn't looking—followed, sticking close to my ankles and rattling its thorns like an angry maraca. It was almost soothing, in a weird sort of way. Here I was, diving back into the unknown, and my rose goblin was coming with me for the ride.

Quentin was asleep almost as soon as his butt hit the backseat. He put his head against the window, mouth hanging open, and fell back into the deep, slow breathing that signified a body fully at rest. May slouched into the other side of the backseat, yawning, and slumped slowly over to rest her head against his ribs. I paused in the act of opening the driver's side door, looking at the pair of them.

"This is going to be a disaster," I said.

"Have faith," said Tybalt, opening his own door. "Perhaps we will all return home with our limbs intact and our souls unbowed."

"Yeah, and maybe I'll finally get that pony," I said.

Spike followed me as I slid into the car. First it scrambled into my lap, and then it leaped onto the dashboard, where it paced and rattled before settling down in a catlike curl. I wasn't worried about any of the human drivers we shared the road with seeing it: the smaller creatures of Faerie are protected from mortal eyes by almost unconscious illusions, making them seem like shadows and tricks of the light, not impossible creatures. It was a nice trick.

Sadly, it wasn't a trick the rest of us shared. All four of us were roughly human, and could probably pass from a distance, but it wasn't a good idea to push our luck. I reached up and grabbed a fistful of shadows and air from the roof of the car.

"I'll do my illusion if you can put a don't-look-here on the car," I said to Tybalt, who nodded. He mimicked my gesture, and for a few seconds the car was filled with the mingled scents of our magic and the slightly disjointed sound of our chanting. We both chose Shakespeare: me, a passage from *The Tempest*, him, one of the sonnets. I couldn't stop my own casting long enough to listen and figure out which one it was. That was a pity. Tybalt reciting Shakespeare was something that should have been savored, not ignored in favor of blunting the tips of my ears and shifting the color of my eyes to something that looked more blue, and less like the fog that hung in the early morning air.

I shouldn't have needed a separate human disguise—

not with a good don't-look-here over the rest of the car—but someone was going to need to go and collect Walther when we got to the college, and that someone might as well be me. It was my fault that he was getting involved in all of this, after all.

My spell gathered and burst, followed by Tybalt's a bare second later. I slid the key into the ignition and started the car, feeling it purr to life around me. Glancing at Tybalt, I asked, "So how much do you know about the Cu Sidhe?"

"The dogs?" He wrinkled his nose. "As much as I must. They're pleasant people, for the most part, if a bit simple. Not stupid, mind: just simple. I dislike their lack of complexity. It makes every interaction feel like a trick. Why do you ask?"

"Tia," I said. "I've never known one of them to get angry that fast."

"Ah." His expression shifted, becoming almost melancholy. "There was a time when not many Cu Sidhe lived in this Kingdom, little fish. This was cat territory, and we mostly avoid one another, when we can. They lived in Silences."

"Until the old King fell," I said, filling in the missing pieces.

Tybalt nodded. "They were of his Court. They came here in the aftermath, and have remained ever since."

"So hearing that Silences had hurt her brother probably didn't help Tia's state of mind." It might well have destroyed it. I shook my head. "I need to think about this. You can get some sleep, if you need to."

To my surprise and relief, Tybalt did exactly that, bracing his arm against the window and resting his head on the platform this created. He didn't enjoy riding in the car under the best of circumstances; something about remembering a time when the streets belonged to horses and carriages kept him from fully relaxing in something that moved faster than either men or beasts were ever intended to. But he was getting used to it, for my sake, just like I was getting used to traveling via the Shadow Roads, for his.

It was nice, that we both had something to get used to. It made things feel more equitable.

I turned the radio on but kept it turned down low as I made the drive from San Francisco to Berkeley, trying to allow the familiar sounds of 1980s rock and roll to ease my nerves. It didn't work. I was wound as tightly as it was possible for me to be, and there was no one for me to blame but myself. I could have been smarter about confronting Arden, for a start—I could have avoided this whole situation if I'd just kept my hands off the Queen in the Mists.

Or maybe not. Arden had been so quick to jump at sending me into Silences as a punishment that I had to wonder whether it would have been her solution even if I hadn't done anything wrong. I was developing something of a reputation as a political wrecking ball. She hadn't built her Court yet, not really, and with Madden out of commission, she couldn't afford to send Lowri away. Who else did she really *have?* I was a hero of the realm. Sending me to Silences might have been her best approach.

"I hate politics," I muttered, and turned onto University.

The central spire of UC Berkeley was visible long before the campus itself came into view. I ignored the posted parking signs and drove up one of the back paths intended for delivery trucks and moving vans, getting as close to the building where Walther worked as possible. Tybalt's don't-look-here was holding exceedingly well. As long as no one tried to bring a U-Haul down the path, the natural aversion to interfering with anything under that sort of illusion would keep the human population of campus from noticing us.

May, Quentin, and Tybalt all remained asleep as I

turned off the engine and eased my way out of the car. Only Spike clambered to its feet, stretched, and leaped after me. "Stay close, okay?" I said, gently closing the door. "I don't have time to chase you around the school. We have a war to prevent."

Spike gave me a reproachful look and rattled its thorns, like it was ashamed of me for even asking. I shrugged.

"I just like making sure we're all on the same page," I said, and started walking.

UC Berkeley is a beautiful school. If I had ever decided to go to a human university, I think I would have liked to go there. Redwood trees studded the grounds, growing thickest around the stream that ran through the center of the school. Squirrels chittered at me as I walked past, and a few of them even pelted Spike with acorns, apparently offended by its presence. The passive illusion that kept humans from noticing my thorny companion didn't extend to the campus wildlife. Spike rattled its thorns and kept walking, apparently unconcerned.

It was early afternoon when I reached the chemistry building. Most morning classes were probably over, while the afternoon classes would get started after their instructors came back from lunch. Still, my association with Walther had taught me that grad students could be found in the halls at all hours of the day and night, taking advantage of whatever free scraps of lab time they could find. I kept that in mind and didn't talk to Spike as I walked down the short hall to Walther's office door.

It was open. I peeked inside, fearing the worst, and found Walther at his desk with his eyes closed and one hand pinching the bridge of his nose. The glasses he wore when he had to interact with his human students were off to one side, next to his laptop's keyboard. I cleared my throat and rapped my knuckles against the doorframe.

"Hey, Walther," I said. "Your ride's here."

"I can't believe she told you. I was never going to go back, you know," he said, as calmly as if he were making an observation about the weather. "I was going to stay here in the Bay Area until I got bored, and then I was going to go somewhere else, but I was never going to go back. You're making me go back."

"And you're delusional," I said. "If you were really never going to go back, you wouldn't have stopped here. You would have gone to Angels, or Lights, or hell, all the way out to Lakes. The Mists are too close to Silences. You were always going to go back. I'm just the excuse that's finally forcing the issue."

Walther lowered his hand and opened his eyes. They were shockingly blue, a shade that shouldn't have existed in nature, not even in Faerie. Not even his reasonably well-woven human disguise could fully blunt those eyes. Hence the glasses, which made him look a little bit less like he was staring into your soul. "Sometimes I don't like you very much," he said.

"That's okay," I said. "Sometimes I don't like me much either. Are you ready to go?"

"Yes." He stood, picking up the briefcase that sat next to his chair. I raised an eyebrow. He shook his head, looking too tired to argue. "Trust me. This contains everything I'm going to need to make it there and back again."

"If you say so. Come on." I turned and walked out of the office, heading for the exit. I didn't hear any footsteps behind me. At the end of the hall I paused and looked back. Walther's door was still open. I waited. A few seconds later he finally appeared, slowly closing and locking the door behind himself. Only then did he turn and walk in my direction.

He was a man of average height, blond, slender, and somehow gawky when he was in his human disguise, even though none of his dimensions really changed. I had to assume it was intentional, something to put his students at ease. Without the illusions concealing his true nature, his eyes would be brighter, his ears would be sharply pointed, and his features would seem subtly inhuman, although there was no single thing that could be pointed to and declared the deciding factor. He was a very classic Tylwyth Teg in all of those regards.

He was also my friend, and as callous as I might have seemed in insisting that he come with me, I was still worried about him. Going back to Silences was going to be dangerous . . . and sadly, I really didn't see a choice. Out of my entire little entourage, he was the one I was most concerned for, and the one I could least afford to leave behind.

When he reached me, I pushed the door open, and together we walked out onto the campus.

"Who's coming with us?" he asked, when we were almost to the car.

"Tybalt, May, and Quentin," I said. Spike rattled angrily. I smiled wryly. "And Spike."

"Portland is good for roses, and for rose goblins," said Walther. "It probably wants to check out the locals. That sounds like a good team. You sure you need me?"

"I need an alchemist, and I need someone who knows the Kingdom," I said. "Maybe I could leave you behind if you were only one of those two things, but since you're both . . ."

Walther sighed. "The curse of my existence. You know, just once, I want a beautiful woman to exploit me for something other than my magic and dangerous political connections. Where's the car?"

"Here." I gestured toward a patch of air that my eyes didn't want to focus on. Spike hopped right into the middle of it, becoming difficult to look at directly as it sat on the car's hazy-seeming hood.

Walther squinted, cocking his head to the side. After a few seconds, he ventured, "Tybalt's work?"

"Yeah." I moved around to where I remembered leaving the driver's-side door and groped in the air until I found the handle. Once the door was open, I could see into the car, where my sleeping passengers had continued to snore their way through my absence. I considered them, and finally said, "Okay, May's practically sitting in the middle of the backseat anyway. You should be able to wedge yourself in next to her. Want me to put your briefcase in the trunk?"

"I'll keep it with me," he said. Putting his hand on the hood, he walked around the car, using the feel of it under his palm as a guide until he reached the back passenger door. Opening it, he dropped onto the thin sliver of seat next to my sleeping Fetch and proceeded to nudge her over with his hip until he had enough space to let him close the door. May grumbled sleepily but didn't wake up. Walther shot me a wry smile.

"I don't know whether to worry about the fact that your brave protectors are so asleep that I could be murdering you right now, or to be relieved that they're getting some rest," he said.

"I would have your heart in my hand before it had stopped beating if I thought you presented even the slightest degree of threat," said Tybalt calmly, without opening his eyes.

I blinked at him as I slid into the car. "I thought you were asleep," I said.

"Ah, but see, I am asleep," said Tybalt. "Note that my breathing has not changed, and that I am not moving. Even asleep, I will protect you. Remember that, and have faith in me."

"I do," I said, and started the car.

"Your boyfriend is scary," said Walther mildly. "I hope you realize that."

"He's my fiancé now, and the fact that he's scary is part of the reason."

"I never did congratulate you for that," said Walther. "I'm really happy, October, for both of you. I've never heard of a Cait Sidhe marrying a member of the Divided Courts. I actually thought it was just one of those weird rumors until I ran into Bridget and she confirmed it."

Walther wasn't a member of Sylvester's Court, but he and Bridget Ames were both on the UC Berkeley faculty. It's funny how rumors travel. Although if Bridget knew, Sylvester probably did, too—so much for keeping a low profile. "We still don't have a date for the wedding. I'm not exactly speaking to Sylvester right now, so I don't want to get married at Shadowed Hills. We can't get married in the Court of Cats, since then I wouldn't be able to have any guests—which is tempting in its own way, but would get me into a lot of trouble. Arden offered to let us use her knowe right before everything started going to shit."

"Are you going to?"

"Honestly, I don't know," I said. "Tybalt gets a vote, when he's awake and we're not heading off to prevent a war. It'd definitely make a statement about the validity of our marriage. Sort of hard to say that a changeling and a Cait Sidhe can't be together when the Queen in the Mists stood witness. At the same time, it feels like she'd be using us to . . . I don't know, make a statement about her own validity as Queen. She *is* Queen. The High King already confirmed her. I don't need to be a political puzzle piece. Especially not on my wedding day."

"You're a hero of the realm now, Toby," said Walther. He sounded almost amused, in a sideways, regretful sort of way. "You're always going to be a political puzzle piece."

I didn't have an answer for that.

Walther took my silence as an excuse for him to close his eyes and settle back against the seat, not going to sleep, exactly, but definitely checking out of the world around him. I turned the radio back on, and focused on the road.

It's a good thing I like to drive. Returning to Muir

Woods meant retracing our path across the Bay Bridge, and then heading deeper, driving across the Golden Gate and into the misty headlands of Marin. My passengers were quiet the whole time, whether sleeping or sunk in thought, and I was grateful. I needed some time to prepare myself.

Being a hero isn't something that's come naturally to me. I became a detective because I was stubborn, and because Faerie doesn't encourage the sort of relentless curiosity that I've always exhibited. That never made me *good* at it—just determined enough that I could usually shake the world until an answer fell out. I'm best at finding things that have been lost. Knowes. Children. Princesses. That last was what earned me the title of "hero," once and for all, and secured my reputation as something more than the street rat I'd once been. I just wasn't sure it was a good idea to approach heroing the way I'd always approached detecting. Can you really shake the world until justice falls out? At this point, did I have a choice one way or the other?

Lowri was standing at the open gate of the Muir Woods parking lot. I stopped about eight feet away from her, looking around for signs of hikers or people who might have come to enjoy the redwoods. Thank Maeve, we were alone. I leaned over and touched Tybalt's shoulder.

"You can drop the don't-look-here now," I said. "We're at Muir Woods."

"And no one's died yet? Truly, it is a day for miracles," murmured Tybalt. He raised one hand and snapped his fingers. The spell burst around us, smelling of musk and pennyroyal.

It had barely begun to dissipate when Lowri raised her hands, sketching a quick series of gestures in the air, and the scent of Tybalt's magic was replaced with hers, all warm barley grass and mustard flowers. Whatever spell she was casting, it was finished in short order, and she stepped to the side, motioning us forward.

Tybalt was sitting bolt upright now, eyes narrowed and nostrils flaring. I put a hand on his arm after I had pulled into the first available parking space.

"We'll find out what she cast in a moment," I said. He liked having others use magic on him without his consent about as much as I did—which was to say, not at all. "She's acting on Arden's orders, whatever she did. If you're going to be mad at someone, be mad at the Queen."

"Believe me, I fully intend to," he muttered.

"Good plan. Hey!" I twisted in my seat, raising my voice as I addressed the rest of my passengers. "Get up. We're here."

Quentin cracked open one eye, looking at me petulantly. He had been drooling in his sleep, and his bronze hair was plastered against his cheek in a matted snarl. He still managed to look like he should have been on the cover of whatever the modern equivalent of *Tiger Beat* was. Daoine Sidhe are always prettier than they have any right to be. "I hate you," he said.

"True," I agreed. "Now get up."

I was the first out of the car, with Tybalt close behind me. Lowri started toward us as soon as I emerged, which made her previous stillness even more obvious. It finally registered that she wasn't wearing a disguise: her tunic was in Arden's colors, belted at the waist, leaving her goatish legs bare. Her goat-like ears hung almost to her shoulders, covered in a thin layer of silver-brown fur, and her eyes had horizontal pupils. No one could ever have mistaken her for human.

"This whole area's been warded off, hasn't it?" I asked.

Lowri nodded. "No mortals, not until you're up the hill and safely in Queen Windermere's Court. She asked me to wait here for you, and add your car to the spell as soon as you arrived. I'm sorry I didn't ask you first. I was following orders."

"Next time, I recommend you search those orders for flexibility," snarled Tybalt, showing the tip of one pointed incisor. His teeth hadn't been that sharp before. He was genuinely angry.

"I will try," said Lowri deferentially. She looked past us to the others, eyes widening as she saw who was staggering out of the car. Then, before either Tybalt or I could say anything, she dropped to one knee, head bowed. "Your Highness."

She wasn't supposed to know that. I turned to look behind me. Quentin met my eyes, expression broadcasting alarm and dismay so clearly that it was a wonder he'd ever been able to conceal his title at all. May was yawning, Spike slung over one shoulder and her suitcase clutched in her other hand. She had left the trunk open after she retrieved it. Walther . . .

Walther had dropped his human disguise and taken off his glasses before getting out of the car. He shook his head, looking resigned. "Not me, I'm afraid. You've mistaken me for my cousin Torsten." He caught my stare and smirked. "Not *everyone* you know can be royalty in hiding, Toby. Arden was about your limit."

He still didn't know about Quentin. I schooled my face back into something more neutral, and said, "You didn't tell me you were related to the royal family of Silences."

"I'm Tylwyth Teg. So were they. By definition, I'm at least distantly related to them." Walther walked over to join us, bending to offer Lowri his hand. "Seriously, get up. I know where Torsten is, and he's not here."

"Dead?" Lowri asked, lifting her head and looking up at him.

"Sleeping," said Walther, still holding out his hand. "I saw him fall. The arrow caught him in his shoulder, and he toppled from his horse, and he didn't get back up. But he wasn't dead. Still isn't, unless the usurper chose to kill them all when they woke."

"Wait—what do you mean, when they woke?" I asked.

"The war was fought shortly after the death of King Gilad," said Walther. "That was more than a hundred years ago. Elf-shot, even when it's mixed by a master, can only put someone to sleep for a hundred years. Any members of the royal family who were elf-shot during the war, rather than being killed outright, would have woken up sometime in the last few years."

"But killing them now would be a violation of Oberon's Law, which is bad, so there's a good chance the current King of Silences just had them elf-shot again instead," I said slowly. Oberon's Law allowed for killing purebloods during times of war. Any other time . . . it was the one thing that was truly forbidden. "Sweet Titania, that's messed up."

"Tell me about it," said Walther. Lowri finally took his hand. He helped her off the ground, smiling wryly, and said, "I'm Walther Davies. Your prince is in another castle."

She looked at him blankly. "What?"

Walther sighed and let her go. "See, this is why I never have anyone to talk to. My students have ruined me."

"This is fun and all, but we should probably be heading for the knowe," I said. "Lowri, is there anyone who can help me with my suitcase? It's pretty heavy."

"I'll get it," she said, and started toward the open trunk of my car. I shrugged and followed her. Glastig are a hell of a lot stronger than they look, and what was almost too much for me to carry would be nothing to her.

As I had expected, she hefted my suitcase like it was nothing. I retrieved the backpack that held my toiletries and the sword I tried my best to avoid wearing. Belting it around my waist made all this feel real. This was happening. Whether I liked it or not, it was happening.

May, meanwhile, was eyeing Walther suspiciously. "Toby's right, though," she said. "You never told us you were related to the ruling family of Silences."

He shrugged. "You never asked."

Lowri walked back over to them, carrying my suitcase in one hand. "If you'll leave your keys with me, we can move your car to a more secure parking space," she said. "Duchess Lorden has agreed to grant us the use of a lot she owns near here."

"Of course the Undersea owns a parking lot near Muir Woods," I said, pulling my keys out of my pocket and dropping them into Lowri's waiting palm. "Why wouldn't they? Mermaids need a place to keep their cars, right?"

"Doesn't everyone?" asked Lowri. She started walking. Lacking anything better to do, and any way to get out of the situation, the rest of us moved with her. Lowri, Tybalt, and I took the lead, while May, Quentin, and Walther lagged behind—May and Quentin because of exhaustion and luggage, Walther because he wasn't in a hurry. I couldn't blame him. He was as trapped as the rest of us.

Lowri glanced back a few times as we walked. Finally, when we were starting up the side of the hill, she said, "I'm not sure he is who he says he is."

"You mean Walther," I said.

"Yes. He looks so much like Prince Torsten . . ."

"If he says he's not your missing prince, he's not. The person who introduced me to him vouched for him. She said he was a good guy, and she never said anything about him being a prince in hiding. I think she would have told me." Walther had started his time in the Bay Area in the Japanese Tea Gardens, which had been held by a woman named Lily. She was an Undine, and had known my mother for years before I was born. She'd always been good to me. If he'd been keeping secrets that could harm me, she would have said so. I had faith in that.

"I thought I knew all the members of the royal family," said Lowri. "I was training to serve in the guard.

Torsten had many cousins, but none by the name of 'Walther.' "

"So he changed his name to keep himself out of trouble," I said. "It wouldn't be the first time. Leave it be, all right? He's coming with me, and I've trusted him with my life before."

"As you say," said Lowri—but she glanced back at Walther one more time, frowning like she knew the answer she wanted was somehow just out of reach.

I shook my head and kept on climbing.

Arden was waiting in the clearing at the top of the hill, standing a good ten feet outside the doors of her own knowe. Her guards were behind her, holding the open door. It struck me that this was the first time since Lowri had left the false queen for the true one when I had seen her on duty but outside of her armor. She really was standing as Arden's seneschal, at least for now.

Madden's sister Tia was also there, holding herself slightly apart, watching the scene with cold eyes. She looked angry. I understood the sentiment.

"Are these to be your companions?" asked Arden, eyes going from me to the small group straggling up the hill behind me. "I'd offer you my guard, but I can't do that. I need you to understand that whatever happens once you leave my lands will be avenged, but it won't be prevented."

"I do understand that," I said. If the King of Silences had me arrested, elf-shot, or even killed, Arden could respond. She couldn't send someone with me to make sure that it never happened in the first place. Pureblood politics are strange at the best of times, and unbearably complicated all the rest of the time. "I need something from you, though."

Arden blinked. "What's that?"

"Blood. I have an alchemist," I indicated Walther, "and being able to access your magic might make the difference between a strategic retreat and a massacre. Nolan's would be better, but yours would be good."

She relaxed marginally. "We anticipated this request. Tia?" The Cu Sidhe stepped forward, handing Arden a carved redwood box. Arden handed it, in turn, to me, indicating that I should open it.

Lifting the lid revealed four crystal vials, each full of a dark red substance that I had no trouble accepting as the Queen's blood. It would hold her power. If Quentin or I consumed it, we could use it to open teleport gates, just like she did. After Walther had treated it, anyone would be able to use it that way, although the power wouldn't last as long for anyone who didn't have natural skill at blood magic. That blood could be our escape route, if things got as bad as I was afraid they were going to.

"Is that enough?" Arden asked. "My brother can't consent, so I'm afraid I'd prefer not to involve him."

"It should be," I said, and passed the box to Walther, who somehow made it vanish inside his coat. "If it's not, I guess we'll find out."

But Arden wasn't done. "Are you sure you should be taking the King of Dreaming Cats?" she asked, her gaze going to Tybalt. "His presence states—"

"You can neither prevent me nor forbid me; I am not yours to command," said Tybalt. His words were dangerously calm. "I will find and inform the local King of Cats of my presence, but so long as I do not enter his Court uninvited, I am issuing no challenge by entering his territory. We are more civilized than you believe us to be. My presence states only that no harm will come to my betrothed, unless it comes first through me. I am very much looking forward to seeing anything try to get through me."

Arden paled slightly. That was the appropriate response. She turned back to me. "I've arranged dressing rooms for all your people, off the main hall. As soon as you're changed, I'll open the portal to see you into Silences. You do your Kingdom a great service on this day."

"Just make sure the Mists are still standing when we come home," I said.

That earned me a small, quick smile. "I'll do my best," said Arden.

"Good," I said, and walked past her into the open doorway, and the inevitable.

SEVEN

THE SKY WAS A bruised purple as we stepped through Arden's portal and onto the red brick esplanade outside the castle and ruling seat of the Kingdom of Silences. The blackberry flower and redwood smell of her magic clung to our clothing, announcing us as hers more clearly than a herald ever could.

I glanced up. There were at least six moons visible: we were in the Summerlands, standing on the fae side of the knowe. Evergreens pressed in on us from all directions, creating a verdant barrier between our small party and whatever lay beyond the castle. We moved closer together without saying anything about it. Our position had us totally exposed—any archer who wanted to appear on the castle wall and put an elf-shot arrow through our hearts would have been able to do so without making any real effort.

"Points for 'I can design an imposing front door,' no points for 'people will want to use it,'" I said. "Where the hell is everyone?"

"Did the Queen tell them we were coming?" asked May. "Maybe we should have called ahead."

Tybalt snorted.

We had all taken advantage of Arden's changing rooms, although some of us had taken it farther than others. Tybalt, Walther, and Quentin were dressed like something from a production of *The Tempest*, in tight trousers, linen shirts, and vests. Their styles didn't quite synch up—Tybalt was more swashbuckler, Quentin more courtier, and Walther a strange sort of combination between scholar and undertaker—but they made a pretty picture, taken as a group. May was wearing jeans and a Golden Gate Park sweatshirt. And I . . . well, I had brushed my hair. That was all the concession they were getting out of me, at least for now.

Arden had provided a small cart for our bags, and had thrown in several trunks of what May assured me were very nice outfits, accompanied by even nicer cosmetics, accessories, and shoes. The look of relief on Arden's face when May had explained that she was acting as my lady's maid had been almost insulting. Spike was riding atop our piled suitcases, paws tucked underneath its body, seeming perfectly content.

The evergreens rustled, but no one appeared. I gave Walther a sidelong look. "Any of this look familiar to you?"

"Yes," he said, shaking his head. "There was no need for a road before. I suppose there isn't need for one now, either. We're being watched, you know."

"Swell," I muttered. Of the three races that hold most of the thrones in Faerie, only the Daoine Sidhe ever bother to *walk* anywhere. Tuatha de Dannan can teleport. Tylwyth Teg can fly, given a bundle of yarrow twigs and the space to push off. I gave the brick esplanade a more critical look. It was broad enough that even young Tylwyth Teg would have been able to use it as a landing strip, and the underbrush surrounding the edges of the area contained an unusually large amount of yarrow for the region and the climate.

Walther followed my gaze and shook his head. "They

didn't even bother to replant our gardens," he said, open bitterness in his voice. "Why should they? We were never coming back."

"Yeah, well. Surprise." I planted my hands on my hips, turned my attention to the door, and said—loudly and clearly, but without yelling—"I am Sir October Christine Daye, Knight of Lost Words, sworn to the service of Duke Sylvester Torquill of Shadowed Hills, here in the name of Arden Windermere, Queen in the Mists. I claim the hospitality of your home for myself and my company, who have traveled with me to negotiate a cessation of hostilities between our lands."

Silence fell. Somewhere in the distant pines, an owl hooted once before getting with the program and shutting up. I tapped my foot against the brick.

"You declared war on *us*, remember?" I called. "That means we get to take our three-day window to try to fix it. Now let us in. I'm allergic to fresh air and moonlight."

Tybalt snorted again, this time sounding almost painfully amused. I glanced at him, raising one eyebrow in challenge. He shook his head, fighting to swallow his smirk. That was a good thing, in its way. If he was busy laughing at me, he wasn't worrying about my imminent demise.

I resumed glaring at the castle. Seconds ticked by, and my frustration grew. Finally, I threw up my hands, and demanded, *"Well?"*

The great wooden doors began to swing inward.

It was a slow process, so slow that at first I wasn't sure what I was seeing. But the crack of light that appeared between them grew wider and wider, until glimpses of the wide, open air courtyard on the other side became apparent. The red brick of the esplanade continued beyond the gates. We would have a level surface on which to pull our little wagon. Bully for us.

It took almost five minutes for the doors to fully open. We didn't move during the process; instead, by silent agreement, we waited to see what would happen next. I was expecting the King's guard, maybe accompanied by his seneschal, to appear and tell us that we weren't welcome—that, or show us to our rooms. It all depended on whether or not they accepted that I had the right to claim their hospitality.

But the doors opened, revealing the deserted courtyard. There was a fountain at the center, made of gold, with stylized Sidhe bodies and stags caught in eternal, faceless dance. The statues were featureless enough that they could have belonged to any of the ruling races, but the yarrow branches etched into the stone around the fountain's edge made it clear that the installation had been originally commissioned by one of the Tylwyth Teg. The walls of the courtyard had been scrubbed as clean as it was possible for granite to be, and there were no tapestries or pennants hanging there, leaving the fountain as the only decoration. It made the little water feature seem sad, almost, like it was trying too hard to brighten a space that was far too large for it to illuminate alone.

Spike leaped from the wagon and trotted over to stand next to my feet, rattling its thorns in a timbre that I recognized as frustration.

"Yeah, I'm feeling pretty jerked around, too," I said. "Come on, guys. Let's walk into the big creepy castle and see if we get attacked by something. Doesn't that sound like fun? I think it sounds like fun." I began to walk.

"She's *your* fiancée," said May. There was a small rumbling sound as she and Quentin began pulling the cart over the bricks. Maybe having them do the pulling was a little unfair, given that Tybalt and Walther had their hands free, but there was a method to my madness. Quentin was my squire: I didn't want him being looked at as anything else. And when a knight has a squire, that squire can expect to be put to work doing whatever irritating or unpleasant jobs the knight isn't in the mood for. May was my Fetch, but she was here as my lady's maid, and it made sense that if two people were needed to do the pulling, she would be the second one. I'd probably hear about this from both of them later. In the moment, they understood as well as I did how important it was for things to appear normal.

Well. As normal as it was possible for anything about our little group to appear.

We walked through the open, unwelcoming castle doors and into the courtyard. There were no visible doors on this level, apart from the one we'd entered through. I shot Walther a hard look, and he shrugged helplessly. It's not uncommon for the people in charge to design their strongholds in a way that makes it clear that *they* make the rules, that anything you do is dependent on their kindnesses. The Mists has always had a lot of Daoine Sidhe in positions of power, in part due to meddling from their Firstborn. As I looked around what was essentially a room with no windows and only one door, I found myself faintly grateful that Evening had been so inclined to stick her nose in. At least Daoine Sidhe had to *walk* everywhere, and hence built strongholds that were useful to the rest of us.

Except for the part where Evening had been indirectly responsible for me being turned into a fish, and had actually caused the death—however temporary—of one of my greatest allies, I could almost forget that she wasn't actually my friend.

The doors slammed shut behind us. May and Walther both jumped. I didn't. Neither did Quentin or Tybalt. That said something sort of sad about the situations we tended to find ourselves in.

"Nice fountain," I said, still speaking louder than was my norm. "I know that if I had a fountain this great, I'd totally set up a whole courtyard just to show it off. Look, the way I see it, one of two things is happening right now. Either you're getting ready to ambush us, in which case you'd better do it fast, or you're not going to like the results. Or you've got a really messed-up way of showing hospitality. One more time: I am Sir October Daye, I am here on behalf of Queen Windermere in the Mists, and you are beginning to piss me off."

The scent of meadowsweet and wine vinegar tinted the air, and a portal opened in the wall on the other side of the fountain. The room on the other side was all polished hardwood and velvet, and I only saw it for an instant before bodies began pouring through the opening.

First came the guards. Eight of them, all wearing the deep pine green and silver livery of Silences. They split, four taking each side as they placed themselves between us and the portal. Then came the courtiers, three this time, two women and a man, a Tylwyth Teg and two Daoine Sidhe, and again, all wearing the colors of Silences, although their tunics were finer and their outfits were accessorized by incredibly silly looking floppy hats.

One of the courtiers produced a scroll from inside her doublet, unrolled it, and read, "By the grace of Oberon, His Majesty, King Rhys of Silences."

Years of courtly etiquette drilled into me by Etienne, and even more years of silently following my mother through the Courts of the Mists, kept me from rolling my eyes or otherwise doing something to offend the king we had come to visit. Instead, I dropped into a deep and proper bow, bent double at the waist, knees bent, one leg extended so that my thigh muscles began almost immediately to ache. Out of the corner of my eye, I could see Walther and Tybalt matching the gesture, their own bows only slightly modified by the variances in custom and region. Tybalt's bow was shallower than mine, since it would have been inappropriate for him to show too much obeisance to a ruler of the Divided Courts. Walther's bow included an elaborate hand gesture that I had never seen before.

I couldn't see Quentin and May from my position, but I had faith that they would be demonstrating the appropriate amount of humility. I had to trust them. If I didn't, we were already lost.

"You may rise," said an unfamiliar male voice, tenor and calm, like its owner had never encountered anything that needed to disturb him.

I straightened up, and got my first look at the King of Silences.

He was taller than I expected, with the glossy black hair and olive skin common among the Tuatha de Dannan. He wore that hair cropped short in a style that was almost disconcertingly modern, given his current surroundings, and which did nothing to conceal the sharp points of his ears. His eyes were the color of slightly tarnished pennies, with bolts of molten-looking copper surrounded by streaky verdigris. He was handsome, I had to give him that, but he looked more like a businessman playing dress up than he did a king, even wearing a fur-lined cloak that reached all the way to the floor. Even with a crown resting on his head.

Spike rattled its thorns and hissed, too quietly for anyone to hear it but me. I took the sound for the warning it was, and I said nothing at all.

The King of Silences appeared to take this as a sign of respect. He smiled, a cold expression that did not reach his eyes. "My friends from the South," he said. "How kind of you to travel hence and see whether our disagreements might be settled like civilized people, instead of clawed from one another's flesh like animals." His gaze flicked, ever so briefly, to Tybalt at the end of his statement.

My shoulders tightened. I forced my expression to remain neutral as I said, "Queen Arden Windermere in the Mists, daughter and heir to King Gilad Windermere in the Mists, recognized in her claim to the throne by High King Aethlin Sollys of the Westlands, sends her regards, and hopes we will be able to lay this matter to rest before any further harm is done to her people."

"No harm has been done to her people, as she has no people to claim," responded King Rhys, without missing a beat. "The throne she sits is not her own. If she wishes to settle this dispute with no loss of life or damage to property, she will admit her crime, step aside, and allow the true Queen of the Mists to retake what is rightfully hers."

"See, that's what we're here to talk about," I said, struggling to keep my voice as genial as I could. "We call upon the hospitality of your home."

"And so you shall have it. We follow the rules set down by Oberon in all his wisdom here in Silences. For three days, you will be honored guests here in my Kingdom. No hands will be raised against you, and we will see to your safety even at the risk of our own. When that time is done, we will part either as friends or as foes, to be determined by your actions while you stand within my walls. Do you agree to comport yourselves as guests, and raise no hands to me or mine?"

"Save in self-defense," I said.

"Then the bargain is struck." King Rhys looked from me to my companions. "Who travels with you? I would know whom I welcome into my keep."

"These are my friends and companions," I said. "The Daoine Sidhe is my squire, Quentin. He's kind of slow on the uptake sometimes, but he's pretty, so we put up with him. The woman next to him is my half-sister, May." Technically true. She was born of my blood and the flesh of the night-haunt she had been. No one could say that we weren't blood relatives, just like no one could say that she had been carried or delivered by my mother. Faerie makes everything complicated.

"I see," said King Rhys. "And the others?"

"Walther Davies of the Mists, my lord," said Walther. "I am Sir Daye's alchemist, and travel at her command."

"King Tybalt of the Court of Dreaming Cats," said Tybalt. "A war in the Mists would of necessity inconvenience my people. I am here to observe, and, should such a war become inevitable, to return home and prepare the Court of Cats for what has been brought down upon our heads."

King Rhys narrowed his eyes, studying Tybalt. I had to admire the artistry of the moment, even as it made me squirm. By going last, Tybalt had prevented the King of Silences from spending too much time dwelling on Walther. If Lowri had been able to recognize him as related to the rightful royal family, there was a chance the King who'd replaced them could have done the same . . . if he hadn't been immediately confronted with a rival monarch that he technically had no power over. It was nicely done. And it was scaring the hell out of me.

King Rhys could deny Tybalt his hospitality, saying that a knight didn't have the right to claim a King of Cats as a traveling companion. Or he could deny me my hospitality and give it to Tybalt instead, which would mean we had made the entire journey for nothing, since Tybalt didn't have the authority to negotiate a peace on Arden's behalf.

Finally, King Rhys said, "I see. We have never hosted a monarch of your Court here; I hope you will not take offense if my people don't know exactly the right etiquette for treating with you."

"Tell them not to pull my tail or kick me, and I will respond in kind," said Tybalt mildly.

"As you say," said King Rhys, with another broad, chilly smile. He stepped to one side. His guards did the same, falling back so that their backs were to the courtyard wall. It was an eerily synchronized motion. I wondered how much time they had spent practicing to make sure that their footsteps would be perfectly in unison. I just as quickly decided to stop wondering about that. It couldn't do anything good for my sanity.

"Welcome to Silences," said King Rhys, gesturing to the portal.

There wasn't really anything we could do at that point. Refusing his invitation would have been rude, and we didn't have anywhere else to go. With another, much shorter bow, I began walking around the fountain toward the portal.

Walther stepped close enough that he could murmur, "Ever been to Disneyland?"

"No," I replied, as quietly as I could. "Why?"

"Because this guy learned everything he knows about crowd control from the Haunted Mansion."

I gave him a puzzled look. He laughed, and kept on walking.

Walking through King Rhys' portal was like stepping through a soap bubble formed entirely of someone else's magic. The urge to hold my breath was great, but I forced it aside and breathed in instead, trying to learn whatever I could about the man whose demesne we were now inside. He was pure Tuatha de Dannan, that much was clear: I could pick up nothing else from his heritage, or from the meadowsweet and wine vinegar traceries of his spell. He was also casting unaided—the magic was entirely his, and he had sustained the portal for the entire process of determining our purpose in his lands. He was strong. Not as strong as Chelsea, maybe, but strong enough to hold his Kingdom.

We came out of the portal in the lushly appointed ballroom we had glimpsed before, our feet and the wheels of our wagon clattering against the polished wooden floor. The dais in front of us held a single central throne, decorated in the same style as the fountain in the courtyard. Walther tensed beside me. Whatever else King Rhys had done since becoming King, and however blameless he may or may not have been in what had happened, he was sitting on the throne that had belonged to the original ruling family. I couldn't even imagine how that had to feel.

There was no matching queen's throne. Either Rhys

was unmarried, or he had chosen to rule alone. There were two smaller chairs, carved from rich pine and detailed with gold leaf, that were probably intended for use by visiting nobility or dignitaries important enough to share the dais with him.

As my companions and I fell into a loose semicircle, Walther to my left, Tybalt to my right, and May and Quentin fanning out to hold up the ends, Rhys walked past us, mounted the dais, and settled in his throne. He braced one elbow on the armrest, slouching into a position as carefully calculated as the motions of his guards. As for the guards themselves, they took up places around the edges of the room, while his three attending courtiers moved to stand near, but not on, the dais.

"My staff has been notified that you'll need to be housed and fed for the next little while," he said. "I assume you'll wish to have adjoining rooms for your squire and your lady's maid, Sir Daye?" His eyes raked over my hair, mouth pursing in a way that made it clear he found everything about my appearance to be wanting.

"Yes, if it please your Majesty," I said, with a quick dip of my head. "I would also like my alchemist to be housed as near to me as possible. He is . . . useful, in certain regards." Let him think I was addicted to sleep tonics. Let him think I was sleeping with Walther. I didn't care, as long as he didn't try to separate us from each other. I might not have been very good at courtly manners, but I was smart enough to know that winding up in opposite wings would be bad for everyone's health.

"Indeed," said Rhys. "As for the King of Cats, we will have to arrange a room suitable for such a luminary, as I would not want to give accidental offense—"

"Then I am not rude in interjecting to tell you that no such arrangement will be necessary, nor would it be welcome if undertaken," said Tybalt, cutting smoothly into the rhythm of the King's speech. Rhys looked nonplussed, but not as angry as he would have been if I had tried the same trick. Tybalt reached out and set a hand gently upon my wrist, so that his fingers traced the line of my pulse. It was nothing as blatant as putting an arm around me or as crass as kissing me in front of a rival monarch, but it was more than enough to get the point across.

Rhys' eyebrows rose. "I see," he said, giving me another assessing look. My lack of cosmetics and clearly unstyled hair was being put into a new light: among the nobility of the Divided Courts, Cait Sidhe have a reputation for being bestial and little better than changelings. If I was screwing the King of Cats, it made sense that I'd be a little unkempt—never mind that Tybalt looked like he could appear on the cover of a magazine without changing anything but the shape of his pupils.

"Sir Daye is my betrothed, and as such, I choose to cleave to her as much as I may," said Tybalt, a dangerous note coming into his voice. It was clear he knew how King Rhys was judging me, and just as clear that he didn't approve. "I'll understand if you cannot place us in the same room, as we are yet unwed, but I will be close to her, or know the reasons why."

"I see." Rhys sat up straighter. "I'll instruct my seneschal appropriately. I'm sorry we didn't have rooms ready for you. My counterpart to the South did not tell me she was sending an emissary to argue on her behalf, perhaps because she knows she has no authority to do so. But no matter." He waved the hand that wasn't supporting his head before any of us could object to his continual characterization of Arden as the usurper in this equation. "You'll be shown to your rooms. My court slumbers, in the main—I was woken to receive you—and you will be summoned again when it's time for our first formal meal of the night."

"I thought you had to tell your seneschal about our rooming arrangement?" I said, slowly.

"His Majesty has just informed me," said one of the

courtiers. She stepped forward, offering a shallow bow in our direction. She had the golden hair and blue eyes characteristic of the Tylwyth Teg, and her expression was so composed as to be virtually blank, a perfect mask betraying nothing of her feelings. "My name is Marlis. I am standing seneschal to this court. Please allow me to escort you."

"Sure thing." I turned back to Rhys, bowing one more time in his direction. "We appreciate your hospitality, and will not abuse it."

"See that you don't," he said. "Marlis, you will return here when you have them settled. I must speak to you."

"Yes, Your Majesty," said Marlis. She gestured toward a doorway on the other side of the hall. "You will follow me."

It wasn't a request. She walked, and after the rest of our group had made their quick, final bows, we followed.

Marlis' entire stride changed as soon as we were in the hall, going from tight and reserved to open, wide, with a heel-first way of striking the floor that made it clear she'd been trained in some pretty serious kick-your-ass techniques. She didn't say a word until we reached the first stairway. A basket of yarrow twigs was hung over the newel post. She began grabbing out handfuls and tying them into quick wreaths, which she tossed to May and Quentin.

"Here," she said briskly. "Put these on the wheels of your wagon, and be quick about it. His Majesty doesn't like things cluttering up the hall."

That certainly explained the lack of knickknacks and portraits: aside from the velvet draperies in the throne room, the knowe seemed to be entirely undecorated. "Is this an extension of that whole 'flying on yarrow branches' trick I've seen some Tylwyth Teg do?" I asked. "I didn't know you could use it on things other than yourselves."

"Some of us have to work for what we receive in this

world, miss," said Marlis. "Some of us have to find ways of making that work easier." She looked back to May and Quentin. Seeing that they had looped the wreaths over the hubs of both wagon wheels, she raised her hand and chanted a quick phrase in Welsh. The smell of ice and milfoil rose in the air around the wagon, which began to lift away from the ground.

May let go of her handle. Quentin did the same, releasing the wagon barely a second before Spike made a mighty leap and landed squarely in the middle of our luggage. It rode there, chirping jubilantly, as the wagon floated up to the top of the stairs and settled on the landing.

"Roller coasters for rose goblins," I said, as mildly as I could. The smell of Marlis' magic was still lingering in the air. I sniffed it, shooting Walther a sidelong look. His magic smelled of ice and common yarrow. Hers was ice and milfoil—otherwise known as fernleaf yarrow. With magical signatures that similar, there was no way they weren't related, and yet she hadn't looked at him any more critically than she'd looked at the rest of us. Something was going on here, and I didn't like not knowing what it was.

"This way," said Marlis, and followed our wagon's trail up the stairs. The rest of us were close behind her, with me in the lead and Tybalt bringing up the rear. He'd be able to defend against any surprise attacks that way. Not that I was actually expecting King Rhys to go for us this soon—if he'd been planning an immediate double cross, I doubted that he would have let us past the front gates. It's much easier to get rid of unwanted guests when you can say, honestly, that they never set foot inside your knowe. Besides, there was a lot of forest in Silences. That meant a lot of places to hide the bodies.

The upstairs hall was as stark and unornamented as the downstairs. The walls lacked the filigree and carving I was accustomed to in most noble knowes. Walther looked faintly sickened when he glanced at the places where the walls met the ceiling and floor, which probably meant that there *had* been decorative carvings here, once. Why Rhys would have had those removed while leaving the fountain and throne was anybody's guess.

We walked through a pair of tall double doors and into a wider hallway. This one had a plush carpet patterned in pine green and rose red covering the floor, instantly muffling our footsteps. The doors swung shut behind us. Marlis kept walking, until we were halfway down the hall, where she stopped at a door set into a particularly ornate frame. It was carved with pine boughs and roses, and looked almost ridiculously out of place against its austere surroundings.

"The visitor's suite is through here," she said. "I apologize if it is finer than you're accustomed to, but you left us little choice, with the size of your party. The main room is yours to do with as you like. I suggest your lady's maid be given the room off the master bedroom, as King Rhys insists upon certain standards at his court functions." There was an oddly pleading note to that sentence, like she was telling us more than she was strictly allowed.

"Cool," I said. "Is there anything else we need to know?"

If I'd been hoping for more rule bending from her, I was going to be disappointed. Marlis shook her head. "No, miss," she said. "Simply come when you are called, and communicate your situation clearly and without prejudice. I think you will find King Rhys to be a generous and compassionate ruler, and you will soon come to understand the reasons for his indignation."

"Let's hope," I said.

"I must to my lord. If you would excuse me?" Marlis offered a quick, shallow bow, barely enough not to be insulting, before she turned and hurried back the way she'd come.

The five of us watched her go, not saying a word. Then I turned to the door and pushed it open, revealing a receiving room easily the size of my first apartment. "At least he's not being stingy with the space," I said, stepping inside.

He wasn't being stingy with the furnishings, either. All the clutter that wasn't evident in the hall had apparently been crammed into the quarters for visiting diplomats, creating a dizzying maze of couches, end tables, and decorative shelves stacked high with vases, decorative statuary, and knickknacks I didn't have a name for. It would have been attractive, if any effort at all had been made to coordinate the things that filled the room. As it was, I felt like I was visiting the Hollywood idea of an antique barn.

Walther and Tybalt pulled the wagon with our things inside while May and Quentin brought up the rear. Walther looked around, sighed, and said, "I was wondering where all this stuff went. It's not like he could sell it, and destroying the possessions of the royal family of Silences would have just been tacky." He didn't sound surprised. More resigned, like this was exactly what he'd been expecting.

"See, I thought conquering someone else's Kingdom was tacky," said May. "Getting rid of their stuff afterward is just good housekeeping." She squeezed around the wagon to begin opening the doors that radiated off the room like the spokes of a wheel.

"What are the odds we're being spied on?" I asked.

"High," said Walther.

"Absolutely we're being spied on," said Quentin.

"There's no one but us physically present right now, but that doesn't mean there aren't listening charms," said May, opening another door. "I mean, they may not have had time to set them, since we surprised them and all, but they could have enchantments primed to activate as someone crosses the threshold."

I paused. Sometimes it was easy to forget about May's weird radar, since it came up rarely and wasn't exactly an active magic. Still, it was good to have the confirmation. "All right. Assume listening charms. Let's go to our rooms and get ready for what's ahead." And figure out a way to find and deactivate anything that was monitoring us. If we were going to plan strategies, we needed to do it in private.

Walther opened his briefcase and took out a notepad, scribbling something before ripping off the top sheet and sticking it to Spike's back. The rose goblin took its new status as a message board in stride, chirping amiably before wandering over to rub against my ankles.

"Found the master bedroom," called May. "It looks like there's only one sub-room. Quentin can have it. I'm happier when I don't have to listen to you snore." Meaning she'd be happier knowing that she was in the exterior ring of rooms, since she was indestructible and Quentin wasn't.

"Got it," I said, resolutely not looking at the note Walther had stuck to my rose goblin.

It only took us a few minutes to get the suitcases into the appropriate rooms. Their owners followed them, with varying degrees of enthusiasm. Walther looked faintly sick; May looked grim. When the door to the master bedroom shut, it was with me, Tybalt, Quentin, and Spike inside.

The bedroom was as opulently decorated as the front room, with a bed large enough to hold six, and a wardrobe that should by all rights have contained a doorway to Narnia, or at least the deeper lands of Faerie. A small door on one wall led to a much less fancy room, with a single narrow bed where Quentin would be expected to sleep. I almost envied him that simplicity. I was so far out of my depth that I was worried about drowning without going anywhere near the water.

Spike rubbed against my ankles again. I bent to pluck

Walther's note from its spines. Unfolding the piece of paper, I read quickly. Then I closed my eyes and held it out for Quentin and Tybalt to see.

Marlis is my sister, read the note. *Be cautious.*

"Well," said Tybalt, tone gone tight and careful. "Isn't this going to be fun?"

I didn't have an answer for that.

EIGHT

WE DIDN'T KNOW HOW long we would have before we were summoned back into King Rhys' presence, and so we focused on the only thing about our situation that we had any hope of controlling: ourselves. Quentin had hauled his suitcase into the small side room that would be his, leaving the door open in case I needed him. Meanwhile, Tybalt and I began unloading our things into the wardrobe.

There was something pleasantly domestic about unpacking together, like we were going on vacation or moving in together for real, not just through slow osmosis. I liked it.

"I hope I was not too forward before, in introducing myself as your betrothed," said Tybalt, hanging a pair of his ubiquitous leather trousers over the rod at the center of the wardrobe. "He would have separated us had I not, claiming that it was in recognition of my 'status' within the Divided Courts. I could not allow that to happen."

I gave him a sidelong look. "What, do you think I'm ashamed of you or something?"

"No." He looked amused. "I know you well enough to find it much more likely that you would declare yourself unworthy of my unstinting affections, and attempt to part yourself from me 'for my own good.' At which point, I assure you, I would follow you about like a lost kitten until you came back to your senses. It is simply that our alliance may not be advantageous for you in all political arenas."

"And won't that be fun for them to deal with after we're married?" I asked. "If you're a political liability, let's elope. Get me out of this gig even faster."

"Get a room," called Quentin.

"Shut your door," I called back. I hung the last of my dresses and stepped back, eyeing the wardrobe like it was a venomous snake. It brimmed with gowns I couldn't fight in and shoes I didn't want to wear, and I didn't have a choice about any of this. Arden had sent me to fight for her on a battlefield I didn't understand and couldn't twist to my own advantage.

Or maybe I could. I fished my cellphone out of my pocket as I took another step back, bumping my thighs against the overstuffed mattress. I sat down, dialed, and waited.

I didn't have to wait long. There was a click midway through the first ring, and the familiar, slightly artificial-sounding voice of April O'Leary, Countess of Tamed Lightning, came on the line with a "You do not call me often. Is something wrong?"

"Maybe," I said. "Probably. Okay, yes. And hello to you, too." April was originally a Dryad, before her adopted mother—the late Countess January O'Leary—spliced her tree into a computer server to save her life. I didn't really understand it, but the process had worked, resulting in April becoming the world's first cybernetic tree spirit. Her grasp of social niceties wasn't the best, which was something she shared with her Dryad relatives: most of them spent more time with trees than they did with people, and they didn't necessarily know how to make conversation about things that didn't photosynthesize. April was willing to fake pleasantries with people she didn't know. She rarely bothered with her friends.

"What is wrong? Is this related to the notice I received from Queen Windermere that a war was being beta-tested, and might be cleared for release? I do not have time to allow my coders to be slaughtered. It seems very inefficient."

Leave it to April to get right to the heart of things. "I've been sent to the Kingdom of Silences as a diplomat, because Arden wants to skip the whole 'war' thing if possible."

"Oh." April hesitated before asking, "Are you the most qualified for this assignment?"

"Nope, but neither is anybody else, so we're faking it," I said. "Anyway, we're in the royal knowe of Silences, and we think we may be being listened in on. Any ideas about what we could do about that?"

"Why do you ask me?"

"You live in a magic electrical network. I thought it was worth a try."

"I see." There was a pause. Then April said: "Please put your phone down and cover your ears. Do not hang up."

"Got it." I dropped the phone on the bed and stood, moving away. "Everybody cover your ears," I said, following my own instructions. Tybalt glanced at me, looking confused, but clapped his hands over his ears anyway.

Good for him: almost at the same time, my phone began to emit a high-pitched screeching sound that made my teeth hurt as it resonated through my skull. Spike hissed and ran into the wardrobe. Quentin slammed the door to his bedchamber. The door to the master bedroom slammed open as May and Walther piled through, both of them trying to cover their ears and get inside at the same time. I mouthed "sorry" at them, but didn't try to speak. The noise April was somehow generating would have prevented them from hearing me, anyway.

The sound lasted for no more than thirty seconds before cutting off as abruptly as it had started, leaving the faint smell of ozone hanging in the air. I cautiously uncovered my ears. When the screeching didn't resume, I leaned over and picked up the phone again. "April?"

"No one is listening to you now," she said serenely.

"Yeah, because if they were, they're probably deaf," I said. "What did you do?"

"Countersurveillance charm. We use them internally to prevent leaks from inside the company to competing firms. Elliot says I am perhaps overly cautious, but I prefer to think of myself as profit-oriented." April's County was also a working computer programming company. I wasn't clear on exactly what they did to make their money, and I didn't really want to know. "Any charms or spells designed to record or transmit the things said within the room you currently inhabit have been suspended for a period of no more than twenty-four hours. If the charms are self-renewing, they will reassert themselves at sunrise, and you will need to either call me again or find another avenue."

I paused, trying to work my way through the complicated twists of April's vocabulary. Then I said, "So no one can hear us in this room?"

"Correct. Please come visit me after you have prevented this war. I have missed your company, and the company of your associates. My remaining mother sends her regards." April said the last as if by rote, and I had no doubt that Li Qin, January's widow, had in fact told her daughter that whenever I happened to call, I should be given her regards.

"Tell Li Qin hi," I said, unable to keep myself from smiling. "Open roads, April."

"Good-bye," she said, and hung up.

I lowered the phone, turning to the others. Walther and May were still standing by the door, looking shaken and disheveled. "Okay, first, close that," I said. They did, although May's expression turned dangerously mulish. If I didn't explain myself soon, I was going to be in a world of trouble. "I'm sorry about the loud noise. April didn't exactly explain what she was going to do."

"You called April?" asked May, her frown melting first into confusion, and then understanding. "Did she clear up the listening devices in here?"

"She says she used a countersurveillance charm, and since I know nothing about that sort of magic, I put it to all of you: do we trust that it worked? April says we can talk freely in this room for the next day."

"I think that if we're being spied on—which we almost certainly are—then King Rhys will be smart enough not to let us know right away," said Walther slowly. "Coming in here to recast his charms would be a giveaway."

"I trust April," said Quentin, cautiously pushing his door open and sticking his head into the room. "She does stuff no one else does, mostly because we're all made of meat, so we don't think the way she does. I know she's paranoid about security, and if she says the charm works, the charm works."

"May? Tybalt?"

"I trust her," said May.

"I'm playing the game of your politics for the sake of peace and nothing more," said Tybalt. "If there's any challenge that could cause us harm, I'll have the lot of us onto the Shadow Roads before a single blow can strike home."

"Then we're trusting her. All right." I turned to Walther. "What do you mean, she's your *sister?*"

May, who hadn't seen the note, looked confused. Walther just sighed. "I mean exactly what I said. Marlis is my older sister. We have the same parents. My father's brother married the old Queen of Silences when she was still the Princess, and their son, Torsten, was heir to the throne when the war happened. Marlis and I were never in the line of succession—if anything happened to Torsten or his mother, the throne would have either gone to his mother's brother, or back to his grandmother, who had stepped down after her daughter came of age. I knew Marlis hadn't made it out of Silences after the war, but I thought she'd been elf-shot, not pressed into service for the new King. The fact that she's his seneschal is . . . worrisome. He shouldn't trust her this much."

"Wait, you never looked for her?" May turned, looking at Walther like she was seeing him for the first time. "She's your *sister*. You should have tried to find out where she was."

"I spent the first twenty years after the war running, hiding, and making sure no one could find me," said Walther wearily. "Marlis and I agreed when we split up that we wouldn't look for each other, because it would be too dangerous. If either of us had been caught, we didn't want to be able to give the other away."

"Looks like she never ran," I said.

Walther shook his head. "That's the problem. I *know* she ran."

I frowned. "Okay. Explain to me why this means we need to be on guard."

"Because if she's here, working for the man who took our aunt's throne, and if he trusts her enough to make her seneschal, something is compelling her loyalty." Walther shook his head again, harder this time. "I'm going to refine one of the potions I brought with me. You need to sprinkle it over everything you eat and add it to everything you drink. It's the only way to be safe."

It took me a moment, but I caught his meaning. "You think she's drugged."

"I think a Queen with Siren powers put a Baron in charge of a Kingdom of alchemists," said Walther grimly. "Mind control is hard, even for the best of us, but suggestibility is easy, and so is memory suppression. Scramble things in someone's head enough, and keep dosing them regularly, and you can bend even the strongest will to your hand."

"Memory suppression would explain why she didn't seem to recognize you," I said. "How long before that potion is ready?"

"Not long," said Walther, with an odd grimace. "It was one of the potions I was using the dawn to finish. I just need to boil off the excess liquid, flash-freeze, and powder the results. Say an hour? That should be long enough to make a supply for all of us."

"Won't the King be offended when we start adding things to our food?" asked Quentin. "I mean, the chefs in Quebec get angry if you ask for *salt*. I can't imagine a royal kitchen ranks below a French restaurant for snootiness."

"He might be, but he won't say anything," said Walther. "Silences has declared war. It's perfectly reasonable for a diplomat from Mists to bring along an alchemist to guarantee there's no poison in the food, since even if the King is perfectly respectable, polite, and law-abiding—"

Tybalt snorted.

"—there could still be loyalists in the Court who wanted to curry favor by being the first to kill a citizen of an enemy kingdom," continued Walther, without missing a beat. "As long as we don't actually *say* that I'm protecting you from mind control, my presence will continue to seem like a sadly necessary evil."

"I hate politics." I sat back down on the edge of the bed. "Seriously, this stuff was easier when I was living with Devin. If you were our enemy, we just came over and beat the shit out of you. No declarations of war, no pretending everything was normal while we plotted your death, just a bunch of street kids with knives and brass knuckles handing you your own teeth."

"You are truly a charming example of what the Divided Courts can produce when given sufficient motivation," said Tybalt, the fondness in his voice sapping the sting from his words.

I shrugged. "I'm one of a kind."

"Thank Oberon for that," muttered Quentin, while May just laughed.

The mood in the room seemed lighter now that we knew we had at least one spot where we could talk with reasonably little fear of being overheard. "Any thoughts on when Rhys is likely to want us to come for breakfast?"

"It's a royal court, which means most people probably went to bed sometime shortly after dawn," said Quentin. "If you figure sleeping for eight hours, and then taking an hour or so to become presentable, I'd guess they're having breakfast right around now."

"We're clearly not being summoned for that, so I guess it's not an 'official' meal," I said. "When do you guess they'll have lunch? Go nuts. Make a prediction."

"Um, probably in like four or five hours? That gives Rhys time to figure out what he's going to do with us."

"Great. That means we can go out and get the lay of the land before we need to be properly formal." Part of me wanted to crawl into that big bed and have a nap, since I rarely got to sleep once things really started moving. The rest of me knew that it was a bad idea. For me, anyway. "Quentin, why don't you grab a few more hours of sleep. I need you fresh."

"No nap for me," said Walther. "I need to finish that potion before we go anywhere near the table. Don't worry—I mix my own energy drinks." His smile was tight but confident. He was an excellent alchemist. He wasn't going to poison himself by mistake.

Well. Probably not.

"I have an idea," said May. The rest of us turned to look at her. She shrugged. "I'm officially here as a lady's maid, and the servants never get to sleep in as long as the nobles. That's just not how things are done. So I figure if I can skip on the sleeping, I can go and get some gossip about the shape of this place before we have to discover it on our own. But, Toby, you should sleep."

"May's right," said Walther. "Right now, there's nothing you can do, and my magic isn't a substitute for real sleep. It doesn't restore the body the way actual unconsciousness would. We need you at your best."

"My best still isn't equipped for this situation," I said.

"And yet here we are," said May. "I'm going to get the lay of the land. Walther's going to do alchemy. The three of you, nap, and I'll be back in two hours to help you get ready for dinner."

"Look at it this way," said Walther. "You're going to be working harder than anyone once things really get moving, so we're not doing you any favors. We're just equipping you to run a little bit faster when the monsters come."

"I hate you all," I groaned, and flopped backward on the bed.

Laughing, May left the room, with Walther close behind her. Quentin remained, standing awkwardly near the door to his private chamber. I raised my head enough to peer at him.

"You okay, kiddo?"

"Can I take Spike with me?" he asked. "I don't want to sleep in here, but I'm not comfortable being alone in a Kingdom I don't know."

I pushed myself up onto my elbows. "Of course. Spike, go with Quentin." The rose goblin, which had settled itself atop one of my suitcases, stood, rattled its thorns, and trotted over to rub against my squire's ankles. Quentin bore the thorny intrusion with a minimum of wincing. "We're right here if you need us."

"Cool," said Quentin. "Sleep well."

"You, too."

He stooped to pick Spike up from the floor before retreating into his room, shutting the door behind him. I looked at it for a moment, feeling obscurely guilty. Quentin had learned a lot since I'd first met him. He was going to be a good King someday, when his father chose to give him the throne, and while I wasn't egotistical enough to think it was because of me, I did believe our time together had taught him to be better than he would have been otherwise. But it had also taught him to be cautious, and that not everything was going to go his way. He would have learned those lessons eventually. They were unavoidable. I still felt bad about the fact that he had needed to learn them from me.

Tybalt removed his boots and unbuttoned his shirt and vest, leaving them discarded on the floor before crawling into the center of the bed. He made the motion look remarkably natural, like bipeds had always been intended to move about on all fours. He stretched, getting comfortable, and then looked at me, raising his eyebrows.

"Well?" he asked. "Time is short, and sleep is precious. I should like to think you'd be allowing the first to expedite the second."

"Sorry." I kicked my own shoes off, and squirmed out of my leather jacket, draping it over the bedside table. Only then did I roll over, still effectively clothed, to snuggle against him. The smell of pennyroyal and musk was comforting, and I pressed my face to his chest, breathing it in.

Tybalt chuckled, although he sounded less amused than relieved. "Times are hard, and this is a battle unlike any you have fought before. Take comfort in knowing that you do not fight alone, and allow yourself to rest."

"I'm trying." I tilted my head back, looking at him. "I'm not equipped for this. I'm going to screw it up."

"My dear, your entire life has been a succession of things you were not equipped for, and while you may have, as you so charmingly say, 'screwed some of them up,' you have, in the main, come through spectacularly well. You are surrounded by allies, and each of us is, in our own way, uniquely suited to the challenges ahead—as are you, or you wouldn't be here. Trust Arden to know her people. Trust us to know your needs. Trust yourself to protect your Kingdom." He kissed my forehead. "And sleep, I beg of you. You were bad enough when you were still drowning yourself in coffee. Now, when you become overtired, you are positively unlivable."

"I love you, too," I said, and leaned up to kiss him.

It wasn't the most romantic kiss. I was fully clothed, he was still wearing trousers, and we were in what was effectively the fanciest guest room bed I had ever seen, with my squire just one thin door away. But his lips were warm and tasted like pennyroyal, and I could feel the purr vibrating through his chest. Sometimes romance is of less importance than the feeling of being absolutely safe: of knowing that nothing and no one can hurt you, because the person who loves you most in all the world will destroy them if they try.

I put my head down on his arm, closed my eyes, and let the world go away for a while. If I dreamt at all, I dreamt only shallowly, and there was nothing there that could hurt me.

Tybalt pulling his arm from under my head rocked me back into wakefulness. I opened my eyes, blinking first at the canopy above me, and then, as I shifted positions enough to look at the rest of the room, at the open doorway. May was standing there, arms folded, a concerned look on her face. She was wearing a dress I'd never seen before, a sedate concoction in gray silk with blue accents, like something out of a Waterhouse painting. I sat up, blinking again.

"Are you awake?" she asked. Her voice was flat, devoid of anything that would tell me how she was feeling.

Tybalt, who had been sitting up and rubbing his face in an effort to wipe his own weariness away, stiffened. I felt him changing positions on the bed next to me, and knew he was moving into a position from which he could maneuver better.

"Yes," I said cautiously.

"Good. I've prepared milady's dress for the meal. May I enter?"

"Yes," I said again, even more cautiously this time.

"You are gracious," said May, and stepped into the room, pulling the door closed behind her. Her posture and expression instantly changed, going limp with relief. "Oberon's ass, I thought I was going to pull something. It's worse than we thought out there, and it's a damn good thing you both got some sleep, because I don't know when that's going to happen again."

"What?" I rubbed my eyes with the heels of my hands, trying to chase the sleep away. It wasn't happening fast enough. "What's going on?"

"Quentin needs to get up." May strode across the room, her new gown snapping at her ankles, and pounded on Quentin's door with the heel of her hand before shouting, "Yo! Get your ass up! We have forty-five minutes!"

Her tone did what all the eye-rubbing in the world wouldn't have been able to do, rocketing me from groggy wakefulness into full alertness in an instant. I hadn't heard my Fetch sound that panicked since before we'd been separated. Once—and only once—she'd thought I was about to die, taking her with me. She'd sounded like this then.

"May?" I slid off the bed, standing. "Seriously, what's going on?"

"What's going on is that this Kingdom is fucked up, and it's our fault." She rounded on me, eyes brimming with unshed tears. "We *knew*, Toby. We knew Silences was a puppet government, and we knew the current king got the throne because he was willing to be an asshole to changelings. We knew that meant things here were probably bad. And we ignored it. It was inconvenient, and we ignored it."

"May, honey." I reached out and grabbed her hands. Behind her, the door to Quentin's temporary room swung open and my squire stepped into the room, blinking blearily underneath the tangled fringe of his hair. I ignored him, focusing on her. "You still haven't told us what you're talking about. We want to help, but you have to explain."

"Almost all the staff here are changelings, Toby," she said. There was something dull, nearly broken, about her voice. May was a pureblood, but unlike most purebloods, she had never enjoyed the privilege of that position. As a night-haunt, she had been exiled to the edges of Faerie, denied the glitter and pageantry of the courts. And when she had finally become a Fetch, she had done so with the memories of two changelings—myself, and Dare—fresh in her mind. Despite her centuries of living, she remembered growing up as a changeling more vividly than she remembered anything else about her youth.

Slow comprehension was dawning at the back of my mind, hampered by an unwillingness to accept what she was saying. But understanding is a cruel beast: it *will* have its hour, no matter how painful.

"No changeling would voluntarily stay in Silences," I said. "Being part human doesn't make you stupid."

"No. But being born to be put into service makes you afraid to run away." May shook her head, a tear escaping to run down her cheek, before she stalked over to the wardrobe where I'd stowed my gowns. She wrenched it open, continuing to talk. "Most of them, their parents are on the staff. They were born in the Summerlands. They never had the Choice, because Faerie was all they knew. Service is all they've ever known. They think . . . they said . . ." She stopped.

Quentin was staring at her, his face pale and his eyes wide. He'd been my squire for years, and most of his early ideas about changelings had faded in the face of *knowing* us. It's hard to reduce people to stereotypes after actually meeting them. But in some ways, I think going from a relatively sheltered boyhood to Shadowed Hills, to me, hadn't done him any real favors, because he'd never been forced to see the way changelings were treated in the rest of the world—and that included places like Silences, which were part of his father's greater Kingdom, and would one day be his.

"What did they say?" I asked, stepping over to May and taking the dress gently from her hands.

She sighed, a long, shuddering sound, and said, "They said you were incredibly generous, letting me run around unsupervised when we'd just shown up here, since there was a chance I could offend someone in your absence. Then they explained what that would mean. They beat their servants, Toby. Like this was the middle ages or something. There are children working in the kitchen. *Children*. They've never seen the mortal world. They've never been to school. And they flinch if any adult raises their hands above shoulder level, because they've been here since they were born, and they know what a raised hand means."

I stared at her. Then I threw my dress on the bed and put my arms around her, pulling her close. She pressed her face into my shoulder and sobbed.

Growing up as a changeling in the Mists was hard. I had never considered that other Kingdoms might have it even worse.

Tybalt's hand landed on my free shoulder. I twisted to look at him. His mouth was set in a thin, disapproving line, and I was reminded—not for the first time—that part of the conflict between the Court of Cats and the Divided Courts was the way that we treated our changelings. Cait Sidhe didn't care so much about blood purity. They cared about strength, and how effectively you knew how to use it. Everything else was secondary.

"I won't claim to be as angry as I know you must be. That frightens me, because I'm furious, and I can't stop worrying about what you may choose to do next," he said. "You must dress. We cannot insult this king at our first meal in his home."

"I'd like to do more than insult him," I said. May pulled away, and I let her, turning to face Tybalt instead. "If things here are as bad as May says, something has to be done."

Tybalt nodded solemnly. "Yes. And yet, nothing will be done if we begin by offending the king. No." He raised his hand as I was inhaling to object. "I am sorry, but no. This is, for once, a situation that cannot be resolved with blunt force, cannot be reconciled through bullheadedness or refusal to participate. We are here to play their game, to go through the dance steps that define the political waltz of the Divided Courts. We cannot refuse. You must put your dress on. You must dry your eyes. And you must ride to battle of a different sort."

I looked at him. I turned to look at May, who was still crying, and at Quentin, standing white-faced and silent in his doorway. I couldn't let them down, no matter how much I wanted to.

"All right," I said. "Let's get ready to meet the locals."

NINE

WE WALKED ALONG THE deserted hall like prisoners on our way to our own execution. Tybalt had his arm locked into place, held out and bent just so, allowing me to rest my hand on the inside of his elbow. Walther and Quentin walked three feet behind us, as was appropriate for servants attending on a diplomatic mission—at least according to Quentin, and I had no reason to argue with him.

May had decided to skip lunch in favor of staying back at the room. She was already approaching the point of total exhaustion, and she needed to sleep more than she needed to eat. The last I'd seen, she'd been crawling into the bed in Quentin's room, where she could sleep without fear of the door opening and someone trying to drag her back to the servants' quarters. I had the feeling Quentin was going to wind up sleeping on the floor for at least part of our stay. I didn't think he was going to object.

"You are digging your fingers into my flesh, little fish," said Tybalt mildly. He was wearing a rough silk shirt and brown leather vest that wouldn't have looked out of place in a *Pirates of the Caribbean* movie. For once, his trousers weren't leather, but brown cotton, and tight enough that they would have been indecent if not for the length of his vest. It was a shame I was too tense to really admire the view.

"Sorry," I said, and didn't relax my hand.

Quentin and Walther were wearing generic jerkin and trousers combinations in shades of blue and gray similar to the ones that May had been wearing. I suspected some minor illusions had been used to change the color of their clothes, since the last time I'd looked in Quentin's wardrobe, he hadn't owned that much that coordinated with the banner of the Mists. I was in a long gray silk gown so pale that it would have looked white if not for the braided red belt that rode low on my hips. It wasn't the belt that had come with the dress—that one had been bright, bloody red, unrelenting and almost gaudy. This one was new, made by May, and it alternated arterial red with a darker, quieter shade, the color of blood allowed to dry on a marble floor.

Matching ribbons were twined through my hair, pulling it up and back into a complicated crown braid that I was going to be wearing until someone else took it down. My makeup was understated enough that I was unlikely to destroy it by mistake, but it played up the human roundness of my features more than the fae sharpness that had been overtaking it in recent years. It was May's subtle way of making sure no one could look at me and forget what I really was, and I loved her for it.

We stopped outside the closed doors to the banquet hall, waiting to be allowed inside. A muffled voice spoke from the other side of the doors. I couldn't hear the words, but I could make out the tone, and it was the loud, measured cadence of a herald announcing an arrival. I straightened, tightening my grip on Tybalt's arm. To his credit, he didn't say anything.

The doors swung open. We stepped inside.

The banquet hall was as austere as the rest of the

knowe, all plain wood and stone floors, like something from a movie full of knights and wizards and dragons to be slain. The nobility of his court looked almost laughably out of place in their silks, velvets, and other fine fabrics, perching on the long benches that ran along either side of the equally long banquet tables. Servants in the livery of Silences circulated with trays of sliced meat, eggs, baked goods, and juices.

All of the people in silk and velvet were purebloods. Daoine Sidhe, Tuatha de Dannan, Tylwyth Teg, and Ellyllon. All of the staff were changelings.

There was a smaller table positioned on a low dais at the head of the room, presumably for the king and his companions. There were two chairs there, and an assortment of foodstuffs had already been set out, waiting for Rhys to arrive. I narrowed my eyes, glancing back to the banquet tables. The nobles already seated there were watching us, expressions calculating, taking our measure. None of them had touched their food. This was a "no one eats before the king does" court, then; good to know.

There was a space open at the end of one bench on the banquet table nearest the dais. Tybalt and I walked over and sat, with Quentin and Walther waiting to see that we were settled. Walther leaned forward, in the guise of straightening my skirt, and pressed a small vial of silver-blue powder into my hand.

"Everything you eat or drink," he murmured. "Don't forget."

I nodded. He retreated, along with Quentin, to a table at the back of the room.

We had barely settled ourselves when the herald posted by the door announced, in that same loud, ringing tone, "His Majesty, by Grace of Oberon, King Rhys of Silences, and his honored guest, the rightful Queen of the Mists."

The nobles around us stood. Tybalt stood, the narrowing of his pupils betraying his unhappiness. A heartbeat later, I followed the rest to my feet, gathering my skirts in my hands in an effort to keep myself from shaking. I didn't expect it to work, but at least it was something I could do, however small, however useless.

A door I hadn't seen before opened in the wall at the back of the dais, and King Rhys appeared. He had his arm held out at his side, just the way Tybalt always held his when he was escorting me. And there, walking next to him, calm and cool and serene as ever, was the former Queen of the Mists.

She was a mixed-blood, part Sea Wight and part Banshee, and her heritage showed in everything she was. Her skin was the color of a dead, waterlogged sailor's flesh, and her hair was the color of sea foam, long and fine and perfectly straight, even as it fell past her feet to trail along the floor. Her eyes were like moonlight shining off the sea, blank and cold and halfway mad. She was smaller than she used to be, thin and frail and fragile-looking. That was my fault. She'd been part Siren, once, and when I'd taken that part of her heritage away from her, I had taken more than a foot of height and all the color she had once possessed.

I should have felt bad about that. I had changed her body without her consent, and it wasn't the sort of thing that could be taken back: so far as I knew, not even my mother could have restored the old Queen's Siren blood. I couldn't bring myself to feel anything more than faintly triumphant. She had tried to kill me. She had tried to destroy the people I loved. All I'd done was what I'd had to do.

King Rhys looked across the assemblage with a mild, content smile on his face, like this was exactly the way the world ought to be. The false Queen looked at me, and only me, and her eyes burned with hatred. She'd destroy me, if she could, and nothing I or anyone else could say was going to make her stop wanting my head on a platter.

On the plus side, I could probably make her want it *more*, if I was willing to really work. It's always nice to have goals.

The King's smile broadened when he saw me standing there in my Court finery. He didn't say anything. He just sank down onto his own seat. The false Queen sat a few seconds later, gracefully settling herself beside him. Then, and only then, did the rest of the nobles retake their seats, doing it with an ease that told me this was the normal way of things around here. The servants began circulating faster, getting food onto empty plates and pouring liquid into empty glasses.

I was at the end of our bench, putting Tybalt between me and the nobility of Silences. I was grateful for that, and still trying to regain my equilibrium, when a familiar smell assaulted my nostrils. I reeled, barely grabbing the table in time to keep myself from falling off the bench. Tybalt's hand clamped down on my leg, adding additional stability, even as it served as a warning of a sort. He was telling me not to react.

He could have skipped it. I was so shocked by what was happening that I couldn't have reacted if I'd wanted to—not beyond slowly turning my head and staring at the man on the other side of Tybalt, who was picking up a crystal mimosa flute filled with dark purple, almost black juice. He sniffed it appreciatively before taking a long sip and extending it back out toward the changeling server, who dutifully topped off the glass from the pitcher she was holding. She wasn't wearing a mask over her mouth and nose, and her eyes were filled with a clutching, clawing need.

I understood how she felt. For changelings, just the smell of goblin fruit was enough to awaken an undying hunger that would gnaw at our bones until it was fulfilled. Even with Tybalt between me and the man who held the glass, it was all I could do to stop myself from reaching over and snatching it out of his hand, claiming it as my own. For the girl holding the pitcher, the temptation must have been unbearable.

Pulling my eyes away from the flute of goblin fruit juice, I forced myself to study the servant. She was thin, yes, but not so thin that I suspected her of starving herself. She'd been able to resist temptation, at least so far. I didn't dare try to breathe in her heritage with the goblin fruit so close. Going by the shape of her chin and the dark green color of her pupils, I guessed she was half Hamadryad, which might explain her resistance. Hamadryads were always better at avoiding poisons than the rest of us.

But the entire kitchen couldn't be staffed by Hamadryads, and there was no way a King who would make his serving girls pour goblin fruit would send a pureblood into the servants' quarters to make juice. My shock and anger hardened into a lump that nearly choked me. I swung my head around to the king. I'm not sure what I expected to see there.

I certainly didn't expect to find the former Queen smirking at me, a triumphant expression on her thin, pale face. She had been watching me the whole time.

The serving girl with the goblin fruit moved on, replaced by other servants, with less dangerous offerings. It would have been an insult to refuse to eat, and so I allowed one of them to place a slice of quiche and a pile of potatoes on my plate—the simplest things on offer, even if the quiche was studded with flecks of rosemary and marbled with veins of rich white cheese, even if the potatoes had been cooked in what smelled like lamb fat and garlic. My own glass was filled with orange juice, pale and bright and obviously untainted by goblin fruit. I sprinkled a pinch of Walther's powder over the plate, and added another to my glass, before handing the vial to Tybalt.

The old Queen was watching me like a hawk this entire time. As soon as the vial left my hand, she pounced, demanding, "Is the food not refined enough to your liking, Sir Daye? Shall we have the chefs whipped for disappointing you?"

"Far from it," I said, raising my head. My voice was calm, but my eyes screamed hatred at the woman on the dais, the woman who had nearly destroyed me so many times. She just wouldn't stop. "I grew up in the mortal world, you see, and so my palette is less refined than it might be. A little bit of salt goes a long way toward keeping me from completely embarrassing myself. My alchemist mixes it for me personally." Which meant I was admitting the "salt" was a protection against poisoning, and daring Rhys to say anything about it.

He didn't. "What of your companion, the King?" King Rhys' tone was milder than the old Queen's; he was still amused by what he saw as my useless antics, while she recognized me for the threat I had become. I had to give her that, at least: maybe it had taken me having her deposed, but at least she'd learned to be afraid of me. "He seems bent on adding the same seasoning to his food. It's difficult not to view this as an insult to my kitchens—unless you'd prefer it be viewed as a failure on their part."

"I simply tailor my tastes to the tastes of my betrothed, because I have to eat her cooking," said Tybalt, tone mild and faintly resigned, like being forced to let me feed him was the worst of all possible fates. Some of the surrounding nobles chuckled.

I punched him lightly in the arm, doing my best to look offended, when all I really felt was relief that he'd followed my lead. More of the nobles laughed, more openly now. Even Rhys smiled, although the expression remained calculating enough to make my stomach churn.

"The course of true love never did run smooth," he said. "I shall have to prepare a special banquet just for you, that we might sit together as Kings and speak of kingly things without the needs of our domestic lives intruding upon our statures."

Then, just in case that didn't make his point clearly enough, he turned, took the old Queen's hand, and pressed a kiss just above her knuckles.

Bile rose in my stomach, followed quickly by cold, chilling rage. This was all a ploy, a play they were performing with themselves cast in the leading roles. The unfairly dethroned Queen goes to her beloved, the ruler of a neighboring kingdom, who was unable to be with her because it would have been a conflict of interests. Now he was willing to sacrifice his happiness all over again, for the sake of putting her back in her rightful place. It was an elegant, epic love story, worthy of any stage, and that didn't change the fact that the whole thing was bullshit. They were trying to sell a fairy tale. I wasn't buying.

"Please, eat," said Rhys, releasing the false Queen's hand. "There will be time enough for politics later, when you're ready."

Nice. He was putting the weakness back on us, implying that our journey from the Mists had left us too exhausted to start doing what we'd come here for. In some ways, he was right. Having more time to learn the lay of the land could only help, and it wasn't like we had any real secrets—with the false Queen beside him, he could learn basically everything about us without trying. She knew May was a pureblood in changeling's clothes; she knew Tybalt would die before he'd hurt me again. About the only thing she *didn't* know was that Quentin was Crown Prince of the Westlands, and that wasn't something I was going to bring up for any reason. He needed to be protected from people like her, and the so-called King of Silences.

The quiche was excellent, sweet and creamy, with just a hint of peppery zing. I barely tasted it as I shoveled food mechanically into my mouth, watching the dais all the while.

Walther and Quentin were sharing their table with

what I took for a variety of lesser nobles. They were dressed mostly in Kingdom colors, and the servants seemed to reach them last, resulting in half empty platters and pitchers that sometimes ran dry while a drink was being poured. I saw Walther add a pinch of powder to Quentin's food, and relaxed marginally. My squire was as safe in this environment as he could possibly have been.

That was more than I could say about the rest of us. I could feel the eyes of the surrounding people on me as I ate. They were watching my motions, taking my measure. I was reaching for my orange juice when a passerby "accidentally" tripped, spilling his own drink all over the front of my gown. The fabric immediately turned a deep, bruised purple, and the smell of goblin fruit struck me like a physical blow, nearly knocking me off the bench.

Mocking laughter rose from the nobles around us. I barely noticed. I was too busy staring at the stain spreading across my chest, remembering the sweet dreams the fruit had given me the last time I'd been tricked into tasting it. I was less human now than I'd been then. It would be less able to destroy me. But "less" didn't mean "not at all," and I was all too aware of what would happen if even a drop made its way into my mouth.

Curing myself of goblin fruit addiction once had required iron poisoning, the blood of a Firstborn, and the sacrifice of more of my dwindling humanity. Not much more—I was still mostly what I had been—but I knew, even as I reeled, that getting clean a second time might require everything I had left.

Tybalt's hands were on my shoulders, half pulling and half lifting me out of my seat. I staggered to my feet, the laughter of the nobles still following me. There was a scrape from the dais as King Rhys stood, his own laughter joining the crowd.

"Oh, my!" he said, clapping his hands. "Sir Daye, I'm terribly sorry and embarrassed by this accident! It's such a pity that anyone can be clumsy, isn't it? I assure you, there was no malice intended, and my laundry will be able to restore your . . . lovely . . . gown to its original condition."

I stared at him, too stricken to speak.

He smiled. It was a terrible thing to see. "You look distressed, milady. Oh, that's right—you have human blood in your veins, don't you? Such close exposure to goblin fruit must sit poorly with your mortal heritage. How foolish of me to have even allowed it at the table. But you must understand that my Court is a pureblood holding, and I have such trouble denying my people the little pleasures that make our exile in these shallow lands more bearable."

For once in my life, I couldn't find any words. I couldn't even open my mouth. The smell of the goblin fruit was so strong, and so distracting, that if I breathed too deeply, I didn't know what was going to happen.

Quentin and Walther were suddenly there, standing behind me and lending what strength they could to the situation. Tybalt kept his hands on my shoulders, and said, "Please excuse us. My lady has learned that I do not care for messes, and has begun taking great pains to keep herself from such mortifying social situations. We will return after she has been restored to her pristine state, and will be glad to begin the conversations for which we came here in the first place."

"Indeed," said Rhys. "The sooner begun, the sooner done, wouldn't you say?"

Tybalt didn't answer, but his pupils narrowed, telegraphing his displeasure. He offered the King of Silences a short, stiff bow, pulling me with him, so that we had both performed the absolute minimum that would be acceptable before leaving the presence of a reigning monarch. Then he turned, pushing me in front of him as I stumbled dazedly toward the door.

"I won't tell you to take a deep breath; that might

harm you more than what's to come," he murmured, lips close to my ear. "Simply trust me, and this will all be over soon."

I nodded mutely, keeping my lips pressed into a hard line and trying to minimize the breaths I took through my nose. The doors swung open as we approached them, forming a shadow in the space where the hinges bent. Tybalt seized the opportunity as soon as it presented itself, swinging me up into his arms and plunging us both down into darkness.

The Shadow Roads were airless, black, and cold. They were also scentless, since taking a breath would have frozen my lungs solid in less time than it took to finish the inhale. I leaned against Tybalt, curling into as tight a ball as I could manage in order to reduce the drag. I could feel him tensing as he ran, covering the distance between the dining hall and our room in less than a third of the time it would have taken by more normal channels.

My lungs were aching when we plunged out of the dark and back into the startlingly bright light of our guest chambers. Tybalt all but threw me against the wall, where I fumbled for the lacings on my gown with half frozen fingers. He cut the process short by raking his claws down the ties, slicing them neatly in half. I immediately yanked the gown over my head, panting slightly as I leaned there in strapless bra and underpants.

The purple stain of the goblin fruit was on the bra, too, although it wasn't as dark; that, and the handy flash-freeze effect of our trip through the Shadow Roads, allowed me to remove it without ripping the clasps. I flung it on the pile of fabric before collapsing backward on the bed, staring at the canopy.

"Are you well?" asked Tybalt.

"As well as can be expected," I replied.

"Then I will see to this, and return." He gathered my discarded clothing from the floor, carrying it with him as he walked into another shadow on the far side of the room. That alone told me how concerned he'd been, even if I had somehow managed to overlook everything else that had happened since the glass fell. Normally, he would never have left me by myself.

Not that I was completely by myself. I rolled off the bed and walked to Quentin's door, feeling my legs shake with every step I took. I should probably have stopped to grab a shirt out of the wardrobe, but I felt shocky and unsure: I needed reassurance. So I banged my knuckles against the doorframe and waited, counting the seconds until the door opened and May appeared, her short hair spiky and disheveled. Her white linen nightshirt fell to her knees in a shapeless line, making her look younger than she was.

She blinked at me slowly, confusion written in her expression. "You're not wearing a shirt," she said, like this was somehow going to surprise me. "Or a bra. Toby, what's—do I smell goblin fruit?" Her eyes widened. "Oh, sweet Titania, what happened?"

I laughed unsteadily. "The King of Silences serves goblin fruit juice with lunch. One of his cronies spilled it on me. I don't . . . I can't . . . I need to wash myself. Can you please come with me?"

I didn't need to explain why, or detail my fears: that I would wipe the stickiness off my skin and start drinking the bathwater, looking for the faintest echo of the dreams the goblin fruit could bring. I'd managed to do the unthinkable when I beat the addiction, but that didn't mean I was cured—I was still a changeling, and it would always be more tempting than anything the mortal world had to offer. It just meant that I'd survived a brush with something that should have destroyed me, and while survival may have made me stronger, it had also left its scars.

"Of course," said May, putting an arm around my shoulder and steering me across the room toward what I presumed was the door to the bathroom. "Just let me grab something for you to wear, all right? I think Quentin would drop dead on the spot if he realized you had nipples under there."

My laughter was a little less strained this time, although it still had a tight, flat edge to it that I didn't like. "I'm pretty sure he knows I'm a girl by this point, May."

"I don't know. He's your squire, and you're pretty good with the willful ignorance. He's learning from the best, is all I'm saying." She paused as we passed the wardrobe, taking her arm away long enough to open it and pull out a clean blouse, bra, and panties. "Let's at least try not to scandalize the poor boy. He's having a hard enough time figuring out what he wants without you flashing your boobies all over the place."

She was trying hard to cheer me up. I recognized that, even as part of me balked at her needing to. She had spent the day trying to gather information and discovering just how messed-up Silences really was; she had barely slept. She deserved better than to have me clinging to her arm like some fainting heroine in a bad gothic romance . . . but I didn't let go, and when she started for the bathroom, I let her lead the way without fighting. It was easier.

I needed a little easy.

The bathroom was large enough to contain an old-fashioned copper bathtub, complete with clawed feet that dug into the tiled floor like they were declaring war on the plumbing. There *was* plumbing, which was a bit of a relief: I'd been half afraid we were going to need to fetch buckets or boil our own water. Instead, May turned on the taps, beginning to fill the tub with steaming water.

"I brought bubble bath, on the assumption that you were going to need to scrub blood off yourself at some point; I guess this is a similar situation," she said, indicating a bunch of bottles arranged on the sill of the room's single window. The glass was cloudy with particulates, but judging by the green on the other side, it looked out on a garden of some sort. We were on the second floor. Make that "it looked out on the trees growing in the garden."

May grabbed two bottles, uncapped them with her thumbs, and sniffed their contents before announcing, "You're going to be the most perfumed princess at the party," and dumping a healthy amount of both liquids into the bath. The water promptly foamed up, smelling of peppermint and rosemary.

I blinked at May. Then, slowly, understanding dawned, and I smiled. She wanted to remove the temptation. With two strong herbs scenting the air, there would be virtually no chance of my smelling the traces of goblin fruit still clinging to my skin.

She smiled back, even as she was tipping another vial of Walther's countercharm into the water. Just in case. "Get in the bath. I need to have you dressed again and ready to go before Tybalt gets back."

"Yes, ma'am." I stood, stepping out of my shoes, and peeled off my underpants before allowing May to help me into the bathtub. I would have felt weird about that, but the tub was twice as high as the one we had at home, and had clearly been designed for someone with attendants to use. She took her hand away as soon as I was in the water, and leaned over to turn off the taps.

"There," she said. "Now clean yourself up, and tell me what happened."

"I'm not sure you really want me to," I said, sinking down so that the bubbles were up to my chin. Then, and only then, I began to speak.

There wasn't much to tell, but it took a surprisingly long time to tell it all, especially since May kept asking me to back up and repeat things that she considered important—some of which were seriously odd. She focused less on the goblin fruit juice than she did on the spices in the quiche, for example, and on the seating arrangement of the room.

When I finished, she looked at me, lips pressed into a hard line, and shook her head. "That's messed up. The etiquette of the room is all off. He's playing at classy, and falling way short."

"I don't know about that, but I know it's messed up. You didn't see . . . is the chef a pureblood at least?" Anything to let me believe, however temporarily, that Rhys wasn't making his changeling servants crush the goblin fruit themselves.

May's expression killed that hope before it could fully form. "I didn't see anyone in the kitchen but changelings. If they're that fond of goblin fruit here, they probably lose one or two a year to addiction. Why should they worry about it? They can always make more." She made no effort to conceal the bitterness in her tone, and I appreciated that. It was easier to feel like my own bitterness was justified when I wasn't the only one.

"The trouble with thinking of living beings as a replaceable commodity is that one day, they may think the same of you," said Tybalt, in the mild tone he always used when he was angry but trying not to aim it inappropriately. I turned my head to find him standing in the bathroom doorway. His expression softened as he looked at me. "Are you . . . well, my little fish?"

"I'm sitting in a tub full of water without having a panic attack about it, so I think I'm doing basically okay," I said. "Where are Walther and Quentin?"

"Walking back with diplomatic slowness," said Tybalt. "Both of them knew you would need to clean yourself, and I think neither wished to offer offense by walking in when you were unprepared."

"I'll go let them know everything's fine," said May, pushing herself away from the bathtub and heading for the door. She patted Tybalt on the shoulder as she passed him, causing him to raise an eyebrow. Laughing, she made her exit, and closed the door as she went.

"I may never understand that woman," said Tybalt,

walking toward the tub where I sat. "Then again, I may never understand any woman."

"Not even me?" I asked.

"Especially not you," he said, leaning forward to kiss my forehead. I tilted my chin back, and he kissed me again, this time on the lips. It was a glancing thing, but it made me feel better. "If I understood you in more than the most basic of principles, it would be a violation of the laws of nature, and the cosmos would be quickly thrown into disarray. What *is* that smell?"

"Bubble bath, two kinds," I said. "May was making sure I couldn't smell anything else."

"Ah. She is a wise one, your incomprehensible Fetch." Tybalt took a step back, leaning against the nearest wall and watching me. "You realize this has all been orchestrated, do you not? Even down to our places at the table."

"Yeah, I picked up on that." I grabbed a sponge from the side of the bathtub, beginning to scrub off the last of the sticky film from the goblin fruit. "I can't tell whether it was a test or a carefully designed humiliation, and I'm not completely sure it matters. The end result was the same."

"Ah, but you see, it *does* matter," said Tybalt. He sat down on the rim of the bathtub, picked up another sponge, and began washing my back. "They only had one chance to do what they did today. You cannot forever be having things spilled upon you, or it becomes intentional offense. The glass was aimed at your clothing, to test your poise and self-control, but not at your face. Why not? That approach has worked in the past."

"Yeah, but with you right there, and Walther in the room, I wouldn't have had the chance to really hurt myself," I said. "We know blood stabilizes me, and I know you want me to be safe more than you want to not be bleeding. I would have stabbed you in the arm and used your blood to stay on an even keel until Walther could hit me with some alchemy." He'd done it before. I had every faith he could do it again.

"So they knew they could not reacquaint you with your old addiction—not in any way that would serve them—and with the false Queen having experienced your magic firsthand, they must also have been aware of the risk that you would simply become stronger in an effort to overcome the fruit."

I twisted to blink at him. "Say what?"

Tybalt leaned over and tapped the point of my left ear. "A person would have to be blind of both the eye and nose to have missed the changes you've undergone these past several years, October. You have traded away slivers of your humanity for many things, all of them worthy, and I'd be lying if I claimed I was not glad. I prefer you among the living, and the more fae you become, the longer you'll stay alive. But that is no matter. Every trade you make increases your power. You think they want that? The idea was never to addict you. It was to shame you, and to remind you that this place is not yours, it is theirs. Their blood is purer than yours, and things which can destroy you cannot hurt them."

"Gosh, Tybalt, if this is supposed to be a pep talk, you need to take a refresher course on inspiring the troops."

He smiled. "Ah, but you see, they neglect to remember that the opposite is also true. What can destroy them cannot hurt you, for you are fae and human at the same time, and your power is not theirs to claim."

I blinked at him, taking in his words. Then, slowly, I began to smile.

The rest of the bath passed quickly, despite the natural distraction that Tybalt represented, and soon, I was out and dry and ready to face the rest of my day. Quentin and Walther were waiting when Tybalt and I emerged from the bathroom, Tybalt only slightly damp, me clean and peppermint-scented and wearing the clothes May had grabbed for me. She hadn't bothered to pick up any trousers, but the blouse was long enough to hang to my knees; I wasn't worried about showing anything I didn't want people seeing.

Walther was pacing when I stepped into the room. He stopped when he saw me, visibly relaxing. "Are you all right?" he asked.

"Damp and cranky, but I'll survive," I said, heading for the wardrobe. "Quentin? You okay?"

"I don't think it's appropriate for me to plot regicide," he said. My squire was obviously fighting to control his voice, which seemed to be on the verge of breaking. He had mostly finished puberty, but sometimes little reminders of how young he was would find a way to slip through. "He *laughed*, Toby. After you and Tybalt left? Walther and I had to walk out on our own, and he was laughing. Like it was the funniest thing that had ever happened."

I didn't have to ask to know which "he" Quentin was referring to. I changed directions, walking over to the bed instead, where I put my arms around my squire and squeezed tightly. Quentin returned the hug with obvious relief.

"Let him think that it's funny," I said. "It's going to be one of the last jokes he ever makes."

"I still think it's inappropriate for me to plot regicide," said Quentin.

"So don't." I let him go. "Regicide is nowhere near as much fun as a good, old-fashioned deposing." I turned to the wardrobe and began digging through my heaped-up clothes.

"Are you planning to replace every monarch on the West Coast?" asked Walther. "Not that I automatically disapprove if you are, I just need to know if I'm clearing my calendar for the next few decades."

I paused. *Was* I planning to replace every monarch on the West Coast? I had never thought of myself as the sort of person who reshaped the political landscape . . . but then again, I'd been doing it all along, hadn't I? Even getting knighted was an act of political rebellion, in its way. I'd accepted the title because I'd wanted to be safe from the sort of people who thought changelings were all disposable. But it hadn't stopped there, and I had already toppled one queen who didn't deserve her throne.

She wasn't the only one in Faerie who didn't deserve a throne. King Rhys of Silences had been hand-picked for the position he now held. Under him, changelings were worse than second-class citizens. They never had a chance. But that didn't mean that we could just walk into his house and start questioning whether or not he had the right to keep it.

"I don't *know* that we're ever going to depose another monarch," I said carefully. "Right now, we're here to prevent a war, and that's what we're going to focus on. But when this is over, and we're not all spilling our literal guts out on the battlefield, I think it might be time to take a trip to Toronto and talk to High King Sollys about the validity of Rhys' claim to Silences. He was given the throne by someone who didn't have the right to her own crown. It's possible that a member of the old royal family could just . . . step in."

All eyes went to Walther. I took the opportunity to pull my jeans on and tuck my blouse in, creating a faintly old-fashioned, but acceptable level of decency.

Walther shook his head. "Don't look at me," he said. "Even if you deposed the man, I couldn't inherit. I keep telling you, I'm several steps away from the line of inheritance. I'd be no more legitimate than he is, and besides, I'm on a tenure track. It's important that I stay in Berkeley."

I blinked. "That may be the best reason for not wanting to be King that I've ever heard. 'I'm going to get tenure.' "

"It's true." Walther shrugged. "So what are we going to do now?"

"The same thing I always do," I said, selecting a lace-up bodice from the wardrobe and sliding it on. "I'm going to go annoy the crap out of the nobility. Now somebody lace me into this thing."

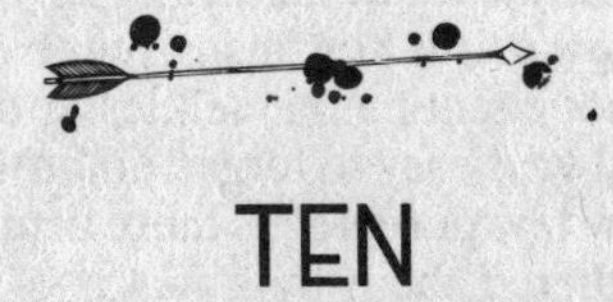

TEN

I WALKED DOWN THE DESERTED hall toward King Rhys' receiving room with Tybalt on my arm and Walther following two paces behind. Quentin was off with May, exploring the knowe. As my squire, he could be reasonably expected to be running around and doing the tasks I didn't want to bother with, and as a pureblood, he was going to be in less danger than a changeling manservant would have been. I'd still insisted he take some of Walther's powder with him, just in case somebody tried to force him to have a friendly cup of tea or something. The thought of Quentin being dosed with a loyalty potion was enough to make my skin crawl.

"I wonder how big this Court really is," I commented mildly, looking at one of the blank walls. I'd never been in a knowe this size with so little decoration. It was like Rhys had ordered the whole thing from Castles R Us, and then never bothered to swing by the local Bed, Battlements, and Beyond for the accessories he'd need to make it believable.

"In what regard, my dear?" Tybalt's tone was artificially plummy and tolerant, like he was speaking to a child he suspected of being slightly slow. I wrinkled my nose, resisting the urge to burst out laughing. We were almost certainly being listened to, and speculating about the size of the Court, while rude, wasn't seditious or otherwise inappropriate . . . except in that it could be considered speculation about the size of Rhys' army.

"Well, I know about how many purebloods there are in the Mists, not counting the Selkies or the Undersea," I said. It was always easy to forget, embroiled as I was in the courts, how few purebloods there actually were. Humans outnumbered them by a factor of tens of thousands. Changelings could have outnumbered them, too, if we'd ever cared to pull away from our human friends and pureblood masters and become an organized force. Luckily for the status quo, most of the changelings I knew were too busy keeping body and soul together to waste their time on sedition. "Silences is a smaller Kingdom, isn't it? So maybe that explains why the halls are so empty."

"Silences is a smaller Kingdom, but Portland is the biggest city in Silences," said Walther. "I know a lot of the local fae don't necessarily take part in Court. That's true in the Mists, too. I think what you're seeing is just the effect of a high turnover in the higher social classes during the war. People who used to be held in good standing aren't always anymore, and some of the nobles who managed to keep their places did so by keeping their heads down and not drawing attention to themselves."

"Oh," I said, and looked thoughtfully around the hall again, trying to fill in the spaces between his words. I knew people, like Walther and Lowri, who had come from Silences; purebloods who had chosen to move to other Kingdoms rather than stay where they were. But I didn't know anyone who had chosen to move *to* Silences. All the mobility seemed to be in the wrong direction.

Idly, I wondered whether King Rhys had one of the still-missing hope chests. If he could turn changeling children into pureblood fae, he might be able to solve his population problem. Of course, he'd have to deal with the fact that his populace had all started out part-human, which might be a bit much for him, given his prejudices, but who knew? Maybe he could adjust.

Two men in full Silences livery were standing outside the receiving room doors when we walked up. One of them looked me up and down, not making any effort to hide his dismay at my blue jeans and bodice. I thought I actually looked pretty good, all things considered. They were dark jeans—the only formal way to wear denim, according to my ex-boyfriend, Cliff, who had worn jeans every day while we were together—and my bodice was a lovely shade of wine red, holding everything in place without turning my breasts into the stars of the show. It seemed more inspired by mortal ideas of the Middle Ages than by actual pureblood fashion, and I appreciated that, too, since the entire point of the outfit was reminding them that they weren't dealing with their own kind. They were dealing with me, and I was done playing around.

"Sir October Daye, Knight of Lost Words and diplomatic representative for Her Majesty Arden Windermere, Queen in the Mists," I said, without preamble. "I am accompanied by King Tybalt of the Court of Dreaming Cats, and attended by my alchemist, Walther. I would like to see your liege now, if you would be so kind as to open the doors for us."

The guard who had been sneering at my clothes blinked. Apparently, whatever he'd been expecting me to say, it hadn't been that. "King Rhys is otherwise occupied," he said.

"Does he get to do that?" I raised an eyebrow as I glanced to Tybalt, my tone making it clear that my question wasn't really a question. "I don't think he gets to do that." I turned back to the guard. "I am the diplomatic representative for Queen Arden Windermere, recognized by High King Aethlin Sollys as rightful ruler in the Mists. Your King has declared war on her Kingdom, which makes her sort of cranky. That's why I'm here. We're hoping this can be resolved without resorting to actual bloodshed since, well, blood is so messy, don't you think?" I took a step toward the guard, who shrank back.

The Luidaeg would have been so proud of me in that moment. Her little troublemaker, all grown up and complicating lives on a grander scale than ever.

"So here's how this is going to go," I continued, not giving the guard a chance to speak. "You're going to open the door. You're going to let us through. You're going to remember that we're here under the rules of formal hospitality, and that barring our way could be viewed as an act of aggression against the Mists. Do you really want to do that? Aggress against us when we're in that polite three-day period between you being dicks and us being allowed to kill you for it?" I was bluffing. I wasn't sure aggressing against us was a bad thing at this stage, since Silences had declared war—it seemed a little unrealistic to expect them to worry about our feelings when they were planning to march in and start slaughtering us.

Thankfully, the guard didn't call my bluff. He fell back another half step, shooting a glance at his compatriot, who seemed to be doing his best to ignore what was going on. I guess when you're not the person being advanced on by the scary changeling, there's very little motive to intervene.

"Apologies," said the first guard. He stepped to the side, grabbed the door handle, and pulled.

I didn't say anything. I just offered him a thin smile, placed my hand back on Tybalt's arm, and proceeded onward.

The receiving room was the room where we had been taken upon first arriving in Silences. Velvet and tassels threatened to strangle the walls. The hardwood floor was polished bright as a mirror. I had to take extra care not to slip as we made our way across the room to the dais where Rhys waited. The last thing I needed was to fall on my face in front of him. He presented exactly the picture I'd been expecting, seated proudly on his golden throne. What I hadn't been expecting was the woman who sat beside him on one of the dignitary's chairs, although in retrospect, I should have been: the false Queen wasn't the sort of woman who would allow herself to be left out of a war of her own devising.

Marlis was standing at attention to the left of the dais. As we approached, she said, loudly, "Sir October Daye of the Mists. King Tybalt of the Court of Dreaming Cats." Walther, it seemed, did not deserve an introduction. I searched her face, looking for any flicker that she recognized the man she was failing to announce. It wasn't there.

"Ah, Sir Daye, how lovely to see you again," said King Rhys, before allowing his eyes to travel the length of my body. He raised his eyebrows slightly, as if surprised. "Were you unable to pack sufficient clothing for your trip? My court tailors would be happy to help you with any deficiencies in your wardrobe. Simply send your lady's maid to them, and they will provide whatever your heart desires."

"I'm good," I said. "It's sort of hard to do much in the kind of dresses people keep trying to put me into, you know? Jeans are much more convenient."

"Convenient, yes; respectable, no," said the false Queen. She leaned back in her chair and snapped her fingers, a cold smile on her face.

The changes I had made to her blood had echoed through her flesh and into her magic. Some of those changes were good ones. She could no longer command people with her voice, could no longer compel us to attack our loved ones or forget our places in the world. Some of those changes were less positive. A cloud of mist enveloped me, so sudden and thick that I found myself separated from Tybalt even though I would have sworn that I hadn't moved at all. I realized, to my dismay, that I didn't really know *what* Sea Wights were capable of. They were technically Undersea fae, and I had never encountered a pureblood.

"He'll leave you before this is done, you know," murmured the false Queen's voice, from deep inside the mist. The air smelled of rowan and tasted of the sea, an indefinable flavor that was salt and rot and petrichor and a thousand other things, all of them mingled into a single element. "He'll leave you to drown, and he won't be there to save you."

"I've never needed to be saved before."

"Oh, my dear. My dear, my delusional darling, no. That's where you're wrong. You have never been the golden-haired girl in skirts of green, and you are always the one who must be saved."

As suddenly as it had come, the mist was gone. My hand was back on Tybalt's arm, and he was frowning at me, eyes narrowed in anger and suspicion. I forced myself to keep my chin up, not allowing myself to look down at my clothing. I could already tell, from the feeling of fabric hanging around my legs, that it had been changed.

"You know I hate it when you do that," I said, eyes fixed on the false Queen. She was reclining in her seat, a smug expression on her face. There was a time when that look would have caused me to compare her to a cat, but I had gotten to know the Cait Sidhe a lot better since then—all sorts of Cait Sidhe, not just my childhood friend, Julie—and I knew no cat could ever match her for underhanded treachery. They could be deceitful, sure, but it wasn't the same thing.

When the Cait Sidhe came to kill you, they did it with tooth and claw, and they did it in the open. They didn't do it with words and dresses and slander.

"Do you?" she asked, her eyes widening theatrically. "I don't believe you ever told me so. Then again, perhaps that's because in the past, when I gave you the gift of a better wardrobe, I was still recognized as rightful Queen of the Mists. It's rude to argue with your monarch, isn't that so? So you must have stayed silent, and now I have overstepped. How terrible. Imagine how this could have been avoided with better communication. Then again, many things could have been avoided with better communication. You could, for example, not have gone looking for an imposter to steal my throne away from me."

I blinked at her, momentarily nonplussed. To cover the silence, I looked down at myself, finally giving her the satisfaction of acknowledging what she'd done.

My jeans, blouse, and bodice were gone, replaced by a pine-green velvet gown straight out of a pre-Raphaelite painting. It was embroidered with gold heraldic roses around the long, trailing cuffs and square neckline. The underdress was pale gold, a few shades lighter than the embroidery, and had its own line of primroses in heather green stitched across the neckline. I kicked out one foot, sending several skirts rustling out of the way, and revealed a green slipper that matched the gown.

"You always did have an excellent sense of color," I said, looking up again. "You know it didn't go down like that. You didn't leave me any choice."

"I left you the world, October." The coy theatricality bled out of her eyes, leaving them icy and filled with the moonstruck madness that had always been her stock in trade. It seemed colder than it used to be, less fragmented and more simply wild. I had done that to her. The weight of it seemed to strike me all at once. So much of who she'd always been was in her blood, in the jagged places where her various heritages rubbed up against each other. And yes, sometimes those edges were sharp enough to cut her, or to cut the people around her, but they'd been hers, and I'd taken them away from her without her consent.

The false Queen wasn't the first person whose blood I had changed. She wasn't even the most recent. But she was the only one whose blood I had changed without her consent, against her will, and while I had done it to save both myself and the people I loved, I suddenly found myself wishing there had been another way. There was a time when I would have found another way, because I wouldn't have had any other choice. Back then, I was too human to have transformed her the way that I had.

Maybe I was losing touch with my humanity after all.

"All I denied you was my Kingdom, and I denied it to you because you pushed too hard," she said, apparently taking my stricken silence for confusion. "You couldn't be still, couldn't be quiet, couldn't remember your place. I gave you enough rope to hang yourself and more; enough rope to weave a bridge that could have carried you beyond the Mists. But you wouldn't go."

"Everyone I know is in the Mists," I said. My lips felt numb.

Her eyes narrowed. "And everyone I know is not? I have allies in Silences—obviously, or you would not be here now—but they are few and far between compared to the comforts of my own knowe, my own *home*."

The knowe she had claimed as her own was standing empty, waiting for Arden or someone else among the nobility to decide what to do with it. The amount of iron in the false Queen's dungeons made it a dangerous place for purebloods, apart from the Gremlins, and no one was sure they wanted to give *them* access to that much iron.

"I found that knowe, remember?" I wasn't sure what I was going to say until I was speaking, and then it was too late. "It was the first thing I ever did for you. I went into the city, and I found you a knowe when your old one was sinking back into the shallowing it had been shaped from. And I think I sort of wondered, even then, how a kingdom as big as ours could have such an unstable royal seat. Because no one had ever told me that King Gilad reigned from someplace different, you know? I thought you were his daughter."

She glared at me, her eyes all but snapping fire. "I am my father's daughter."

"No, you're not." I shook my head. "I mean, technically I guess you are—whoever your father was, you're his child, but you're not King Gilad Windermere's daughter. He was a pureblooded Tuatha de Dannan, and you have no Tuatha in you."

"Because you stole it from me!" She sat up straighter, expression going triumphant. "You reached into my blood and you ripped away my heritage, all so you could give my throne to someone else! Betrayer! I made you a Countess, I elevated you above all others of your kind, and this was how you repaid me. With unspeakable treachery."

"I see how we're playing this," I said. "You keep saying things that are true, because they don't have any context. Yes, you are your father's daughter, but your father was never King in the Mists. Yes, I changed the balance of your blood, and I'm genuinely sorry to have done it without your permission, but I did it to save my friends, and what I took away from you was Siren, not Tuatha. It's not against the Law for us to use magic against each other. Sometimes I wish that it was. We might do a little less damage that way. Since it's not, under the Law, I've done nothing wrong."

"Wait." King Rhys leaned forward on his throne, breaking into the conversation for the first time since the false Queen had started speaking. "Is what she says true? Did you really lay hands upon her, and take her heritage from one thing into another?"

"Yes." There was no point in lying. We didn't go around advertising the fact that I wasn't Daoine Sidhe, as I had always assumed, but the more fae I became, the more obvious it was that my heritage had nothing to do with Titania. Everything about me was wrong for one of her children, and perfect for one of the children of Oberon. "When I placed my hands on her, she had three bloodlines in her. Siren, Sea Wight, and Banshee. She was using the abilities she inherited from her Siren bloodline to harm the people I love. I had no other solution that wouldn't violate the Law, and so I took those abilities away from her." Oberon's Law said that we weren't allowed to kill each other. It never said anything about getting creative with our magic, which was how elf-shot was invented, and why so many of us had passed a few centuries as trees, or boulders, or white stags that only appeared at sunrise.

"And this is something you could do again?" He leaned forward a little more, looking at me with more interest than I was really comfortable with. "You could just . . . change someone?"

"Yes," I admitted. "But I can only work with what's already there. I couldn't make myself part Cu Sidhe, or turn a Tylwyth Teg into a Tuatha. I'm . . . sort of an alchemist, I guess, in a weird way. I can't actually transform anything into something that it's not."

"I haven't heard this power attributed to the Daoine Sidhe before," he said, raising one eyebrow inquisitively. "Are you a prodigy of some sort? Or are you a danger? Is this a thing any Daoine Sidhe could do, were they not limited by their own safeguards?"

There was a time when I could pass for something other than what I was, and thus protect my mother's first big secret: that she was Firstborn, a daughter of Oberon himself, and hence the parent of a whole new race. That time was long past, and if Mom wanted me to keep my mouth shut, she should have given me a reason. "I didn't say I was Daoine Sidhe," I said. "I'm Dóchas Sidhe. We're blood-workers, but our powers run along different lines."

"I see. Fascinating." King Rhys settled back in his throne again. "Forgive me if I'm a little slow to fully grasp the implications of these . . . powers . . . of yours. Are you saying you can't return my lady's true heritage to her?"

"That's correct," I said. "There's no Siren left in her blood. I can't create something that isn't there."

"If you looked for it, would you even be able to find traces of it? Would there be any sign that it had ever existed?"

"I don't know," I said, slowly. "I've never had reason to look for a bloodline that had been removed from someone. I think there would probably be signs. She'd have to consent to my looking, though; they'd be delicate and hard to find, and would require her cooperation." There were watermarks in my blood, showing the places where my fae and human heritages had slid back and forth, fighting for dominance. There was no reason to believe that the false Queen would be any different.

"I see. What about the process of the removal itself? Could it have, ah, 'washed away' any of those marks that were made before you laid hands on her?"

Too late, I recognized the trap that I was walking into. "Yes," I said.

"Then you don't *know* that my lady is not King Windermere's daughter and rightful heir. What makes you so sure that what you did to her had not been done before? Hope chests have always existed. In fact . . ." He turned to the false Queen. "Wasn't there a rumor that a hope chest had been found in the Mists? In the care of the Countess Winterrose?"

"It's no rumor, my lord," she said, with open satisfaction in her voice. "It was brought to me by Sir Daye, and placed in my royal treasury. I don't know where it is now, of course, denied as I am the right to access my own home and goods. But it was a true thing, and one which I saw with my own eyes." Her gaze slanted back to me, mouth thinning into a hard line. "Until recent events caused me to realize that I had been deceived as to Sir Daye's heritage, I had assumed that her growing purity of blood was due to her having used the chest herself, before she handed it over to me. I considered raising the question with her, if I am being entirely honest. The hope chest is a powerful artifact, and should not have been left cavalierly in the hands of a changeling."

"Doesn't make it yours," I said, as calmly as I could. "According to the official records, it was given to the care of the Daoine Sidhe Firstborn by Oberon himself. I guess that means it should be held by the Daoine Sidhe, if by no one else. Since you've never claimed to be Daoine, and at the time I thought I was, I would have had more right to keep the thing than you did. And I didn't. I handed it off to the Court of Cats while I finished dealing with the business at hand, and then gave it to the woman who stood as Evening's liege—you. I never used it."

At least, I hadn't used it on purpose. The delicate balance of my blood had been disrupted when I'd touched it: there was no denying that, and it would have been foolish to try. My whole life had been a ride from one end of my heritage to the other, with forces—the hope chest, my mother, the goblin fruit—tugging me first one way and then the opposite. I was finally in a position to do the tugging for myself, and if that meant I was choosing to stay exactly where I was, well, that was my prerogative.

"I believe we're getting off the subject," said King Rhys. "Sir Daye, you claim that Arden Windermere is rightful Queen of the Mists, by virtue of being the eldest child of Gilad Windermere, who died without announcing an heir. Is this so?"

"Yes," I said. It seemed like a simple question, which meant it was probably anything but. I breathed in through my nose, trying to calm myself, and was hit again with the mingled magical scents of the people around me. Tybalt's pennyroyal smelled, soothingly, of home, while the false Queen's rowan and seashore warned me that the danger was very far from over.

"You have also admitted that you don't know whether you would be able to tell, now, if someone else had manipulated the balance of my lady's blood, given the violence of your attack." He leaned forward, expression suddenly predatory. "As *you* can manipulate blood without a hope chest, and have allies who can walk through shadows and move through walls, who knew where a hope chest was to be found—and you have a mother, do you not? Someone who, presumably, shares your capabilities; Amandine, I believe her name was—why am I to believe that my lady is not *also* King Gilad's daughter?"

"My mother was of mixed-blood," said the false Queen piously. "The Undersea refused her, because her father had been a Banshee, and Banshee are not creatures of the sea."

"Wait. Wait just one moment." I put my hands up, palms turned outward. "Are you trying to claim that she's actually the legitimate heir to the throne?"

"I am the elder among us: none will question that I was born before Arden," said the false Queen. "Why didn't you ask if Gilad was my father? Why didn't you test my blood, look for those markers you claim you can see? You could have told for certain whether part of my heritage had been stolen—and by your own words, once it was taken, it couldn't be returned. So you stand here and admit, instead, that you destroyed the evidence of such a crime."

"If that evidence existed," I snapped. "You *never* said you'd been part Tuatha and lost it. There's nothing to support that idea."

"But there's nothing to contradict it, either," said King Rhys. "You're here because you want to prevent a war between my Kingdom and yours. I can't blame you for wanting that, any more than I can blame the usurper for sending you. After all, power cleaves to power, and you're quite enjoying the change in regime, aren't you? From a powerless changeling to a diplomat. Respected, attended by pureblood servants, allowed to take a squire of your own, even betrothed to a man whose power outstrips your own . . . I'm sure you can see why I find it difficult to believe that you acted solely out of the need to protect your Kingdom."

"I never said I didn't have reasons to want Arden on the throne," I said. "If you don't think she's legitimate, take it up with the High King."

"I don't have to," said Rhys. "I am a valid monarch, holding a throne that was given to me by my liege, and I have held that throne well for over a hundred years. No one is going to challenge my right to declare war on my neighbors when they threaten me."

"How did we threaten you?" I demanded.

"The Mists has threatened me by allowing you to live, Sir Daye," he said calmly. "You are a threat to my throne, and to my people's way of life. If Arden's first step after taking 'her' throne had been to order your execution for laying hands in anger upon a pureblood, my lady might have finally accepted my age-old proposal and agreed to sit beside me as my Queen. But Arden didn't do that. She welcomed you as a part of her Court, of her political structure. And you are, quite simply, too dangerous to be allowed to run about as you do."

His smile was sudden, and predatory. "You see, Sir Daye, I know you are here to prevent a war, and I would very much like to give you the opportunity to do so. I'd like to offer you a solution."

"What's that?" I asked warily.

"Bleed for me." King Rhys kept smiling. That was possibly the worst thing of all. "Go to my alchemists, and let them bleed you dry. Let us make talismans of your bones, and antidotes from your liver. We'll let everyone else you brought with you leave—and as you are not a pureblood, we won't even have to accuse them of standing idly by while Oberon's Law was broken. Die for us, Sir Daye, and we will let your loved ones live."

The false Queen had never looked so triumphant. Not even when she was banishing me from the only home I had ever known, not even when she was sentencing me to death for breaking the same Law that would now fail to protect me.

"The choice," she said, "is yours. But then again, it always was, wasn't it, October?"

ELEVEN

I TURNED AND STALKED OUT of the receiving room, leaving King Rhys' terrible proposal unanswered. Tybalt and Walther were close behind me. We walked in silence until we turned the corner of the hall, passing out of sight of the guards on the door. Tybalt looked at me. I nodded, and he grabbed us both—me by the arm, Walther by the collar—before yanking us onto the Shadow Roads.

We emerged less than a minute later on a narrow pathway lined with pine trees. Walther pulled away and Tybalt let him go, watching with some interest as the alchemist staggered, wheezing, to lean against the nearest evergreen. He didn't look as frozen as I was, just winded, which leant some credence to my belief that Tylwyth Teg were self-defrosting. It was the only way to explain the stunts they could pull with yarrow branches not ending in frostbite or worse.

Tybalt looked at me gravely, studying my face, before pulling me into an embrace that lasted longer than we'd been on the Shadow Roads.

"That could have gone better," said Walther, voice still strained from the lack of oxygen. His words seemed to break some temporary spell of peace, bringing us crashing back into a world where time was passing and I had to start thinking about the future.

Damn. Sometimes it was nice to have a few minutes where all I had to do was live in the past. Now I had to go back to living in the present, and since the present seemed to want me dead—again—I would have been just as happy to put that off for a little longer.

I pulled away from Tybalt, turning to face Walther. "I guess I shouldn't have been surprised," I said. "We all knew she was here. We knew she'd kill me if she could. I just didn't expect her to be quite so blatant about it."

"The ways of the Divided Courts grow more distasteful by the hour," said Tybalt. "It is a pity you cannot, as you say, introduce a thing that is not present into the blood. I would beg you to come and be a cat with me, and leave this terrible way of doing things behind."

"I never thought that would sound so tempting." I tried to run my hand through my hair, only to run into the braids May had put in it earlier. I groaned instead. "I don't think we should be talking out here. It's too open."

"Yes, exactly," said Walther. "Being out in the open is a form of protection. It's hard as hell to cast listening charms on living trees, and I haven't seen any pixies. That means they'd need stationary stones, which I can check for, or something else."

"I can think of what that something else might be," I said slowly. "Tybalt, why are we here, specifically? Instead of back in the room?"

"I was aiming for familiarity, and the roads here are not yet as known to me as I would prefer," he said. "I thought the door would open on something that belonged to one of us."

I paused, looking at him flatly. "Okay, wow. I knew the Shadow Roads were sort of an art, rather than a science, but I don't think I needed to know they were *that* much of an art."

Tybalt smiled. "As long as we come out of the dark each time, why should you be concerned?"

"I don't even know where to start." I walked over to the edge of the brush and knelt, peering into the green. Had something moved in there? It was difficult to tell. "You can come out now," I said. "We're not going to hurt you."

"Who are you talking to?" asked Walther.

"Something else," I said, and made a little clucking noise with my tongue. "Come on out."

And they came.

Only one at first, pink-thorned and purple eyed, like something out of a very strange Lisa Frank painting. But three more were close behind it, and three more close behind *them*, until rose goblins were pouring out of the brush. They rattled their thorns and made inquisitive chirping noises as they surrounded us, sniffing at Walther and Tybalt's ankles, and at basically everything I had, since I was still crouched almost to their level. Most were within the "housecat" range, size-wise, although a few were substantially larger, big enough to look like exceedingly strange dogs.

"Well," said Tybalt, sounding faintly nonplussed.

"Told you Spike wanted to check out the locals," said Walther. He knelt, offering his fingers to one of the larger rose goblins. It sniffed them cautiously before making a delighted chirping noise and leaping into his arms. Walther made an "oof" noise, but managed to catch the rose goblin before its thorns could shred his shirt. He stood, now holding the outsized, thorny creature against his chest. "Well, hello to you, too."

The rose goblin—which was the same mossy green as peat, with eyes the color of yarrow flowers—pressed itself against his chest, making a happy chirping noise. I raised an eyebrow.

"It seems to know you."

"Probably because it does," said Walther, stroking the

goblin's head. "Rose goblins live until something kills them. For this fellow to be the size it is, it must be a few centuries old. So yes, you have this sort of size to look forward to from your Spike."

"Oh, goody," I said mildly. "I assume I'm correct in calling the rose goblins the 'something else' that Rhys is going to use to listen in on us out here?"

"Probably," said Walther, and gave his goblin's head another careful stroke. The goblin chirped happily. "There used to be a few Dryads on the groundskeeping staff. Since no one cuts down a Dryad's tree if they can avoid it, I'm assuming they're still here. They'd be able to translate what the rose goblins say, and they're too naïve for anyone to think that they're lying."

"Right," I said. Most Dryads were more interested in being trees than they were in being people. They weren't stupid, but they were . . . distracted might be the best word. Constantly distracted by the strange situations that came with the incarnate condition, and always keeping half their minds back in their tree. Our friend April was a Dryad who didn't have those issues, but she was also half computer, which made her a bad model to go on. "Is there any way we can convince the rose goblins not to tell the Dryads what we talk about out here? We could go back to the room, but . . ."

"But if we're constantly walling ourselves up in there, Rhys is going to figure out that we're up to something, and he's going to come looking," said Walther. "Give me a second."

"You speak rose goblin?" I asked. I was starting to feel like I needed a list of who could and couldn't interrogate my house pets.

His smile was brief, and amused. "Not quite. But the ones here in Silences . . . we have ways around language." This time, he sat down on the path, still holding the large rose goblin against his chest. Once he was settled, he transferred it to his lap and began digging through his vest.

Tybalt put a hand on my arm. I glanced at him. He nodded toward the other side of the path. I nodded in turn, and followed him away from Walther and the gathering of goblins, stopping just before the trees took over. We were still close enough to be together, but by lowering our voices, we could at least pretend to a modicum of privacy.

"Are you all right?" asked Tybalt.

I laughed, unsteadily. "Let's see. The woman we thought was done threatening my life and transforming my jeans into elaborate formalwear is not only still in the business of doing both, but she's managed to produce a King who'll back her up—and oh, right, they want to take me apart."

"You cannot allow them to do this thing, of course," said Tybalt, matter-of-factly.

"Right, I—" I paused, blinking at him. He had sounded so calm, like we were talking about where to go for lunch, and not whether I was going to be brutally murdered over the course of several days in order to prevent a war. "What?"

"All my many personal objections aside—and they are *many*, beginning with my disinterest in marrying a corpse, and continuing onward from there—you cannot allow the king of a demesne famed for its alchemists to have access to any part of your body. Even if your escape requires leaving one or more of us behind, you *can't*."

Tybalt sounded so serious, and so upset, that I couldn't say anything to that. I just stared at him.

He sighed, shaking his head. "I'd tell you to run, if I thought we could get away with it. I'd say to gather up our people, and those things which we cannot bear to lose, and flee for the hills. Do you not understand what they could make of you?"

"I'm starting to," I said, in a very small voice.

Blood-workers—like me, like the Daoine Sidhe—could sometimes "borrow" the magical talents of others through judicious sampling of their blood. Tap a vein and hey, presto, suddenly we could teleport, or transform, or do any number of other things that didn't come naturally. For us, blood was the ultimate wonder drug, opening all doors and removing all barriers—as long as it was the *right* blood. But it had its limitations. I had never yet been able to borrow magic from blood that wasn't coming straight out of a living person. I could awaken memories in dried blood, but that was about it; anything more complicated than a few flashes of the past was beyond me. If you wanted to preserve the magic in a person's blood, or better yet, if you wanted to make that magic accessible to *anyone*, not just your local blood-workers, you needed something special.

You needed an alchemist.

Alchemists could "freeze" the magic in blood, refining and strengthening it until they found themselves in possession of potions, charms, and powders capable of lending that initial magic to someone else. With a good enough alchemist on your side, you no longer needed a blood-worker: all the magic of Faerie could be at your fingertips for as long as you wanted it to be. And my blood held the power to rewrite a person's heritage.

Not enough to make humans out of purebloods or vice-versa, but enough to weaken changelings, turn them human or fae on your whim; enough to strengthen or resolve the confusion that already existed in a mixed-blood's veins. Both changeling madness and the instability that sometimes came for those with exceedingly mixed heritages were functions of the blood. With fae, you're not dealing with issues of race; you're dealing with issues of *species*, completely dissimilar creatures that could, thanks to magic, somehow interbreed. Children of Maeve reproducing with children of Titania wasn't like apples mixing with oranges—it was more like apples mixing with cheese graters, or rainbows with hardware stores.

Magic was enough to make the way Faerie worked possible, but magic couldn't necessarily make it functional. Changeling madness was proof of that. Mixed-bloods had just as many issues—more, in my experience—but we didn't talk about them as much, because they were still pure fae, and that made it a politically sensitive subject. Give King Rhys and his nameless mistress access to my blood, and they could parlay it into control of Faerie. I meant that literally. Anyone with human heritage would be in danger of being turned mortal. Anyone who had made peace with the balance of their blood would be at risk of having that peace ripped away.

Much like I had ripped the false Queen's peace away, such as it had been, when I had reached in and unraveled the delicate tapestry of her heritage. I still didn't feel bad about that—she had brought it on herself, in the truest meaning of the phrase—but I was starting to feel bad about what it had revealed to her. She knew how to hurt us now. She knew how to hurt everyone.

"Oh, oak and ash," I said, with a shake of my head. "We *can't* let them have me."

"Or May," said Tybalt. "I dare say they would be able to do fascinating things with the blood of your lady Fetch, given that there's nothing else like her in all of Faerie. Whether those things did them any good at all would doubtless matter little to May, after she had been exsanguinated for their pleasure."

Across the path, Walther stood. I switched my attention to him. It was better than dwelling on Tybalt's uncomfortable, if accurate, words. "What's up?" I asked, loudly enough to be heard.

"The rose goblins here remember me, which is always nice," said Walther. "I was starting to feel like a ghost." He was still holding the big one against his chest. The others surged around his ankles, moving like a strange and landlocked tide. Some of them were stropping up against him, using the odd, hopping dolphin-like stance that Spike always used when it wanted to show affection without actually breaking my skin.

"That's weird," I said, trying to keep my tone neutral. "I'm used to people being a little better with the visual perception."

Walther looked faintly uncomfortable. "I didn't grow up the way people expected me to is all. Anyway: the rose goblins remember me, they're not huge fans of the new management, and they'll keep whatever we say secret from King Rhys. In exchange, they'd really like your rose goblin to come out and play. They don't get to meet many cuttings from Luna."

Cuttings . . . I blinked. "That's right: rose goblins are cuttings from a Blodynbryd. Luna's the only one I've ever met. Who did these come from?"

"Me," said a light, pleasant voice, faintly accented with the echoes of Wales. Its owner followed it out of the trees a heartbeat later, stepping out onto the path and offering a dazzling smile in my direction. "Hello. It's lovely to meet you."

She was tall, slim, and facially so similar to Luna that I would have known them as sisters even if there'd been some other option. Her skin was a fascinating shade of silvery purple, and her hair was almost exactly the same shade at the root. It darkened as it fell down her back in a waterfall of curls, ending in a purple deep enough to seem virtually black. Her eyes were bright pink, the color of primroses, with a thin ring of pollen yellow around the irises.

"Um, hi," I said. "You're . . ."

"Blodynbryd, yes," said the woman. "My name is Ceres. You would be?"

"I'm October Daye; this is Tybalt," I said.

"A pleasure to meet you both," she said. A smile suffused her face as she reached over to caress Walther's arm. "Any who travel with my dear Waltrune are friends to me."

Walther looked briefly panicked. The panic faded, replaced by profound embarrassment. "It's 'Walther' these days, Aunt Ceres," he said.

"Ah," she said. "My apologies; it's been so long since you bothered to visit that I'm afraid I'm not so well-informed as to what you wish to be called, or when, or by whom." The look she leveled on him was pure aunt.

I couldn't help myself. I burst out laughing. Both Walther and Ceres turned to look at me. "I'm sorry, I'm sorry," I said. "You just really reminded me of Luna for a moment. But in a good way, honest." I wasn't sure how much gossip from the Mists had traveled this far up the coasts, and I didn't want to start my association with the second Blodynbryd I'd ever met by implying that I disliked her.

Gossip is interesting. In the human world, thanks to cellphones and the Internet, a rumor can travel around the world in less time than it takes to check your facts. In Faerie, for all that we have people who can teleport or fly, it still takes a little longer—mostly because very few of us have figured out how to turn on our cable modems. It'll probably change in the next decade or so, as more and more changelings start setting up data centers within their lieges' knowes, but for right now, it was entirely possible that Ceres didn't know about my fight with her sister.

Ceres smiled. "Mother's youngest rose. I hear she's back in her proper pruning these days? No longer twisting herself into topiary for the sake of appearances?"

"Yes," I said. "She's Blodynbryd again."

"That's good." Ceres tilted her head to the side, frowning speculatively. "October . . . I know I've heard that name before."

"It's a month in the current calendar," said Walther. His note was mild, and a little dry, like he wasn't being helpful so much as seizing on an opportunity to be sarcastic. "Has been since the Romans got hold of the thing."

"I keep abreast of current events, you naughty child," said Ceres, shooting him a look before swinging her attention back to me. "You're the one who killed my father, aren't you?"

Oh, great: this again. Killing Blind Michael was something I didn't regret in the slightest. It was also something I was going to be dealing with for the rest of my life, if the last several years had been any guide. "I did," I said.

"Good." Her nod was brief and firm. "He was a good man once, but that was so long ago that only the roses remember. Mother has been to visit me twice since he died. Twice, after centuries without more than a whisper on the wind! Our family owes you a debt that can never be repaid, no matter how long we may struggle to do exactly that. Thank you for what you have done for us. Truly."

I blinked at her, nonplussed. Apparently, growing up surrounded by Firstborn didn't instill the same dislike for saying "thank you."

Ceres wasn't done. She stooped to pick up one of the rose goblins that crowded the path, glanced in the direction of the distant castle, and said, "Come. I would sit with you. I would share tea and stories with my family's savior, and with her friends." She kissed the rose goblin's head, making no effort to avoid the angle of its thorns. If I'd done that, I would have sliced my mouth open, but she barely seemed to notice. The goblin made a low purring sound. "As for you, my little spy, go tell the king I have found his wayward diplomats. Paint the picture of a woman greatly troubled, overcome with the duties of her position. The better your portrait, the better your rewards shall be. Do you understand?"

The goblin made a trilling noise. Ceres smiled.

"Excellent. You are very dear." She set the goblin back on the ground. It took off like a shot, vanishing into the brush as Ceres straightened. Making a beckoning gesture, she started down the path. "Come," she said again.

Tybalt and I exchanged a glance. Walther was already following her. It was my experience that he was a pretty good judge of character, and once we knew where we were going, I could always ask Tybalt to go back and tell Quentin and May what was going on. I shrugged and, together, we followed.

Ceres led us along the pine-choked path for about a hundred yards before she turned and stepped onto a narrow dirt trail winding through the forest. As before, Walther followed her, and so Tybalt and I followed him, trusting that whatever their relationship was, it wouldn't cause him to lead us to our certain doom. Maybe that was overly optimistic of me, but I felt like I had earned a little optimism after the day that I'd had.

The trees closed around us like a curtain. The trail was covered in pine needles, and we couldn't avoid stepping on them, causing the rich, syrupy scent of pine to become even stronger, until it was like we were walking through the distilled essence of Christmas. I've always liked that smell, which is a good thing; if I hadn't, I would have been sneezing and cursing my life choices before we were halfway through the wood.

Rose goblins flickered through the underbrush, their thorny faces seeming to bloom like strange flowers as they peeked back at us. None of them stayed long enough for me to pick out individual features—just thorns and bright, floral colors, and those vivid, staring eyes. Ceres moved through the wood like it had been designed for her private use, and in a way, it had. Her mother, Acacia, was the Firstborn of both the Dryads and the Blodynbryd. When she spoke to the forest, the forest responded. Ceres might not have quite such a close connection to the trees, but she was a relative, however distant, and they seemed to respect her.

I wasn't so lucky, and I was walking through a pine

forest in a formal gown. At first I tried to keep my skirt from dragging on the ground, but I gave it up as a bad idea before we'd gone very far. Either the palace laundry would be able to save it or they wouldn't. I didn't give much of a damn either way. Although I was going to miss those jeans.

Tybalt shot me an amused look after the third time I had to wrestle one of my sleeves back from a tree. "You know, in all my years, I've never known a woman with such talent for wearing unsuitable finery into the wilderness."

"Really?" I eyed him dubiously. "You're going to tell me no Cait Sidhe woman has ever wound up in the woods while she was dressed for Court?"

"No. But if you were a Cait Sidhe woman, you would have removed your gown by now."

I didn't have an answer for that. Tybalt laughed as my cheeks flared red.

"I do so appreciate knowing that I can still make you blush," he said.

Any answer I might have given died as the trail ended, widening out into a clearing straight out of a Disney movie. It was small, perfectly round, and even more perfectly designed. Pine trees created the edges, but they were barely visible under the rioting roses that climbed them, treating them as a natural trellis and pathway to the sky. High overhead—easily fifteen or twenty feet—those roses reached out and twined themselves together in a series of gravity-defying lover's knots, creating a latticework of living branches. It shouldn't have been possible . . . but Ceres was Blodynbryd, just like her sister, and I had seen Luna do quite a few impossible things with her roses.

The flowers themselves came in every color of the rainbow and a few colors the rainbow hadn't received the memo on yet. Some were modern, cultivated roses, blooming in that familiar shape that has sold a million

Valentine's Day bouquets. Others had older, wilder silhouettes, opening in ragged cups or in tiny starbursts. But they were all roses. The air in the clearing was thick with their perfume, and they turned toward Ceres as she walked.

At the center of the clearing was a tiny cottage that might as well have been made of gingerbread for as much as it resembled something that should have housed a fairy-tale witch. The door was held shut by twisted rose boughs, all in a state of full bloom. Ceres stopped in front of the door, raising her hand and waving it across the span of the doorway. The roses promptly furled themselves, becoming tight buds. Then, and only then, the boughs unknotted and pulled away, revealing the actual door one inch at a time.

When the last of the roses retracted, Ceres pushed the door open and looked over her shoulder, smiling at the rest of us. "Enter freely, and be not afraid, for there is nothing that will harm you here." Then she stepped inside.

"I think that was meant to be reassuring," I said distantly. "I am not reassured. Tybalt, how about you? Are you reassured?"

"Unlike you, I come from an era where that was a common welcome into someone's home," he said. "I am reassured."

"Ceres usually has lavender cookies," said Walther. "I am *totally* reassured." With that, he went in, leaving us with no choice but to either follow or wait outside for his return.

I have charged headlong into portals, sealed lands of Faerie, and experienced more dangers than any one woman can reasonably be expected to both encounter and survive. I sighed, and stepped into the quaint little forest cottage.

"Huh," I said a moment later. "It's bigger on the inside."

"Many things are," Ceres agreed. She was on the opposite side of the large parlor, arranging a tea service on a sideboard that appeared to have been designed for exactly that purpose. Despite the size of the room—it was easily bigger than my first apartment, but then again, what wasn't?—it was modestly appointed, with most of the furniture carved from rosewood, left unpainted to allow the wood's natural beauty to shine through. I called it a parlor, because I didn't have a better word for a space that seemed to be receiving room, living room, dining room, and foyer all at the same time.

It was an elegant, economically designed space, and I wouldn't have found it strange in almost any demesne, if not for one small thing: there was no floor, just hard-pressed dirt that filled the room with its characteristic earthy scent. It mingled with the roses, creating a perfume that was at once common and impossible for any lab in the world to replicate.

"It hasn't changed a bit," said Walther happily. He walked over to the table that occupied one side of the room, pulling out a chair and dropping himself into it. There were three covered dishes on the table. After a moment's consideration, he lifted the center lid to reveal a pile of pale purple cookies, dusted with sugar. "Lavender cookies. Ceres, you're the best."

"So you've been telling me since you sprouted, but that didn't stop you from leaving me for a hundred years." She carried the tea service over to the table and set it down, smiling indulgently as Walther snatched a handful of the purple cookies. He didn't do anything to them before taking a bite of the first one. Either he trusted Ceres not to poison or bespell us, or she already had him ensnared.

The Blodynbryd didn't have any sort of enthrallment or persuasion powers, at least not that I was aware of. If they had, Luna would probably have made sure her daughter's marriage ended in something other than annulment and murder—the annulment on the part of Raysel's ex-husband, Connor, who was also the one who wound up getting murdered. If Ceres had that sort of power, we were already screwed. I shrugged and walked over to join Walther.

Somehow, despite us both starting at the same time, Tybalt managed to beat me to the table. He pulled out a chair for me. I shot him an amused look and sat, only to find Ceres watching us approvingly.

"Manners are rare in this day and age, or perhaps only in this kingdom," she said. "Too few people remember that they are the glue that binds our society together. Please, have some cookies. I have tea, or there is lemonade, if you would prefer."

"Lemonade would be fantastic, if it's not too much trouble," I said. Tea was complicated for me. Lily—a friend of my mother's who had become a friend of mine, in the fullness of time—had always insisted on preparing tea when I came to visit her. Sometimes she'd even been able to catch glimpses of my future in her tea leaves. I hadn't really drunk tea since her death. It was too hard, and I wasn't up for risking that sort of emotional trauma over a beverage.

Tybalt settled next to me and smiled lopsidedly, revealing the tip of one fang. "Tea would be lovely. I've had little enough since I came to the Colonies, lo these many years ago."

"I always forget how many of the older among us came from somewhere else," said Ceres. She turned to open a cupboard, and withdrew a pitcher of lemonade, condensation beading on its sides. It was a nice—and necessary—trick. The Summerlands aren't usually good about being wired to the local electrical grid, which means the locals keep their food cold with either magic or old-fashioned icehouses. Both had their advantages.

"Didn't you?" I asked.

Ceres smiled. "Yes and no. My father linked his skerry

to this land long before anyone from Europe decided to 'discover' it. The humans who lived here then gave him a wide berth, and he gave them the same. I spent my childhood wandering these forests, as well as my mother's. I was the third of their children, you see, and when I was a girl, they were still more open to the idea that someday we would grow up and leave them. Luna was the last of us. None of us realized how tightly Father would cleave to her, once all others were gone, or how far she would have to go to get away. I like to think we would have chosen differently, had we known what it would cost our little sister to choose as we did. But that was long ago, and no one knows for sure."

"Right," I said. Walther was still nibbling on his purple cookies. I reached out and took one, turning it between my fingers as I tried to figure out what to say next. Of all the ways I had expected my day to go, fleeing from a homicidal ex-Queen and then taking tea with the second Blodynbryd I'd ever met definitely hadn't been near the top of the list. "So you were born here?"

"Farther down the coast. I moved here because it was good for my roses, and because I could no longer bear the company of my parents. Even once Silences was settled, Father let me be for centuries. He thought he was punishing me by refusing to let me see his face. He forgot that I did not want to."

Briefly, I wondered whether we could chart the world's Blodynbryd by looking for the places where Blind Michael had chosen not to go hunting. I dismissed the thought. It wasn't my job to organize a family reunion for Acacia, and if the other Blodynbryd were living quiet, untroubled lives, I should leave them alone. Instead, I ate a cookie.

Walther was right. They were excellent.

Ceres finally took a seat at the table, placing a glass of lemonade in front of me, and teacups in front of Walther and Tybalt. There were flecks of mint all through the lemonade, deep green and inviting. I watched as she poured tea for the two men, and then for herself. Sugar and cream had already been placed at the center of the table: she took her tea plain, Walther took his with sugar, and Tybalt, who had once chided me for doctoring my coffee, added enough milk that his tea turned a pale shade of brown.

"So, how is it that you know my dear Walther?" asked Ceres.

"He came to live in the Mists a few years ago, and his first stop was at a knowe that belonged to a good friend of mine," I said. "She died not long afterward. We sort of bonded over the whole situation. It was nice to have someone who could understand just how much I missed her." Lily had even suggested that Walther and I would be a good match at one point—that my mother would approve. We'd never pursued that, for a lot of reasons, but she'd been right about how well we got along. As friends, nothing more.

"As for me, I know who October knows, or else ask the reason why she's hiding such charming and diverse people from my eyes," said Tybalt. He took a sip of his tea, bobbing his head in apparent satisfaction, before asking, "And what of you, milady? This is your home, there can be no doubt, but I would have expected a woman of your breeding and manners to have chosen a new home when the government was overthrown."

"I would have, believe me, but I have been here a very long time, and my children thrive in this climate." Ceres glanced to an ottoman on the other side of the room. I followed her gaze, and found a pile of rose goblins the size of kittens all mounded up, sleeping peacefully. Ceres continued, "Transplanting all the bushes would require an army of gardeners. To leave, I would have to leave the little ones, and I can't quite bring myself to do it."

"Not all your little ones are rose goblins," said Walther quietly.

Ceres looked to him and smiled. "No. Not all of them. I was tutor to the children of the Davies and Yates lines—heirs to the throne and born stewards, the lot of them. I expected young Walther here to be a court alchemist by now, brewing love tinctures and potions to clear up the complexion."

"Love tinctures are unethical, and the mortals make this stuff called 'Proactiv' these days. It does a decent job with the pimples," said Walther, sounding amused. "I teach chemistry to human kids, and I do alchemy for the people who need it. It's a good life, Aunt Ceres. I like it. Promise."

"As you say," said Ceres. She was smiling as she turned her attention back around to me. "The rose goblins would have been difficult, even impossible, to transplant in their current numbers, and I would have needed to find a place where the ground was fertile and the climate was kind. And as Walther reminds, not all my charges were so easy to move. Some still slumber in the castle deeps, waiting for the day they are released from durance vile."

"Not so vile," said Tybalt. "Elf-shot does not dictate dreams."

"No?" Ceres raised an eyebrow, looking at him. "Can we be so sure of that? Many are the methods to force sleep, and I would not be surprised if at least one came complete with unquiet dreams."

"My niece is an oneiromancer, and she hasn't said anything about people who've been elf-shot having nightmares," I said. "That doesn't mean it doesn't happen. Nightmares are ordinary things that can happen to anyone, and I guess you could make a type of elf-shot that forced them." It seemed like a form of torture to me—and it was, really. There was no other word that described being trapped in a realm of unending nightmares, with no way of waking up.

"I haven't forgotten them," said Walther quietly. "I've never forgotten them. I'm keeping my word, Aunt Ceres."

"Good," said Ceres.

I looked between the two of them, frowning. "Somebody want to fill the rest of us in? Because I have no idea what's going on right now."

"When I left, I promised Aunt Ceres that I'd find the counteragent to elf-shot," said Walther. "There's always a counteragent. It's just a matter of figuring out what it is. I've been working for the last hundred years on a way to wake the sleepers up. I'm almost there, I am. If I could just find someone who knew who brewed the original tincture—"

"Eira Rosynhwyr," I said, without thinking. Walther and Ceres turned to stare at me.

Tybalt took another sip of tea.

A moment passed, and then Walther asked, slowly, "What do you mean?"

"Eira Rosynhwyr is the Daoine Sidhe Firstborn, and she was the first person to make elf-shot. The Luidaeg said so." She hadn't mentioned Eira—better known as "Evening"—by name. I'd been forced to put the pieces together myself, a little bit at a time, due to the geas the Luidaeg was laboring under. She couldn't tell lies, but there were things she couldn't say out loud. "She's the reason the stuff's fatal to changelings. According to the Luidaeg, it didn't have to be. Eira's just a bitch."

"You . . . I . . ." Walther stopped. Then he started to laugh, shaking his head slowly from side to side. "Of course you know who created elf-shot. Of *course*. And why would you have told me? It's not like I ever asked."

"You didn't," I said.

"I don't suppose the Luidaeg also told you what Eira's magic consisted of, did she? What the elements of it were?"

It had taken me years to realize that most people in Faerie weren't as sensitive to the distinct elements of a person's magic as I was. Knowing someone's magic was part and parcel of knowing their bloodlines, which made it as easy as breathing for me. "She didn't, but I've met the woman. Her magic smelled of roses and snow."

"What kind of roses?" Walther leaned forward, expression eager.

"Red ones," I said. "Not wild roses—cultivated ones, although they don't smell like the kind of hothouse roses you can get today. It's like they're an early kind of garden rose? Walled gardens. Ones where people could breed and breed their flowers, and not worry about how they would thrive in the outside world." I stopped, unsure how much further I could go—and how much further I would want to.

Tybalt had put down his tea and was looking at me, eyebrows raised. "I'd always wondered how it was that you could insist that everyone's magic was so different, when you said the same words over and over again. Roses and pine trees and all the flowers of the forest. But if you know them that intimately, then there really is no wonder."

"I don't know them all that intimately," I protested. "I have to think about it to start getting details like that." Tasting Evening's blood had probably also helped, but I didn't need to bring that up. It wasn't something I was proud of.

"Still, that should be more than sufficient detail to let me find the roses in question," said Ceres. I gave her a blank look, and she smiled. "All the world's roses are brought to Portland. Didn't you know? We have a thing the mortals call a 'test garden,' where the new cultivars are coaxed to open for the sun and show their secrets clearly as a morning breeze. They grow the new, but they treasure also the old—and there are roses none of them can explain, roses that seem to have arisen naturally around the corners of their carefully planned plots, their delicately designed gardens. My siblings and I, we have played at curators in a great museum, coaxing long-past roses from our bodies and planting them where they have the chance to flourish."

It took me a moment to realize what she was saying. Finally, I ventured, "So you're saying my old red rose might be growing somewhere in the gardens?"

"I would stake my eye on it."

The phrase was unnerving, and not just because of who her father was. Some of the old pureblood oaths involved staking an eye, a hand, even a heart—and when the oaths were broken, it was generally expected that the person who made them would actually give up those body parts. There's a reason swearing on the physical has fallen out of favor, replaced by the cleaner, safer swearing on the abstract. "Okay," I said. "What good would that do us?"

"If Ceres can find the right kind of rose—the kind of rose you say this Eira woman's magic smelled like—then I can use that, and I can figure out the counterformula for elf-shot." Walther put down his last cookie, leaning forward. There was an unfamiliar intensity in his eyes. "I can *do* it. I can wake them up."

I blinked before looking to Tybalt, only to find that he was blinking, too, looking as nonplussed as I was. Elf-shot was . . . elf-shot wasn't supposed to be forever. It was the holding pattern of the fae world, the injury that took enemies out of the fight for a long time without actually breaking the Law and killing them. It wasn't something that could be undone by one alchemist with access to the proper rose garden. That wasn't possible.

But then, when has Faerie ever settled for the possible? "I'll do my best to make sure you have the right rose, but I can't promise anything," I said, looking back to Walther. "This isn't something I've done before."

"Narrow it down to ten and I can take it from there," he said. "I—"

The cottage door slammed open, and Marlis stormed into the room, half-drawing her sword. "Get away from my aunt!" she shouted.

Well, hell. And things had been going so *well*.

TWELVE

"MARLIS, DEAR HEART, PLEASE don't threaten my guests: it's neither proper nor polite, and I raised you better than that," said Ceres. She picked up her tea and took a dainty sip, as if to emphasize how calm she was. She wasn't being attacked: she was having some people over for tea. I admired her serenity, even as I tried to decide whether she'd be pissed off if I hit Marlis with a teapot. I didn't have any better weapons at hand, except for Tybalt, and I didn't want to *kill* the girl.

"They shouldn't *be* here," snarled Marlis, glaring daggers at the rest of us. "They're here on the King's sufferance, and that sufferance does not extend to troubling you!"

"How'd you know we were here, Marley?" asked Walther, reaching for another lavender cookie. The pink ones and the yellow ones were still relatively untouched, but he'd eaten nearly a dozen of the purple cookies. "All the rose goblins are either here with us, or they're off telling the King all about how Ceres is leading us astray and shouldn't be interrupted. You shouldn't have been able to find us."

Marlis' head snapped around, eyes narrowing as she

focused on him. "My name is *Marlis*," she spat. "As for King Rhys, he is preoccupied with the preparations for war, and as he had no need for me, he generously allowed me to come and see my old nursemaid. Now rise, and answer for your trespasses!"

"No," said Walther mildly. "Eat a cookie. We saved the saffron ones for you. I know those were always your favorite. Here." He reached for the tray of yellow cookies. It was only because I was so close to him that I saw the light dusting of powder fall from his hand to mingle with the thin layer of powdered sugar atop the cookies as he picked up the tray and held it out toward his sister. He was using the countercharm.

Ceres was as close to him as I was: she must have known what he was doing. She didn't say anything about the powder. She just took another sip of her tea and said, "You're too tense, my darling. Have a cookie. Stop threatening my guests, who are here by my invitation, and not for any other reasons."

Marlis hesitated. At least she took her hand off the hilt of her sword. I appreciated that.

But Ceres wasn't done. "If you do not have a cookie, I'll have to assume that you don't respect my hospitality, and remember that slight when next you seek solace in my chambers. I love you, Marlis, but you're not the girl I raised. You haven't been since that outland King came and took your open eyes away."

"I don't believe this," muttered Marlis. She strode across the room and snatched two cookies from the tray—one in each hand. Taking a large bite of the first, she chewed with an exaggerated motion meant purely to make sure we all knew that she was eating the cookie. Ceres watched without comment.

Marlis swallowed.

"See? You always feel better when you have a cookie." Walther picked up one of the purple cookies.

Following his lead, I snagged a pink one and took a bite. Candied rose. Naturally.

Marlis looked at him blankly. There was an open confusion in her face that hadn't been there a moment before, like some thin, undefinable veil had been stripped away.

"Have another cookie, dear," said Ceres, her voice holding the note of command that has been used by parents and teachers since the beginning of time.

Automatically, Marlis put her second cookie in her mouth. This time, her chewing was less exaggerated and more mechanical, like she didn't know exactly what she was doing. Ceres glanced to Walther.

"What did you do to your sister?" she asked.

"Isn't that a question that should have been asked before you fed her the second cookie?" I asked. "As, you know, a thought?"

"Walther has never poisoned Marlis before, so it seemed unnecessary," said Ceres.

I really didn't have an answer for that. I sat silently for a moment, trying to come up with one, before I finally shrugged and reached for another of the rose cookies.

"Do I know you?" Marlis was still staring at Walther, making no effort to hide her confusion. "Do I . . . you look like my cousin."

"It's me, Marley." Walther put his last cookie down and stood. They were almost the same height. She was a tall woman, and he was of relatively average height, for a man. Expression sheepish, he spread his hands, and said, "I go by Walther now—that's my name—but you used to call me 'Waltrune.' If that helps."

"Truny?" Marlis squinted at him, like she was trying to confirm what he was saying to her. "But that's silly. Truny was my sister."

"And now I'm your brother," said Walther. "Technically, I always was. I just needed some time to get that sorted out properly. I thought you were going to run. I ran, because I thought you were going to run."

"I couldn't leave the rest of our family behind; I told you I was going to run because I didn't want you to wait for me," said Marlis. "You were my baby sister. It was my job to look out for you. That meant getting you out of the Kingdom before the new regent took—Waltrune, really? Are you really Waltrune?"

"Not anymore, and always," said Walther. He offered her his hands, smiling. "It's good to see you, Marley. I've missed you."

"I . . ." Marlis took his hands, and frowned. "What did you put in the cookies?"

"Standard anticompulsion charm. If you were being compelled by King Rhys—and of course you were being compelled by King Rhys—it would cancel out the potion. Who does he have making his tinctures, Marley? I thought the whole family was asleep, except for you."

"Yes, except for me," she said bitterly. "I do all his blending and brewing and binding. Just me, in Mother's workroom, enspelling a Kingdom for the sake of a man who should never have sat this throne." She gasped then, yanking one hand free and clapping it over her mouth. "Oh, sweet Oberon, those words just left my mouth. Truny, what have you done? What have you done to *me?* He'll know! I'm his seneschal, his eyes are everywhere, and he'll *know!* My disloyalty will be punished!"

"His eyes are not here," said Ceres calmly. "His eyes have never been here. I am on these lands at his sufferance, or so he pretends, but he knows full well that he'll never move me if I do not wish to be moved. My roots are deep in this land. I support his kingship solely to retain access to the castle where my charges sleep. They deserve more than to have me desert them before they wake and remember me."

"But his eyes are everywhere else." Marlis lowered her hand. "He'll know. He'll *know*."

"Only if you slip up," I said, finally interposing myself into the conversation. I pushed my chair back and stood, offering Marlis my hand. "Hi. I feel like we didn't really meet before. I'm Toby, I'm a friend of your brother's, and I'm here to keep the man who's been drugging you from leading your Kingdom to war against mine."

"Marlis," she said, taking my hand and shaking. Then she laughed bitterly. "And he only drugged me once. Maeve knows who mixed the potion for him, but it was strong, and it worked well, and my resistance disappeared like sugar on the snow. I've been drugging myself to make him happy ever since."

I couldn't quite conceal my wince. It was an elegant solution to the captive alchemist: drug her into loyalty and then tell her that the thing you wanted most was for her to drug herself *better*. "All right. Do you remember what you did while you were drugged?"

She grimaced and turned her face away without answering me. Which was an answer in itself.

"Walther tells me you weren't in line for the throne of Silences, but that you were more sort of . . . throne adjacent. That means you learned the manners and the dances and the rules right alongside your cousins, because you were always going to wind up being seneschal, or court alchemist, or whatever, right? Well, that means you know how to play a role. That's all court politics are. A great big game of let's pretend where winning means you don't get your head chopped off this round."

Marlis slowly turned back around to look at me. "Go on," she said.

"Just play the role of a good, chemically modified seneschal," I said. "No one in this room is going to get mad at you for pretending Rhys is still the boss of you. It's the only sensible thing to do."

"But the only reason for me to go back to him, to not flee the Court at once for fear of discovery, is to foment revolution," said Marlis. "Are you asking me to join a conspiracy against my King?"

I grimaced. "Not in so many words, but sort of, I guess. I'm here to prevent a war, through whatever means necessary."

"Trust October to feel that dethroning a monarch to prevent a small border skirmish falls under 'whatever means necessary,'" said Tybalt, sounding amused. He was still seated, as was Ceres. I shot him a look. He smiled at me, and took one of the saffron cookies.

"Cats," I muttered, looking back to Marlis. "You don't have to help us. I'd ask only that you not work against us too enthusiastically. The woman who has the King's ear was never rightful Queen in the Mists. She has no claim to the throne."

"But she gave *our* throne to Rhys," said Marlis hotly. "If she had no claim to her own, how could she have given ours to *him?*" The way she said "our" made it clear that she meant her family's throne, and not just her Kingdom's.

"At the time, she was Queen, and no one was questioning her, maybe because we'd just had half our Kingdom fall down and catch fire in a giant earthquake. That sort of thing makes people pretty tired," I said. "After that, she had just been in charge for so long that nobody questioned her about whether or not she had a right to be there."

I certainly hadn't. Not until she'd forced my hand. Even then, all the questioning in the world wouldn't have done me any good if not for the Luidaeg, who had stepped up to make sure I knew Arden wasn't dead. A lot of factors had combined to see the nameless Queen relieved of her throne. As I watched Walther and his sister starting to reconnect, I wondered how many of those factors were combining right in front of me. Silences was a corrupt house. It needed cleaning.

"If you keep doing this, monarchs will cease allowing you to enter their demesne," murmured Tybalt, voice low enough that I knew his words were intended for me alone.

I snorted. "This is the first time I've ever left the Mists. I don't think it's something we need to worry about becoming a habit."

"Everything about which you have ever said, 'oh, this will not become a habit, no, not for me' has become a habit—even me," said Tybalt. "My little king-breaker."

I twisted to wrinkle my nose at him. Before I could say anything, Marlis said, "She's already got that reputation."

"What?" I looked back to her, blinking. "What do you mean?"

Marlis shrugged. "Rhys speaks freely in front of me. He knows I'm too deeply enspelled to turn against him, and I think it amuses him to stand before the last waking member of the royal family—however removed from the throne—and speak of things I'll never have, or even remember wanting. When the Queen in the Mists sent notice that she was dispatching a diplomatic team, and that you'd be leading the group, he went white as whey and started whining about what you'd done in the Mists. He's afraid of you. It's why he orchestrated that spill at breakfast. He wants to get you out of here as fast as possible."

So Rhys had been lying about being surprised by my arrival. Somehow, that wasn't all that shocking. "All he has to do to get me out is agree not to go to war against the Mists," I said. "It's that simple."

She shook her head. "Even if it were that simple," and her voice told me it wasn't, not really, "he wouldn't do it. He seeks the favor of your deposed Queen. He took this throne for her. And for power, of course—some men will do anything for power—but the power he *wanted* was the power of sitting at her right hand, in his homeland, not being exiled to kingship in our damp and forested lands."

"Careful, Marley," said Walther. "You're starting to sound like you agree with him."

Marlis turned to look at her brother. There was no anger in her eyes: only bone-deep exhaustion, and the quiet resignation that comes with too many defeats. She had the eyes of a woman who'd never won anything in her life, who'd simply stepped through the patterns that were demanded of her, all the while praying she could survive them. "A hundred years," she said softly. "More than a hundred years. I held our mother down while his people stabbed the arrow into her shoulder, less than a decade past. You got away. You became the man you'd always wanted to be. You grew *up*. I didn't. I stayed here, with the man who overthrew our family, and I learned to be a pet. You were my little sister, but if we compare the things we've seen, the things we've done . . . I'm the little sister now. I can't say whether I agree with him or not, because I haven't been allowed to have my own ideas about anything in a *hundred years*."

Walther paled. "Marley, I'm sorry. I didn't . . . I didn't think . . ."

"Why should you? You're the one who got out. Did you ever even look for me? Or did you just assume I was in hiding somewhere, because if you really looked, you knew you'd find me here?" Marlis shook her head. "I'm not mad at you for getting away. I could never be mad at you for that. But I'm disappointed that you're so quick to point fingers at me for echoing the only opinions I've been allowed to have for a century."

"Okay, let's all take a breath." I stood, taking a step forward—not quite putting myself between them, but making myself much harder to ignore. "I'm sorry, Marlis. This has been a long night, and it's not over yet. We didn't know how bad things were here."

"Silences keeps to itself," said Marlis bitterly. "We always have. We were that quiet alchemist's Kingdom before Rhys took over, and now we're just quiet because we have nothing to brag about. All our friends and allies left us. The Cu Sidhe. The Huldra. All of them turned and walked away, and left us. All the ties we worked so long to build have been severed. Everything our family built has been broken."

"Maybe we can put it all back together," I said. "We have glue. You said they made you help put the members of the royal family back to sleep when the elf-shot wore off?"

Marlis nodded. "Our mother and father; our aunt and uncle, the rightful Queen and King of Silences. And our cousin Torsten, the Crown Prince. If they ever woke . . ."

"If they woke, they'd be within their rights to try to take back their throne, especially now that we know that the woman who gave it to Rhys didn't have the authority to make that sort of decision," I said. "They're all alive? None of them have been injured too badly?"

Marlis looked away again.

I frowned. Walther, on the other hand, seemed to know what her silence meant. "Marley, what did they make you do?" he asked, voice barely rising above a whisper.

I appreciated the fact that he hadn't asked her what she'd done—what she had done was have a century of her life stolen from her by drugs that she'd been forced to manufacture—but the message was the same. Marlis dropped her head, looking down at her feet. She stayed that way, silent as a statue, while Ceres rose from the table and walked around to stand behind her, putting her hands on the smaller woman's shoulders.

"Your mother was Amandine of Faerie, was she not?" Ceres asked, attention fixing on me. "She must have taught you the importance of blood."

"I've got a pretty good idea," I said. Amandine hadn't taught me much at all about the importance of blood—or the importance of anything else, really. Amandine's lessons had always focused more on how much of a disappointment I was to her, too fae to be human, too human to be fae. The fact that she'd chosen my father without any input from as-yet-unborn me didn't seem to be a factor in her judgments.

"Then you know that some potions work better when they contain it. Some potions wouldn't work at all without it. And if blood is good, bone could be said to be even better . . ."

I went very still. Her words made sense, taken individually, but as a whole, they painted the beginnings of a picture that I didn't want to see.

Oberon's Law forbids killing. Just killing: nothing more, nothing less. Elf-shot is allowed. Loyalty potions and brainwashing are allowed. And anything that doesn't quite kill, well, that's all right, too. That's not a death. All he ever told us not to do to each other was murder. Everything else is still on the table.

"How much, Marley?" asked Walther softly.

"Uncle Holger's left hand, to the elbow; Mother's right foot, to the knee. An inch at a time, over the course of a century. He . . . he likes to talk about how much he wants their eyes, their tongues, all the pieces that could make the potions stronger, but he won't take them. Not yet, not while anyone remembers the war. He leaves them lying on their biers in the crypt. He says anyone who wants to see the faces of their old oppressors is welcome, and he makes me take people down to see them. Sometimes, if they're trying to curry the King's favor—and everyone wants to curry the King's favor, because the only thing worse than having it is knowing that you never will—they spit on them. They *spit* on our family, Wal—Walther. Even people who should still be *loyal* spit on our family, because doing anything else risks the King's wrath, and I just . . . I did it, I didn't tell him no, and I didn't even think that what I was doing was wrong, because he t-told me to . . ."

Finally, at the end of her speech, Marlis burst into tears. Walther put his arms around her and held her close, letting her sob out a century of abuse and frustrations against the fabric of his shirt. Marlis clung to him like she was afraid he was an illusion. I couldn't fault her for that. After as long as she'd been dealing with King Rhys and his loyalty tinctures, anything that smacked of freedom or independent thought had to feel like a dream—a beautiful one, but not one that could ever possibly last.

Ceres stepped away from the pair, moving to stand next to Tybalt and me. "If you have any compassion in your bones, you will fix this," she said mildly.

I started, glancing up at her. "What?"

"You are, as your cat says, a king-breaker. You defeated my father. You've done impossible things, and I choose to view your presence here as the beginning of one more impossibility. You could free Silences."

"I'm not sure how you'd want me to do that," I protested. "I'm just one person. I don't have an army."

"You have a King of Cats and an alchemist who has spent a hundred years perfecting his craft," said Ceres implacably. "Even if this were all your resources, here in one room, you would have the makings of a revolution."

". . . oh," I said. She wasn't even accounting for Quentin and May—the boy with the High King's ear, and the woman who couldn't be killed.

Maybe she was right. Maybe I *did* have the makings of a revolution. The only question now was whether I wanted to start one.

Marlis was still clinging to her brother, still weeping in huge, shuddering gasps that seemed like they would shake her entire body into pieces. Only Walther's arms were keeping her from breaking. Rhys had done this to her—and he'd done it on *purpose*. He'd done it because he thought that it was *funny*. Oberon might not have been willing to forbid the things that we did to each other, but maybe he should have—and maybe that was why so many of his descendants were heroes. Because we had to fix what he couldn't, or hadn't, or wouldn't.

"Yeah, okay," I said. "Let's do this."

THIRTEEN

WALTHER HAD LEFT MARLIS with a supply of the antidote he'd dusted on her cookies, and a promise that he'd find a way to make her long torment end. I think that even if I hadn't been willing to stand up against Rhys, Walther would have been plotting a revolution all by himself. The tearstains on his shirt made the reasons exquisitely clear.

Ceres escorted us to the edge of the forest, leading us through the trees until the path that would bring us to the palace appeared out of the green. There were rose goblins lounging there, basking in the moonlight and "coincidentally" keeping an eye on the distant keep. I had every faith that, had Rhys sent people looking for us, the rose goblins would have come to warn Ceres. The fact that they would have warned us at the same time was almost an accident.

"Remember," she said, and then she was gone, melting back into the green like she'd never been there in the first place.

"It's amazing how quickly a purple person can disappear when she really puts her mind to it," I said. The path stretched out in either direction. Thanks to the way the forest bent, both ways seemed to lead to the castle. I turned to Walther. "Which way?"

"This way," he said, and started walking. Tybalt and I followed, letting him set the pace. We'd all had a hard night, and it wasn't over yet, but of the three of us, he was definitely the one who had suffered the deepest and most painful shocks.

After we had walked in silence for several minutes, Walther said, "You didn't ask."

"What?" I turned my head enough to see the side of his face. "What do you mean?"

"Sorry." He rubbed his face with his hand, spreading his fingers so as to cover the whole thing before lowering his arm and saying, "When she thought I was her sister, you didn't say anything. And now you're not asking. It's not the response I expected."

"Ah." We kept walking, me taking advantage of the pause to put my thoughts in order. Finally, I said, "I guess I didn't know how to respond. I still don't. You're you. You've always been you. If who you are used to be someone different, that's your business, not mine."

"There have always been members of my Court whose parents named them one thing, but who were in truth another," said Tybalt. "When I was younger, they would go to the stage. Only men were permitted, you see, so a man who was in truth a woman could live a woman's life, petticoats and powders and all, under the guise of playing pretend. And few who would enforce the law looked critically at the stagehands—I suppose they assumed it would not have been worth the dangers of being a woman in the theater if you never took the stage. They did not understand that the attraction was in having the freedom to be themselves, free from judgment, free from social laws."

"You know, sometimes I forget how old you are," said Walther.

"But I never forget how old I am, even as I am surrounded by the children of this modern world, who do not understand the trials of those who came before them," said Tybalt. He sounded amused, which meant he was probably being clever—or at least thought he was.

I elbowed him lightly in the ribs. "We get it. You're a creepy old man, and I'm way too young for you. Now quit it."

Tybalt laughed.

Walther rubbed the side of his face this time, rather than the whole thing, and sounded relieved as he said, "I didn't expect this to be quite so easy, if it ever came out. I was expecting . . . I don't know."

"Is this because I'm a changeling?" I asked gently.

"I feel like a jerk for saying it, but yeah," he said.

"I understand." And I did. Faerie could be backward in a lot of ways—the absence of indoor plumbing in many knowes was a big one—but having a population of semi-immortals with a very low birth rate meant that in other ways, Faerie had always been ahead of the mortal world. No one batted an eye at May and Jazz's relationship; they would have been normal and accepted in any Court in the world a hundred years ago, or five hundred years ago, all the way back to the beginning of Faerie. The odd part would have been May's history as a night-haunt, not the fact that they were both women. The only limit Faerie really put on who someone loved came when it was time to produce heirs . . . and since adoption and fosterage were both acceptable within the nobility, even that wasn't required.

But I wasn't solely a child of Faerie. I'd been born and raised in the human world, in the 1950s. Yes, I'd moved to the Summerlands when I was very young, but that didn't mean I had escaped without a fun assortment of human prejudices on top of the fae ones I'd learned during my adolescence and adulthood. Some pure-bloods, when they were making the case for why they were better than their changeling cousins, would point to our supposed "small-mindedness" as proof that we would never be good enough. And in some ways, in some cases, they were right.

"I'm sorry you had to be afraid of how I'd react," I said, when the silence got to be too much for me.

Walther flashed me a quick, crooked smile. "It's cool. We're cool."

"Cool," I said, and then burst out laughing at the ridiculousness of my own reply. Walther blinked, looking nonplussed, before he started laughing as well. Tybalt didn't join in, but smirked, shaking his head.

"I am to be forever surrounded by the young," he said. "I would bemoan my fate, but I am not yet sure whether it is intended to be punishment or paradise."

"Here's a tip," I said, still half laughing. "If you call me a punishment, you're going to spend our wedding night sleeping on the couch."

"But ah, you see, I will *have* a wedding night. So long as you do not steal that from me, I can endure any trial the world sees fit to set before me."

"Right." I glanced to Walther. "Marlis mentioned the Cu Sidhe as a major tie. Do you think we should have brought Tia after all?"

"I don't know," he said. "Everyone who made it out of Silences scattered after the war. There were always Cu Sidhe in the Court, but most of the time, they were dogs. They seemed happier that way. No one really questioned it . . ." He trailed off as we came around a bend in the path.

The mouth of King Rhys' gardens appeared before us, marked both by the tall topiary archway that separated cultivated paths from forested wilds, and by the guards in the livery of Silences who stood across the opening. There were four of them, two armed with short swords, and the other two armed with nasty looking polearms that probably had some fancy name but really just looked like giant manual can openers on sticks. Whatever they were, they meant business.

The three of us stopped dead. It seemed like the best way to prevent *actual* death from occurring. "Can I help you?" I asked.

"Sir October Daye, you are under arrest for sedition and conspiracy to commit treason," said the guard in the middle. He was tall, black-haired, and silver-eyed, with the sharply pointed ears and harsh cheekbones of the Tuatha de Dannan. Not part of the original guard, then, and not another relative of Walther's being forced to work for someone who wanted to destroy him.

"See, this is familiar ground," I said, glancing to Tybalt. "We should have arranged for me to be arrested earlier. I always do so much better when I'm being arrested."

"And yet you do so much damage to the hearts of the people who love you when you insist upon spending so much time in gaol," said Tybalt stiffly. "If it is all the same to you, I would like for you to minimize your periods of incarceration."

"I'll keep that in mind." I turned back to the guard, who looked increasingly annoyed. There was a script that normally accompanied arrests, and I wasn't following it. I wasn't even following the basic themes of the play. "So I'm being arrested for sedition and treason, right?"

"That is correct," said the guard. "Will you come quietly, or must we use force?"

"That depends. Where will we be going?"

"To King Rhys, that you might plead his mercy and receive your sentence." The guard's tone made it clear that pleading for mercy wouldn't do me much good—although it might provide vital entertainment for the members of the Court, who didn't seem to have much to do with their time.

"Straight to the King? No stops to have dungeon funtimes or examine your torture chamber?"

The guard blinked. "Yes. Straight to the King."

"In that case, let's go." I smiled sunnily. One of the guards took a step back. The others looked like they wished they had the courage to do the same.

"Er," said the lead guard.

"This is where you take us prisoner, despite the fact that I have diplomatic immunity and you can't legally arrest me," I said, in a helpful voice.

"I would prefer not to be taken prisoner, as I *am* a visiting monarch, but I will gladly accompany you as you lead my betrothed off to a travesty of justice," said Tybalt. "Perhaps a second war can be declared today."

"Stop sounding like that would be fun," said Walther.

"Shan't," said Tybalt.

"Come with me," snapped the lead guard, who had apparently realized that we could do this until the sun came up. The other three guards moved to form a rough circle around us, and together they led us into the garden.

It was a lovely area, all landscaped hedges and blossoming roses, some in colors I had never seen before, not even in Luna's gardens. That had to be Ceres' work. She had the advantage of age, and access to the test garden she'd been telling us about—and if she'd been nursemaid to the previous royal family, she must have been doing *something* for the new regime in order to retain her access to the palace and grounds. Tending the garden seemed like the easiest thing for her to do.

People strolled here and there along the garden paths and down the central promenade. There were too many of them for it to have been coincidence: they had come to watch my arrest. Some of them looked amused by the sight. Others looked disappointed, like I was supposed to be crying and trying to get away by this point. I considered telling them that I'd been arrested by the best, and that their palace guard needed to step it up, but decided against it. There was no point in taunting the men who'd been sent to get me. They were just doing their jobs, and it's never a good idea to needlessly antagonize people with swords.

One thought led inexorably to another. I snorted. Tybalt gave me a sidelong look. "What is it now?" he asked.

"Just thinking about how long it's been since I've managed to wind up covered in blood," I said. "It's like a new trend. A blood-free trend."

"Pray keep it up; I find it a refreshing change," he said.

I laughed, and we kept walking.

The guards didn't like the fact that we weren't treating the whole situation as dire and filled with ominous portent: I could tell that from the way they looked at me, stealing glances out of the corners of their eyes as they waited for me to break down and start crying. I smiled when I caught them looking at me, but I didn't taunt them or laugh in their faces. Under the circumstances, that seemed like the best that I could do.

Of the three of us, Walther came the closest to behaving the way he was expected to behave. He walked silently, watching the faces of the people we passed like he thought he could uncover the secrets to the Kingdom if he just looked deeply enough. He didn't look like a defeated man, but he definitely looked like a man who'd been hit more times than was fair, and was still trying to recover his footing.

More guards met us at the entrance to the castle, presumably to make sure we didn't try anything in the presence of the King. I smiled politely as they joined the formation around us, and we walked, en masse, to the receiving room doors.

Marlis was already waiting there, her face composed into a mask of utter disdain. "You are entering the presence of His Highness, King Rhys of Silences," she said. "Should any of you raise hand or voice against the King, the penalty will be sleep for one hundred years. Should any of you present a clear and present danger to the King, the penalty will be sleep for one hundred years.

Should any of you refuse the justice of the Crown, you shall have no recourse. Do you understand?"

I tried to meet her eye, to figure out whether she was back under the King's control, but I couldn't manage it. That, more than anything, convinced me that she was still free. She was being too careful to have been anything else.

"We understand," I said. "We do not accept this arrest, but we understand."

"Then enter, and plead your case before the King," said Marlis. The doors swung open, apparently independent of any hand, and the guards moved through, pulling us with them.

As soon as the last guard was past the doorway, the doors slammed shut, rattling their frame with the force of their closure. I didn't look back to see if Marlis had accompanied us. My attention was fixed on the front of the room, and on the feeling of slow rage blossoming in my chest like a poisonous flower. King Rhys was there, as I had expected, sitting on his throne like he belonged exactly where he was. The false Queen was next to him, a smug smile on her pale face. Neither of them was worthy of my attention, or my outrage.

It was only when I looked at the people standing in front of the dais that my anger found a purpose. May and Quentin were off to the side, their hands bound in front of them with delicate-looking loops of morning glory vine. As I watched, Quentin shifted positions and grimaced, looking pained. Whatever that vine was, it was nothing as innocuous as morning glory. It was hurting them.

"Sir Daye," said King Rhys, rising. He struck a pose that was worthy of the King he was pretending to be: feet apart, shoulders square, arms crossed over his chest like his disapproval was his most powerful weapon. His guards continued marching us toward the throne, and he watched us come with a disappointed look on his face, clearly heartbroken by my supposed betrayal.

Bastard. "King Rhys," I replied. I didn't bow. He had lost the privilege of having me bow to him. "You want to tell me what this is all about? I'm here under the hospitality of your house. Maybe you do things differently in Silences, but in the Mists, we don't arrest our guests unless they've actually done something wrong."

"You have done something wrong," said Rhys, still sounding profoundly disappointed. We had let him down; we had failed to live up to his lofty ideals. And if I had possessed any respect for the man whatsoever, that might have mattered to me. Sadly, under the circumstances, all he was doing was pissing me off. "You have plotted treason against my throne; you have brought seditious elements into my demesne. How do you plead, Sir Daye? What possible excuse can you have for what you have done?"

I folded my own arms, feeling a little silly in the trailing sleeves the false Queen had saddled me with. It's hard to look like a force to be reckoned with when wearing something that a Disney princess would think was cute. "Since no one's *told* me what I've done, I plead get your head out of your ass and start explaining yourself. I'm here to prevent a war, remember? What good would plotting treason do? I didn't bring an army. I don't even know how we're getting back to the Mists if you don't open a portal for us." The bus, probably. Greyhound would be a real adventure with this bunch. "Also, there's the whole 'diplomatic immunity' aspect of things. I have it, and so do my people. Plus we're not your subjects, so while we can plot insurrection, we can't be guilty of treason."

"One of my maidservants stopped off at your quarters to clean and remove the laundry, as is only proper within a noble household. She was sparing you the effort of performing such menial chores yourself. But in her attempts to gather the washing, she found this." Rhys unfolded his arms and gestured at one of the guards. The woman—whose face didn't betray a flicker of emotion—moved to pick up a small chest from the edge of the dais. She turned back to us, holding up the chest like it was supposed to mean something.

Apparently it did, to at least one member of my little posse: Walther groaned, reaching up to pinch the bridge of his nose with one hand as he said, "That's mine. It's not treasonous for an alchemist to carry his supplies with him."

"But it *is* treasonous for an alchemist to serve the deposed rulers of this land." Rhys leaned over, opened the chest, and pulled out an amethyst bottle. It looked like it had been carved from a single impossibly large stone, with gold filigree around the top and bottom. Rhys held it up like it was proof of a crime. "Or do you deny that this is yours as well?"

"I am a cousin of the Yates family," said Walther. "I never claimed I wasn't. I never changed my last name—the only line of Tylwyth Teg to go by 'Davies' has long been known as related to the Yates line. But I don't serve them. I didn't come here to overthrow you. My service is to the Kingdom of the Mists, and I am here as Sir Daye's private alchemist, to supply whatever potions or posies she requires."

"I need a *lot* of potions and posies," I said. "My complexion isn't great—human blood, you know—and my hair gets frizzy when people use too much magic around me. And hoo, boy, you do *not* want to know about my digestion problems." I gestured to Quentin. "And my squire over there—you *do* know that's my squire, right? That you have detained and restrained my squire, without my permission, despite him being underage and hence my responsibility, rather than someone who's capable of plotting treason on his own? I'm just checking, I don't mean to imply that you don't understand your own rules—anyway, he's a teenage boy. Acne, weird rashes, chafing, they're all on the table. You'd travel with your own alchemist, too, if you didn't own a whole Kingdom full of them."

Rhys blinked. Whatever response he'd been expecting, it apparently hadn't been a bucket of refutations and denials.

Then Tybalt stepped forward.

It was a small gesture, as such things go: he moved less than a foot, bringing himself even with me. He didn't even put himself in front of me. But as soon as he moved, the atmosphere in the room changed. King Rhys stiffened, attention going to Tybalt, and everything went very still.

"It may interest you to know that I have been a King of Cats for several hundred years," said Tybalt. He didn't raise his voice. He didn't need to. Everyone in the room was listening. "During that time, I have had cause to learn much about the Divided Courts. Your quaint ideas of how Oberon would have us treat with one another. Your strange rules and aspirations toward power. I have enjoyed the company of your monarchs, even sat for a time at the High King's table, back when the Westlands were still a novelty. I have seen corruption, and deceit, and all the other lovely ills to which the monarchy is heir. It is remarkable, really, how much effort you put into damaging the positions you create for yourselves. Does it entertain you? Is this how you fritter away the centuries?"

Rhys frowned. "I am sorry, but I don't take your meaning."

"My betrothed announced when she arrived here that she traveled with an alchemist. His relation to the family which once ruled here is public knowledge, as is his contented service in the Mists. He is no revolutionary, no redeemer; just a man who has no claim to the throne you hold, and no desire to hold it. She *announced him to you*, and now you rummage through his things like a common thief because . . . what reason could you possibly have?"

Tybalt's expression hardened, turning cold, until he was looking at Rhys the way he might look at a mouse. I didn't see that expression much anymore, and every time I did, I was grateful that it wasn't directed at me. "Given that you have spoken openly of wanting to exsanguinate Sir Daye in order to use her in your own alchemy, you'll forgive me if I state that this seems less a matter of protecting your Kingdom, and more one of enriching your treasury through the body of the woman I love. If you do not present further evidence of this 'treason,' I shall have to assume I am correct in my reading of the situation—and I shall be forced to take that as any King would take such a thing, were it to be aimed at his lady love. I will take it as a declaration of war."

"The Court of Cats will not go to war against a throne of Oberon's declaration just because you bid them to, Your Majesty," said Rhys. There was an oily coating on his words, making it clear that he thought Tybalt had just given him back the upper hand. "That would be foolish in the extreme, and if there's one thing the Court of Cats has never been, it's foolish."

"I recommend you do not test my resolve unless you are sure you know my people more intimately than I do," said Tybalt quietly.

Rhys paused. The false Queen, still seated on her throne, wasn't smiling anymore. In that moment, I knew we'd won—the battle, at least. The war was still ongoing, and it wasn't going to end until we left Silences. "It is . . . possible there was some mistake regarding the possessions of Sir Daye's alchemist. It's true that he announced his surname upon arrival; it's also true that sometimes my people can be overzealous in their desire to please me. They are *very* loyal, you understand." Rhys spoke slowly, choosing his words with much more care than he had only a few moments before.

"I understand loyalty well," said Tybalt. "Many credit the Cu Sidhe as the most loyal souls in Faerie. Those people have never experienced the loyalty of the Cait Sidhe. Once someone is under our protection, they will remain there for the rest of their days."

I cleared my throat. "Excuse me. If we've established that I'm not *actually* under arrest for harboring a traitor, could someone, I don't know, *let my people go?* Because if my squire and my assistant are tied up for one more minute, without valid reason, I'm going to have some really interesting things to say about your Kingdom when I get home."

Rhys glared at me. I glared back.

Silences might have the bigger army—would definitely have the bigger army, since Rhys wasn't above using loyalty potions to get people to do what he wanted, while Arden actually had a moral core, however warped it had been by her slapdash upbringing—but it didn't have bigger allies. If I went back to the Mists with stories of false allegations and abuses against purebloods, stories I could back up by giving blood memories to the Daoine Sidhe attached to the various Courts, we could join their armies to ours. Dianda would never stand for this sort of thing. I was willing to bet that whatever Undersea Duchy bordered on this part of Oregon wouldn't be too happy about it either. And that didn't even account for Angels and Golden Shore to the south, or Evergreens to the north, or Falls to the east. There were half a dozen Kingdoms and free Duchies that could become involved with this, if Rhys pushed me into it. Now the only question was . . . was he really that stupid?

Rhys might have gotten his Kingdom through politicking and appointment, but there was a reason he'd been able to hold it for a hundred years. He wasn't a foolish man. A little hasty, maybe, with the false Queen spitting poison in his ear and making him feel invincible, but not foolish. He looked away, and I knew that we had won.

"Release Sir Daye's people," he said. "Return her

alchemist's things to him. Nothing has been taken, or broken."

"Good," said Walther. He stepped forward to claim the little chest, clearing his throat when King Rhys didn't seem inclined to put the amethyst bottle back. Looking faintly offended, Rhys returned the bottle to its place. Walther closed the lid of the chest and retreated to his original position.

I noted all this out of the corner of my eye: the bulk of my attention was on the guards approaching May and Quentin, neither of whom had spoken through this whole ordeal. One of the guards removed a glass vial from his pocket. He uncorked it, and dripped three drops of clear liquid onto the vines holding May's wrists. They promptly writhed and curled into a small green ball, like a flowered bezoar, which dropped to the floor. The guard repeated the process with Quentin.

Still neither one of them moved. King Rhys turned his head, facing them, and said in a loud, clear voice, "You may go."

They both walked forward, their steps measured so that they moved together, as smooth and soulless as automatons. I swallowed the urge to shout even as it rose in my throat. I didn't *know* that what I feared was happening was real. Maybe they were just staying quiet out of protest, and the desire not to make things worse.

Then they got close enough for me to see their eyes. Their pupils were dilated, and their normally sharp, focused gazes were soft and blank. I turned to Rhys, glaring mutely. He met my eyes and smiled. Just a little. Just enough that I knew he was my enemy. If everything that had come before had been politics, this was personal.

"They had to be sedated in order to keep them calm while we awaited your return," he said. "Had you not run out of here the way you did, it might not have been necessary. You have my sincere apologies for any trouble this has caused. I'm sure you can understand why I would be wary of deceit from a diplomat belonging to a Kingdom we are on the cusp of war with—a diplomat who has already been known to depose monarchs she did not approve of."

"Not sure this is how I'd go about making me approve of you," I said tightly. I wanted to say more, but the eager way he watched me made me rein myself in. He was waiting for an opportunity to strike. Tybalt's threat had been enough to cow him for the moment. That didn't mean he wouldn't move if he thought that he could get away with it. I swallowed my fury, cleared my throat, and said, "Don't do this again."

Rhys raised an eyebrow. "I beg your pardon?"

"I'm not raising my voice, I'm not yelling at you, and I think I've earned a moment of speaking on my own behalf, considering what you just tried to pull, so let me say it one more time, for the sake of clarity: don't do this again. If you want to arrest me, fine, you're the King here, you can arrest me. But if you don't want it to be the biggest mistake of your political career, you'll arrest me for something I *did*, rather than trying to trump up a crime you know damn well I didn't commit. This wasn't smart of you. It makes us both look bad. So don't. Do it. Again."

There was a long pause before Rhys nodded. "I will take your words under advisement, Sir Daye. You are free to leave my presence, as are your people. The night has been long, and we are planning to push it further. Return for a late dinner at the stroke of noon. We shall have a grand feast in your honor."

"We wouldn't miss it," I said. I took Quentin's hand, which he let me have without protest, and gestured for Tybalt to do the same with May. My fury raged against my breastbone, begging for its freedom, and the fact that I couldn't grant it what it wanted was worse than the anger itself.

Together, the five of us walked out of the room, May

and Quentin staring vacantly off into space, Walther clutching his chest as tightly as I held my squire's hand. None of us spoke. If we had, I think Rhys would have found a lot more grounds to arrest us for treason. All he'd really needed to do was wait.

FOURTEEN

"HOW MUCH LONGER?" I glared at Walther as I paced back and forth across the bedroom. May and Quentin were sitting on the edge of the bed, staring at the wall in front of them. Even waving my hand in front of their faces hadn't been enough to make them track my motion or acknowledge my presence. Only direct orders did that, and I didn't like commanding my friends when they couldn't refuse me.

"Almost done," said Walther, adding another pinch of brightly colored powder to his mortar. "This would be a *lot* easier if I had access to my lab back at the University."

"Well, you don't. Work faster." I kept pacing.

Walther didn't dignify my words with a reply. That was probably for the best. He had checked the room for new listening charms when we first got back, and hadn't managed to find any; either King Rhys had charm-crafters who were so far outside of Walther's league that he couldn't recognize their work, or no one had yet figured out that they weren't getting anything useful out of this room.

Tybalt was gone. He hadn't told me where he was

going, but he'd kissed me before diving into the shadows behind the bed, and I trusted that whatever he was doing, he'd come back and explain it when he was done. I would normally have been a lot more agitated about him running off without explanation during a crisis, but Walther had still been checking for new listening charms when Tybalt had opened the Shadow Roads. Explanations hadn't been safe yet.

I was still wearing my latest involuntary ball gown, since I hadn't been able to figure out how to remove it on my own. The more things changed, the more they inevitably stayed the same. Most court gear seems to have been designed to hobble women, making us easier to catch—and honestly, easier to kill. I'm sure there are people who know how to fight in floor-length gowns with six layers of crinoline, but I do not know their secrets. I just know that I'll take denim over damask any day, and I was looking forward to May being able to help me with the ties on my current dress.

"Done," said Walther.

I whirled around to face him. "Done?"

"Done," he repeated. He stood, leaving most of his kit behind as he started toward the bed. "I'm not sure how they're going to react. You might want to stand back."

"No. They're my responsibility. If this stuff doesn't require magic to use, let me do it. I can take a lot more damage than you can."

Walther paused for a moment, said, "Good point," and handed me his mortar. It was filled with a white, faintly luminescent dust, like embossing glitter. "Just blow a pinch of this in their eyes and they should snap out of it. It's a broad-spectrum anti-hypnotic, which means it'll work on a dozen different kinds of base enchantment, but some of them will leave them not remembering anything that's happened since they were whammied."

"Which is why there might be hitting, got it," I said. "Step back."

Walther stepped back.

I set the mortar down on the table next to the bed and placed a pinch of powder in the palm of my hand, where it created a glittering white smear. It didn't have a smell, but it chilled my skin slightly: the mark of Walther's magic. Once I was sure I had enough I bent, just a little, and blew the powder into Quentin's eyes.

The effect was instantaneous. Quentin's pupils snapped back to their normal size and shape, his shoulders went from drugged stiffness to his normal, natural good posture, and he punched me in the face without hesitation. There was a resounding "crack" as the cartilage in my nose gave way. It was accompanied by a bolt of pain and a sudden hot gush of blood from both nostrils, which coated my chin and soaked into the front of my dress as Quentin was pulling back to hit me again. I was ready for him this time, and caught his wrist before he could begin his swing.

"You're safe, you're with me, stop *hitting*," I said. My voice was mushy and distorted by the damage he'd done. I couldn't help feeling a little bit proud. My squire was all grown up and breaking noses. I just wished he wasn't breaking mine. "Now stop punching me and help me set this before it heals all crooked and weird."

"Toby?" His eyes widened as he realized who he was hitting, shock transforming almost immediately into guilt. "Oh, oak and ash, Toby, I'm sorry! I didn't know who you were! I thought—"

"You thought I was the King, or one of the King's men, I know. It's okay." Quentin didn't look like he was going to help me set my nose any time soon. That was probably asking a little much. I placed my index fingers to either side of the break, feeling for the places where things were out of alignment, and shoved until everything lined up. This was accompanied by another bolt of pain, even more vivid than the first, and a fresh gout of blood. The pain faded almost immediately. My body was already putting itself back together, healing with the ludicrous speed gifted to me by my heritage.

"I didn't realize it was you," said Quentin, sounding miserable. "I would never ever hit you. Please believe me."

"Kiddo, it's okay. You don't need to convince me that we're friends, and sometimes friends have to hit each other in the process of discharging our duties. Remember all those times I slapped Tybalt?"

"I certainly do," said Tybalt dryly. I turned to find him behind me, a resigned expression on his face. "I leave for half an hour and return to find you covered, head to toe, with blood. Perhaps you would be better suited to be a Bannick's wife. At least then you could be cleaned via supernatural means, rather than depending on the vagaries of the laundry."

"I'm surprisingly good at getting blood out of cotton," I said. "Velvet may be a little harder. It's an adventure. Come here. My hands are all bloody, and we still need to snap May out of it."

"Why are you covered in blood?" pressed Tybalt.

"Quentin broke my nose," I said. I couldn't keep the pride out of my voice.

"Sorry," said Quentin.

Tybalt blinked slowly. Then he sighed, and said, "Each time I tell myself you have reached the summit of your strangeness, you find a way to climb still higher."

"Look at it this way: being married to me will never be boring." I pointed to the mortar. "Take a pinch of that and blow it into May's eyes, will you? Just be ready to duck."

"Yes, dear," said Tybalt, his flat, toneless delivery making it clear that he was mocking me. He picked up a pinch of Walther's powder, spread it thinly across his palm, and blew it into May's eyes. He jumped backward at almost the same time, leaving a glittering cloud hanging in the air for May's hand to sweep away as she directed an open-palmed slap at the place where he'd been a moment before. When her hand struck nothing but the empty air she stopped, blinking, a look of profound confusion on her face.

"You see, some of us understand the meaning of the word 'dodge,'" said Tybalt. "Perhaps you should enlighten yourself. You might keep more of your blood within your body, and thus tax my poor heart less." He turned his attention to May. "Milady Fetch. Welcome back to the land of the self-aware. I trust you have enjoyed your stay in the land of the insensate?"

"I'm going to kill him," said May, in a slow, wondering voice. "I'm going to commit regicide. I hope none of you have a problem with that, because I'm going to do it."

"Sorry, but I can't let you," I said. "We don't have all the pieces we'd need to kill a King, like, I don't know, consent from Oberon himself to violate the Law."

"The penalty for breaking the Law is death," said May. "I can't be killed. It'll work out fine."

"The fact that you *can't* die doesn't mean they can't try to kill you, and I'm pretty sure that you wouldn't enjoy, say, decapitation," I said. "While you were getting arrested, we were gathering information. Now settle down, and listen."

It only took a few minutes to explain what had happened when I went to speak with King Rhys. It took longer to describe what happened next: the meeting in the wood with Ceres, the reunion between Walther and his sister, and most importantly, the possibility that Walther would actually be able to engineer a counterpotion for elf-shot. If the rightful holders of the throne could be awakened, we'd be in a better position to petition the High King to make things better.

When I finished, there was a moment of silence. Then Quentin asked, "Why did they come for me and May? We weren't doing anything."

"No, but as my squire, you're the best hostage against

my good behavior. And May looks like my changeling sister. I've been careful not to say that she wasn't, although the false Queen knows, so we can't discount the possibility that Rhys does as well. Either way, she's clearly family, which makes her a good hostage, too."

"And as your family, I command you to give me your dress," said May, sliding off the bed and holding out her hand.

I blinked at her. "Excuse me?"

"You said Rhys wanted to take you apart. Have you noticed that he has an army of alchemists, including Walther's sister, ready to do his bidding? You can't just go leaving your blood around like it's not a big deal. Give me your dress. Give me everything that has blood on it." May continued to hold out her hand. "I'm going to make sure it can't be used against you."

"I can take you to a proper laundry, if you would like, rather than run the risk that Rhys will save and reuse your wash water," said Tybalt calmly. "We have need to go into Portland regardless."

I turned to look at him. "Is that where you went? To Portland?"

"Yes," he said. "I've been making many promises. It was time to see whether they could be kept. The local King has agreed to see us. He has already seen me, you understand, but is interested in meeting the woman who could sway me toward marriage. Apparently, our union will settle some sort of bet." He wrinkled his nose at the end, like this was so unbelievably crass that he didn't know where to begin.

"Fair enough," I said. I looked down at my blood-soaked bodice and sighed. "I need help getting out of this, and then we can head for Portland. Quentin, Walther, do you want to come with us? I'm not sure I like the idea of you staying here alone."

"I'm coming with you," said Quentin.

"I'm not," said Walther. The rest of us turned to look

at him. He shrugged. "I need to spend more time with Aunt Ceres, and to work on finding that rose. Until I have it, I can't make any more progress on my counter-potion. I can get to her without having any issues. I know this castle better than the people who currently hold it—I'd be willing to stake my life on it."

"You will be," I said grimly. "If you have any trouble, or if Rhys threatens you in any way, run, all right? None of this is worth it if you get yourself killed."

"Yes, Mom," he said, and smiled. "Now get yourself cleaned up. You look like a crime scene."

"That's how you know I'm feeling like myself," I said. I walked to the wardrobe, fished out jeans, my leather jacket, and a clean tank top, then started for the bathroom with May close behind me.

It took us five minutes to undo all the stays and ties holding the dress together. There was a bloodstain on the left cup of my bra, but it wasn't bad enough to make me want a clean one. I had every confidence that it was going to be joined by more before this trip was through. May took custody of the dress as soon as it was peeled from my body.

"Wash the blood off your face," she said, and left me to get dressed.

The others were waiting when I emerged. May had produced a laundry bag from somewhere, and had it slung over her shoulder. "At least you didn't get blood in your hair," she said.

"I'm not a barbarian," I said.

"Barbarians bleed less, because barbarians know that actions have consequences," she countered. "Maybe you should try being a barbarian."

"We're going to Portland," I said. "Let's be hipsters instead." I turned to Tybalt. "How do you want to do this? Taking three of us through the shadows at once is a lot to ask."

"You have asked more of me with less cause, and I do

not want the local regency to realize that something is happening," he said. "We are close to the mortal city, all but overlapping its bounds. You will hold fast, and not let go. I will run as fleetly as I may, and together, we will come through the other side, bent and bowed, but nowhere near to broken."

"You're nervous, too, huh?" I asked, reaching over to put my hand on his shoulder.

He folded his fingers over it, lifting it to his lips and pressing a kiss against my knuckles. "I am in a constant state of what you would term as 'nervousness,' and it is most often your fault."

"A girl's got to be good for something." I turned to look at Walther, who was standing near the door. "Be careful, okay? You know they're out to get you, and you know Rhys is a bastard. He'll do whatever he feels he has to do in order to accomplish his goals."

Walther smiled slowly. "Lucky for me, I'm as big of a bastard as he is. I just have less reason to show it. Now go. Enjoy Portland. Don't get yourselves killed."

"Right." I turned back to Tybalt, who was still holding onto me. Quentin stepped up and took my free hand in his, while May took Tybalt's free hand and held it tightly. Then Tybalt stepped backward, into the shadows cast by the hanging curtains, and out of the world where light and air were possibilities.

Running along the Shadow Roads with multiple people was never easy. There was too much chance that someone would trip or lose hold, and consequently be lost—possibly forever—in the darkness. Tybalt set the pace and the rest of us did our best to keep up, our lips sealed tight against the airless void and ice crystals forming on our hair and eyelashes with every step that we took. The cold was bad enough that I closed my eyes reflexively, shielding them from the worst of it. As always, I found myself wondering how everyone else was doing, whether the Shadow Roads were kinder to them than they were to me, or whether the opposite was true. It was better than dwelling on the nothingness surrounding us, infinite and empty.

Then we were falling back into a place where the air was warm, and more importantly, *breathable*. I lost my grip on Quentin's hand. I lost my grip on Tybalt's half a second later. There wasn't time to worry about it, as my head's impact with a brick wall followed almost instantly. The ice was knocked from my hair and eyelashes, jarring my eyes open, and I found myself looking at a narrow alleyway. A dumpster stood between us and the street. Tybalt was standing behind May, his hands in her armpits, and her face only a few inches from hitting the wall like mine had. Quentin was on his back on the ground. Fortunately, it either hadn't been raining recently or the alley had excellent drainage: there was no standing water for him to have landed in. After the day we'd been having, if there had been an available puddle, he would have gone into it.

The sun was up, and it was early morning, based on the shadows. The Summerlands had been distorting time again. That made me worry about how Rhys was calculating the days. If his knowe burned hours faster than the world outside, our three days could be up before we even knew it.

"I'm the fiancée. Why am I the one you let risk concussion?" I asked, peeling myself away from the wall and rubbing the back of my head with one hand. It didn't feel like I had knocked anything loose inside my skull, and my nose hadn't started bleeding again. There was probably a layer or two of skin remaining on the brick, but that was a small thing. Any scrapes would be healed before we made it to the sidewalk.

"Because you're also the one who heals like she's trying out for the magical Olympics," said May, pulling away from Tybalt. She retrieved the laundry bag from where it had fallen next to Quentin. "If I'd eaten wall the way you just did, my face would look like roadkill for the next week."

"Aren't you sweet," I said, and offered Quentin my hand. He took it, letting me pull him off the alley floor. "You okay there, kiddo? Didn't whack your head too hard?"

"I'm fine," said Quentin. He raised his hand and whistled a few bars of a sea shanty as he brought it down again. The smell of steel and heather filled the alley as the thin veil of a human disguise settled over him, softening the lines of his face and stealing some of the metallic sheen from his hair. His tunic and trousers also blurred, becoming jeans and a T-shirt advertising a band called Great Big Sea. He looked like any human kid, standing on the border between high school and college, and ready to take on the world.

My ears itched. I reached up to feel the side of my right ear, and found that it was gently curved—human. "Good work," I said.

Quentin smiled. "No problem. Um, I know you're going to see the local King, so you can dispel it if you need to by clapping your hands twice."

I raised an eyebrow. "You're learning conditional illusions now? *Excellent* work. That tutoring with Etienne is really working out."

"It'll go faster once he has access to his own magic again," said Quentin, cheeks reddening with pleasure.

"Still. Better than I could do."

Everyone knew that illusions were harder for me than they were for Quentin or May. They were predominantly rooted in flower magic, which descends from Titania, although you can accomplish the same things through a slightly different route if you had access to water magic, which descends from Maeve. Lucky me, I didn't get either, since the Dóchas Sidhe descended solely from Oberon. If you want blood magic, I'm your girl. If you want an illusion cast quickly and well, I'm really not.

Tybalt—his own face now hidden by a human mask, and the smell of musk and pennyroyal attending him like my favorite cologne—walked over to us and slid one arm around my waist. "Your clothing needs no alteration, as you are always more inclined to dress for the mall than for the presence of Kings."

I wrinkled my nose as I turned to give his own altered attire a once-over. He looked good in jeans and a flannel work shirt, but let's be serious here: this was Tybalt I was talking about. He would have looked good in a burlap sack, a sentiment I have expressed before and will no doubt express again, when the opportunity arises. "See, I find that I spend more time grocery shopping and running for my life than I do making nice with royalty."

Tybalt raised an eyebrow.

"You don't count," I said.

"Yeah, because half the time you're naked when he's around," said May, sashaying over to our little cluster. Her face was hidden by a human disguise, but her clothing was still Court finery, making her look out of place and out of time in the dingy little alley. I blinked. She smirked. "This is Portland, honey. They pride themselves on keeping it weird here. I could probably add a pair of bunny ears and a basket full of teddy bears before anyone looked at me twice, and even then, they'd just want to know if I was the Shakespearean Easter Bunny. Trust me, I've heard about this town."

"If you say so," I said. "Just please don't get us in more trouble than we're already in, okay?"

"I won't." May turned to Tybalt. "Meet here in two hours? That gives me time to get the laundry done and dry, and maybe do a little shopping. I want to find those food trucks they're always talking about on TV."

"I'm going with May," said Quentin. "Well, I mean, at least until I can find a bus or taxi that will take me to Powell's."

"Powell's?" I asked blankly.

"It's a bookstore so big it takes up an entire city block. They have a rare books room bigger than the Safeway near the house. I'm going to ship things home, don't worry."

I grimaced. "Please. Okay, meet us back here in two hours. That leaves plenty of time for us to change our clothes and get ready for dinner. And be careful, all right? I wouldn't put it past Rhys to have people out here in the city looking for a chance to get the upper hand. Avoid, I don't know, empty streets and archery ranges."

"Will do," said May. She slung the laundry bag over her shoulder and started for the mouth of the alley. Quentin followed her. I turned to Tybalt.

"Well?" I asked.

"We must walk a short distance, but I assure you, it will be no hardship, for I will be with you," he said, offering me his arm.

I laughed as I took it. "Wow. Your ego has grown since we've known each other, hasn't it?"

"Ah, but, you see, I have wooed and won the woman of my dreams. Admittedly, some of those dreams would be more properly termed 'nightmares,' but I don't believe we get to be that picky when talking about such things." He led me out of the alley and onto the tree-lined street. I didn't know Portland well enough to know where we were—I didn't know Portland at all, really—but he walked without hesitation, and I followed him. Whatever strange methods Cait Sidhe used to mark their holdings for each other, I trusted him to know how to interpret things. "If my ego had not grown, it would surely be a sign that I was no true cat, and you would leave me for another."

"I don't know," I said. "I love you, but the cat part has never been the most important thing to me."

The corner of Tybalt's mouth curved upward. "And, truly, that is excellent to know. I was considering becoming a horse, or a stag, or perhaps a dairyman."

"You know, if I ever forget that you're a weirdo, the fact that you class 'dairyman' with horse and deer will remind me."

"Stag, please," said Tybalt. He tried to sound wounded. The laughter sort of spoiled the effect. "Do not shame my manhood, I beg of you."

"Stag, then," I said. We turned a corner, starting down a street packed with odd little shops. Half of them had candles in the window. Sobering, I asked, "Tybalt . . . are we doing the right thing? Getting involved, I mean? We could go home and start rallying our allies."

"Preventing a war is always the right thing to do," he said gravely. "War is not a game, for all that some would play it as they would a round of whist. War is a tragedy in motion. Everyone is innocent, and everyone is guilty, and the crows come for their bodies all the same. The only ones who benefit in war are the night-haunts, and even they would rather their feasts came in smaller portion."

I thought of May, who had willingly left the night-haunts to become my Fetch, and the way the night-haunts sometimes spoke of death: like it was a waste. They lived because other fae died, and even they understood that living was better. "I just feel like we're starting to interfere on a level that's sort of . . . extreme."

"But that's what heroes do." He stopped in front of a comic book store. There were no candles in this window: only men in tights and women with improbably good, improbably invisible bras, striking heroic poses that seemed much more sincere than my own weary resignation. I didn't have time to dwell on that, however. Tybalt pulled his arm out of mine, put both hands against the sides of my face, and kissed me.

No matter how many times I kissed Tybalt, no matter how many situations and places I kissed him in, part of me always marveled at the fact that I was allowed to do it at all. He wasn't the sort of man who kissed scruffy changelings in tank tops and tennis shoes—and yet somehow, he was exactly that sort of man, because he had kissed me over and over again, with the same delicate amazement that I felt when I kissed him. Like we were getting away with something that should, by all rights, have been forbidden. Like we were *winning.*

The taste of pennyroyal and musk on his lips was stronger than usual, thanks to the human disguise he had crafted and was still powering. It overpowered any lingering trace of Quentin's magic, which was good; I would have been a little unnerved to suddenly have my squire involved in our embrace. Tybalt kissed me slowly and thoroughly, until my ears and cheeks were burning red and felt like they must be hot to the touch.

I was panting a little when he pulled away, smiling smugly. I glared at him.

"That was entirely unfair," I said. "You can kiss me like that, but we're not going to be able to *do* anything about it for days."

"We have a bed," he said.

"And we are not doing anything in it when we're in the house of a man who wants to collect my bodily fluids for icky alchemical purposes, okay? Nothing's going to happen, bed-wise, until we get home."

Tybalt sighed extravagantly. "You see, even now, you torment me so." He stepped back, taking my hand in his. There was something purposeful about the gesture, like it was less casual affection and more a statement of ownership. That feeling grew stronger as he turned toward the comic book store and started for the door, pulling me along with him.

"Tybalt?" I asked, in a low voice.

"Yes?"

"Did you just kiss me to show off for whoever's inside here?"

A small, regretful smile touched his lips. "Perhaps," he said, and opened the door.

I've never been much for comic books. I don't object to them as a medium, and having two teenage boys effectively living with me has meant getting used to finding them piled on the coffee table, but it's hard to get too excited about a world where a cheap domino mask is all it takes to hide your secret identity from everyone around you. If it had been that easy for me, my life would have been very different.

The shop was small, made narrow by the huge racks of comics and graphic novels that took up every inch of wall space below seven feet. Above that, the shelves gave way to posters and to tall, expensive statues, for the person who just *has* to have a bust of Batman watching their every move. A few racks of action figures and other, odder merchandise stood here and there among the periodicals. I blinked at a display of purses made from superhero-themed fabric. I hadn't realized there were so many different ways to wear a cape, or so many different styles of bustier that people would consider appropriate to wear into combat.

Tybalt kept hold of my hand, guiding me past the glass-topped counter where a bored-looking girl was flipping through something about robots. The deeper we got, the stronger the smell of paper became, until we reached the back of the store. A half-open door afforded a glimpse into a small office packed with filing cabinets and cardboard boxes. A trim, silver-haired man sat at the room's sole desk, typing rapidly.

Tybalt motioned for me to be quiet before raising his hand and rapping lightly on the doorframe. "I believe we had a lunch appointment, if you would care to put your papers and quills aside, you old rapscallion."

"Rand!" The man was smiling as he turned, the expression carving deep furrows into the skin around his lips and eyes. If not for the faint glitter of a human disguise hanging in the air around him, I would have assumed that he was somewhere in his mid to late sixties, young enough to still be healthy and spry, but old enough to be slowing down. With that glitter, he could have been any age, from sixteen to six hundred. Immortality makes everything difficult. "So you weren't kidding when you said you'd bring your new girlfriend to meet me."

"Indeed, and here she is," said Tybalt, lifting our joined hands ever so slightly, like he was showing me off and asserting ownership at the same time. I swallowed the urge to pull away. No one owns me, and I don't like it when people pretend they do. At the same time, what little I understood about the Court of Cats told me he was trying to protect us both. He knew my feelings on the subject, and that I'd be yelling at him later. He'd done it anyway.

Belatedly, I was starting to realize that marrying a King of Cats was going to mean learning a lot more about how the Cait Sidhe worked. I was never going to be part of their world, but I was definitely moving into the subdivision next door. "Hi," I said, smiling at the man as sincerely as I could manage. "I'm October."

"And you can call me 'Joe.' Give me just a second." The man—Joe—stood, leaning out of his office, and called, "Susie! You've got the store for the next hour or two. My lunch date's here."

"Yeah, whatever," called a female voice from the front of the shop. Presumably, the bored clerk we'd seen before was just as bored now that she was in charge.

Joe stepped back into his office, beaming. "There, that's sorted. Come with me."

The office was small, and had no visible exits. "Won't she notice that we didn't go out through the front . . . ?" I asked hesitantly.

"The new issue of *Atomic Robo* just came in. Susie's a great employee, and I love her dearly, but I'd be lucky if she noticed an armed robbery right now. We're fine. Now come on." His smile faded a few degrees, and a warning glint came into his eye.

Tybalt stepped into the office. I followed. Joe reached past me to close the door before turning off the light and casting the entire room into shadow.

"Hold your breath," he said, and we were plunged into cold.

The transition lasted only a few seconds. Then we were standing in ankle-deep grass, surrounded by trees that had twisted and tangled together until they became an impassable wall. Tybalt released my hand and snapped his fingers, allowing his human disguise to waft away into nothing. I took his lead, clapping my hands as Quentin had instructed. I hadn't cast the illusion, so I couldn't feel it give way, but my ears stopped itching, and I assumed that meant the release had worked.

A voice chuckled from the shadows near the base of the trees. "What an odd young lady you've found, *Rand*. She's lovely, but so unique. Whose bloodline is she? Whose name claims her?"

"Come out, Jolgeir," said Tybalt. There was an edge of impatience in his tone, so thin that I only heard it because I knew to listen. "We are here at your sufferance, and for that, I am grateful, but we are not here to be your playthings. You have plenty such, and finer than we."

"I don't know that I'd trust you to assess the value of my toys," said Joe—Jolgeir—from his hiding place. But he strolled out into the open all the same, giving me my first look at Tybalt's local equivalent without his human mask on.

Fae tend to stop aging in their mid-twenties, thanks to whatever quirk of impossible biology makes purebloods immortal. Jolgeir was no different. He was recognizably the frame on which the older human man had been constructed: his facial features were a little finer, and his ears, now sharply pointed and subtly feline, would have looked wrong on the pleasant human proprietor of the little comic book store. His hair was still silver, although now it was the mottled silver of a gray cat, shot through with veins of purest white. His eyes were a shade of blue never seen in a purely human face, and his pupils were vertical slits, like Tybalt's.

He was still wearing brown slacks and a button-down shirt, which explained why Tybalt hadn't suggested I change my clothes. Kings get to set their own standards, and the standards of the people around them. Of the three of us, Tybalt was the one who looked slightly overdressed. That wasn't so unusual. He usually dressed better than I did.

Jolgeir looked me thoughtfully up and down, less like he was looking for something wrong, and more like he was trying to take a fair and accurate measure. Finally, he said, "Forgive me for my earlier rudeness, but I truly must ask, what bloodline bore you? You look most like the Daoine Sidhe, but you are *not* Daoine Sidhe, and no other race so fine in face and form would suit you half so well."

"I think that was a compliment," I said. Jolgeir smiled, revealing one pointed incisor. I relaxed a little. A King of Cats who was relaxed enough to be smiling at me was a King of Cats who wasn't planning to disembowel me any time soon. "Do you know Amandine?"

"Amandine, the blood-worker? The one who claims to be Daoine Sidhe, and is such a liar that I can't bear her company? That Amandine?"

"That's the one," I said. "She's my mother. She's also a Firstborn daughter of Oberon. Surprise, and all that."

Jolgeir frowned. "It seems odd that she could be Firstborn, and I not have heard."

"Like you said, she lied about it for a long, long time. She even lied to me, until I figured out what she was doing. These days, it's not quite common knowledge, but she doesn't get to make it a secret anymore, either. If she didn't want people to know she wasn't Daoine Sidhe, she shouldn't have left me in the position of needing to figure out my magic on my own. Makes it sort of hard to keep things on the down-low."

"I see." Jolgeir's attention shifted to Tybalt. "I suppose I can see the appeal of a novelty. It's always nice to have something that no one else has."

Tybalt's eyes narrowed, but his tone was pleasant as he said, "I would watch myself, were I you, old man. Some people might say that senselessly baiting me was a sign that you wished to be rid of your Kingdom entire."

"Only if you could take me, kit, and I doubt you can. You couldn't do it last time." Jolgeir moved closer, until he and Tybalt were almost nose to nose. They stared at each other for a long moment, long enough that I was starting to consider shoving my way between them. I might regret it for a moment, but I could recover from whatever damage they did to me. The same couldn't necessarily be said of the damage they would do to each other.

Then something changed in the air between the two men, and they burst out laughing. Tybalt put his hand on Jolgeir's shoulder; Jolgeir bent forward until his forehead was resting against Tybalt's, his entire body shaking with merriment. I stared at them, baffled.

"Oh, Rand, your sense of humor remains your best quality! Never let it go, and don't let marriage change you. The temptation will be there, but I assure you, you and your lady will both enjoy matrimony more and for longer if you remain exactly as you are."

"You old cat," said Tybalt, and pounded Jolgeir on the back. "To speak to me of marriage so! How is your Libby? Still wild and full of mad ideas?"

"Older than she was, but lovelier every day than she was the day before." Jolgeir pulled away from Tybalt, gathering his dignity—such as it was—back around himself before turning to me. "My lady wife, who will not be joining us this day, is of the mortal persuasion. Thirty years she's been a bride, and three children she's borne me, and never have I questioned my good fortune. See to it that you and your husband-to-be feel the same."

"Do my best," I said. "So is there a rule that says Kings of Cats have to talk like they're in a BBC production, or am I just lucky with the ones that I run into?"

Tybalt snorted. Jolgeir looked amused. "Being here makes it easy to fall into the old ways of speech. Remember, the modern world is a moving target. For centuries, men of learning and sophistication spoke the way we do."

"In certain parts of the world, anyway," said Tybalt.

Jolgeir rolled his eyes. "Must you always make corrections?"

"It is my one true joy; begrudge me not such a simple thing," said Tybalt.

"I will begrudge you whatsoever I like on my own lands," said Jolgeir, and offered me his arm. "Walk with me, if you would, milady October? I will show you what lies beyond the briars, and you may tell me what it is that brought you hence. Rand has given me some of the story, but I always like to hear it from the source when possible."

"If you turn down the romance novel dialog a little bit, I'd be happy to," I said, and placed my hand on his arm as he roared laughter. Behind him, Tybalt nodded approvingly. I was doing the right thing, then: good. I hated to think what would happen if I acted wrong.

"As I was saying, the modern world is a moving target," said Jolgeir, recovering his composure and starting toward the thorn wall, tugging me along with him. "Once, modernity was measured in horses and carriages, then in steam trains, and now in cars. I have a station wagon. I bought it in 1984. It still runs like it was made yesterday, and the man I was in my youth would have seen it as impossible magic, too powerful for mortal hands to steer, much less build. Everything changes. I can talk like the men you see on the streets—I do, in my shop, although most of my younger patrons will tell you that I'm old-fashioned. They think I'm quaint."

"If only they knew," I said, smiling.

Jolgeir matched my smile with one of his own. "Precisely so."

We were still walking, and should have reached the thorns by now. I looked up, and was unsurprised to see that we were now in a tunnel of brambles. When I looked back, I could see the clearing behind us, still ringed on its far side by the original thorn wall. Tybalt walked behind us, seemingly relaxed, and looking pleased with how this whole encounter was going.

"So," I said, turning my attention back to Jolgeir. "You own a comic book store. That's an interesting choice."

"Why?" he asked. "Because I should have opened a rare book store, crumbling and cobwebbed, to frighten off anyone younger than the age I pretend to, which is so much younger than my own? Comic books appeal to children, and children understand the era they are born to. When the time comes for my current mortal face to die—and it will come, much as I might wish this time could last forever—I will understand the man I must manufacture as my next self all the better because of the children, and their comics. And besides, the X-Men offer many powerful life lessons to which even the eldest among us should attend."

"Uh, okay," I said. "I'll take your word for that."

Jolgeir was still laughing when we stepped out of the tunnel. There was the twist and stretch that I associated with transit inside knowes, and we were suddenly standing in an old, somewhat repurposed Chuck E. Cheese's. The stage was still there, although the animatronic animals had been cleared away. There was no throne. Instead, where it should have been, there was a burgundy leather armchair, complete with footrest. Dusty old picnic tables cluttered the room, some in their original positions, waiting for birthday parties that would never begin, while others had been pushed off to the side and piled into towers of furniture.

And then there were the cats. They lounged on the piled-up tables; they prowled the floor. A few had stretched out on the steps leading up to the stage, although none had set foot on the stage itself. They understood the limits of their freedom, and if they were anything like the Cait Sidhe Tybalt was responsible for, they appreciated those limits. Total freedom was terrifying. Boundaries made it controllable, and hence enjoyable again.

"If you will excuse me," said Jolgeir. He took his hand away from my arm and calmly walked up onto the stage, where he draped himself across the chair. His posture changed subtly, becoming regal without becoming formal. Before, we had been in the presence of Tybalt's old friend—and, I got the feeling, sometime rival. Now we were in the presence of a King of Cats, and we would do well to remember that.

"Your Majesty," said Tybalt, bowing.

I didn't bow. Instead, I dropped into the deepest curtsy I was capable of holding, bending my knee until it nearly brushed the floor and lowering my head so that I was bent virtually double. I stayed in that position, breathing as deeply and slowly as I could manage in order to distract myself from the slow burn starting in the muscles of my thighs.

Jolgeir whistled. It was a long, low sound. "You found a girl from the Divided Courts who would curtsy to a King of Cats. Again, Rand, I must salute you for the novelty of it all, even as I continue to question the sense of it. You may both rise. You have shown sufficient respect to amuse me, and that's really what this is about."

"That's what I always say. If you can't impress them or dazzle them, at least leave them laughing." I straightened up, feeling my thighs all but sigh in relief. "Your Majesty."

"Sir Daye," replied Jolgeir, with a small smirk. "You came to Silences hoping to meet one King, and here you've been so fortunate that you've met two! Are you overcome?"

"No, Sire. Just relieved. I came to Silences hoping to meet one King, and until this moment, I wasn't sure I was going to meet any."

Insulting Rhys to his Cait Sidhe contemporary's face was a calculated risk. Jolgeir ran a comic book store and had a mortal wife. Those things put him almost exactly opposed to Rhys, with his anti-changeling policies and his disturbingly ornate Court functions. If I was right about relations between the two men, I was making myself an ally. And if I was wrong . . . well, I've functioned in situations where everyone hated me before. It wasn't fun, but I didn't die, so I'm calling it a victory for my side.

Jolgeir looked at me thoughtfully for a long moment. Then he grinned, so wide that I could see both his incisors, along with a great white sweep of supporting teeth. "Oh, Rand, I *like* her. Are you implying that the great King Rhys is less of a King than I am?"

"Implying, no. Stating outright, yes. He's on the throne because a woman who had no right to make decisions about this Kingdom put him there. I'm here, in your territory, because my Queen sent me to prevent a war. Do I look like the kind of person who can just stroll in and prevent a war? Cause one by accident, maybe, but prevent? Not my strong suit. The fact that I worry him should be enough to prove that he's no true King." I shrugged. "Now here I am. It's an honor to be in your Court, by the way. I know the Court of Cats is private, and I'm grateful to be allowed to pass here."

"My wife and daughters pass here frequently," said Jolgeir. He turned his attention to Tybalt. "What of you? Do you find this King of the Divided Courts to be worthy of the name?"

"He is a mewling child playing at the monarchy, making demands he has no right to make and fussing like a kitten when denied," said Tybalt. "In all these regards, he is as so many of their Kings have been, across the centuries. It's difficult to look on him and see anything beyond the destiny they have graven for themselves. But my lady speaks true when she says his throne was granted to him by one who had no right to do the granting. It is possible a sea change is coming, one which will reorder the heavens and the earth, or at least the political structure of Portland."

"Mm," said Jolgeir. His eyes flicked back to me. "Forgive me if my question is rude, but you have human blood, do you not? I can see it in your lips, in the angle of your cheekbones and the way you hold your hands. It's dilute, but it's there."

"My father was human," I said. "I've never hidden it."

Jolgeir sat up straighter, making no effort to hide his bemusement. "You lie, lady, you lie; you aren't a human's child. You have far too little mortal in you to be a human's child."

"Nope. I don't lie. My father was as human as any man who's ever lived." He died for it, too, alone, thinking himself a widower who had buried his only child. I will never stop regretting that. "I told you my mother was Firstborn. Her children are Dóchas Sidhe. We're bloodworkers. For lack of a better explanation, we're hope chests that walk. I changed my own blood. It was necessary to save my life."

He sat up straighter still. "And that is the extent of your powers? To slide yourself back and forth along a scale from human to fae and back again, as you like?"

Just like that, I realized what I was being asked. I glanced to Tybalt, who wouldn't meet my eyes. He'd known this would happen when he brought me here, and he hadn't warned me, maybe because he was afraid I wouldn't agree to come, and maybe just because he, like everyone else in my life, was in the habit of keeping secrets that didn't need to be kept.

We'd have to talk about that later. For the moment,

there was a King of Cats who needed an answer. "No, Sire, that's not the extent of my powers," I said politely, focusing my attention back on Jolgeir. "If you're asking what I think you're asking, yes. I can adjust the balance of someone else's blood, if given their consent. I can pull the mortality out of a changeling—or I can make them fully mortal, and let them be human without needing to be killed."

"I have three daughters," he said. His voice dipped at the end, turning more serious than anything he had said since we walked into his store. "The eldest of them is twenty-eight. She's so beautiful. She looks so much like her mother."

"Have all three of them made the Choice?" I asked.

His nod was brief. "All three of them chose Faerie. Libby encouraged them, although she didn't know what the consequences would be if they chose the human world. She loves me. She's loved me since I was just silly old Joe at the library. How could I tell her I would have been forced to kill our babies if they had chosen to be like she was?"

He sounded so anguished that I almost forgot myself and approached the throne—a diplomatic misstep that would have been hard to recover from. But even my sympathy was mixed with rage. Oberon had created the hope chests to prevent situations like this one, and what had happened to them? They were locked up in treasuries and lost in private collections, and no one could use them for their intended purpose. Amandine could have filled some of that gap, but she'd chosen to hide instead, pretending to be Daoine Sidhe, while countless changelings died of old age or at the hands of their parents when they made the wrong Choice.

Not all Cait Sidhe offered their children the Choice. Those who did apparently offered it in all its aspects . . . even the fatal ones.

"You couldn't tell her," I said. "Yes, Sire. I can give

them the option. It's painful. It takes a lot out of me—and because of that, I'm afraid I can't promise to do anything before this war between the Mists and Silences has been averted. But once that's done, yes. I can let your girls Choose again, and whatever they decide, I can help them make it real."

"I've always thought my middle daughter could have been a Princess," said Jolgeir, collapsing backward in his seat and staring at me. "She's so strong, even with human blood in her veins. Take that away . . ."

"If she chooses to be fully fae, I'll help her," I said. "But not until we avert this war. Or win it, I suppose."

"Well." He looked to Tybalt. "My Court stands with yours. If this war can't be avoided, the Cait Sidhe of the Court of Whispering Cats will fight for the Mists, and we *will* win."

"Oh," I said. "Well. Um. Good."

We still might go to war. But I was beginning to feel like, if we did, we might stand a chance.

FIFTEEN

TYBALT AND I WERE nowhere near the comic book store when we left the Court of Cats. That was normal. I hoped Jolgeir at least had ended up back at his place of business, since otherwise Susie was going to be minding the front of the store for a long damn time.

"Stupid nonlinear space," I complained.

We were standing next to a bright pink storefront that smelled strongly of sugar. Tybalt nudged me onto a bench and vanished inside, returning a few minutes later with a bakery box as violently pink as the business that had produced it.

"Here," he said, pressing the box into my hands. "You should eat something before you yell at me. You'll be able to work up a better head of steam if you fuel yourself."

I eyed him sidelong before opening the box. It was full of donuts. That was normal. The donuts were covered in cereal, M&Ms, and in the case of one large maple bar, bacon. I blinked. "Tybalt?"

"Yes?"

"You know I'm mad at you, right?"

"Yes. I intend to apologize, but in this case, I had reasons for bringing you to my old friend without telling you how I believed the discussion would unspool. I—"

"Stop right there. I didn't ask you to start explaining yourself, I asked if you knew that I was mad."

Tybalt sighed. "Yes. I knew you would be angry."

"Okay. So did you take me to Willy Wonka's donut factory because you were hoping to distract me so much with laughter that I wouldn't yell at you?" I stabbed a finger at one of the donuts. "Captain Crunch, Tybalt. This donut is covered in Captain Crunch cereal."

"I admit it was a small hope of mine, that sugar might lessen your anger," said Tybalt. "But no, I did not expect to escape your wrath entire. Would not want to, in fact. That was a mean trick I pulled, and I am sorry."

I looked around. There were people, human people, strolling past with their own pink boxes, or sitting on the benches nearby, enjoying their donuts. A man was feeding a cruller to a large red macaw, which struck me as probably being unhealthy for the bird. No one was paying attention to us, and why should they? We had replaced our human disguises before we left the Court of Cats. Tybalt was still a handsome man, but his human form lacked the irresistible attraction of his true face, and I was just another brunette in tank top and jeans. We blended.

It was an odd feeling. I wasn't used to fitting in. Still, I kept my voice low as I leaned closer and said, "You know I would have agreed to help your friend anyway. Why did we need to go with the whole cloak-and-dagger routine? It wasn't necessary. It made me feel like you thought of me as something to use. Like a tool."

The stricken look that flooded his face was too real to have been forced, starting with his eyes and moving outward until every inch of him was washed in regret. "Oh, October. I'm so sorry. I didn't intend—I knew he would, given time, find his way to that topic. I knew what your answer would be. I also knew that, for him to take that answer as sincere, he had to reach it on his own, and I feared that if I were to prime you for meeting him, you would have done what you do best, and simply offered."

"Which would have been too blunt, and left him looking for the catch," I said slowly.

Tybalt nodded. "Yes. He's been here, in this political situation, for a long time. Longer than you or I can imagine—my response to such things has always been to leave, to find another place to be, but he has put down roots and done his best to thrive despite adversity. Such a thing makes a man pleasant to talk to, and wary of things which seem too good to be true."

I looked at Tybalt for a moment before reaching into the pink box and pulling out the maple-bacon bar. I offered him the box, as a peace offering, and he took out a chocolate cake donut crowned with a thick layer of Cocoa Puffs.

"I understand your reasoning, but I don't appreciate it," I said, putting the box next to me on the bench. "Please don't do that again, or if we're in a situation like this, where it's genuinely important that I react without prejudice, warn me somehow. Okay? That's enough to keep me from feeling like I'm being used."

"I will do my absolute best," said Tybalt. "Again, you have my deepest apologies."

"It's okay. We just have to keep doing better, that's all. Everything is about doing better." I took a bite of my donut, giving the crowd another look. Most of the people I'd noticed before had moved on, except for the man with the macaw, which was now holding the cruller in one claw and feeding itself. Still, I kept looking. Tybalt and I had been remarkably circumspect in our conversation, saying nothing that violated the provisions against revealing Faerie's existence, and yet I couldn't shake the feeling that something was wrong.

"What is it?" asked Tybalt.

"I don't know." I took a deep breath, but all I could

smell was sugar. The lingering taste of maple didn't help. "Look around. Try to be sort of casual about it. Just . . . tell me if anything seems off to you, okay?"

Tybalt nodded before leaning over to put an arm around me and kiss me theatrically on the cheek. Then he settled back on the bench, an expression of pure smugness spreading across his face. If I hadn't been close enough to see the worry in his eyes, I would have believed that he was the happiest man alive.

After a moment, he murmured, "By the door. There is a man, blue shirt, brown hair. He has walked past three times. Each time he pauses just long enough to see that we remain, and then moves on again. If he's not watching us, he's planning to mug us later."

"Let's hope for a mugging," I said, and shifted to rest my head against Tybalt's shoulder, pretending to take a bite from my maple bar as I watched the spot he'd indicated. People wandered past, some going inside, others escaping the lure of fried dough and sticky frosting. Almost a minute ticked by, long enough for me to start considering an actual bite of my donut, before the man Tybalt had described appeared.

He was average-looking, almost to the point of becoming unrealistic. Brown hair, brown eyes, tan skin, and clothes straight out of a Macy's ad—jeans, a polo shirt, and plain white tennis shoes. The smell of sugar was too strong to let me pick up any hints about his heritage, but now that I was looking, the faint glitter of his human disguise was impossible to ignore. He glanced our way, confirmed that we were still sitting there, and walked on.

"He's not of my kind," murmured Tybalt, voice close to my ear. "If he were, he would have come to announce himself to me. I have no authority here, but I am still a danger to those who would surprise me."

"Right," I replied, equally quietly. The man was continuing onward, apparently following a preset loop. "As soon as he turns that corner, we move. Got it?"

"Yes."

The man turned the corner. We moved.

Dropping the maple bar back into the pink box—which I regretted leaving, I really did, but we couldn't slow ourselves down with almost a dozen donuts, no matter how weird they were—I pushed myself off the bench. Tybalt rose at the same time, grabbing my hand, and together we took off across the little plaza and down the street, nearly knocking several bystanders over in our rush to get away. We weren't being subtle; if our observer wanted to ask where we'd gone, plenty of hands would be pointed in our direction.

That wasn't going to be a problem. We turned a corner, running onto an empty stretch of street, and Tybalt grabbed my hand. He didn't bother telling me what was going to happen next: I already knew, and had time to take a deep breath before the world dropped away and we were running through the dark. It only lasted for a few seconds. Then we were back in the mortal world, in a parking lot behind what looked like a large grocery store. Tybalt stopped, his heels skidding in the gravel. I ran on for another few feet, using my momentum to turn myself around and start scanning for signs that we had been followed.

The only signs of motion came from the crows picking at the grass on the edge of the pavement. There was no guarantee that they weren't working for King Rhys—living in Faerie means never knowing what is or is not spying on you—but they were far enough away that I was pretty sure they couldn't hear us.

"Don't-look-here, Tybalt, now," I said, voice tight. My fingers were itching to go for my knife. I didn't mind being watched while we were in the Court of Silences. I had expected that; it was part and parcel of being a diplomatic attaché to a Kingdom that didn't want me. But the fact that we were being followed out into Portland itself, and followed by people who could track us even after we had passed through the Court of Cats? That wasn't good. That showed a level of dedication to keeping me under surveillance that made me uncomfortable in ways I couldn't even put into words.

Tybalt nodded. He pressed his hands together, rattling off a quick line of what sounded like Middle English. The smell of pennyroyal and musk rose and burst around us as he separated his hands, reached over, and grabbed my wrist. "Keep hold of me," he said. "It works better when the spell doesn't need to labor across open ground."

I raised an eyebrow. "And there's nothing in that casting about wanting to minimize my chances to go off and get myself hurt?"

He rolled his shoulders in a shrug. "I admit your nearness is a convenient side benefit, but no. I wanted to make the spell as strong as possible. That meant accepting certain limitations."

"Okay." I stepped closer. He switched his grip on my wrist to something a little less awkward. "Where are we?"

"Half a mile from our last known location, give or take a bit. We're too far from the alley where we are meant to meet with the others, if that's the true core of your question. We'll need to take the Shadow Roads again." He frowned a bit as he spoke.

I gave him a sidelong look. "How much are you wearing yourself out? You're not a taxi service, Tybalt, and I don't want you hurting yourself just because you're trying to keep me safe. I'm harder to kill than you think I am."

"Having been at your deathbed twice, I tend to disagree."

"Having *seen you dead*, I don't think you get to claim the moral high ground here." I looked around again, and sighed. "All right. I have a solution. I don't think you're going to *like* it very much, and I don't much care."

Tybalt gave me a sidelong look. "What is this solution?"

"We're going to walk until we find a bus stop with a bus that's going in the right direction. Then, when the bus comes, we're going to get on behind whatever passengers are coming on or off, and we're going to make our way across Portland like ordinary people."

Tybalt blinked slowly, looking like he couldn't quite believe what he was hearing. "You want to take the *bus*," he said.

"Yup," I said. "I know, it's pedestrian and plebeian and lots of other things that start with the letter 'p,' but it also works. Buses are designed to get people from one place to another. And more, if Rhys sent whoever it is that's following us—and I think we can both agree that's what's going on here—then he's never going to dream we would take the *bus*."

Tybalt blinked at me again, even more slowly than before. Then, almost against his will, he began to smile.

"Very well," he said. "Take me to your bus."

The nearest bus stop was about a block away, on a corner where the pavement was cracked and the trees were less well-tended than the ones near the donut shop. I guessed that meant we'd been downtown before, and were now somewhere out near the fringes of the city. There was a map of the bus routes served by this stop, and one of them was definitely the one we wanted. That was good. There was no one at the bus stop. That was bad. I sighed, checked the direction of the bus we needed to take, and started walking again.

"Far be it from me to sound as if I am *eager* to 'catch the bus,' but where are we going?" asked Tybalt. "That was a bus stop. I saw it with my own two eyes."

"Then you also saw that we were the only people there," I said. "Buses don't stop everywhere along their route. They stop to pick people up, and they stop to let people off. Bus driver isn't going to be able to see us, remember? There's no guarantee anyone would *want* to get off at that stop, so we need to find a place where there's someone waiting. Hence the walking. We'll come to the next bus stop on the route within a few blocks."

Tybalt threw his free hand into the air, shooting a beseeching glance upward to the sky. I managed not to laugh, but it was a near thing, and I only made the effort because I knew he wasn't trying to be funny. "How do mortals function in a world grown so complex?" he demanded.

"One day at a time," I said. "Now come on."

The next bus stop was on a slightly nicer stretch of road, reinforcing my belief that we had wound up in a part of town that was, if not bad, at least a little bit neglected. There were people at this one, three of them, standing in the weary, not too close clump known to bus riders everywhere. Tybalt and I slipped into position behind them, careful to stay just far away enough that we didn't upset the delicate balance of the bus stop. The don't-look-here Tybalt had cast would keep people from noticing us, but it didn't render us invisible. Blending in mattered, and would make the burden on the spell lighter, which would help it to last longer.

According to the schedule, the bus was slated to arrive about eight minutes after we did. I pointed out the time to Tybalt, who nodded understanding. "See?" I whispered, keeping my voice low. "You're a natural."

I didn't need to bother. Bus riders are a rare breed, aware of their surroundings but also aware that they're about to share a vehicle with a bunch of strangers, vague acquaintances, and people they have no actual interest in knowing. As long as we kept our voices down and didn't seem inclined to murder anyone, we would have been semi-invisible to these folks even without the magic that made us that way.

It was nice, actually. I used to ride the San Francisco buses frequently, before I got a private parking spot and a boyfriend who could break the laws of linear space. I won't pretend it was my favorite thing in the world, but it was familiar. The Portland bus system doubtless had its own quirks and oddities—every bus system does—but it was still public transit, with all the little slings and arrows that such a thing is heir to. Call me weird, but it was relaxing to spend some time doing something so beautifully mundane.

The bus pulled up only three minutes after the sign said it was due. The waiting passengers pushed themselves forward, and we pushed forward with them, me hauling Tybalt by the hand. Our don't-look-here spell kept the driver from seeing us well enough to demand that we pay, but also kept him from closing the door on Tybalt's leg. He did flip the lever as soon as Tybalt was clear, so that the doors hissed closed dangerously close to his ankles, but that was only to be expected. On some level, the bus driver knew we were there, we were fare jumpers, and hence, we were the enemy.

I pulled Tybalt down the center aisle as the bus rumbled away from the curb, finding us an empty seat to snuggle into. I put him on the inside, by the window. "See the cord?" I murmured. "That tells the bus someone wants to get off. When you start seeing things you recognize, yank it, and the driver will know he needs to take the next stop."

"But we're invisible," he whispered back.

"Not to the bus," I said. "Trust me."

Tybalt nodded, looking like he wasn't sure about all this, and turned his attention to the window. Portland scrolled by outside, greener than its Californian equivalents, but otherwise similar, in the way of modern cities built on the West Coast, where the weather is milder and the chance of earthquakes is higher. It's a delicate balance that has defeated more architects than anyone can say, resulting in a lot of single-story homes that might as well have "please don't fall down" stenciled across them in electric yellow. But for all the similarities, there were differences as well: different sorts of gingerbread and decorative wainscoting on the houses, different sorts of quirky independent businesses sandwiched between the chain stores and the municipal buildings. If there was a Portland style, I couldn't recognize it well enough to describe it yet—and at the same time, I knew we weren't in San Francisco anymore.

We had been on the bus for about ten minutes when Tybalt pulled the cord, sending a long tone reverberating through the bus. He pulled it again immediately after. The tone was not repeated. Scowling, he pulled twice more before I managed to reach up and snag his arm.

"No," I hissed. "The bus knows. Come on."

I slid out of the seat, tugging him with me. He came reluctantly, eyeing me the whole time like he was sure that this was some sort of a trick. I didn't have the time to explain, and raising my voice enough to be heard over the hiss of the bus' brakes would have meant risking the spell that concealed us, so I didn't say anything; I just pulled him into the small safe haven of the bus' rear door, waiting for the vehicle to come to a full stop. There was already a woman standing there. As soon as the doors unlocked, she pushed them open, and we all but fell out of the bus behind her.

Pulling Tybalt out of the way before we could be trampled by the other commuters, I moved us to the edge of the sidewalk, out of the way. The idling bus engine was loud enough to cover my voice as I said softly, "Hold here. I want to be sure no one followed us."

Tybalt nodded. The bus pulled away, and I watched as our fellow riders moved off down the street, some doubling back to get to a destination a short ways behind them, others turning corners or just walking away. In a matter of seconds, they were all either gone or going, and we were alone.

The sidewalk wasn't deserted. I scanned the people

who remained in view, looking for any who seemed to be distorting the air or accompanied by unexplained glitter trails. Everyone I could see appeared to be human. I relaxed a little, turning back to Tybalt. "I think we're clear," I said. "Where to now?"

"This way," he said. He started walking, and I walked with him, allowing him to lead me down a side street to a small, tree-lined shopping promenade. It opened on a courtyard packed with food trucks. My stomach rumbled and he paused, smiling. "Hungry?"

"A little," I admitted. "Breakfast was a long time ago, and I didn't get to finish my donut."

"These kitchens on wheels are definitely safer than Rhys' private dining hall; we could stop, if you would like."

I shook my head. "I need to eat at the knowe. I basically skipped breakfast, and I'm supposed to be preventing a war, not insulting the King's hospitality so badly that he invades us twice as hard."

"If Arden did not want to risk being invaded, as you say, 'twice as hard,' she would have sent someone else." We emerged onto a stretch of street that I recognized. The alley where we were supposed to meet the others was right up ahead. I felt myself untense. Maybe we were going to make it back to King Rhys' Court without any serious damage done.

I should really learn to stop hoping. We stepped into the alley to find ourselves alone . . . but the faint smell of ashes and cotton candy hung in the air. May had been here recently. I stopped, bewildered, and took a deep breath. I could smell the faint, nearly indefinable strains of her heritage, mixed with an overlay of Daoine Sidhe. Fear gripped me in an almost physical hand, squeezing until I felt like all the air was being forced out of my lungs.

"Tybalt, drop the don't-look-here," I said, making no effort to keep my voice down. If May and Quentin were in the alley, I didn't want them to be surprised by our sudden appearance.

Tybalt nodded. He clapped his hands, and the spell burst around us, filling the air with the musk and pennyroyal scent of his magic. Not for the first time, I wished that Quentin shared my sensitivity for magical signatures. He could pick up the broad strokes, but there was no guarantee he'd be able to smell the spell from wherever he was and know that we had arrived.

"Quentin?" I called, taking a step forward. "May? Are either of you here? It's Toby and Tybalt. You can come out now."

There was a scuffling noise from behind the dumpster. I took another step forward.

"I'm sorry we're a little late; we had to take the bus in order to get here, and that slowed us down . . ."

Silence. Then Quentin's face peeked around the dumpster's corner, eyes narrowed warily. "How do you take your coffee?" he demanded.

"I stopped drinking coffee after I got hit with an evil pie," I said. "Before that, I took it however I could get it. The more the merrier. Look, do you want a blood sample? That'll confirm my identity faster than any quiz you can give me, and maybe then you can explain why you're hiding behind a dumpster instead of greeting me like a normal person." I couldn't keep the edge from my voice as I reached the end of my sentence. Something was terribly wrong. Quentin had been my squire long enough to have learned that sometimes bravery gets you killed, but he didn't hide for no reason. If I didn't encourage senseless bravery, I didn't encourage senseless cowardice either.

"I, too, am happy to give you a taste of my blood, if it means you will be able to relax yourself and tell us what has happened," said Tybalt. He didn't step forward, recognizing that Quentin wouldn't find his presence as comforting as I did.

Quentin closed his eyes, an expression of relief washing across his face, only to be quickly replaced by bleakness. "Come over here," he said, and withdrew behind the dumpster again.

That was when I knew. There was only one reason he could be acting like this, only one thing that could have happened that would explain his skittishness and his sorrow. So I knew, but I still didn't admit it to myself: not until I had stepped around the dumpster and seen with my own eyes, which had lied to me in the past, when they'd had good enough reason. They weren't lying to me now.

May, still draped in the hazy outline of her human disguise, although it was beginning to fray around the edges, was propped against the alley wall like a forgotten toy, limp and unmoving. The arrow protruding from her left shoulder formed a tight seal against the skin: there wasn't even any blood on her shirt, and wouldn't be until someone pulled that arrow out. Her eyes were closed, and her chin rested comfortably against her chest. She looked like she had just stopped to take a nap, pausing for a moment before she resumed racing through her life.

It was really a pity that the nap was going to last for a hundred years.

My hand was clapped tightly over my mouth. I didn't remember putting it there, or putting my other hand against the dumpster for balance. All I could see was my Fetch, my sister, lying on the ground in an enchanted slumber that no true love's kiss or glass coffin could fix.

"Oh, sweet Oberon," I said, my voice devoid of strength. "What happened?" Night-haunts were immune to elf-shot. May had even said so.

Apparently, Fetches weren't.

"I don't know," said Quentin. He was still standing in the shadow of the dumpster. He looked younger than he had when we left King Rhys' Court, like all his strength and confidence had been ripped away when the arrow entered May's flesh. I knew I should put my arms around him, that I should pull him to me and tell him that I was going to find a way to fix this, but I couldn't make myself move. All I could do was stare at May, so pale and small and unmoving.

My Fetch was *never* unmoving. Even when she slept, she tossed and turned and squirmed, like she was secretly a hurricane forced into a girl-body and told to exist as best she could among people who had no idea what it meant to secretly be a weather pattern. But now, thanks to the elf-shot in her shoulder, she could no more move her body than she could turn back into a night-haunt and fly away on the wings she had traded for solidity and size. She had become a Fetch because I was her hero, and because she wanted to warn me that death was coming. Somehow that single, selfless choice had led us here, to this alley, and to silence.

"October." Tybalt's voice was low. "We cannot stay here. We must move."

"How can we get her back to our room?" I lowered my hand, turning to look at him. "She can't hold her breath. You have to be awake to hold your breath. I don't even know how to get into the knowe from this side."

"Does it matter if she holds her breath?" Quentin's question was hesitant. I turned to look at him. He bit his lip before saying, "She can't . . . I mean, she can't suffocate, right? She can't die that way. She can't die at all. So does it matter if she holds her breath?"

"Not if I go quickly. I will take her first, and return for the two of you, if you can hold yourselves safe that long." Tybalt spoke slowly, like every word was being ripped out of him. In a way, I suppose they were. He didn't like leaving me alone when there was any chance I might be in danger, and this was sort of the definition of a bad situation. And at the same time, if he tried to run the Shadow Roads with May in his arms and the two of us holding onto his shirt, he ran the risk of losing us.

"Go," I said. "We'll be here."

Tybalt nodded once before walking over and scooping May into his arms. She dangled limp, with no muscular resistance or rigor to keep her in place. As I watched, he gently lifted her head, bracing it against his chest to keep from hurting her. Then the shadows against the alley wall parted like a curtain, and he stepped through and was gone.

I frowned. Something was wrong—apart from the obvious, which was very wrong, and almost enough to keep me from noticing subtleties. I crouched, looking at the place where May's body had been propped. There were no other arrows. Either our archer had managed to catch her on the first shot, or whoever it was had been careful to clean up after themselves. We still had an arrow, since there was one embedded in my Fetch's arm, but it would have lost much of its potency when its poison rubbed off into her blood. Tracking the person who mixed the spell would be easier with an arrow that hadn't been used.

There were no footprints, either. The dryness I had been so happy about when Quentin fell in the alley was a problem now. At least mud and wet ground would have increased the odds of someone leaving a trace of themselves behind.

"Toby?" Quentin's voice was hesitant, like he was afraid of interrupting me. "Did you find something?"

"Not yet," I said. I had to struggle not to snap at him, but he didn't deserve that. He was the one who had found her lying there—I paused, turning to look at him. "Why didn't you call me when you found her? I had my cellphone."

"If someone was able to track May back to this alley and put an arrow in her, they had to have been following us," he said. "I didn't want to bring you back here if it meant they might get you, too."

"That was brave and stupid," I said. "You should have hidden yourself and called me. Next time, you call me, understand? You're my squire. It's my job to protect you, not the other way around."

"I thought we protected each other," he said, in a very small voice.

I thawed, just a little. "We do, honey. But sometimes you have to remember that it's my job to protect you. It's basically the most important thing a knight does for their squire. We teach you how to be better knights, sure, but that doesn't matter if you're dead." I turned back to the alley wall. Something was wrong with this picture, something apart from the obvious. It was gnawing at me, biting down with sharp little teeth and refusing to let me go.

It was almost hard to imagine how carefree we'd been when we were first all together in this alley. Tybalt and I were going to meet his friend, Quentin was going to the bookstore, and May was going to—

"The laundry." I straightened up, feeling as if I had just been electrified. "She didn't have the laundry bag when Tybalt picked her up, and it's not here. Did she leave it at the dry cleaner's? Do you know which dry cleaner's she went to?"

"They're right up the street," said Quentin.

"Do you have the name?" I pulled out my phone. When he blinked, I said, "If I send you to check and stay here, I feel like a coward. If I go to check and leave you here, Tybalt loses his shit when he gets back to find me gone. Neither of these is a good thing. So I'm going to pretend I'm a normal person, and *call* them."

"I . . . that makes really good sense," he said. "Sunshine Cleaners, on West Burnside."

"Got it." I dialed information, and when the polite, faintly robotic voice of the computer-generated "operator" picked up, I gave the address. Thirty seconds later, the phone was calling the cleaner's for me. Sometimes I really do feel like we're living in the future, and just haven't fully accepted everything that means.

"Sunshine Cleaners, we put the sun back in your shirts," said a voice that clearly felt it had better things to do with its time than answer phone calls, even if it was being paid to pick up the phone.

"Hi, this is October Daye. My sister, May, was supposed to drop off some laundry for me a few hours ago, and I was just wondering if you were able to get the stains out of my dress? I really love that dress." I tried to match the voice's disinterest with earnest need-to-know. Standing in the alley where my Fetch had been elf-shot and pretending that the most important thing in my world was laundry.

"Please hold." There was a clunk as the phone was set down. I heard rustling. Then the phone was picked up again, and the same bored voice said, "No one named after a month has dropped anything off today. Either your sister sucks at doing her chores, or you need to call another cleaner. Have a nice day."

The connection went dead. I lowered my phone, turning to look at Quentin. "She didn't drop off the laundry, and she's been elf-shot," I said. "You know what this means?"

"Yeah," he said, looking miserable. "King Rhys has an awful lot of your blood, and May's going to be asleep for a hundred years. Toby, what are we going to *do?*"

I looked at him, and I didn't have an answer.

SIXTEEN

WE EMERGED FROM THE Shadow Roads into the master bedroom of the diplomatic suite. May was already stretched out on the bed. Spike was curled on her chest, thorns flat with distress. Walther was standing next to her, crouching as he trimmed the ends of her hair into a small bowl. He stopped and straightened when he heard my butt hit the floor. Spike made a whining sound, but didn't move.

This time it was Quentin who managed to keep his balance, largely by grabbing hold of the bedpost and hanging on for dear life. Only Tybalt—winded and wheezing—remained upright, his baleful glare going to Walther as the only moving target in the room.

Walther was unmoved. "Good, you're back," he said. "I need you to come help me extract this arrow."

"Rhys sent people after us into the city, and they got the laundry, which means they have a *lot* of my blood," I replied. "What can they do with it?"

"Whatever they want," said Walther. "Now come help me. We have too many emergencies to deal with them all at the same time, and I can't start trying to provide May with medical treatment until I have the arrow out."

I picked myself up from the floor. "I hate this Kingdom," I announced. "I hate everything about it. There is nothing in Silences that I do not hate."

"Noted, and under the circumstances, not offended," said Walther. He handed me a piece of red leather. "Wrap this around the shaft and push as hard as you can. The idea is to force the arrow out through the back of her shoulder, not yank it toward us. That could break her collarbone, and she's going to have enough problems without adding broken bones to the mix."

I narrowed my eyes at him, even as I followed his instructions. "You're calm."

"I'm furious, and I'm scared out of my mind," said Walther. "May's my friend. Don't mistake my calm for anything other than anger, and the need to focus."

"Got it." I pushed down. The arrow slid through her flesh with sickening ease. I could feel it break the skin on the other side. I stopped pushing. "Now what?"

"Let go." Walther waited until my hands were clear. Then he reached over, shifted the leather up slightly, and twisted until the remaining shaft snapped in two, leaving the part with the fletching in his hand. He offered it to me. "I'm assuming you'll want to confront the King about shooting her. This proves the elf-shot came from his armory."

"I know how to read arrows," I said. "Still, I appreciate it. This is probably better than carrying the whole arrow into the presence of the King." Angry as I was, I didn't want to give him an excuse to try and arrest me again—and I knew that the false Queen would be more than happy to encourage him to do it. She'd hated me even before I took her crown away. I couldn't imagine how much she had to hate me now.

Then again, maybe I didn't need to. I watched Walther lift Spike off of May's chest. The rose goblin whined as it slunk off to the side, thorns rattling. Walther lifted her halfway into a sitting position before he reached around with his leather washcloth, wrapping it around the point of the arrow. It came free of her flesh with a wet sucking sound that turned my stomach. He placed the arrow on the nightstand, still wrapped in red leather, and eased May gently back down to the bed. Spike immediately leaped back onto her chest.

"I'll wrap and bandage her shoulder, and I have some herbs that will help to prevent infection," he said.

"What about the antidotes you were working on?" I asked. May wasn't moving. I felt like I couldn't breathe. I heard Tybalt move up behind me, but he didn't say anything or put his hands on me, and for the first time, I was grateful for his restraint. If he tried to offer comfort, I would break, and then I wouldn't be any good to anybody.

"I'm still working on them." Walther turned to look at me, expression grave. "I have five different rose strains that fit your description. One of them might be the answer, or none of them might be. I'm not going to stop, but I can't make it happen any faster."

"Try." I stood, looking at the broken arrow shaft in my hand. "We came here to prevent a war, not to get picked off one by one by an asshole with an ax to grind. I need to talk to the King."

"I will come with you," said Tybalt.

"No." The word was out before I was even fully aware that I was thinking it. I turned to find Tybalt staring at me. "I want you there. I want you there more than *anything*. But you can't be. Having the monarch of a political structure completely outside our own standing next to me is actually a political weakness. It implies that I can't take care of myself. I'm taking Quentin, because he reinforces my place in this political structure, and because I want witnesses. But I can't take you. I'm sorry."

Tybalt looked at me flatly for several seconds. Then, seemingly against his will, he smiled. It wasn't a big thing: his lips barely moved, and while the smile touched his eyes, they remained sad, too dark with all the troubles of the past few days to ever lighten. "You *are* learning, and I can't fault you for that," he said. "If anything, it will keep you with me longer. But be careful, and don't be afraid to run. Do you understand? If your safety is threatened, run. I refuse to wait a hundred years to be married."

"You won't have to," I said. I looked down at my tank top and jeans, and shook my head. Rhys no longer got to make me dress up for him, and if the false Queen wanted to transform my clothes again, she could go right ahead. Every spell she cast sapped a little of her power. Let her exhaust herself on things that didn't matter.

But only on the things that didn't matter. I shrugged out of my leather jacket, draping it over the foot of the bed. "I'll be back. Quentin, you're with me."

I didn't wait to see what Tybalt would say to that. I just turned and stalked toward the exit, Quentin dogging my heels like he was afraid letting me out of his sight for a second would mean letting me out of his sight forever. I didn't blame him for feeling that way. I sort of shared the sentiment.

Leaving Tybalt behind to protect Walther and strengthen my own position might have been the smart thing to do, but as we stalked along the empty, echoing halls, I felt the hairs on the back of my neck rising and my muscles tensing, every inch of me preparing for an attack. There was a time when all my grand confrontations involved me and me alone. That time was in the past. I had grown accustomed to having backup when I went to bait my metaphorical dragons, people who would fight with me, rather than against me. I still had Quentin, but that was almost worse, because even if he tried to jump between me and someone's sword, I wouldn't let him. I could *never* let him. He was my squire. He was my friend. He was my semi-adopted son, and I loved him too much to be the cause of his suffering.

Almost as if he could read my thoughts, Quentin said quietly, "You can order me to go back if you want, but I'm not going to listen." I shot him a surprised look. He shook his head. "I know you. This is about where you start realizing you left your big guns behind, and start thinking I'd be better off if I was somewhere safer. That usually means you're forgetting that I'm your squire."

"I never forget that," I protested.

"No, you never forget that you're my knight, and that it's your responsibility to protect me and stuff," said Quentin. "But me being your squire means it's also *my* responsibility to protect *you*. I'll never be a knight if I let you run off and get yourself killed without at least *trying* to keep you in one piece."

"I'm hard to kill," I said.

"So am I," said Quentin, in a voice that made it clear he didn't want to argue about this anymore.

I still considered it. Getting the Crown Prince of the Westlands elf-shot because I didn't want to talk to the King of Silences alone struck me as a bad plan. At the same time, Quentin's parents had known the risks when they had agreed to let him try for his knighthood—something that wasn't required for him to become King one day. And they did have a backup heir if I got this one put to sleep for a century.

"I hate my life sometimes," I muttered, and kept walking.

The doors to the receiving room were closed, flanked by two guards in the livery of Silences. They moved to block me as I started for the door. I marched straight up to the closer of them, making no effort whatsoever to conceal my fury.

"You will *not* fuck with me right now, do you understand?" I snapped. "I am here as a diplomatic emissary, and you are going to start respecting that title if I have to punch every single one of you assholes in the throat. Now I am *going* to talk to your King, and he is *going* to give me some answers, or I'm going back to Arden and kick-starting this war all by myself. Do I make myself perfectly clear?"

The guards stared at me. Quentin smirked.

"She's using human profanity," he said. "She learned that from her close personal friend, the Luidaeg. Just in case you were wondering if you needed to be concerned right now. I would be, if she was talking to me like that."

The guards exchanged a look. Then they stepped back, allowing me open access to the doors. I paused, looking at them. "You should get out of here, you know. Things are about to get ugly." Before they could react, I shoved the doors open and marched inside, Quentin once again at my heels.

There were people in the receiving room, men and women dressed for Court and milling around the edges. Going by the time, they were probably getting ready for dinner. Meals seemed to be the focus of all the action around here, maybe because there was nothing else anyone could do that didn't run the risk of the King stepping in with an elf-shot arrow and an admonition about bad behavior. Some of those same people gasped when they saw me, pointing at my outlandish human world attire and covering their mouths like they had never seen anything more shocking in their lives. Quentin, who was dressed similarly, walked beside me with his head held up, every inch the prince he had been born to be. If their stares concerned him, he didn't show it.

I couldn't have cared less about the petty concerns of a bunch of fops, courtiers, and political leeches. All my attention was on the man at the head of the room, King Rhys, sitting on his throne and smirking—yes, *smirking*—as he watched me approach. The seat reserved for the false Queen was currently empty, which explained how we were able to make it all the way to the foot of the dais without someone turning my jeans into a ball gown.

Rhys composed his expression as we drew closer, but it was a hollow gesture: he knew we had seen his true face, and he didn't care. We were of no more concern to him than the rose goblins in his gardens, and he wanted us to know it.

Oh, I knew it. And I was going to make him pay for it. I held up the broken arrow, showing him the feathers.

"Does the hospitality of your halls always extend to pursuing visitors into the streets of Portland—into the *mortal world*—and leaving them in alleyways with elf-shot inches from their hearts? Because where I come from, that is neither showing respect to your guests nor to the rules which keep us safely hidden." My voice was cold as ice, and I was actually proud of myself for that: until I'd started speaking, I'd been afraid that I would scream. Raising my voice to the King of Silences might be the last thing I'd do for a hundred years.

"I assume you refer to your 'lady's maid,' the Fetch," said King Rhys. His voice was calm, even reasonable, like he was negotiating side dishes for the meal to come. "You did not inform me when you arrived in my lands that you traveled with an oddity never before seen in Faerie. A Fetch with no living tether? It seemed impossible to me. But my lady insisted that this woman who accompanied you was no changeling, no distaff sister; that she was, instead, something entirely different and hence potentially dangerous."

"May *is* my sister, named and accepted by the First-born of my line," I said. It was stretching the truth a bit, but not so much as to break it. "The fact that she started out as my Fetch is irrelevant. In what world is an elf-shot arrow to the body a part of proper hospitality? You break the laws that we all live by, and you do it without remorse."

"I broke no laws," said Rhys. He waved his hand carelessly, as if he was brushing away my petty, uninformed concerned. "Portland is my city, the crown jewel of my

Kingdom, even as San Francisco is under my lady's right and proper rule. I am allowed—no, I am *required*—to protect it as I do my own lands, my own halls. When my guard saw a strange woman carrying a mysterious bag in a dark alley, they acted according to their orders, and they subdued her before she could do any damages. Imagine my surprise when they came back to me and reported that they had silenced your maidservant."

"Oh, I'm imagining it," I said darkly. "This is an act of aggression during a time when we are supposedly under your protection. As to the bag she carried, I'd like it back, please."

"Is it really an act of aggression?" He leaned forward. "She walked my streets under a mask that hid her true face, after failing to divulge her nature upon her arrival. She carried such contraband as could fuel an army of alchemists. Is this an act of aggression on my part, or an act of treason on hers? Be glad I am an honorable man, Sir Daye, or I could have the lot of you arrested—and this time, there would be no argument to free you from my chains." He didn't mention my laundry.

"*Everyone* fae wears a mask when they go out into the mortal world," I said, through gritted teeth. "If you don't, you run the risk of attracting human aggression. She's *not* plotting treason against the crown. Not yours. Not anyone's."

"We'll ask her, when she wakes up," said Rhys. "If you would like to have her kept here, to prevent the need to set up a room for her slumbers, we would be glad to discuss this with you. We have well-established bedding and care for our sleepers."

I stiffened, mouth opening as I prepared to rip into him for his treatment of those "sleepers." Then I stopped.

We only knew about his harvesting alchemical supplies from the sleeping members of the royal family because Marlis had told us. Marlis would never have said anything if Walther hadn't broken the spell of obedience that had been placed on her. If I said *anything* to indicate that I knew what he was doing to them, I would be outing Marlis as free of his control, and more, I would be revealing an actual act of treason. If he was willing to interpret carrying my laundry as hostile alchemy, how would he take Walther using alchemy to free his sister from enspellment?

My mouth was already open: I had to say something. "What did you do with my laundry?"

"Oh, is that what the Fetch was carrying? It has been destroyed. We don't allow dangerous alchemical materials to be left lying around where anyone could get to them." Rhys looked at me, challenging me to call him a liar.

He *was* a liar. I knew that, as sure as I knew that I couldn't prove it. There was no way he'd been handed a bag of my blood and decided that it should just be thrown away—not when he'd been so eager to get his hands on it. Maybe it would be better straight from the source, but that didn't make my blood-soaked clothing worthless.

"I see," I said. I looked at him. He looked back, utterly calm. The bastard was practically smirking, he was so delighted to have the upper hand. And there was nothing I could do about it. "I will see to my own people's comfort, and my sister *will* be returning to the Mists with us when this is done. If you will excuse me, I must prepare my remaining retinue for dinner."

"You *will* tell me before you venture back into the city, will you not, Sir Daye?" Rhys' voice was mild, but not so mild that I couldn't recognize the command it contained. "I would hate for this to happen again. Your King of Cats, of course, is free to come and go as he wishes—I wouldn't want to restrict another monarch in his movements—but it's safer for the rest of you if you make sure I am aware of your movements."

"Yes, Sire," I said. I bowed, as shallowly as I could without giving offense. "May we go?"

"Yes," said Rhys. This time, he didn't bother hiding his smile. He had won. He knew it, and so did I.

I turned, Quentin close behind me, and left the receiving room as quickly as I dared without seeming to run from the presence of a sitting King. The false Queen did not reappear. The courtiers tittered and pointed after us, their laughter following our exit, until the doors had slammed on our heels and we were alone in the hallway. Mostly alone: Rhys' men were still there, flanking the door and watching us with narrow, wary eyes.

"Come on," I said, unable to stem the growing feeling of dread in my stomach. "Let's go."

"Go where?" asked Quentin.

I had to force my next words out. Each one was a rock against my teeth. "We have to get ready for dinner." *I'm sorry, May,* I thought. *We still have to play his game. I'm so sorry.*

Quentin looked at me and nodded. Together, we walked back down the hall toward the stairs that would take us to our room. We were in deep trouble, and getting deeper all the time—and, Oberon help me, I had no idea how I was going to get us out of this one.

I had no idea at all.

SEVENTEEN

WITHOUT MAY, GETTING ME ready for dinner was a much simpler, much less elegant process. I pulled a dress from the wardrobe, checked to make sure it didn't have any visible bloodstains, and retreated to the bathroom to put it on. Tybalt had seen me naked often enough not to care, but I didn't feel like stripping down in front of Walther and Quentin. I emerged from the bathroom as Quentin was vanishing into his own room to put a clean vest on, and blinked at the sight of Tybalt, already in a clean jerkin, shirt, and black leather trousers, sitting on the bed next to May's unmoving form.

"How the *hell* did you get changed faster than me?" I demanded. "Those pants look painted on."

"I will never reveal my secrets, save to remind you that I have been an actor in my day, and sometimes the turns between scenes are very tight." Tybalt's voice was forcedly light, like he was trying to sound like his old, unconcerned self.

"Right." I walked over to where he was sitting and leaned over to place a kiss on the top of his head, between the black stripes that marked his otherwise brown hair. "Walther, what's the situation with you? Are you coming to dinner?"

He shook his head. "No. I figure most of Rhys' men will be there, so I'm going to sneak out to see Aunt Ceres, see if she can't help me get those roses. Once I can start testing them against the elf-shot that was used on May, we'll be able to find out pretty quickly whether or not I'm going to be able to come up with a counter."

"You will," I said. "I know you will." I wasn't as sure as I was trying to sound. I couldn't imagine a world where Walther failed. May was . . .

May was my sister. She was a part of our family, and there was no way we were going to leave her asleep for the next hundred years. Even if I could justify it to myself, there was no way I could explain the situation to Jazz. "Sorry I took your girlfriend off and got her elf-shot" wasn't a conversation I had ever wanted to have.

"Here's hoping," said Walther. He leaned back and offered me a wry smile. "You look lovely. Finally, we know what it takes to get you into a dress several times in a row."

"This is just reinforcing my belief that dresses are a form of torture," I said flatly. I was wearing the silver spider-silk gown that I had previously worn to Arden's Yule Ball, back before there had been any whisper of the possibility of war. That hadn't been a perfect night—they so rarely were—but it had been a better one than this.

"It is difficult to believe we've been here for such a short period of time," said Tybalt. He slid off the bed, offering me his arm. I took it automatically, moving more on autopilot than anything else. He smiled, just a little. "Indeed, if we can bring about a kingdom's downfall in less than a week, I feel sure Arden will give you some sort of reward."

"Yeah, like a plane ticket to someplace really far away from the Mists," said Quentin, emerging from his room. "Maybe a nice tropical island."

"With our luck, the nice tropical island would be filled with dinosaurs," I said dryly.

"Still less annoying than what we're dealing with here," said Quentin.

"Sad but true." I paused, pulling my hand away from Tybalt's arm. "We need to walk to the dining room. Arriving through the shadows makes us look too dependent on Tybalt to do everything for us."

"Twice you reject me, in quick succession," said Tybalt. "Truly, my heart is broken."

"Don't break so fast. I need you to do me a favor."

Tybalt raised an eyebrow. "Do tell."

"The route from here to the dining room is pretty straightforward. Quentin and I aren't going to get lost if we start walking on our own. Can you take Walther to Ceres? It's not that I don't trust you to sneak out, Walther," I hastened to add. "It's that Rhys has eyes everywhere, and I'd rather be safe than sorry right now."

Walther nodded. "That's actually a good idea. We'll have to leave May here, but if Tybalt wards the door from the outside, opening it becomes an act of aggression against the Court of Cats. I think we can trust Rhys not to be that stupid—yet. He may get worse once he's backed into a corner."

"So we make sure we don't do that until we're ready to go in for the kill," I said, as reasonably as I could manage.

Tybalt sighed. "You are bound and determined to get yourselves killed. Yes, I will take Walther to his aunt, but only if you promise to be careful in walking out without my company to protect you. If you reach the dining hall before I return, you must not go in. That is what I will ask of you, in exchange for my forbearance in this matter. Are we in agreement?"

"Yes, we are," I said. "I doubt we'll beat you there, but if we do, we'll wait."

"I am a man beset by devils of my own making,"

grumbled Tybalt. "Well, Sir Alchemist? Are you ready to call upon your aunt and change the world? Because I am ready to have this errand set and done."

"Coming," said Walther. He grabbed his valise as he moved to stand next to Tybalt. "All you have to do is get me to the clearing."

"Let's get out of here so Tybalt can ward the door." I leaned up, kissed Tybalt on the cheek, and started for the exit. Quentin followed. I only looked back once, my eyes meeting Tybalt's for a brief, painful moment. He didn't like letting me go alone: that much was obvious to anyone who knew either of us. The fact that he was allowing me to walk away without him for backup twice in one day said more about the direness of our situation than anything else.

May had been elf-shot. Walther was being watched for signs of treason. We couldn't run back to the Mists, or war would follow—and now that I'd seen the way Rhys treated his changeling subjects and responded to any possible threat to his power, I knew the war would be brutal beyond imagining. Even if we rallied every possible ally to our side, called in the Undersea and the Court of Cats and Kingdoms both near and far, people would die. Elf-shot would rain down from the heavens, and there would be no escaping the carnage.

Quentin offered me his arm as we left our temporary quarters, dressed for court, with our vials of countercharm tucked into our clothes. He was shaking a little, his nerves getting the best of him. I slid my right hand into position, using my left to gather my skirt enough to make walking easier. Doing this revealed my tennis shoes. Quentin glanced at them, blinked, and then snorted.

"Really?" he asked. "You can't even wear heels when your life is on the line?"

"I can barely walk in heels," I said reasonably. "I certainly can't run in heels. Given a choice between shoes no one can see, but that don't leave me at risk of a broken ankle, or tiny torture devices strapped to my feet, I'll go with sneakers every time."

"Your mom didn't do you any favors when she skimped on the early etiquette training," he said.

"No, no, she did not," I agreed. "But on the plus side, if I were a more polite person, I wouldn't be able to associate with most of my friends."

Quentin snorted, but didn't say anything. We were well past the safe zone now; we had to assume Rhys was listening to everything we said, and watching everything we did, waiting for one of us to show weakness. It was an uneasy, awkward way to exist, and I had to wonder how his people could bear to live this way. I would have expected a lot more of them to follow the trail blazed by Walther and Lowri. Then again, maybe it had already been too late by the time most of them realized how bad it was getting. There were loyalty potions in the water, and no one was going anywhere without consent of the King.

It was a good way to run a Kingdom without conflict or risk of political upheaval. How could anyone challenge your leadership when they were no longer capable of thinking for themselves?

"Ever notice how the tenser Tybalt is, the more he sounds like he just escaped from a Jane Austen novel?" asked Quentin.

"How many Jane Austen novels have you read?" I asked.

Quentin shrugged. "A few. Enough. All of them."

"Got it. Yes, I've noticed. I think it's endearing. Although it can get a little difficult to understand him sometimes. If you wind him up far enough, he stops making any sense at all." I slanted a tight smile toward Quentin. "Wait for the wedding. I plan to get him so freaked out that he sounds like a Royal Shakespeare Company production of *Emma*."

Quentin snorted again.

People began appearing in the halls around us as we drew closer to the dining hall. I kept my face turned forward but stole glances at them out of the corners of my eyes, trying to get an idea of what we were walking into. My ball gown would have been too much for a dinner at Shadowed Hills or in Arden's Court, but here, I fit right in. Some of the women were wearing dresses infinitely more complicated than mine. Their outfits were made of feathers, stitched-together moth's wings, snakeskins, and other, stranger things. I saw three separate women in gowns made of rose petals held together with tiny loops of silver wire, like floral chain mail. Several of the men were wearing vests of the same manufacture, making me suspect that this was a local fashion brought on by idleness and access to too many rose goblins. It was also, in an odd way, an insult to Ceres: no matter how hard she worked to grow her gardens, they would be decimated over and over again by courtiers looking for a new outfit.

"Wow," muttered Quentin, as a man walked by wearing a tailcoat that appeared to have been made entirely from evergreen boughs. "How does he get that to lay flat?"

"Don't know, don't want to know, not going to ask," I said, still watching the crowd.

There was a homogeny to them that was even more unnerving than their attire. There were no changelings, and more, there were no visible mixed-bloods; no Centaurs with feathers in their hair, or Glastigs with white hair inherited from their Coblynau grandparents. Everyone in sight was pureblooded, and most of them were either Tuatha de Dannan or Tylwyth Teg. There were a few Daoine Sidhe scattered through the crowd, and seeing them made me realize what else was wrong: none of them had animal features. There were no Satyrs, Hinds, Fauns, or Huldra in the crowd. There weren't even any Cornish Pixies or Harpies. Everyone fit the same basic mold of tall, bipedal, and pretty.

It was weird, it was disturbing, and it made me wonder whether Lowri hadn't been *allowed* to leave. Maybe all the part-animal fae in Silences had been "allowed" to leave, possibly with encouragement from their King. "We need to see those bodies," I said, very softly.

Quentin shot me a startled look, followed by a small nod. Even if he didn't know what I was talking about, he was willing to go along with it. I appreciated that. He was a good squire, and he deserved better than me.

There was a soft rushing sound beside me, like air being displaced, accompanied by the faint scent of musk and pennyroyal. I let go of Quentin's arm and reached calmly out to my other side. As expected, Tybalt's arm was right there, ready for my hand.

"All is well?" I asked.

"I don't believe that statement can apply to our current situation, but my errands have been run, and I have nothing more to do apart from accompanying you to our repast," said Tybalt.

At the word "repast," Quentin snorted for a third time. It was starting to become a habit.

Tybalt blinked, looking around me to Quentin, who was once again staring innocently forward. I offered him a sunny smile. Tybalt shook his head, and turned his attention to the hall.

It was a good thing, too: as we got closer to the dining room, the crowd grew even denser, until it seemed like everyone in Silences was there with us. Despite that, there weren't *that* many people present—a quick count gave me somewhere between fifty and sixty warm bodies. That was a lot for a dinner party, but for a Kingdom that was pulling out all the stops to impress a visiting diplomatic detachment? It was about the same size crowd that Arden could have scraped up on short notice, and while she had an established Kingdom, she was severely understaffed where her actual Court was concerned. Once again, I found myself wondering just how small Rhys' circles really were.

Then again, if he was winnowing people as severely as he seemed to be, it probably shouldn't have been that much of a surprise. If anything, the surprise was that he still had this many people he was willing to allow inside his knowe.

"Be alert," hissed Tybalt, next to my ear.

"Way ahead of you," I murmured, and stepped into the dining hall.

The layout was very similar to the one from lunch, with long tables set up at the center of the hall in a neat square. No benches this time; instead, there were individual chairs, making it easier for the women to sit in their elaborate gowns, some of which could have taken an entire bench all by themselves. Once again, King Rhys and the former Queen of the Mists were seated behind a short table on the dais. There were no servers. Tables laden with platters of cold food, braziers of hot food, and pitchers of drinks had been arranged around the outside of the hall. No one was going near the food. Everyone who had arrived before us was milling around the tables, apparently waiting for someone else to sit first.

Fine. If someone had to start the cascade, it might as well be us. I marched to the table closest to the dais, bowed deeply to King Rhys, and plopped my butt into the first open chair I saw, which just so happened to put me where I could keep an eye on our host and his companion. Smirking, Tybalt settled on my right, while Quentin took the seat to my left. King Rhys raised an eyebrow as he watched me sit. I smiled sweetly back at him, and waited to see what would happen next.

I didn't have to wait long. Rhys raised a hand in a seemingly casual gesture, and one of his servants all but materialized next to him, stepping out of the shadows behind the throne so quickly that if I hadn't known better, I would have taken the girl for one of the Cait Sidhe. King Rhys murmured something to her, glancing meaningfully to me. The serving girl nodded, bobbing a curtsy at the same time, and stepped down from the dais.

I didn't say anything as she approached, but I sat up a little straighter, watching her approach. For what, I wasn't sure, but when she finally reached me and spoke—in the small, trembling voice of a child who had been beaten too many times to ever truly believe in the absence of pain—I knew that I wasn't ready.

"The King requests the pleasure of your company at his table."

Oh, oak and ash. I glanced to Tybalt and Quentin. Both of them looked back at me, their expressions as close to blank as they could get them. If I didn't know them as well as I did, I would have missed the tightness around Quentin's lip and the fractional narrowing of Tybalt's pupils. They knew this was a trap, even if none of us quite knew what sort of trap. And they knew, just as well as I did, that there was no way for me to avoid it.

"I would be delighted," I said solemnly, and rose, gathering my skirt in both hands to keep my fingers from shaking. The servant girl smiled in relief before turning to escort me to the dais.

We were almost there when I realized the true nature of the trap. I couldn't refuse to eat while I was in the King's presence; it would be a grave insult to his hospitality, and the sort of thing that was just rude enough to be unforgiveable. At the same time, I couldn't season my own food while I was sitting at the King's table. It would be an insult to the King's kitchens, and while that wasn't quite as bad as insulting his hospitality, it sure as hell wasn't good. I was stuck.

Walther can make a counteragent, I thought, and stepped up onto the dais, where King Rhys' smile was waiting to greet me.

"Hello, Sir Daye," he said. "I thought we could use this opportunity to talk—in full sight of your friends, naturally, since I doubt they would trust me to speak with you alone. I wanted to apologize again for the error involving your friend. I understand now that she wasn't acting against the throne, but these are dangerous times."

"Yes," I agreed, as neutrally as I could manage. "Dangerous times, indeed." I sank into the seat at the end of the table, my mind racing as I tried to calculate doses and safe margins. Some potions were so potent that a single drop could be enough—like goblin fruit, where the smallest taste was enough to addict a changeling. Others required a higher dose. If I ate only sparingly, and restricted myself to things that I saw Rhys and the former Queen putting in their mouths, I might be okay.

"You look nervous, October." The former Queen leaned forward to smile at me around the King of Silences, her eyes narrowing in a way that was anything but friendly. "Is there something you had wanted to say to the King, perhaps? It's never good to keep secrets from royalty. They always find out, in the end."

"Funny, that's almost exactly what High King Sollys said when we presented Queen Windermere before him," I said mildly. "He was really surprised to learn that King Gilad had had children before he died, and that we had plenty of proof those children existed. I guess he figured someone should have told him."

The former Queen's eyes narrowed further. "I am a guest in these halls."

"Yes, and I'm a diplomat—which I'm sure you can agree is pretty ridiculous, since I'm about as diplomatic as a kick to the face, so hey. We're all learning how to do new things." I looked to King Rhys. "Of course I'm nervous, Your Majesty. This is a Kingdom of alchemists, and I've left my personal alchemist in our rooms to avoid offending you, after the little dustup we had earlier today. I didn't want him getting arrested again. I'm sure you understand."

"I do, indeed," said Rhys. "It seems you are lacking in

certain defenses that one might have expected you to bring to such a formal and important meal."

"If you mean I can't counter anything you decide to put into my food, you're right." I was tired. I was angry. I was done candy-coating things for this man, who seemed more amused by my attempts to be diplomatic than anything else. "I'm starving, and I'm afraid to eat."

"Well, we can't have that," he said. "It speaks poorly to my hospitality, and I'll not have your mistress, however illegitimate her claims to my lady's throne, say that we treated you poorly. May I assume your alchemist has provided you with a counter to anything I might have put in your meal?"

"You can assume," I said cagily.

"Excellent. In that case please, feel free to use it however you like. Coat your cutlery in whatever powder or potion you have with you, and I will pledge, on my honor, not to slip anything into your meal that would be too powerful for a little country alchemist to overcome. I want to you to come around to my way of thinking fairly, Sir Daye, and not through the application of magics."

I blinked at him. I'd been expecting a lot of reactions to my sudden bluntness, but "okay, I promise not to drug you" hadn't been on the list. "I . . . see," I said finally.

Rhys looked at me with something that might have been pity. "You don't. You're willfully blind, because you do not like my lady, and because you are accustomed to a Kingdom where things are done differently. You judge me by the standards of something I have never been. I'm sure you think me a despot, an uncaring tyrant who refuses to let his people have a voice of their own. You aren't wrong. But you should also see me as a caring patriarch, someone who understands that he is in a delicate position. The old rulers, the ones who held this Kingdom before they were legitimately overthrown in a just war, they ruled carelessly. Few pureblood children were born, because they made no effort to keep the bloodlines clean. They allowed cavorting between fae of different races, ignoring what this would mean for the powers and stability of the children born to such unions. And changelings! They allowed their mortal-born children to aspire to places far beyond their station—no offense meant, of course, Sir Daye. Your case is somewhat different from the norm."

"Yeah, I guess Mom being Firstborn buys me a little bit of leniency," I said.

Rhys snapped his fingers. Servants began to approach the table, dishing delicacies onto his plate before serving me from the same dishes. The false Queen got a different assortment, but Rhys was apparently planning to keep his word to me: whatever I ate, he was also eating. I was still going to douse every bite with Walther's counterpotion. There's safe, and then there's sorry. I prefer it when the two don't meet.

"You have been allowed to form some inaccurate ideas about the makeup of our world," said Rhys. "My lady has always been generous to a fault when dealing with those who are of less power and importance than she is, and so she may have allowed you to dream above your station out of kindness, not malice. I can't say either way. But you need to understand that changelings are, by nature, transitory; they are here for the blink of an eye and no longer, and their wishes and desires cannot be allowed to shift Faerie away from its true course. Humanity is a disease. It thinks in hot, fast moments—too hot and too fast for Faerie, which requires cool languor to thrive. We can't make decisions based on an uncertain future. We make them based on a present that will never end."

I blinked at him for the second time in almost as many minutes, trying to figure out what he was trying to say. Finally, I asked, "What, do you mean we shouldn't listen to changelings because they're mortal?"

"Precisely so." Rhys beamed at me like I was a child

who had just managed to solve a particularly difficult math problem. "Changelings are temporary creatures, here to go. Fae are permanent. We live forever, and we should plan accordingly."

"So where do the prohibitions against crossbreeding come from?" My stomach was a solid knot, which solved my worries about the food nicely. I didn't think I could eat if I wanted to. "If fae are permanent, shouldn't you just be happy that they're choosing to have children at all?"

"My lady, beautiful as she is, should answer that question for you," said Rhys. "Had her mother been Tuatha de Dannan, there would have been no way to steal her heritage from her. Anyone who looked upon her face should have known her for Gilad's daughter, and known her claim to the throne for the valid thing that it was. Instead, her blood was such a jumble that a deceitful soul was able to pretend she had no claim to her own throne. Can you imagine how much easier Faerie would be if we didn't blend and blur the forms we were intended to have? It would be the shining beacon it was meant to be, and not this . . . hodge-podge."

"Is that why there are no fae here with animal parts? Humans are animals, too, you know, and a lot of us sure do look human." I pulled the pouch of powder Walther had given me out of the bodice of my dress and began sprinkling it over the contents of my plate. Maybe I wasn't going to be able to choke anything down, but again, it was better to be safe than sorry.

"Humanity is a mask that we are particularly well-suited to wearing," said Rhys. "Wings and hooves and tails are untidy. They mark their owners as bestial, and while they may find a place in some Courts, they have no place in mine. It's our duty to stay within the lines drawn by our lost lord and ladies."

"Really? Because it was good enough for Oberon, you know. He had Cait Sidhe in his Court." And Roane, and Swanmays. "Pretty sure he banged a cat, even, since that's where the Cait Sidhe came from."

Rhys made an expression of distaste. "There's no need to be vulgar."

I glanced to the table where Quentin and Tybalt sat. They were pushing food around their half-empty plates in a way that I recognized from my time with Gillian. She'd been a toddler when we lived together, and she had been an expert at moving food around her plate without letting it get anywhere near her mouth. I looked back to Rhys.

"Do you think Tybalt is bestial?"

The King of Silences paused, pursing his lips. He clearly knew that whatever answer he gave me, I was going to relay it to my fiancé; he just as clearly didn't want to start a second war, this one between his Kingdom and the Court of Cats. I raised an eyebrow, waiting for his answer. *Come on,* I thought. *Show me how much of a bigot you really are.* Hating changelings affected me personally, but it was almost accepted within Faerie: it was the sort of bigotry that no one would question, especially not when it was coming from a King. Even looking down on the Cait Sidhe was generally accepted.

But there are limits.

"I think he is a fine monarch for his own Court," said Rhys finally. "I have heard little of the Cait Sidhe of San Francisco that would lead me to think them anything other than the very best and brightest among their own kind. Do I think their kind should mix with the rest of the fae? No. I've never made any secret of my desire to keep Faerie pure. Please don't take this as my attempting to discourage your marriage—"

"I wouldn't dream of it," I said.

"—but the mere fact that you are part human means I can't be as against it as I normally would be. Your blood is already tainted. It doesn't need any help from me."

I stared at him. "Are you real?"

Now it was Rhys' turn to blink at me. "I beg your pardon?"

"Are you a real person? I thought no one really talked like this. My blood isn't 'tainted.' I got it from my parents. My father loved me. Why shouldn't he have helped make me? And if Tybalt and I have kids, they won't be tainted either. They'll be our children, and we'll love them no matter what their heritage looks like."

"Really." The false Queen leaned forward, fixing me with her pale gaze. "Can you truly look at me and say that you won't pick the humanity out of your babies like a bad line of embroidery, leaving them to grow up immortal and slow, heir to all the glories Faerie has to offer? Overly mixed blood can lead to complications of its own. Will you hold your babies in your arms and condemn them to in-between lives, neither Cait Sidhe nor . . . whatever you are? Tell me lies, October. I promise to pretend that I believe them."

For a moment, I didn't say anything at all. Finally, I said, "I am not here to discuss my future children with either one of you. If Tybalt and I decide that we're going to have kids, we'll have these conversations the right way: with each other, in private, as a family."

"You can't even lie to me." The false Queen leaned back again, radiating smugness. "You'll save your children from growing up the way you did, the way I did, and you'll continue to pretend that Faerie is healthy. But we'll know the truth, won't we? You and I, we've always known the truth."

I looked at her for a moment before turning my attention to my plate. I picked up a fork and speared a chunk of potato, the thin gleam of Walther's counterspell covering the hot fat and rosemary that the potato had been cooked in. I'm sure it was delicious; Rhys wouldn't have employed any cook who couldn't handle something as simple as a potato. I didn't taste anything at all. I was a sea of rage and disorientation, and I didn't know how to make it stop.

Arden should never have sent me to negotiate for her. Sweet Oberon, I hoped this was part of some incredibly clever plan on her part, that while I was away she was bolstering her defenses and finding ways to stop Rhys' army at the border, because more and more, I was sure that nothing I did was going to make a difference. I was going to tie myself into knots, and nothing was going to change. This war was going to happen no matter what I did.

"Is my hospitality not to your liking, Sir Daye?" Rhys' question was mild, but it had teeth, and they were poised to bite. "I've promised not to try to change your mind magically. Why does it look as if you aren't enjoying your food?"

"Sitting with people who think I'm inferior just because my father was human tends to spoil my appetite," I said. I forced myself to lift my head and meet Rhys' eyes. "How can you be this cold? We're all part of Faerie."

"Ah, but you see, some of us were born to this great and ageless land, and others stumbled into their places by mistake." He leaned over and speared a piece of pale white melon from the edge of my plate, looking at it contemplatively before he popped it into his mouth. He swallowed, and continued, "Some of us don't understand how to honor hospitality or show the proper respect, even when we're treated better than we deserve. You are an inferior creature in a world full of superior beings, and you can't even seem to acknowledge that the rest of us are making an effort with every day that we allow you to draw breath."

"I don't think Oberon would agree with you." It was a small, almost pitiable statement, but it was all I had left. Oberon had given us the Law, and the hope chests.

Out of all the Three, he was the one who had looked at Faerie and realized that we needed heroes. If anyone would have understood that Faerie needed to be what it was, and not some sterile, perfect mockery of itself, it would have been him.

Rhys smiled indulgently. "But, you see, that's the difference between myself and our missing Father. He believed Faerie could be balanced, that there was a place for everyone. I believe he was wrong—and since it seems I remain while he is gone, I must assume that I was right."

I stared at him. For once, I couldn't think of a damn thing to say.

The problem with arrogant assholes is that all too often, they'll take silence as agreement. "You understand, then," said Rhys, his smile widening. "I'm so very glad. It's going to make the rest of this process ever so much easier."

I frowned. "Process?"

"Yes. You see, my lady was indulgent with the Mists, and look where it got her. Deposed and dishonored and treated as a traitor to a land which she only ever strove to improve upon. It will not do. It will not stand. I know you have come here to plead the case of the Mists, and while you have done poorly, you have navigated these waters better than I expected you to."

"See, I know you think you're complimenting me, and yet somehow I still feel insulted," I said.

"That's because you are smarter than your breeding justifies," said Rhys. "Please understand, I do not harbor you any specific ill-will. Changelings have their place in Faerie. Someone should remain belowstairs, otherwise, what value will it have to be above them? But you represent the decay and dissolution of the Mists, and I am afraid I'll be sending you home as a failure. The war is going to happen, Sir Daye. Unless you are prepared to negotiate the surrender of your regent and her people, your work here is done."

I stared at him again. I hadn't been expecting to change his mind—not once I'd seen Silences, and the way that changelings were treated in his Kingdom—but this casual dismissal didn't seem to fit with his earlier demand that I bleed for him. "I thought . . ." I began, and stopped, unsure how I could continue that sentence without locking myself into a promise I didn't want to keep.

His smile widened still further, until I began to worry that his head would come unzipped and split in two. "Oh, you mean you actually want to prevent the war? I told you how you could do that. How you could call it all off with a single word. All you need to do is tell me 'yes,' and all of this can go away forever. It will be a bad dream that threatened your precious Arden briefly in the night before wisping away into nothingness."

All I had to do to save countless lives was die. I picked up my napkin, making a show of touching the corners of my mouth, and stood. "Your kitchens are superb," I said. "All praise to your chefs. If you will excuse me, it seems I have packing to do."

Then I turned and descended the dais, trusting Quentin and Tybalt to follow as I made my way toward the door. I didn't look back.

I didn't dare.

EIGHTEEN

QUENTIN AND TYBALT CAUGHT up with me in the hall outside the dining room. They moved into the flanking positions that had become so natural for us, and we continued through the knowe as a small, tightly contained wedge.

We were halfway up the stairs when Tybalt spoke, asking, "Did he request your death again?"

"He made it clear that there's no other way I'm going to broker peace between Silences and the Mists," I said. My voice was strangely thin, like I was being strangled. I forced myself to swallow, trying to chase some of the tension away, before I said, "I don't think we're going to accomplish anything more here. But we need to try."

Tybalt looked surprised before he nodded, understanding chasing his confusion away. If we left Silences now, Walther would have to come with us. He wouldn't be able to finish working on his current countercharm for elf-shot, and his family—and May, and Madden—would sleep out their hundred-year terms without anyone coming to save them. War would disrupt everything. Even if the Mists managed to win, which was something I wasn't sure of, it would be years before Walther could get back to work on the project. Rhys could do anything he wanted to his hostages in the meantime, as long as he came short of killing them, and if he saw that he was losing, even that barrier might come down.

It was now or never.

"Our window of hospitality lasts for three days, so unless we're actually being kicked out of the Kingdom, we have two more days of protection," said Quentin.

"You'll forgive me if I don't put much stock in our 'protection,'" I said. "May's asleep for a hundred years, and the King already tried to arrest Walther once. I'm not really feeling safe he—" My sentence devolved into a squawk as hands reached out of the wall, grabbed my arm, and yanked me into darkness.

Not absolute darkness: we weren't on the Shadow Roads, but in a narrow passageway lit by a single hanging globe of pale white light. Its glow revealed Marlis' anxious, tightly drawn face. She pressed a finger to her lips, signaling for me to be silent, before leaning to the side and thrusting her arms through the apparently solid wall a second time.

Pain transformed her face from anxious to agonized, but she didn't make a sound. She just leaned back, pulling Tybalt through the wall. He had his hands latched around her forearm, claws extended and piercing her flesh. There was so much blood. The smell of it filled the space, hot copper mingled with the ice and milfoil smell of Marlis' magic. I reeled, buffeted by the sudden desire to taste it, to know her life and her allegiances all the way down to the core of me. I had never felt anything like that before. It was terrifying. Tamping down that harsh, almost irresistible need took everything I had—at least until Tybalt looked wildly in my direction, pulled himself away from Marlis, and wrapped his blood-streaked arms around me.

"I thought I'd lost you," he whispered, mouth close to my ear. "Did she hurt you?"

"No, but you hurt her," I said. "I'm okay. I'm fine."

"Please, quiet," begged Marlis, and it was hard not to take a small degree of satisfaction from the obvious pain in her tone. She shouldn't have grabbed me and, more, she shouldn't have surprised Tybalt. We were all tense. She was lucky she was getting away with nothing worse than flesh wounds.

Marlis turned to thrust her now bloody hands through the wall again, and stopped as Quentin stepped through. She blinked at him. He glared at her before dismissing her as completely as a member of the nobility could, turning toward me and Tybalt instead.

"Are you all right?" he asked. "I'm sorry I didn't realize what was going on faster."

"Is this another kind of servants' hall?" I asked.

Quentin nodded. "It's a shallow standing illusion, like the kind we use to hide the mouths of some knowes, only it's designed to remain static and buffered from the dawn, so it doesn't take regular recasting. Coblynau work, probably. It's usually part of the heating system, since air moves through but light doesn't."

"Sound also moves through," hissed Marlis, shoving between us. Her left arm was cradled close to her body, and the smell of blood was getting stronger. "Please, be *quiet.*"

"If you wanted us to be quiet, you shouldn't have pulled us through a wall," I whispered. "Why didn't you just come to our quarters?"

"Because I would have been seen. I'm sorry I had to intercept you this way, but I needed you to come with me, and this was the only method I had of contacting you without endangering us all."

Right. "I don't know if you've noticed, but startling Tybalt is absolutely a good way to endanger yourself," I whispered. "Your arm needs medical attention."

Marlis glanced at her wounded arm like she was seeing it for the first time. Then she shook her head, a small, wry smile creasing her lips. "Time was that bleeding in these halls would have been a signal to the Cu Sidhe and the Cait Sidhe and the Huldra that there was something wrong. Now it's just an inconvenience. Come with me." She turned on her heel and walked off down the hall.

Tybalt, Quentin, and I exchanged a glance. Tybalt raised an eyebrow, apparently leaving the decision of whether or not to follow entirely in my hands. Swell. I do so love being the one who has to choose to follow the maybe-ally, maybe-enemy people down dark hallways.

"Root and branch, I hate my life sometimes," I muttered, and stalked after her. My skirt snagged on the heel of my shoe. I grabbed the fabric in both hands, yanking it upward until my knees were exposed and my walking was unimpeded. I might not have looked very dignified, but I wasn't going to eat floor.

The light from the single globe faded behind us, only to be replaced by a dim glow from up ahead. I could make out Marlis, but barely: she was more shadow than woman, sketched on the fabric of the world. The light grew brighter as we walked, and Marlis continued to move up ahead, never coming fully back into the light. It was enough to make me nervous, but it was too late now; if we exited these narrow hallways, I didn't know where in the knowe we would reappear. With my luck, it would be inside King Rhys' private chambers, or worse, in front of his guards. We'd find ourselves arrested for treason a second time, and this time, it would stick.

Marlis stopped walking. She was easily twenty feet ahead of us by that point, and it took a few seconds before we caught up. A large door blocked the hallway, barring us from going any further. There was no knob or keyhole: its only feature was a gold plate set where the peephole should have been. Marlis turned, studying the three of us, before peering down the hall behind us, eyes narrowed, like she was looking for signs that we were being followed.

"Sir Daye, I apologize for placing demands upon you, but I understand that you are skilled at the art of wind-reading," she said, in a low, deferential tone. "Can you please taste the air, and tell me whether we are alone?"

I blinked at her. "I've never heard anyone call it that," I said. Then I closed my eyes and opened my mouth, breathing in deeply as I looked for signs that we weren't alone.

Marlis was still bleeding. That made things harder: I'd become so attuned to blood that forcing my way past it was virtually impossible. But Quentin was next to me, and he was Daoine Sidhe. I've spent most of my life in the company of the Daoine Sidhe, often while trying to convince myself I was one of them, and I could find that bloodline through anything. Once I had him, it was easy to find Tybalt, and to breathe deeper, confirming that no other bloodlines or magical signatures appeared in the hall. I opened my eyes.

"We're alone," I said.

"Good," said Marlis, and turned to press her bloody hand against the gold plate. The metal seemed to pulse, drinking in her blood as fast as it smeared against the door. Marlis pulled her hand away. There were no traces of blood remaining on the gold plate.

"Nice trick," I said.

"This one's better," said Marlis, and blew on the door. It opened, seeming as insubstantial as a feather, even though I could see that the wood was thick and sturdy, and probably weighed at least fifty pounds. She flashed us a quick, satisfied smile, and I saw Walther in the bones of her face. Until that moment, the fact that she was his sister had been somewhat academic, but now I could *see* it, and see the woman she would have been if her Kingdom hadn't been taken over by someone who was determined to grind her and her family beneath his heel.

"Come on," said Marlis, and stepped through the now-open door, leaving the rest of us with no choice but to follow if we wanted to keep her in sight. And I very much wanted to keep her in sight. I needed to know why she'd risked herself to bring us here, and what she was hoping to achieve.

Although it wasn't like losing sight of her would have meant actually losing her. I could have followed the smell of her blood for a hundred miles, and always known exactly where she was. That was a little bit disturbing, if I allowed myself to think about it too hard, and so I tried not to think. I just followed, with Quentin and Tybalt close behind me.

The light didn't reach past the door. I heard Quentin mutter something, and the smell of heather and steel briefly overwhelmed the smell of Marlis' blood. Then a small ball of light drifted over my head to hover in front of me, bobbing in the air a few inches below the ceiling, which looked rough and rocky, like it had been carved from the body of the earth. I glanced back at Quentin, slanting him the briefest of smiles. He smiled back, although the expression did nothing to remove the tight lines around his eyes. He was worried. That was good. Failure to be worried when following a strange woman down a dark tunnel would have shown a deep and catastrophic lack of self-preservation, and I wanted to keep him around for a little longer.

Marlis was visible up ahead of us. I focused on walking, silently cursing her for grabbing us while we were in transit from the King's company, and not waiting until after we had reached our quarters and had the chance to change our clothes. My shoes were sensible, but my dress was ridiculous. Formal gowns were not designed to be worn in underground tunnels—and I was becoming increasingly sure that when we had stepped through that door, we had transitioned from the stately, manicured halls of Silences to something older and rougher, probably intended as an escape route if things went poorly.

Marlis stopped. When we reached her, she was standing next to another door, this one made entirely of rose brambles. It was clearly Ceres' work, and Marlis was just as clearly unhappy about the idea of opening it. There was no doorknob or keyhole.

I'd seen doors like that one before. Blind Michael—Ceres' father—had used them in his stables, probably courtesy of his wife, Acacia, who was the Firstborn of both the Dryads and the Blodynbryd. "Does it need your blood, specifically, or will any blood do to open it?" I asked.

Marlis jumped, like she had forgotten that we were there. "Any blood will do," she said. She was speaking in a normal conversational tone now: apparently, we had moved outside the sphere of the King's surveillance. That, or we had moved deep enough into his trap that she no longer needed to pretend to be quiet. "Only a member of our family can open the door to the tunnel, but Aunt Ceres' roses are less picky. They don't care who bleeds for them."

Behind me, Tybalt sighed. I smirked. He was clearly anticipating my next move, and while he didn't approve, he wasn't going to stop me.

"Let me," I said, and reached into the brambles. As I had halfway expected, they writhed, repositioning themselves around my hand, before driving their thorns like needles into my skin.

Healing quickly doesn't mean I don't feel pain. If anything, it means the opposite. I don't get nerve damage and I don't build up scar tissue: I can recover so fast from an injury that I experience it again for the first time while it's still ongoing. It seems like a blessing, and it has been, in a great many ways—I would never have been able to live this long if it weren't for the fact that I can bounce back from things that should by all rights have killed me. But sometimes, when it seems like the pain is never going to end, I wish I'd gotten a different suite of magical talents from my mother. Like the power to avoid situations that end with me willingly jamming my arm into a door made entirely from animate, apparently angry rose briars.

The thorns bit into my flesh until it felt like they were touching the bone. I gritted my teeth, asking, "Does it *always* do this?" I tried to keep my voice from shaking. If Tybalt or Quentin decided I was in trouble, they might come into range of the door. I didn't need to deal with multiple people being attacked by the architecture.

Marlis didn't answer with words. She just raised her arm and rolled down her sleeve, showing me the hundreds of tiny white scars pocking her skin. Some of them were old and almost faded, while others were glossy and as pale as birch bark.

Seeing them both made me feel better about what the door was currently doing to my arm, and made me worry once again about whether we were walking into a trap. Marlis had been under Rhys' spell for a hundred years, and some of those scars were substantially fresher than that.

She must have seen the doubt in my eyes, because she lowered her arm, rolling her sleeve back down, and said, "He couldn't hold me all the time. Even when I was dosing myself, it's dangerous to layer loyalty over loyalty. Sometimes, I came back to my senses. Never for long—never long enough to decide that I could run, that I could leave my family and go. But long enough for me to do certain things that needed to be done."

"Right," I said. The thorns dug deeper. Then, as if they had finally found the key they were looking for, the briars began to loosen, finally unspooling and dropping away. I pulled my arm, now effectively shredded, out of the thorns. The smell of my blood washed over the smell of Marlis' blood, concealing it. That was almost a relief. My blood was at least familiar, and didn't take as much effort to block out.

Speaking of blood . . . I raised my hand to my mouth

and sucked the blood off my wrist, centering and strengthening myself. There was no sense in letting it go to waste when it was right there. I didn't even need to cut myself.

"You're bleeding on your dress," observed Quentin. He sounded unhappy, but not shaken. Me bleeding all over everything was practically normal these days.

"I'll give it to Tybalt to dispose of on the Shadow Roads," I said, the blood making my voice sound positively giddy. The thorn door was still opening, unwinding itself one knot at a time. It was a slow process that was probably supposed to look impressive, but really just made me wonder what would happen if someone ever got cornered down here. An escape route that took too long to open was almost as bad as no escape route at all. "I never liked this dress anyway."

"Ah, but you see, I did, which is why I will be concealing it in the local Court of Cats, to recover later," said Tybalt. "I'm sure May will be able to get the blood out, once she wakes, and will have some fascinating things to say about your heritage while she works. I treasure the idea of hearing her insult you."

"Right now, so do I," I said. I looked toward Marlis. She was staring at my arm, eyes huge in a suddenly pale face. I glanced down. The blood covering my arm was thick and bright, but it was possible to see the unbroken skin beneath it. I ran my clean palm across the arm, wiping a swath of blood away, and held it up for her to see. "Good as new," I said. "Can we start moving again, or do you have a door that requires a kidney?"

"Nothing heals that fast," she said.

"Faerie always changes," I replied. I wiped my bloody palm on my dress. Let May enjoy a real challenge for once.

"I . . . I see," said Marlis. "This way." She turned and dove through the opening created by the retracting vines, which had barely pulled back far enough to let her through. I followed, gathering my skirts close to keep them from getting snagged. Getting the blood out was going to be hard enough without adding physical damage to the dress itself.

Quentin and Tybalt followed me, Tybalt swearing softly as he navigated the space between the thorns. Quentin's little ball of light continued to dart ahead of us, brightening the tunnel until I could make out the finer details of the walls. They were as roughly hewn as the ceiling, and glittered here and there with flecks of pyrite and quartz. We were walking through the body of the Summerlands, surrounded by stone, and I wasn't sure whether that was comforting or terrifying.

"You said this would have signaled the Cu Sidhe, Cait Sidhe, and Huldra once," I said. "How tightly tied were they to your wards?"

"The Cu Sidhe and the Huldra were tightly tied; the Cait Sidhe had access as a courtesy, and so they wouldn't turn against us," said Marlis. "There were never many of them, anyway. Cats don't stay where there are so many dogs." She smiled, just a little, seemingly lost in the pleasure of having unfettered access to her own memories, and the feelings that went with them.

A pale light began to filter through from ahead, different in both quality and quantity from the small, bright glow of Quentin's ball. He snapped his fingers and it guttered out, leaving the presumably natural brightness to guide us. We were close enough to the exit that there wasn't much change. We continued forward, until we stepped out of the mouth of the tunnel and into a garden taken straight from a botanist's dream.

The sky overhead was a smooth sheet of velvet black spangled with so many stars that they chased away the deepest of the shadows, casting the entire world into a crystalline twilight. The air smelled so strongly of roses that I almost lost track of the smell of blood—both my own and Marlis'. Everyone around me could have been casting spells and spinning illusions, and I probably wouldn't have been able to tell. The smell of roses was too strong.

The sight of them was even stronger. They grew everywhere around us, spiraling out in a wheel of colorful blooms and thorny boughs. Some climbed trellises or tangled themselves around statuary, while others grew in vast, fragrant bushes. I recognized many of the varieties from my visits to Luna's gardens. There was even a plot of my beloved glass roses, the starlight lancing through their petals and casting colored shadows on the soil below them. Other varieties were new to me, roses that glowed blue like swampfire or burned with actual fire, somehow sustaining their own flame without being consumed. I couldn't count the varieties in front of me. All I could say was that they were beautiful beyond measure, each in their own unique way.

"Good; you made it." Ceres appeared from behind a trellis as casually as if we were at her cottage, and not at some secret rose garden at the end of a long tunnel. She was carrying a red rose in each hand. Both had the wide, loose-looking petals that I associated with wild roses, rather than the tight swirl of cultivated blossoms. "Marlis had no trouble finding you, I trust?"

"Marlis nearly got herself gutted by my fiancé when she surprised us, but apart from that, it went just fine," I said mildly.

Ceres raised an eyebrow. "I would have expected you to be the sort of woman who did her own gutting, after the things Walther has told me about you."

"I normally would be, but she grabbed me first, so I had time to get over my surprise." I rubbed my hands against my dress again, trying to get rid of the tacky feeling of blood drying on my skin. "Where are we?"

"My own test garden. I cultivate my roses here, in privacy, and plant what grows well around my cottage for others to enjoy." Ceres stepped closer, holding her two roses out toward me. "Smell these."

I raised an eyebrow. "That's why we're here? So I can smell a couple of roses? No offense, but I could have done that in my room, *without* bleeding all over everything in sight."

"Aunt Ceres, I told you: you can't be mysterious with Toby, all it does is piss her off." Walther emerged from a cluster of rosebushes. He looked tired, but there was a light in his eyes that I recognized from my visits to his office. He was an alchemist before he was anything else, and alchemists thrive in the presence of puzzles. "Hi, Toby. Can you please smell those not at all mysterious roses for me, and tell me which one smells more like the rose we're looking for?"

"For you, yes," I said. I stepped forward to where Ceres waited, and sniffed the roses in her hands, first the right, and then the left. Then I frowned. "Neither one of these is right. They smell great, but they don't smell like *her*."

"I told you," said Walther. He sounded oddly triumphant for someone who had just had both his roses rejected. "You can't trick Toby's nose. It's weird, but it works." He opened the pouch attached to his belt and withdrew a third rose. It was smaller than the others, only half-open, and while the petals were red, they were patchy and bruised-looking, like it hadn't been grown to be picked and hadn't been prepared to be separated from its bush. He held it out toward me, almost reverently. "Smell this."

"Right," I said, and leaned forward, sniffing the rose. Then I recoiled, atavistic revulsion rising in my throat, so strong and fierce that I almost slapped the flower out of his hand. It might have seemed like a melodramatic reaction to something so small, but the rose's smell was so close to the scent of Evening's magic that I couldn't help myself. It lacked the depth and power of her signature. It was just a rose, with no undertones of ice or snow. But I had never smelled a rose like that one, old and deep and somehow primal, the sort of flower that would have grown on a grave in a folksong, or provided the perfume to a figure from a fairy tale.

Walther watched me, assessing my reaction with a faint gleam of satisfaction in his eyes. "Well?" he asked, needlessly.

"That's the one." I wiped my mouth with the back of my hand, leaving flecks of dried blood on my lips. That helped a little. "It smells so close to her magic it makes me want to throw up. Where did you find it?"

"In the oldest of my rose gardens, in a corner, where the sun only shines fully for a few months out of the year," said Ceres. "I've thought it dead several times, but always it returns."

"Yeah, well, it and the woman whose magic smells like it have that in common," I said, resisting the urge to wipe my mouth again. "That's the one. That's the rose that smells like her magic."

"And you're *sure* this is the woman who created elf-shot?"

I hesitated. "Yes and no," I said finally. "The Luidaeg is the one who told me about her making the elf-shot, and the Luidaeg is sort of laboring under a geas, where she can't say her sister's name or identify her directly. But she told me it was her oldest sister who created elf-shot, and Eira Rosynhwyr is her oldest sister. Maybe more importantly, Eira is really hung up on position and power and all that fun stuff, and whoever brewed the first elf-shot designed it to be fatal to changelings when it didn't have to be. It was her."

"We need to be sure," said Walther. "If I brew this wrong, it could do more harm than good."

"Define 'more harm,'" I said.

"Elf-shot doesn't normally kill unless the potion is altered to add poison," he said. "I'm not worried about turning it fatal, but I *am* worried about tripping a failsafe and extending the length of time that the sleepers are out."

I stared at him. "So if we do this wrong, we could put everyone to sleep for even longer? How much longer?"

"How does a thousand years strike you?" Walther shook his head, the lines of weariness in his face suddenly making perfect sense. "This isn't just some brute force compound. It's one of the most complicated spells I've ever tried to reverse-engineer. I feel like I'm trying to replicate a cobweb from a blurry picture. I can do it—don't get me wrong—but it's the hardest piece of work I've ever attempted."

"You were always Daddy's little prodigy," said Marlis. Her tone was equal parts amusement and bitterness, like she had spent years coming to terms with her own words. "I was good, but you were better."

"I had to be," said Walther. "I was going to break his heart one day, when I told him why I wasn't going to marry and provide him with heirs. Being the best alchemist I could be seemed like the least I could do."

Marlis nodded. "You did good. You got out."

I looked between them, hand going automatically to the pocket where I usually kept my phone—only for me to realize that I didn't have a pocket, and I didn't have a phone. I was wearing a blood-drenched ball gown. They aren't known for their copious storage capacity. "Oh, oak and ash," I said. "Look, I can confirm that Eira brewed the original potion, but I'm going to need to borrow somebody's phone."

"Phone?" asked Ceres blankly.

"Mortals have started carrying portable communication devices," explained Marlis. "No one in this Kingdom has anything so . . . déclassé and human."

"See, you say 'déclassé,' I say 'I can order Chinese food without getting out of bed. I resisted at first, too, but the convenience of having one outweighs the irritation of remembering to keep it charged." I turned to Quentin. "You. I know you have a phone. Fork it over."

Quentin's cheeks reddened as he dug into his pocket.

"Okay, just don't go poking around in my files, all right?" He produced a phone that was newer and sleeker than mine, with a glass front. It wasn't the phone he'd had a few weeks previously. I raised an eyebrow, and he reddened further. "April upgraded me. She said I was shaming Tamed Lightning by carrying around something so out of date."

"Your phone was less than six months old," I said, taking the space-age rectangle from his hand.

Quentin shrugged.

The phone wasn't locked, thankfully, and a sweep of my thumb across the screen woke it up and displayed Quentin's wallpaper at the same time: a picture of him with Dean Lorden, the current Count of Goldengreen. They were sitting on the dock of Goldengreen's private beach, Dean with his arm slung carelessly around Quentin's waist, Quentin with his head resting on Dean's shoulder.

This wasn't the time or the place to start grilling my squire on his social life, but I glanced from the picture to him, just long enough to be sure that he got the message that we'd be discussing this later. Quentin nodded, accepting his fate, and I called up the keypad.

Dialing on these new phones with their virtual keys is easy. Using it to channel the spells necessary to reach the Luidaeg is somewhat less so. I drew a starburst pattern across the keys, chanting, "My lover's gone to sea, to sea, my lover's gone away; may he come back to me, to me, for this each night I pray." The smell of cut grass and copper rose in the air around me, strong enough to overwhelm the scent of roses. Only briefly—the roses were already slipping back by the time the spell coalesced and popped like a soap bubble, sending a thin bolt of pain lancing through my head.

I raised the phone to my ear, and heard nothing. That was another thing about those new phones: they didn't come with dial tones to tell me when my spells weren't working. But my head hurt, and the smell of copper was still hanging in the air. I waited, until faintly, I began to hear the sound of waves battering themselves against a distant beach. Jackpot.

The sound of the waves grew louder as connections were thrown and magic tunneled its way through the phone lines between me and the Luidaeg. Nobody loves a special effect like a pureblood, and as the Firstborn daughter of Oberon and Maeve, the Luidaeg was about as pure as they came. I counted silently to ten, and had just reached nine when the waves crashed loudly enough to be startling, and the Luidaeg's voice demanded, "What now?"

"Hi, Luidaeg," I said. "I'm still in Silences, and I have an awkward question that's probably going to run up against your geas. Sorry about that."

There was a pause. "What?"

"I don't really have time to explain right now. I'm standing in a rose garden with a Blodynbryd named Ceres and a whole bunch of flowers, and King Rhys is probably going to notice that I'm missing pretty soon. So if I could just ask my question, that would be swell." I didn't beg or try to convince her that she should tell me what I needed to know. Our relationship had long since progressed past those little formalities.

This time, the pause was longer. Finally, the Luidaeg asked, "Is it important enough to make me answer you?"

"Evening has been elf-shot, Luidaeg. She's not going to come back just because I ask something that involves her."

"Spoken like someone who never really knew my sister," said the Luidaeg. There was no mistaking the bitterness in her voice for anything else. Then she sighed, and said, "All right. Go ahead and ask. If it wakes her, then it's on your head."

"Did Eve—did Eira create elf-shot?" The correction pained me, just a little, but I wanted to leave as much distance as possible between the woman I had believed to be my friend and the Firstborn that she had turned out to truly be. I had lived my entire life in the shadows of Faerie's giants, and I had never even known that they were there.

"Ah." The Luidaeg paused, taking a deep, slow breath, like she was trying to center herself. Then she said, "Yes. Father wanted a weapon that wouldn't kill. He wanted to know that we'd still be here when he came looking for us. And she—the person you're asking about—said she had just the thing. A period of sleep, for reflection, followed by waking renewed and refreshed and ready to face the world more fairly. She made it sound like some sort of vacation."

"You told me it didn't have to be deadly to changelings," I said carefully.

"That was her own little twist on the formula," said the Luidaeg. The bitterness was back, and stronger than ever. "She was happy to preserve our brothers and sisters, because Father wanted it, but human-born? They were worse than useless in her eyes. So she made sure that for them, there would be no slumber. Only death."

"Okay." I closed my eyes. "That was what I thought."

"Toby . . ." The Luidaeg sounded hesitant. That was unusual enough to make me open my eyes again. "Are you about to do something stupid?"

"Well, that depends." I looked at my allies: Walther and Ceres, with their hands full of roses; Marlis, with her bloody arm; Quentin and Tybalt, who I would have willingly followed into the Heart of Faerie itself, if that was what was required of me to keep them safe. "How much common sense do you think I have?"

"Oh, for fuck's sake. Just try not to die, all right? No one gets to kill you but me." The line went dead.

I lowered the phone, holding it out for Quentin to take. He didn't quite snatch it from my hand, but it was a close thing. With this small, centering transaction done,

I looked to the others, and said, "I was right about who created elf-shot, and I'm right about the rose. You have everything you need. What do we do now?"

Walther smiled, just a little. "Now's when things get interesting."

NINETEEN

"WHEN YOU SAID THINGS were going to get interesting, I thought you meant you were going to do a lot of complicated alchemy, not that we were going to break into Rhys' private morgue," I hissed, staying close to the wall. Tybalt had stepped into the Shadow Roads, returning in short order with a tank top and jeans from Old Navy. Literally from Old Navy: both had still had the price tags attached. They were the right sizes, too, which had earned him a speculative look. He had answered with a smirk, and I had gone behind a curtain of hanging roses to change my clothes while he got rid of my bloody dress.

I might have done better to stay behind the roses. When I came out, Walther had been waiting with his full kit and a basket of cut flowers. The basket had been pressed into my hands, and Ceres had done what only a Blodynbryd can do, and opened the Rose Road into Rhys' knowe. All of which led to us walking through a narrow tunnel made entirely of thorns, trying to navigate our way into the heart of Rhys' knowe without dropping back into the Summerlands proper. Ceres wasn't going to be able to open a second Road to get us *out*—she had remained behind in her garden after opening the tunnel. I couldn't blame her for that. If she got elf-shot for treason, who would take care of her flowers, or the surviving members of the former royal family? She had responsibilities in this Kingdom that needed her to remain above reproach.

But, Maeve's eyes, we all had responsibilities. Tybalt had a Court to care for; Quentin was going to be the King someday; Walther had his students, who would never know what had happened to him if he disappeared while on a sabbatical to Portland. As for me, I had the people who were walking through the rose-scented darkness by my side, and at least a dozen more who counted on me to be there to save them. I didn't sign up to be a hero. It just happened. That didn't mean I could pretend it didn't matter.

Marlis had also stayed behind. She needed to bandage her wounds, clean off the blood, and prepare to return to the receiving hall, where she would stand right in front of King Rhys and act as if nothing unusual was happening in the knowe. I didn't envy her the task. I just hoped she was an incredible actress. If she so much as hinted to the King that something was up, we were all going to get caught—and this time when he charged us with treason, there wasn't going to be any miracle save. He'd have us dead to rights . . . or maybe just dead.

"We're almost there," said Walther. He was walking at the front of our uneven little line, while Tybalt walked at the back, leaving me and Quentin in the middle. I would normally have been offended by the implication that I couldn't take care of myself, but in that moment, I was just glad that someone who knew the way was taking point. I didn't need to bring up the rear; there was no one I trusted more than Tybalt to hold that position.

"Why did we agree to this again?" I asked.

"Because I may need your blood to quicken the spell, depending on how complicated the counteragent turns out to be," said Walther. "And I'm doing the final mixing in the dungeon because I need to be able to use this tincture immediately. Anything that has to be chilled to work isn't going to sit well."

"I know nothing about alchemy," I said.

"I know," said Walther. "That's why you have to trust me."

We walked on in silence after that, until Walther held up a hand, signaling for the rest of us to stop. He was looking at a stretch of thorny wall that looked exactly like the thorny wall all around it. "We're here," he said, and reached out to touch a single thorn with the tip of his index finger. The smell of his blood, faint but unmistakable, wafted back to tickle my nostrils as the brambles began to unwind.

"Please tell me that wasn't all that was required to unlock the other door," I grumbled.

Walther shot me a quick, tightly amused look. "No, that one takes sacrifice, and intent. This is a one-way door. It doesn't demand as much." The brambles were still unknotting themselves, opening a narrow slit in the side of the Rose Road. I couldn't see anything through the opening; it was like it looked out on absolute blankness.

"That's encouraging," said Quentin. It was the first time he had spoken since we'd left the garden.

"Look at it this way, young squire: if we plummet into unending blackness, we will be falling into shadow," said Tybalt. "Stay close to me, and I will be able to yank the three of us onto a more suitable Road before anyone is hurt."

"Three?" asked Walther.

Tybalt looked at him flatly. "If you lead us into unending blackness, I feel less than obligated to rescue you."

"Fair enough," said Walther. "I guess that means I'm going first." He slipped through the opening, and was gone, taking the faint but lingering scent of blood with him.

I sighed. "There's only one way out. Come on." I stepped through the opening after Walther. There was a moment of disorientation, like I was riding an extremely fast, totally dark elevator—

—and I was standing on a rough cobblestone floor, surrounded by gray granite walls. Stone biers studded the room, spaced out like display cases in a strange museum. There were at least a dozen of them, each with their own motionless figure lying atop them—the jewels in these inhumane displays. Walther was standing next to the nearest bier, his head bowed and his hands clenched into fists. I spared a glance behind me and, seeing that there was no opening, stepped out of the way. My instincts were correct: Tybalt and Quentin appeared out of thin air a second later.

Tybalt stopped as soon as he had his bearings, looking warily around the room. "This is dangerous," he said, eyes narrowing. "Do what needs to be done, and let us be away from here."

"I still don't understand why we couldn't start with May," I said, walking over to Walther. I stopped when a few feet away, feeling my stomach drop toward my feet. I put a hand over my mouth, unsure of what I could possibly say in response to the scene in front of me.

The woman who was sleeping on the bier, her hands folded over her chest and a faint grimace on her otherwise peaceful face, couldn't have been anyone but Walther's mother. The shape of her cheekbones, the subtle composition of her features, even the angled points of her ears, they all mirrored his like some sort of sideways mirror. She looked more like Marlis than she did like him, but together, the three of them formed a family unit so unbelievably clear that there was no point in pretending it wasn't there.

She was dressed in the pseudo-Medievalist fashion so common among the Courts, and if her gown was a hundred years out of fashion, I certainly couldn't tell; one of the side effects of choosing all your clothes like you were getting ready to put on an extremely classy production of *Camelot* was that everything became subtly timeless, impossible to measure. But there were smears of dust at the corners of her eyes, like whoever was responsible for cleaning her hadn't been as careful as they should have been, and I had no trouble believing that she'd been asleep for a century or more.

Her right leg ended at the knee, leaving that side of her skirt to fall straight down and puddle on the table. Walther followed my gaze to her missing lower limb. Then he looked back up, reaching out to carefully wipe the dust away from her eyes with the side of his thumb.

"We're starting here, and not with May, because if I'm not exactly right, no one will notice," he said. "Everyone in this room is already expected to sleep for a century. More than a century—as long as Rhys is in power and willing to keep putting them under. So if I test my tincture on one of them, and they don't wake up, we haven't lost anything. If I test it on May and put her to sleep for a thousand years, you'll probably kill me."

"Walther, I'm so sorry." The words seemed awkward and out of place. They were the only things I had to offer. I had known that his family was here, sleeping, but I'd never thought too hard about it, because there hadn't been anything I could do. Now . . . this was his *mother*. I didn't even like my own mother most of the time, and I couldn't imagine what it would do to me to know that she might never wake up again.

"I can't start with my aunt or uncle, because we're going to need them to challenge for the throne before the High King," he said. "My cousin Torsten is next in line to be King, so I can't start with him either. Mother was never the best alchemist in our family, but she was always the most adventurous. I remember her turning her hair purple when I was a kid. She laughed and said fashion couldn't come before science, not if we wanted to understand what we did. She was the first one I told when I really started to understand that I was supposed to be a boy, because I knew she wouldn't say 'let's just cast a transformation spell and make it all better.' She'd tell me to use my alchemy, to do it myself and make it *permanent*. Because she believed in me."

"We don't have to start with her," I said softly.

"Yes, we do," he said. "If I don't wake her up, I can try again. I can find the right formula, I can wake up my father, and together, we'll be able to undo whatever it is I've done. But if I start with him and I've got it wrong, there's no one I can safely try to wake who will actually be able to help me save him. She has to come first."

I couldn't tell how much of his logic was sincere and how much was his need to see his mother again, to feel her arms around him and hear her voice telling him it was going to be okay. In the end, it didn't matter. He was the alchemist: he was the one who understood the risks, and the possible costs, of what we were about to do. All I could do was follow his lead. "What do you need from me?"

Walther offered me a wan smile. "I'm going to need you to bleed for me."

"That's something I can do." I looked toward Tybalt and Quentin, who were standing quietly a few feet away. Neither of them looked happy with our situation. Neither of them was telling me not to help. I think we all knew that ship had sailed long ago, and not one of us had been on board.

"Good. It'll be a few minutes." Walther opened his kit, beginning to unpack it one piece at a time on the edge of his mother's bier. Some of the things were familiar—mortar and pestle, little jars of assorted herbs, syringe. Other pieces were strange to me, weights and presses and oddly-shaped vessels that didn't hold anything but potential. The rest of the world seemed to drop away from him as he bent over his work.

I turned and walked back to Tybalt and Quentin. "I don't know how long this is going to take, and I'm not comfortable being unarmed, or leaving May by herself," I said. "Tybalt, do you think you can get Quentin back to our room, and come back here with my knife?"

Tybalt scowled. "No good ever comes from sending me away."

Quentin looked resigned, and a little relieved, like this was the answer he'd been hoping for but hadn't quite dared to suggest. "She's right. Someone should be with May, and if things go wrong here, I probably shouldn't be caught where the alchemy is happening. My parents would be pissed if I wound up getting elf-shot."

"You've left me on my own several times since we got here, and I've been fine," I said, leaning up to kiss Tybalt on the cheek. "Just trust me, okay? I need my knife, and May needs someone to protect her. I can take care of myself in the nice, empty dungeon until you make it back."

"You tell me you no longer yearn for death, but sometimes, you do things that make it difficult to believe you," said Tybalt. He had the resigned tone that meant he was going to do what I was asking, thank Maeve. Quentin was looking more uncomfortable by the minute, and the threat of discovery was making me twitchy. I didn't want to get the Crown Prince of the Westlands busted for treason if I could help it.

When I first found out Quentin was going to be High King someday, I had promised him I wouldn't let the knowledge make me treat him differently. For the most part, I'd kept my word. But there were certain things that had made me unhappy when he was just my untitled squire, and now that I knew who he really was, they were unbearable. Situations like this made the list.

"I love you, too," I said. "Quentin, stay with May; don't let anyone in."

"Got it," he said. "Don't do anything *completely* stupid, okay?"

"I'll do my best," I said. Quentin smiled tightly as Tybalt took him by the arm. Then my boyfriend and my squire stepped backward into the shadows, and they were gone, leaving only the faint scent of musk and pennyroyal hanging in the air.

I walked back to the bier where Walther was working, standing silently off to one side and watching as he mixed powders and liquids, ground rose petals in a mortar, and generally worked his own quiet brand of magic. There are races in Faerie that are uniquely well suited to the art of alchemy—Tylwyth Teg, Kitsune, Huldra—but anyone can learn it, if they're willing to put in the time, and even the races with a natural talent require years of training and practice before they can really claim to be skilled alchemists. Walther had been practicing for more than a century. He had reshaped his body with his art, and he was a living testament to what kind of alchemist he had become.

At the same time, he was trying to unmake a spell first woven by one of the Firstborn, a spell that had been used throughout Faerie for millennia without being broken or undone. He was going to need every bit of skill he possessed, and then some, if he wanted to make this work.

"Toby?"

The sound of his voice snapped me out of my thoughts. I looked up. "Yeah?"

"It's time." He held out a scalpel. Its edge glittered too softly to be stainless steel; it was silver, as sharp and pure as any fae dueling blade. "I don't need much."

"I've got plenty." I took the scalpel from his hand, testing the weight of it before I brought it down across my arm, cutting lengthwise to get as much blood as possible before my body started to heal. He held out a chalice, and I bled into it, turning my face away. I still don't like the sight of blood, despite how often I bleed. One more thing to thank my own mother for.

"That should be enough," said Walther.

"Okay. Just tell me if you want more." I turned back to face him, holding out the scalpel for him to take out of my hand. He did, and I wiped as much of the blood off my arm as I could. Problem: this left me with a blood-coated palm, which I promptly rubbed against my brand new jeans. The amount of time a piece of clothing could expect to be in my possession before being ruined was going down all the time. "What happens next?"

"You let me work, and we both pray that I got the recipe right," he said. He turned back to his equipment, beginning to add blood—one drop at a time—to his mashed rose petals. He must have added a powder to the chalice that would keep my blood from clotting, because it seemed strangely liquid, even for as fresh as it was, and very, very bright.

The smell was overwhelming, a mixture of blood and roses that was so reminiscent of my mother that it sent shivers down my spine. I moved away, starting to walk a slow patrol around the edges of the dungeon.

Each of the biers was occupied, most by Tylwyth Teg who shared a faint familial resemblance with Walther. There were a few others—a Glastig, a Daoine Sidhe, even a Tuatha de Dannan whose glossy cherrywood hair made her look more like Etienne and Chelsea than Rhys or Arden—but the Tylwyth Teg were by far in the majority. This hadn't just been a conquest: it had been a rout, and I wasn't sure, even now, how it had been accomplished. The Mists had possessed the larger army, but Silences had been the aggressors. How could they have underestimated their position so dramatically?

"Walther, you remember the war," I said, turning. "How did the Mists win?"

"No one knows," he said, still working. "We were fighting, and it seemed like we had all the advantages. Then we just . . . started to lose. It was like people didn't have the will to fight back. Entire parties were wiped out without raising a finger to defend themselves. We lost half the Cu Sidhe. The ones who didn't die just vanished. They're probably still asleep in a basement somewhere."

"That's not good."

Walther chuckled humorlessly. "Tell me about it. Now hush, and let me work."

I hushed. But I continued walking around the edges of the dungeon, marking the entrances, and the position of the biers. There wasn't much here that could be used as cover. I was on my third circuit of the room when I heard a sound. It was faint, like a footstep on a distant, stony floor. It was loud enough to be a concern.

"Walther, hide yourself."

"What?"

"You're a good enough illusionist to hide yourself, and you share blood with most of the people in this room; even a Daoine Sidhe won't be able to sniff you out. Now *hide*." I kept my voice low, but my last word verged on a snarl.

Walther didn't argue. The scent of yarrow flared in the air and then was gone. I looked over my shoulder, and I didn't see him, or the array of alchemical supplies that he had been using to prepare his counterpotion. Good. There were more powerful people than I was in Faerie, and some of them might have been able to spot him, but only if they were looking. With this many Tylwyth Teg in one room, they hopefully wouldn't be looking.

That just left me. I grabbed a handful of shadows out of the air, weaving a blur as fast as I could. Anger usually made my illusions easier to cast. I didn't have anger, but I had the burgeoning seeds of panic. I threw it into the magic, spinning and twisting the spell as fast as I could. I wanted to chant—spoken spells have always helped me to focus my magic and make it obey me more quickly—but I didn't know how close company was. The last thing I wanted to do was conceal myself magically and give myself away through mundane means.

The spell rose, solidified, and burst around me. I

pressed myself to the wall and tried not to move more than I had to. Blur spells don't make you invisible, but they make you damn hard to see, like those little brown lizards that infest the mortal park outside of Shadowed Hills. As long as I was perfectly still and didn't make a sound, there was a good chance I'd be overlooked.

Seconds ticked by. I was starting to think that I had been overly-cautious when the footsteps started up again, moving closer. I stopped breathing.

Tia stepped into the dungeon.

Madden's sister had changed since I'd last seen her, in Arden's Court, demanding strident justice for her brother. The pigtails and peasant blouse were gone, replaced by unbound waves of red-and-white hair and a long silver-gray gown that hugged her curves and erased any traces of the hippie girl she had seemed to be when she stood before the Queen. Her amber, distinctly canine eyes were narrowed, and she was sniffing the air with every step she took. Two of Rhys' men were behind her . . . and behind them was Rhys himself, still wearing his Court finery, his hands folded behind his back like he was afraid he would touch something and dirty himself.

Tia's nose wrinkled as she took in the biers. "You kept them?" she demanded. She turned to Rhys. "You told me they'd been killed, all of them, even down to the suckling babes. You *promised* me."

"I told you they had been disposed of," said Rhys. "What could be worse than an eternity of sleep at the hands of one who bears you no good will? They've woken once, and we put them down again. They'll sleep forever, and each time they wake, they'll find more of themselves missing, carved away for purposes they will never know. I have made their lives a processional of nightmares and horrors. Would you really rather that they were dead?"

"I suppose not," sniffed Tia. "Whatever you give them, they deserve. Bastards, all of them."

"I've kept my word to you otherwise," said Rhys. "I even started with your brother when it came time to declare war on the Mists. Now keep your word to me. Find my enemies."

"I gave you the opportunity to put an arrow in Madden. I'm not sure you can claim that was a favor to me; you'd have done it for free if I'd promised you there would be no retaliation."

"And yet I did it because you asked me to, which makes it a favor. All I ask is that you do the same favor for me. Do what I've asked."

I didn't dare breathe. I had been expecting treachery, treason, all sorts of terrible things, but I hadn't been expecting Rhys to walk into the room with a Cu Sidhe by his side—not when his Court was so blatantly devoid of fae with animal traits. I'd only been thinking about Daoine Sidhe reading the air for the heritage of those present, or Gwragen looking for the cobweb sheen of illusions. I hadn't considered the fact that they might just look for the physical.

Tia sniffed the air, her nostrils flaring in a way that was subtly, anatomically inhuman. "Blood, and magic," she said. "They were here."

"Where did they go?" Rhys sounded anxious. He didn't like not knowing where we were.

I didn't have much sympathy for him. My heart was hammering against my rib cage, beating so hard and fast that I was honestly amazed it hadn't given me away. If Tia's ears had been as sensitive as her nose, surely she could have just followed them to me. I stayed as motionless as I could, unsure whether I should be praying for Tybalt to arrive and pull me out or praying that he would stay as far away as possible, avoiding this entire situation. We didn't both need to get caught. Neither of us needed to get caught.

Sweet Oberon, please get me out of this, I thought.

Then Tia turned toward Walther, still sniffing the air,

and took a step in his direction. "It's freshest this way. Is there a secret passage? Those Yates bastards riddled their home with holes, and their Davies cronies weren't any better. They could have dug straight down through the stone, just to give themselves another place to beat their dogs . . ."

Two more steps and she would be on top of Walther. Walther, who was the only chance we had of unmaking the potion that powered the elf-shot. Without him, we'd never be able to wake any of the sleepers—not Madden, not May, and not the true heirs to Silences. He was so close. He could fix it all, as long as he could have just a little bit more time. That was all he really needed: just a little bit more time. He wasn't going to get that if Rhys caught him. He was going to get an elf-shot arrow to the shoulder and a long sleep in this same dungeon, and the victims of elf-shot were going to sleep out their sentences, no matter where they were.

I couldn't let that happen. No matter how much I wanted to stay safe and hidden, I was a hero of the realm, and that meant I had to choose the greater good. *Tybalt, I'm sorry,* I thought, and raked the palm of my left hand against the rough stone of the dungeon wall, leaving a layer of skin behind.

The pain was immediate and intense, followed almost as fast by the dull ache of healing. The smell of blood filled the air around me, hot and unmistakable. Tia's head whipped around, her nostrils flaring and her pupils dilating as she scented blood in the air. "There," she said, and pointed, so much like a hunting hound that a bubble of desperate, angry laughter tried to raise in my throat. "She's against that wall."

"Excellent," said Rhys. "Men?"

His men reached into their jerkins and withdrew cheesecloth bags, like party favors at a wedding. They flung them at the spot Tia had indicated. I ducked away, but couldn't avoid the cloud of pale blue dust that exploded around me as the bags burst, filling the air with the taste of evergreens and smoke. I coughed. I choked. And finally, I collapsed, hitting the floor so hard that I felt the impact all the way down into my bones.

The last thing I saw before everything went black was Tia's face, looming in my field of vision like a mountain. "And they call me a bitch," she said, and spat on my cheek. I felt the dampness. I felt the stone floor beneath me.

And then I didn't feel anything at all.

TWENTY

EVERYTHING HURT. IT WAS like someone had taken my nerves and dipped them in fire ants, all of which were now industriously working to chew their way through my flesh. The pain wrenched me out of sleep, pulling me back into a world full of nothing but suffering. At the same time, the pain kept my body from listening to my commands: it was too busy trying not to writhe in involuntary agonies to do anything as simple as letting me open my eyes.

There was a time when I would have thought that no one could endure that level of pain and survive. I had learned a lot since those easy, innocent days, back when I believed a bullet could be merciful enough to let me die.

"This is taking too long," said a voice. It sounded familiar, although I couldn't place it, not quite. "You promised me this would go faster."

"And I told you, cur, that I am a king, and I don't take orders from my dogs." Rhys. Bastard. "You've already betrayed one master. If you want me to trust you, you will do as you are told."

"We need this war. You *promised*." There was a growl

lurking in the unfamiliar voice now, allowing me to place it: Tia. Tia? But she wasn't supposed to be here . . .

Wait. No. She was the reason they'd been able to find me. Memory coursed back into my body, and I gasped, just a little.

It was enough.

"I think she's awake," said a voice—the false Queen. She sounded faintly interested, but not terribly concerned. "Do you think she's awake?"

"She might be. Faoiltiarna, you are dismissed. I'll speak with you later." There was a pause, broken by a huff, and the sound of footsteps. When Rhys spoke again, his voice was closer, only a few feet away from my head. "Sir Daye? Can you hear me? If you can hear me, open your eyes."

I did not open my eyes. I couldn't. The pain was too constant, and I still couldn't get a grip on my own body.

"Hmm. You see, the trouble with this sort of situation, my dear, is the uncertainty. Is she awake and ignoring us, or is she unconscious? It's so difficult to tell rebellion from oblivion. But I have an idea!" His voice came closer still as he said, very kindly, very cruelly, "Sir Daye, if you do not open your eyes, I am going to put a rosewood spike through the flesh of your left hand. I will not concern myself with the placement of the bones. I'm sure several of them will be broken, and the pain will be unbearable. Now, will you do as I say?"

I tried, I really tried. I'm proud, but I'm not stupid, and I've never been a fan of additional pain. My eyes refused to open.

"I see." He sounded genuinely regretful. I couldn't tell whether it was sincere or not. It really didn't matter.

New pain exploded in my left hand, so intense that it made the old pain seem inconsequential. My eyes snapped open, my body straining as it tried to lift up into an involuntary arch, pulling as far away from the pain as it could. I barely got my butt an inch off whatever it was that I was sprawled upon. Something was holding me down, and I was weak as a kitten besides: all the strength had gone out of my muscles, leaving them limp and agonized.

I think I screamed. It was hard to say.

"You see, we still don't know whether she was awake before, but she's awake now, and isn't that what matters?" Rhys didn't make any effort to conceal how pleased with himself he was. Why should he? He was winning. The winners are allowed to gloat.

I collapsed back into limp motionlessness. I couldn't really turn my head, but my eyes were willing to respond to commands, and so I glanced from side to side, trying to get an idea of where I was and what was going on.

Rhys and the false Queen were standing off to my left. He was wearing a heavy leather butcher's apron, which didn't inspire confidence about what was going to happen to me next. She was wearing white—she was always wearing white—and there were a few spots of blood on her bodice, standing out like brands against the fabric. She was smiling, her moon-mad eyes filled with delight . . .

And Marlis was there, too. She was standing a few feet behind them, holding a wide silver bowl in both her hands, her eyes fixed straight ahead. She was wearing a butcher's apron, which just made it harder for me to imagine that anything good was going to happen next. I couldn't tell from looking at her whether she was back under Rhys' control, or whether she was just playing along until it was safe to do something different. I hoped like hell for the latter.

The room was decorated in Rhys' usual austere style, and the walls were plain wood, easy to clean. I strained until I could see my shoulder. There were no chains or straps holding me down: just a thin string of yarrow flowers tied together with golden thread. They shouldn't have been strong enough to keep me from moving. "Should" is a word with very little power in Faerie.

"Amazing," said Rhys, leaning forward. "Sir Daye, were you aware that you heal so swiftly that your body rejects foreign objects? Your flesh is trying to push out my spike. It's quite remarkable. I wonder what part of you contains this property. I wonder whether I can bottle it."

"That's not the first thing you're going to bottle," said the false Queen. There was a faint whine in her voice that hadn't been there before. It was the first time I had heard her sound anything other than completely confident in her hold over the King of Silences. Her smile vanished, transmuted by suspicion. "You promised me, Rhys, remember? You promised you would get me what I needed."

"I will, my dear, I will, but you can't blame me for showing interest in all the other wonderful things that we have resting at our fingertips, now can you? Healing tinctures, complexion potions . . . we have immortality, but we've never had indestructability. Now, with a little work and a little cleverness, we can. We can ascend to the level of Oberon himself: untouchable, eternal, never dying or suffering any of the predations of mortality. All we have to do is find the right combination to coax it all out of her." Rhys leaned forward, grabbing something outside of my limited frame of view.

The pain in my hand, which had faded to a background note in the overall symphony of pain coming from the rest of me, suddenly flared into bright new agony. Rhys held up a wooden spike. It was dark with blood, and there were shreds of something that looked a lot like skin sticking to the sides. "You see? Your body couldn't decide whether to expel it or consume it, since it was so large, and tried for both. Your healing powers are incredible, Sir Daye, but they're not very smart."

"You don't have to keep using her title," said the false Queen. "She never deserved it in the first place, and she's certainly not going to use it again. Are you, October?"

"Go . . . fuck . . . yourself," I said, my voice barely above a whisper, my lips resisting even that small command. The pain wasn't getting any better. Aside from moments like the one where Rhys had pulled the spike out of my flesh, it also wasn't getting any worse.

Pain and I have an interesting relationship. I've spent so much time dealing with it over the past few years that it wasn't quite as incapacitating as it probably should have been. Every nerve I had was still on fire, and every inch of my skin felt like it was being flayed, but as long as those were constants, I could adapt.

"Human and obscene even to the last," said the false Queen. "Can you do anything with her tongue? It could be an excellent potion ingredient, and more importantly, it would silence her."

"It would just grow back," said Rhys. "I'll save it until I need it; we know she regenerates blood and skin with the same degree of strength, but I'm worried that the rest of her organs will only be fully effective when they're the originals. What do you think, Sir Daye? Have you experimented with your own limits? If I start removing fingers, will your body know to make more bone, or will it just patch the holes?"

Swearing at the false Queen had exhausted me. I glared at him mutely, hoping that my face would be enough to broadcast my hatred and anger at the situation.

"Ah. A pity. If you'd been willing to share what you knew, we might not have to test you. Now we'll have to put you through your paces before we know what we can safely do. If you were anything else, I'd just take what we needed—but then, if you were anything else, you wouldn't be so appealing. So I suppose there's a consequence for everything." He put the spike aside. "Marlis. A knife, if you please."

"Yes, Your Highness," she said. Her tone was virtually flat, like she was disengaged from the scene. Hearing it answered one question and opened a whole host of new ones, as well as a whole new slate of worries.

Marlis wasn't back under her supposed King's control. She hadn't sounded like a robot when he had her: she had sounded perfectly normal, just loyal to the man who had overthrown and tortured her family. Now she sounded like she was burying everything just to keep from blowing her own cover. If she wasn't careful, that was going to be the thing that gave her away. I couldn't help her if the King turned on her. Not while I was tied down and fighting against my own randomly misfiring nervous system.

She stepped closer, holding a blade out toward Rhys, handle first. For one giddy moment, I allowed myself to hope that she was going to flip it around and bury it in his gut. We were in a Kingdom full of alchemists. Surely someone would be able to save him before he died and put her in violation of Oberon's Law.

He took the knife from her hand without anyone getting stabbed. I hoped my disappointment didn't show, and was briefly glad for my ongoing agony, as it was probably doing a lot to prevent my face from showing what I was thinking. Only briefly: the man responsible for my pain was now holding a knife, and as worried as I was for Marlis, I was somewhat more concerned for myself.

"Do it," said the false Queen.

"Patience," he said, and lowered the knife toward me. I tried to pull away, I really did, but my body wouldn't obey me. It may have gotten easier to think, but it wasn't getting any easier to move.

The line of pain he drew along my collarbone was almost soothing in comparison to the agony flaring in my nerves. The smell of my blood filled the air, hot and sweet and coppery. I inhaled greedily, trying to focus on the blood, which I could feel running down my shoulder. There was a soft plinking sound as it dripped onto something metal; presumably a bowl, since he wasn't likely to be bleeding me without a collection method handy.

My strength has always been in the blood. It would have been better if he'd been cutting my face, where there would have been at least a chance of a drop hitting my lips, but I'd take what I could get. I didn't bother arguing with my eyelids, which were now as stubbornly unwilling to close as they had previously been unwilling to open. I just let my eyes become unfocused, and tried to concentrate on the blood.

The downside of being the first—effectively—of a new breed is that there's never been anyone to tell me what I could do. I've learned most of what I know through trial and error, sometimes with assistance from the Luidaeg. Recently, I've been getting almost as much assistance from May. She seemed to understand my magic better than I did sometimes, maybe because she had my memories but not my powers, giving her the luxury of objectivity.

Rhys cut me again, slicing through my hard-won distance and tearing it away. I gritted my teeth involuntarily, trying to find my focus through the pain. The blood wasn't plinking into the bowl anymore. As it fell, it landed with the thick, muddy sound of liquid dropping into liquid. He almost had enough for whatever he was trying to do. He had to—he couldn't be intending to bleed me dry one slice at a time. Could he?

"Is it ready?"

"Almost, my dear, almost. Have you never learned patience?"

"I was a Queen for more than a century. Any patience I might have learned, I forgot long ago. Now is it ready?"

"Almost." There was a soft clatter as he put the knife down, and Rhys began to chant. He spoke in a language I didn't know, full of rolling vowels and muted consonants. The smell of meadowsweet and wine vinegar began to grow in the air, itching where it touched my skin.

I could almost see his magic, if I didn't focus my eyes, if I kept the smell of the blood in mind. It swirled around me, colorless and cruel.

Then it burst, and the false Queen laughed, high and delighted and utterly pleased with the world. "It's beautiful! You've done it!"

"For you, my sweet," said Rhys. Then: "Marlis, move her head. She should see the sort of wonders she'll be enabling me to perform."

"Yes, Your Highness," said Marlis. She stepped closer, and stumbled, catching herself on the edge of my temporary bed before putting her hands on the sides of my head and turning me to face the King. Her thumb grazed my lips, and I realized the reason for her stumble.

Where she touched me, she left blood behind.

It wasn't much—just a smear, presumably wiped from the knife that Rhys had set aside—but it was so much more than I had had only a few seconds before. I forced my tongue to move, licking the blood away before she withdrew her hands. The taste of it exploded in my mouth like everything that was good in the world. In that moment, I felt like I could unmake any spell, overcome any obstacle, and do it all without getting a scratch on me.

The trouble with feeling invulnerable is that it's never true. When Marlis moved, she revealed Rhys and the former Queen of the Mists standing a few feet away. The false Queen had a jeweled chalice in her hands, so tacky and crusted with filigree that I had no doubt that it was real. Things like that are either plastic or platinum, with nothing in between. She looked at me, smirked, and raised the chalice to her lips, drinking deeply.

The smell of my magic filled the room, overlaid with a sharp, vinegary note that was acrid enough to bring fresh tears to my eyes. I recognized it objectively as the stamp of Rhys' magic marking his alchemy, but the rest of me raged against it. How *dare* he put his magic over mine? How *dare* he steal something that was so deeply and intrinsically my own, that was supposed to be unique in all of Faerie?

"Look for what's missing, and call it back," said Rhys, in the low, encouraging tone of someone who was trying to coach a recalcitrant pupil. "You have her power, you should be able to heal yourself."

And just like that, I knew what he was doing—what the false Queen had asked him to do. She wanted her Siren blood back. She was stealing my magic because she wanted to restore what I had taken away from her. There was just one problem.

She couldn't.

Dóchas Sidhe can do things no one else in Faerie can do. That's true of every race descended from Oberon or his wives. But we can't create what isn't there. We can't make a pureblood mixed, or turn a human into a changeling—and that means that when we remove something from the blood, it's gone forever. The false Queen wasn't going to be able to restore her Siren blood, because it was no longer there to be restored. I had taken it away. It was gone.

The smell of my magic began to fade. She lowered the chalice, looking disbelievingly at Rhys. "It didn't work," she said. "Why didn't it *work?* You told me this would work!"

"We must be missing something," he said soothingly . . . but when he turned to me, there was nothing soothing in his face. "What are we missing, Sir Daye? How may I restore my lady? Speak, or be sorry that you stayed silent."

I tried, I really did. I swallowed, feeling the precious blood that Marlis had managed to give me run down my throat, and forced my lips to open. No sound came out.

"Your Highness, your binding may be preventing Sir Daye from answering your questions." Marlis' comment was calm, even deferential, but it struck me as dangerous all the same. She was disagreeing with something her liege had done. What would happen if he realized that was unusual?

"Let her speak," hissed the false Queen. She grabbed his arm, digging in her fingernails. "She has to tell us how to fix this!"

"Oh, very well." Rhys walked back to me, leaned down, and touched the rope of yarrow flowers that stretched across my shoulders. The pain didn't stop, but it decreased so dramatically that I gasped, feeling as if a huge weight had been removed from my chest. I could breathe again.

Rhys waited a few seconds, watching with an analytical eye as I panted. Finally, he said, "I know this is not going to be a pleasant process for you. Pain is unavoidable. But how much pain is up to me. Do you understand? Answer my questions, and I can keep things pleasant. Like this. We can work together."

I stared at him. "This isn't working together," I said, and was only half surprised to discover that my voice was working again in the absence of the bulk of the pain. "This is you asking me to be good while you cut me up for parts."

"You make a fine point," he said. He looked to the false Queen. "She makes a fine point." Then he looked back to me, and smiled. It was a terrible expression, filled with edges, and with knives. "I suppose I didn't make myself very clear. Right now, we're planning to cut you up for parts. That's true. I won't try to sugarcoat it. That would insult both of us, and there's no need for me to do that. But here's the thing you're missing. Right now, we're planning to cut *you* up for parts. Not your pet death omen, not your squire, not that animal you've been bedding. Just you. That could change. Do you understand me? I could easily send my archers after the members of your little team who aren't yet asleep, and tell them that we've proven your treachery, and that your diplomatic immunity has been revoked in the face of crimes against the throne. Once they're all asleep . . . ah. Oberon was quite clear that we mustn't kill each other, and I am very, very good at not killing the people who come before me. Some of them may wish I had, when they finally wake. But I never break the Law."

For a moment, the urge to spit Quentin's true identity at him was so strong that I had to grit my teeth to keep it in. He'd never be this cavalier about slicing up the Crown Prince.

But he might be willing to use the Crown Prince as leverage to get what he really wanted: the false Queen back on the throne of the Mists, and no one to challenge what he'd been doing with Silences since he made it his own. I couldn't bring Quentin any deeper into this than I already had. All I could do was hope that Tybalt was smarter than he was loyal: that when he realized I'd been taken, he'd get Quentin the hell out of here, and tell Arden that I was lost.

"Go to hell," I said.

Rhys sighed. "I hate that you make me do this," he said. He produced another spike from inside his apron. I had time to tense—barely—and then he was driving it into my stomach, so hard that it seemed like he was pinning me to the table, a moth under glass, at the mercy of the biologist who had netted me out of the air. I screamed. I couldn't help myself, and I didn't really try; failure to scream would have meant that I wasn't playing along, and might have made him even crueler.

It was getting hard to remember why I didn't tell him about Quentin, or about Walther, or about *anything* that would make him stop hurting me.

"I hate that you make me be a monster for you," said Rhys. He didn't pull the spike from my belly, and his hands, as he pulled them away, were dripping with gore. "You see how hard I'm trying to be reasonable? I'm offering to make the pain as minimal as I can. I'm promising safe passage for your people. And all I need you to do is explain how I may help my lady. Why is that so hard for you? Can't you just go along?"

"Let me have her," said the false Queen, stepping up behind him. "I'm still part Banshee. I can make her hurt in ways that never break the skin."

There was a threat I hadn't considered, and didn't really want to think about. I took a breath, feeling the motion tug on the spike now embedded in my stomach, and managed to speak. "What's your name?"

She blinked at me, looking nonplussed. "What?"

"You must have a name. No one looks at a baby and says 'fuck her, she's so ugly that she doesn't get a name.' I don't know what your name is. I've never known what it was. You were always a queen, so I couldn't ask. What's your name?"

Now her eyes narrowed, expression turning wary. It was more familiar a look for her than confusion. "Why do you want to know?"

"Because you're going to be dead soon. Maybe I am, too, but I'd like to go to the night-haunts knowing who you were." I smiled. It was one of the hardest things I'd done in a long time. "Call it a last request?"

"I am not going to be dead soon, you stupid little mongrel bitch," she said, and sneered at me. "You've lost, October. You've finally, fully lost. I'm going to enjoy watching Rhys slice you so thin that you could be hung as ribbons from the trees, and I won't mourn for you. And as for my name, you can't have it, because I don't own it anymore. I sold it years ago, in exchange for everything I'd ever wanted, and I have never regretted my decision. Not for a moment."

"Now tell us what we need to know," said Rhys. "My patience wears thin."

"Your patience?" I demanded, lifting my head and shoulders away from the surface beneath me. It was all I could manage—even with the pain reduced, the chain of flowers still bound me tight. "*Your* patience? You're not the one with a spike sticking out of your stomach! Oberon's balls, you have some fucking nerve! Don't you dare stand there and talk to me about *your patience*, you arrogant—"

Rhys' hand caught me across the face, slamming my head back down against whatever was beneath me. I choked on a mouth that was suddenly full of blood, hot and sweet and exactly what I'd been hoping for. A man who likes to tell you about his plans is a man who can be goaded into lashing out. Years of dealing with villains and misguided despots has taught me that.

"See what you made me do?" He sighed. There was nothing soft or sorry in that sound. "Now answer my question, Sir Daye. Why didn't it work?"

I swallowed. My mouth was still bleeding, and I swallowed again, unwilling to let any of the precious blood escape. Finally, as my mouth healed enough to make speech possible, I said, "It didn't work because it *can't* work. She has no Siren blood to restore. I took it all away from her. It's like I told you before. My magic can't create—it can only manipulate what's already there."

"You're lying!" The false Queen lunged for me, and only Rhys' arms around her chest kept her from clawing my throat open. She struggled against him, face set in a mask of hatred that had nothing in common with her mild amusement of only a few minutes before. "You give back what you took from me! You give it back right now!"

"I can't." I didn't take any pleasure in the words, strange as that might sound. She was clearly desperate, and I was starting to wonder whether I had made things that much worse for her. Sirens and Sea Wights were both descended from Maeve, while Banshee were descended from Titania. When she had been the daughter of three bloodlines, she might have been in a strange sort of internal truce, tilted so much farther toward Maeve than toward Titania that she had been able to remain relatively at peace. Now her bloodlines were equally weighted, and there was a good chance that they were tearing her apart.

I took a breath. "I can't," I repeated. "But I can take more away. I can make you purely Banshee, or purely Sea Wight. I know you're hurting. Maeve and Titania . . . their bloodlines don't blend. If you let me take one of them out of you—"

"You'll touch me again over my dead body," she snarled. She broke free of Rhys, and there was a knife in her hand, the silver clean and glinting in the light from overhead. She slammed it into my chest in a hard overhand arc, and I gasped, shock racing through my body only a few beats behind the pain, which was immense and unrelenting.

She must have hit a lung, I thought desperately. I couldn't lift my arms to claw at the blade. I couldn't do anything but close my eyes, and let the world drop away.

So I did.

TWENTY-ONE

THE WORLD CAME BACK like the fuzzy picture on a badly tuned television, gradually illuminating itself until I could see the room around me in washed out, under-defined color. It wasn't the right room. This was my living room at the house, complete with thrift store sofa and dozing Cait Sidhe still gripping the remote control. Raj looked utterly at peace, and utterly unaware of my presence, which meant I was either dead or dreaming. There was no other way I would have been able to sneak up on him.

"Let's go with dreaming," I said, and my voice echoed like I'd been shouting down a long tunnel. My mouth still tasted like blood. I swallowed. The taste remained. Not dead, then. I couldn't imagine that my death would be as bloody as my life had been.

Then again, when I died, I would go to the night-haunts. It didn't get much bloodier than that.

"Dreaming is close enough," said a voice behind me.

I turned. "May!"

My Fetch was standing behind me, wearing a long gray dress belted with a length of rope. Her hair was as long as mine, and the colored streaks were back, blue and green and lovely. She smiled at me, but not happily; she looked like her heart was breaking. "Sort of. Technically. Karen's here, too. She's just staying out of the way because it's all she can do to shift me from my dreamscape into yours. Adding herself to the mix would complicate things too much, and she might lose her grip on the whole house of cards. She says hello, by the way."

"Karen's here?" Karen was the middle daughter of my friends Stacy and Mitch: sweet, friendly, fifteen years old, and an oneiromancer. She could move through dreams, manipulate them, and use them to communicate with others, even when those others were supposedly outside of her reach. No one knew where the gift had come from—according to the Luidaeg, there hadn't been any oneiromancers in Faerie in centuries.

We'd first learned about Karen's talent when she was taken by Blind Michael. There was nothing like being kidnapped by the monster under the bed to make you really embrace what you could do, no matter how strange it might seem.

May nodded. "She came as soon as I'd been elf-shot. I guess she keeps an eye on us."

"That's good to know." I paused. "Wait—have *I* been elf-shot?"

"No." May's expression sobered, her heartbroken smile dying. "You've been stabbed in the heart. I know you think you're immortal, Toby, but you're not. Your body's trying to fight through this. I'm not sure it can."

"What?" The sucking feeling in my chest. I'd been assuming it was because the false Queen had hit my lung, but my heart . . . laughter rose unbidden to my lips. "Oh, man. I never thought this was how it was going to end. That's almost stupid, it's so predictable."

May scowled and folded her arms. "Maybe you think this is funny, but I don't. You think I want to wake up to a world where Tybalt is blaming me for letting you die, when you could have prevented it? That is not a fun world. That is a world full of bitterness and anger and dead mice in my shoes."

"So what do you want me to do about it, May?" I demanded. "I'm not exactly in a position to negotiate, here. I've blacked out from shock, or I wouldn't be talking to you, and there's a *knife* in my *heart*."

"You were starting to look for the keys to his spell when she stabbed you, weren't you?" May's question stopped me cold. She allowed herself the sliver of a smile. "See, I can be a smart girl sometimes. Marlis fed you some of your own blood, and you needed more, so you goaded him into hitting you. That way, you got what you needed, and you could start looking for a way out. It was a good plan. It's not your fault she stabbed you before you could finish."

"Still stabbed," I said. "Still blacked out. What do you want me to do, May?"

"I want you to wake up," she said. "Do what you were planning. You have a few seconds. Time's different when you're asleep."

"I don't know—"

"And tell Jazz I'm sorry, okay? I didn't plan on this. I'll see her when I wake up." May's smile grew, turning sad again. "Everything gets messed up sometimes. Now close your eyes, and live."

I wanted to argue. I wanted to tell her that this was futile, that I couldn't accomplish anything but looking foolish in my own dreamscape while my body was bleeding out back in the waking world.

I closed my eyes.

The world was replaced by blackness. There was still no pain, but that didn't necessarily mean anything: if I was close enough to bleeding out, I might have reached the point where pain couldn't reach me. There was something incredibly alluring about that thought. I could just stay where I was, and the pain would never touch me again.

But neither would the pleasure. I'd never see Quentin crowned; I'd miss my own wedding. I squinted my eyes tighter, blocking out all traces of light . . . until the light appeared in a glowing web of pale yellow strands, crossing and crisscrossing my body like a spider's web. They covered parts of me that I couldn't possibly have seen, but I saw them anyway. They were the logical extensions of each other, and once I knew what they were, I couldn't have missed them if I'd tried.

Two of the lines came together and crossed over my fingers, tying them down. I flexed my hands, carefully at first, and then with more force, straining against the lines. They stung where they touched me. It started out light, and then it flared into a burn. Pain flooded back into my body, like it had been invited in when I started fighting against the lines. I welcomed it. If there was pain, I still had a body that was capable of hurting: there was a chance I'd be able to make it to all the things I didn't want to miss. I strained harder.

Follow the lines, I thought, and then: *Don't let the bastards win.*

The lines across my fingers snapped.

The smell of meadowsweet and wine vinegar assaulted my nostrils as I moved my hands, clearing more of the lines away. The pain wasn't receding, but it wasn't as all-consuming as it had been: I was starting to hear voices. A male voice, raised in anger; a female voice, raised in a plaintive whine that sounded somehow familiar. I knew these people.

Rhys and the false Queen. If they were arguing, it was probably over the fact that I was supposed to be his undying font of alchemical providence, and she had gone and stabbed me in the chest. I wouldn't be nearly as useful if I was dead. They might as well have stuck with my laundry.

My eyes wouldn't open. That . . . wasn't a good sign. Before, it had been pain keeping my body from responding to my demands; now it was weakness, plain and simple and all-consuming. My mouth wasn't bleeding anymore. There was nothing to lend me strength but stubbornness, and so it was stubbornness I seized upon, using it to force my now-unbound hands to keep moving. If I had hands, I must have arms; that was the logical extension. If I had arms, they were going to do what I told them to do. They were going to work.

It was a relief when my hands touched my chest. Until I felt the fabric of my cheap tank top, tacky with blood and sticking to my skin, I hadn't been sure the movement was anything but my own dying imagination. Slowly, with fingers that felt like so much dead weight at the end of hands that weren't much better, I began feeling around for the knife. When I finally found it, I gripped as best I could, and began trying to pull.

Arthur pulling Excalibur from the stone got him a kingdom and a legend and a whole bunch of crappy knock-off stories. Hell, it got him a Disney movie. Me pulling a knife out of my own heart got me pain, pain, and more pain, until I felt like I was on the verge of blacking out again. I gritted my teeth and kept pulling. If I lost my grip, I wasn't going to get it back.

The knife moved.

It was a small thing at first, just a shift, but it was a shift that pulled an infinitesimal fraction of the blade out of my heart. I could almost feel my flesh beginning to knit back together, moving faster to save me than my body was moving to die. I pulled again, and the knife shifted more, almost coming free.

The false Queen had never been a fighter. Her attack had been intended to kill—there was no doubt of that—but she'd never really had the strength to drive the knife as deeply as she would have needed to. She only got it between my ribs because I couldn't move away and luck was on her side. While she'd been able to pierce my heart, she hadn't been able to fully bisect it, which explained why I was still alive to pull the damn thing out.

"—attack her like that!"

"She deserves it for what she did to me! You don't know how I've suffered since that little whore put her hands on me! You'll never understand the pain she's put me through."

"She *purified* you!"

The sound of flesh striking flesh covered up the sound of the knife finally coming free of my chest. It couldn't cover the sound of that same knife dropping from my hand and clattering to the floor. There was a sickening pause before Rhys laughed, sounding utterly delighted.

"Look at that! You didn't exaggerate when you described how difficult she was to kill. She's amazing."

I forced my hands to move again, raising them, shaking, to my mouth. I had a few seconds. That was all. Rhys would get over his delight: he would realize I was moving, which meant that his spell had broken. Once that happened, all hell was going to break loose.

The blood I sucked from my fingers tasted darker than it ever had before. My death had seeped into it, flavoring it until it was barely recognizable as my own. I still swallowed greedily, pulling it back into my body and yanking out every last scrap of strength. I could feel my heartbeat, steady and strong and slightly frantic, like it was as angry as the rest of me.

I opened my eyes. I reached down and ripped the spike out of my stomach. I sat up. I had been lying on a bier like the ones in the dungeon. There were channels cut into the stone to coax my blood toward the bowls Rhys had set up at the corners. I ran my fingers through one of them as I swung my legs over the side of the bier. The blood that had pooled there was still half liquid, and stuck to my skin. Good. I was going to need it.

"You stabbed me," I said, eyes going to Rhys and the false Queen. She was standing so that his body shielded her from me. That was probably smart; I wanted to strangle her more than I had wanted anything in a long time. It was too bad I was also too weak to stand. "I didn't expect that. I didn't appreciate it, either."

Marlis was standing behind the pair, the heavy jeweled chalice still in her hands. She met my eyes and nodded, almost imperceptibly. I didn't dare return the gesture. I just hoped she would take apparent disregard as agreement.

"I am a diplomat from the Kingdom of the Mists," I said, sliding slowly off the bier. I kept my hands braced against the stone, trying to look like I was just steadying myself, and not holding myself up completely. It wasn't an easy balance to strike. "I am here in the name of Her Majesty, Arden Windermere, Queen in the Mists. And it is not *nice* to stab your diplomats."

"You troublesome little bitch," said Rhys wonderingly. He took a half step forward, one hand going to the pocket of his apron.

He was still reaching when Marlis hit him across the back of the head with the chalice. I could hear bone crack from across the room. Rhys wobbled, looking startled. And then he fell, opening a portal beneath himself as he dropped, so that he fell through the floor rather than crashing into it. The former Queen of the Mists stood frozen for a few precious seconds, eyes gone wide and pale with terror, before she whirled and bolted for the door. She grabbed it, slamming it open—

—and ran straight into Tybalt's open, outstretched hand. She screamed, and the sound was cut off as his fingers closed around her throat. His face was contorted into a twisted mask, more feline than human. I couldn't hear him snarling. That was probably not a good sign. The louder he was, the easier it was to talk him down.

"Tybalt!" I took a step forward, and almost fell as my legs tried to buckle underneath me.

His eyes flicked to me, widening in concern. Some of

the feral fierceness went out of them, leaving the man I loved visible in the face of the furious King of Cats. Then the false Queen squirmed, and his attention snapped back to her, eyes narrowing again. He tightened his grip, lifting her off the floor. Her feet kicked helplessly, finding no purchase, while her hands clawed at his arm, trying to make him let go. It wasn't going to happen. Unlike him, she had no actual claws: she couldn't hurt him enough to get what she wanted.

He was going to kill her. He was going to kill a former monarch of the Divided Courts in front of me, and I wasn't going to be able to stop him.

"Don't do this!" My legs were still weak, but I was standing, and that was enough for me. I half-walked, half-fell toward him, gaining strength with every step, until I was virtually running. Marlis appeared next to me, offering me her arm, and I took it. She had attacked her King for me. At this point, I would have trusted her even if she hadn't been Walther's sister.

"Why not?" Tybalt gave the false Queen a shake. She moaned, the sound garbled and distorted by the pressure of his hand against her throat. "She earned this. She paid for every scrap of it. She *hurt* you."

"I got better." I let go of Marlis' arm in order to touch his, trying to keep my hands gentle. It was hard—I had so little balance, and the world was still so unsteady—but for Tybalt, I would try. "I always get better. You're better than she is. Don't do this. Don't break the Law."

"No one would ever know," he snarled. He shook her again. This time, she didn't waste air on moaning, although her hands continued to scrabble against his grip.

"You would know," I said softly.

"I have an alternative," said Marlis.

We both turned to look at her, Tybalt holding the false Queen off the floor and me covered in my own blood. We must have made a pretty pair, because she flushed red, taking a small step backward before straightening her shoulders and holding her ground.

"I have an alternative," she repeated. She dipped her hand into one pocket of her butcher's apron, producing a small, leather-wrapped bundle. The Queen began kicking and squirming even harder, her eyes almost bugging out of her head. Marlis ignored her. Instead, she calmly unwrapped the leather, producing a short, stone-tipped arrow fletched in the colors of Silences. She held it out to me. "Let her sleep."

"I would rather let her bleed," said Tybalt.

"But the Law says you can let her sleep." Marlis looked to the false Queen, and there was no softness in her eyes. "Believe me, this isn't any better."

"Mercy rarely is." I reached out and took the elf-shot gingerly by the shaft, careful to avoid the point as much as possible. I looked to Tybalt. "Please."

"She has hurt you too many times."

"Yes," I agreed. "Don't let her hurt me by taking you away."

He stared at me for a moment, instinct and intellect warring in his eyes. Then he lowered her to the floor, hand still clamped around her throat, and looked away.

The false Queen glared hatred and fury at me as I pressed the arrow's tip against the skin of her collarbone. "Sweet dreams," I said, and drove it home.

The tension went out of her instantly as the magic of the elf-shot washed through her body, driving her down into sleep. Tybalt dropped her a heartbeat later, letting her fall to the floor like so much trash. Then he turned to me, took a single step forward, and wrapped his arms around me, crushing me against his chest. He was shaking. The vibrations seemed to radiate out from his center, making them impossible to ignore, and so I didn't try. I just put my arms around him, and let him hold me until the shaking slowed to something more manageable.

He made a small, unhappy noise when I began to pull

away, but he didn't stop me. He knew better. I left my hand on his arm, unwilling to fully break the contact between us. I needed him as much as he needed me.

"Where's Quentin?" I asked.

"In the Court of Cats," said Tybalt. "Jolgeir handed him a stack of graphic novels and told him not to touch anything. We may never get him back."

"Good. That means he's safe. Where's Walther?"

"Still working," said Marlis.

"That means we only have two loose ends." I looked at the false Queen, sleeping on the floor, and at the room, where I had been intended to spend the rest of my life bleeding for the King's pleasure. Then I turned back to Marlis. "Rhys ran. Where did he go? We need to find him, and then we need to find Tia. She betrayed us." She betrayed all of Silences.

They both needed to pay.

"Why?" Marlis asked. "You're free."

"Yeah, but he's not." I smiled thinly. "I have diplomatic immunity from being cut up by assholes. He broke it, even if he wants to claim that finding me in the vault was proof of treason. The High King isn't going to let him keep his throne, and I intend to deliver the fucker to Toronto myself. As for Tia, she's a bad dog, and bad dogs get punished. Now let's go."

The room where I'd been destined to be sliced and diced was connected to a hallway that connected, in turn, to the main hall. Marlis led the way. We didn't see anyone as we walked the halls like something out of a horror story, me drenched in blood, Tybalt still more cat than man, and Marlis in her butcher's apron, which she had refused to remove before we left the surgery room. "I'm done hiding what he made us do in his name," she'd said, and now she stalked ahead of us, a scalpel in her hand and murder in her eyes. If she found Rhys first, there might be a violation of the Law after all—and I couldn't say it wasn't earned. After what the bastard had done to her family, I would have been happy holding him down while she killed him.

But I didn't have that luxury. I'd see him deposed, elf-shot, and shunned by pureblood society before I'd see him dead. He didn't deserve to turn me, or anyone else, into a killer.

"That blow to the head should have broken the skin," I said. "If he's bleeding, I'll find him."

Something touched my shoulder. I turned just enough to see that it was Tybalt's hand. His eyes were still fixed straight ahead, his pupils narrow slits of black amongst the green. There was a tremble in his fingers that worried me, but this wasn't the time to ask him about it, or to do anything but keep on walking. We had to find the King of Silences. We couldn't fall apart now.

"So I'm thinking this isn't where we're going to go for our honeymoon," I said quietly.

Tybalt almost jumped, turning to stare at me like he had just noticed my presence—even though his hand was still resting against my shoulder, even though he hadn't been more than a few feet away since we'd been reunited. "I would prefer something drier, and less filled with intrigue," he said.

"That means Disney World's out, too," I said. I offered him a smile. He didn't return it. "I'm okay, Tybalt. It's almost over." He didn't know how close I'd come to bleeding out. Sure, I was covered in the stuff, but that didn't mean anything—I'd been covered in blood before, lots of times. It wasn't always life-threatening. Not to me. As long as May didn't tell him the false Queen's knife had actually pierced my heart, he never needed to know.

Sometimes silence is a greater form of mercy than the truth.

"Is it?" he asked, and I didn't have an answer for him.

Marlis stopped at a blank stretch of wall. I almost expected her to walk straight through it, like she had before, but instead she reached out and touched a patch of wood, her fingers tracing the grain. "There used to be a gold yarrow branch here," she said. "*He* had it removed. He had everything but the fountain removed, and he would have taken that, too, if it hadn't been connected to the foundation of the castle."

"Home décor is not currently our priority," I said.

She shook her head. "It should be," she said, and pushed inward.

The wall swung open, revealing, not a hidden passageway, but an entire hidden room. It was empty, and smelled of dust and long, lonely days, hours where no one walked within it, or even remembered its existence. Marlis stepped inside. Tybalt and I followed her, his hand remaining on my shoulder right up to the moment when I stiffened, sniffing the air, and turned to point at a narrow doorway on the room's far wall.

"That way," I said. "He went that way." The smell of blood hung in the air, faintly tinged with wine vinegar and meadowsweet. That could have been the residue of his magic: if he'd teleported here, the smell would naturally have lingered.

This time, I took the lead, crossing the room and heading down the narrow hall with Tybalt so close at my heels that if I stopped, we were going to have a collision. I didn't let it slow me down. The smell of blood and magic might be lingering now, but it wouldn't last forever; it never did. If we were going to find Rhys, we needed to do it soon.

My hand went to my belt, instinctively reaching for the knife that wasn't there, and I realized that I was unarmed. Of course I was unarmed: who takes someone hostage and conveniently gives them weapons? Rhys was a bastard and a butcher, but he wasn't stupid. He never had been, except possibly in who he loved. If he hadn't been so fond of the false Queen, he would never have declared war on the Mists—but then, he would never have been King, either. Maybe he thought it had all been worth it. I'd have to ask him, before I let Tybalt voice his displeasure with the hospitality we'd received.

The hall was long and dimly lit by sconces set near the top of the wall. Their pale, steady glow was enough to keep me from tripping or walking into anything, but only just; my night vision isn't as good as a pureblood's. I forced myself to keep walking confidently forward, following the blood trail. Rhys was going to ground. He wasn't going to be slamming into walls while he did it.

The trail ended at another blank wall. "Let me through," said Marlis. Tybalt and I stepped to the side, and she repeated her earlier trick, spreading her fingers against the wood and pushing inward until there was a click and the wall swung open. The smell of wine vinegar and meadowsweet was stronger on the other side. Marlis shook her head. "He's been doing this for years. He teleports around the knowe like we would have built it without doors, and he never asks himself why a place that wasn't meant for him would come so perfectly tailored to his abilities."

"Sounds like a King to me," I said, and stepped through the newly opened door before Tybalt could push in front of me.

The smell of blood was basically gone now, only providing the faintest of undercurrents to the much stronger scent of Rhys' magic. It trailed after him like a string, and I followed it without hesitation, seeking the minotaur at the center of my own private labyrinth. I could feel the weakness in my knees and the lightness in my thoughts; if I didn't finish this soon, my friends and allies were going to be finishing it without me. Even I have my limits. My body was cooperating for now, but that was more a matter of stubbornness and shock than anything else.

"This way," I said, beckoning the others on. I was so focused on the trail I knew, the blood and magic and the promise of a conclusion, that I didn't check my surroundings the way I should have. Tybalt would normally have caught the scent, but he didn't have my skill at distinguishing blood from blood: I was covered in the stuff, and that was hiding Rhys' scent from him. I stepped forward.

Rhys lunged out of an alcove to my left and grabbed me, his arm locking around my neck, pulling me backward into his chest. I gasped as the air was knocked out of me. Then I tensed, bracing for an impact that didn't come. Tybalt was still standing exactly where he had been before, not making any move toward me or the man who held me. It didn't make sense.

"Move, and I break her skin," snarled Rhys. I tensed more, my eyes tracing the line of his arm until they reached his hand, and the arrow he was holding just above my shoulder.

Oh. That made sense after all.

"You don't want to do this," I said. "I'm a diplomat. Any act of aggression toward me is an act of aggression toward the Mists."

"And I am a *King*," spat Rhys. "You disgusting little bitch. You could have cleansed your own blood long ago, but instead you choose to remain mortal, and for what? So you can come here and taunt me with your filth, even as you plot my downfall? Stay back!" I felt him stiffen behind me.

Tybalt, who had been inching forward, stopped. "Let her go," he said softly. "If you let her go, I will not pursue you when you run."

"And if I don't?" demanded Rhys. "You're an animal. What can you do to me?"

"Follow you to the ends of the earth. For a hundred years, if I must, because I will have no better way to spend my time. When she wakes, I will press your heart into her hand, and tell her I am sorry I was not a better man." Tybalt's smile was slow, and terrible, and had nothing to do with joy. "I have tried to be a better man, you see. For her. But I could be a better monster, for you."

The arrow was barely an inch above the skin of my shoulder. If I moved at all, or if Rhys did, it was all going to be over. I would either die as the potion fought against my humanity, or I would sleep for a hundred years when my magic automatically pushed me all the way toward Faerie. Tybalt would break the Law, and High King Sollys would have no choice but to put him to death.

But if Tybalt let Rhys go to save me from elf-shot, then it would all have been for nothing. Silences would remain frozen in the rule of a man who allowed changelings to be treated like chattel, who sliced up his enemies for parts—and who had, thus far, managed to serve the letter of Oberon's Law, never going too far, never crossing the line. The war might happen or it might not. It wouldn't really matter. For the people of Silences, the last War still hadn't ended. Either way, we would lose. We would all lose.

Or I could put my faith in Walther and in my magic, and I could end it now.

I moved my chin just enough to let me meet Tybalt's eyes. His smile died, replaced by horrified understanding. Then, before he could react, I slammed myself hard to the side, taking advantage of Rhys' rigidity. The change in our positions put the arrow above the flesh over my collarbone. As I had expected, Rhys brought it down, piercing my skin. I fell forward, hooking his ankle with mine. He wasn't prepared, and my weight drove the arrow deeper as we both tumbled to the floor, passing through the muscle of my shoulder and into the flesh of his chest.

"I win," I said, and closed my eyes. The pain began a moment later, electric and all-consuming. I welcomed it. The pain meant my body was fighting the elf-shot, and the elf-shot was fighting my body, and as long as I was at war with myself, I was alive.

It was only when the pain began to ebb that I realized I might be losing.

TWENTY-TWO

I AWOKE WITH A GASP, one hand flying up to check the curvature of my ear while my eyes were still struggling to find their focus. It was familiar, no sharper or softer than it had been before I went and stabbed myself in the shoulder with an arrow. Either I was dreaming, or I hadn't changed the balance of my blood at all.

Hands clamped down on my shoulders, and then a mouth was pressed over mine, kissing me with such fierce intensity that I didn't need to be able to see to know that it belonged to Tybalt. I looped my arms around his shoulders and kissed him back, not really caring who else was in the room. I wasn't dreaming. I dreamed about Tybalt kissing me sometimes—I dreamed about it a lot—but it was never like this, never shaking and scared and holding me so tightly that it felt like air couldn't slide between us. I was awake.

My eyes had finished focusing by the time he pulled back and let me go. I blinked, several times. His cheeks had seemed rough when he was kissing me, and now I could see why; they were peppered with stubble, which grew in bands of alternating black and brown, like his hair.

"Even your face is striped," I said, half-laughing. He smiled, but it didn't reach his eyes. That was when the fear began. "Oh, oak and ash. How long . . . how long have I been asleep?"

"Now you begin to worry," he whispered. "Can't you learn to worry sooner? For my sake, if no one else's?"

"A week," said a voice from my left. I turned. Walther was standing there, looking exhausted but pleased with himself. He raised one hand in a small wave. "Hi. Welcome back to the land of the living."

"You did it?" I raked my hair out of my face with one hand, staring at him. "You actually did it?"

"You mean did I, Walther Davies, find the solution for elf-shot? Yeah. I did."

"Wow." I couldn't think of what to say after that. I settled for looking down at myself and confirming that yes, once again, my clothes had been changed while I was unconscious: my tank top and jeans were gone, replaced by a long white chemise that probably wouldn't stay white for long, if my recent adventures were anything to judge by. I recognized the bed as the one I had been given when we arrived in Silences. I looked up. "We're still here? Where are May and Quentin? Did we ever find Tia? Is she still on the loose?"

"May is awake and helping Marlis get an accurate count of the household staff. Rhys didn't really have any records, and even as his supposed seneschal, she had very little idea of who all the changelings were, how old they were, or what kind of health they were in." Walther made no effort to hide his expression of disapproval. "He thought it was improper for purebloods to spend time belowstairs like that. Some of them are so terrified of us that they can't even speak in our presence."

"They'll come around." Changelings inherited one major trait from our human ancestors: we were flexible, capable of adjusting to incredible changes in our situations. They would come to realize that not all purebloods were their enemies. "Some of them . . . Rhys was really casual about his goblin fruit usage. Some of them are addicted."

"And you want to help?" asked Walther.

I nodded. "Once I can stand unassisted."

"I would expect no less, from a hero." There was a new formality in Walther's tone. I didn't like it.

"As for Tia, we found her attempting to flee the Kingdom," said Tybalt. "I was . . . not gentle in apprehending her, I am afraid."

"You were gentler than you had any reason to be." For once, it was Walther whose voice was as cold as death. "She's being held for trial. She's confessed to betraying my family during the War. The Cu Sidhe led the forces of the Mists straight to us, and we never knew."

"Why?"

"Because she thought that we treated them like pets, and not like allies." Walther's mouth turned down at the edges. "I don't know whether we did or not. I always thought that we were friends."

"I don't think Tia believes it's possible for the Cu Sidhe to be friends with their regents," I said, and tried to push the blankets off. Tybalt moved them back into place. I realized for the first time that he was kneeling on the edge of the bed, not sitting; he was ready to move.

"No," he said. "Stay where you are."

I frowned at him. "What aren't you telling me?"

"You've been asleep for a week," said Walther.

"I knew that."

"I've been trying to wake you up for six days," he shot back. I stopped. "You had seizures. You shifted your own blood back and forth so fast that I could *see* your features changing. You kept returning to the point you're at right now, but it took longer every time, and we were afraid that if it didn't stop, you were going to tear yourself apart. So you'll forgive us for being sort of nervous about you passing out again. You were trying to do what your mother did, and shift the elf-shot out of your blood. It was going to kill you before you succeeded."

"You woke once before," said Tybalt. "You said my name. And then you went back to sleep."

"That was then," I said. I felt bad about essentially brushing off their genuine concerns, but I didn't see that I had a choice. "Let me up. I have to call Arden. I have to tell her—"

"She's here," said Walther.

I stared at him. "What?"

"Queen Windermere is here," said Walther. "The Queen of Silences contacted the Queen in the Mists this morning to rescind the declaration of war, and ask for help in rebuilding this Kingdom. Queen Windermere arrived an hour ago."

I kept staring at him. *"What?"*

He smiled, looking a little frayed around the edges. "I didn't wake you up first, remember? I started with my mother, and then moved on to the rest. You actually took longer, because every time you pulled yourself toward mortal, I had to back off. Aunt Siwan is back on her throne, with Uncle Holger beside her. It's going to be a while before they're comfortable. They'll have time."

"And . . . and Quentin?"

"Your young squire has been getting to know the younger people of Silences, and reporting back on what he learns," said Tybalt. "He has been invaluable to the cause of knowing who might yet turn against the throne, and who is simply relieved to see Rhys the bastard gone at last."

This time, when I swept the blankets aside, Tybalt let me. He rose as I did, offering me his arm. I took it. My whole body felt too light, like the center had been pulled out of things. "Is there a robe or something I could borrow? I think I need to eat before I get dressed."

"You didn't have to get out of bed for that," said Walther.

"No, but I have to get out of bed to see Rhys and the false Queen." He frowned at me. I shook my head. "I need to see them. I need to *know* that they're asleep." I needed to know that Tybalt hadn't responded to my loss of consciousness by killing them both.

Tybalt clearly understood the reasons for my insistence. He folded his hand over mine and said nothing, only joined me in looking at Walther, who sighed.

"You're not content unless you're running yourself to death, are you?" he asked. "All right. Follow me."

The difference in the knowe was apparent the moment we left my rooms. There were people, for one thing, moving here and there with quick purpose. Some of them were stripping tapestries off the walls; others were installing golden filigree in holes and corners that had clearly been designed to hold those specific ornaments. Everything smelled of yarrow and roses, a perfume that was explained by the vases of fresh flowers that had appeared on every flat surface that wasn't the floor.

A few curious glances were cast at me and Tybalt, but people were polite enough not to stare. Walther, on the other hand, got blatant pointing, and even a brief round of applause. His cheeks reddened. He kept walking.

"I've told everyone that this is on you as much as it's on me," he said, voice pitched low. "You took out Rhys; you confirmed the roses I needed; you gave yourself up to buy me time. But they keep insisting that I'm their savior."

"I don't mind if someone else is the hero for a change," I said. "I'm just glad I'm not going to be asleep for the next hundred years."

"You are not alone in that," said Tybalt.

I squeezed his hand, and kept walking.

We were descending a flight of stairs when a voice from behind me shouted "Toby!" I turned in time to see Quentin racing toward us, and braced for impact. Tybalt even let go of my hand, moving to position himself just below me. My squire slammed into me, knocking me back a half-step; Tybalt caught us both, saving me from needing to do anything but return Quentin's embrace. I held him tight. He held me tighter. That was our relationship, in a nutshell.

When he finally pushed me away, it was to look me critically up and down, and proclaim, "You've lost weight."

"I'm going to eat something after I see them." I didn't need to explain who I meant, or why I wanted to see them with my own eyes: Quentin nodded in clear understanding, taking his hands off my arms. I turned to retake Tybalt's hand, and asked, "Coming with us?"

"Never leaving again," said Quentin. Now four, we walked the rest of the way down the stairs. At the bottom, we found a hallway; at the end of the hall, there was a door. It wasn't locked.

The room on the other side was small and austere, furnished only with two plain stone biers. Rhys lay atop one; the false Queen of the Mists, whose name we might never know, was on the other.

"They'll sleep out their enchantments before they stand trial," said Walther, watching me as I looked at them. "A hundred years isn't much, but it's a start."

And they would wake into a world where fair, considerate stewardship had wiped away any legacy of their hatred. Arden in the Mists, and the Yates family here in Silences. In a way, the torture of knowing that they had failed to remake Faerie in their own image would be worse for our sleepers than anything else could have been.

"Toby?" Arden's voice was soft and familiar, and most of all, expected. I still tensed before I turned to see her standing in the doorway. There was a woman next to her, golden-haired and blue-eyed, with a circlet resting atop her head. One of her hands was missing several fingers.

"You know, the bastard," I gestured toward Rhys, "swiped some of my laundry after I bled all over it. I heal pretty fast. A good alchemist might be able to make something from my blood that would help you grow those back."

The woman smiled. She looked tired. "Not the greeting one usually offers to a queen, but given what I know of you, I'll take it as given. Hello, Sir October Daye, Knight of Lost Words, sworn in service to Duke Sylvester Torquill of Shadowed Hills, Hero in the Mists. My name is Siwan Yates, Queen of Silences, and my family owes you a debt we will never be able to repay."

"But we'll still take the laundry," said Walther quickly. Siwan shot him a sharp look. He smiled guilelessly. "Hey, if Toby wants to help us grow back all the parts Rhys stole, I say we let her. She's got more blood."

"Because you are our trusted allies, I'll allow it," said Arden.

Siwan nodded. "Then we are even more deeply in your debt, Sir Daye. If ever you need anything, you need only ask."

"I need you to let me talk to your changelings." The words burst out in a rush. Siwan looked startled. So did Arden. I pressed on: "Most of them have never seen the mortal world. They never got the Choice. All of them have been exposed to goblin fruit, and some of them are already addicted. We have a hope chest, in the Mists, and if Queen Windermere isn't willing to risk bringing it here, we have me. I can offer them a Choice, a *real* choice, one where they get to belong completely to whichever world they want. It'll cure the addictions. It'll give them a chance."

Siwan looked from me to Arden, brows raised. "Can she really do that?"

"She can," confirmed Arden.

"She *won't*, for several days," said Tybalt firmly. "She needs her rest."

"But after I've rested, please," I said. "Let me help them."

Siwan turned back to me. Tears were running down her cheeks, but her smile was still serene. "Thank you," she said. I managed not to flinch from the words. The fact that I felt like hell probably helped. "I never thought to have my Kingdom back, and now . . . thank you. All of you. You are heroes here."

"We have more to do, Your Highness, and Sir Daye looks exhausted," said Arden respectfully. "Shall we?"

"We shall," said Siwan. The two queens turned and walked away. They didn't say good-bye.

Quentin broke the ensuing silence first. "Huh," he said. "I guess that happened."

"I guess it did," I agreed. I turned to Walther. "Are you going to be staying here after the rest of us go home?"

He shook his head. "Hell, no. I have classes to teach, and kids who depend on me. And I meant it about the tenure."

"Good." I leaned to the side, resting my head against Tybalt's shoulder. There was so much left to be done. I had a promise to keep to the local King of Cats. I had a lot of changelings to talk to. I needed to eat my own body weight in sandwiches. And none of that really mattered, because we'd done it. We'd prevented the war. We'd saved the people of Silences.

We'd survived.

"Have you seen enough?" asked Tybalt quietly.

"I have," I said. "Let's get going. I want to go back to bed."

Together, the four of us turned and walked out of the room, leaving the past to sleep behind us. It was time to head into the future.

It had been waiting long enough.